road trip summer

Also by Lauren Barnholdt

Watch Me
One Night That Changes Everything
Sometimes It Happens
The Thing About the Truth
Through to You

road trip summer

TWO-WAY STREET and RIGHT OF WAY

LAUREN BARNHOLDT

Simon Pulse

New York London Toronto Sydney New Delhi

SIMON PULSE

An imprint of Simon & Schuster Children's Publishing Division

1230 Avenue of the Americas, New York, New York 10020

This Simon Pulse paperback edition May 2016

Two-way Street copyright © 2007 by Lauren Barnholdt

Right of Way copyright © 2013 by Lauren Barnholdt

Cover photograph copyright © 2016 by Chris Gramly/Getty Images

All rights reserved, including the right of reproduction in whole or in part in any form.

SIMON PULSE and colophon are registered trademarks of Simon & Schuster, Inc.

For information about special discounts for bulk purchases, please contact Simon & Schuster Special Sales at 1-866-506-1949 or business@simonandschuster.com.

The Simon & Schuster Speakers Bureau can bring authors to your live event.

For more information or to book an event contact the Simon & Schuster Speakers Bureau at 1-866-248-3049 or visit our website at www.simonspeakers.com.

Cover designed by Russell Gordon

Interior designed by Mike Rosamilia

The text of this book was set in Cochin.

Manufactured in the United States of America

2 4 6 8 10 9 7 5 3

Library of Congress Control Number 2016930109

ISBN 978-1-4814-5992-1 (pbk)

ISBN 978-1-4169-5477-4 (*Two-way Street* eBook)

ISBN 978-1-4424-5129-2 (*Right of Way* eBook)

These titles were previously published individually by Simon Pulse.

CONTENTS

Two-way Street   1

Right of Way   295

road trip summer

Two-way Street

For my sister, Kelsey, because she begged
and begged to have a book dedicated to her
(and also because she's amazing and wonderful
and makes my book signings a lot more fun)

ACKNOWLEDGMENTS

Thanks to:

My agent, Nadia Cornier, who puts up with my scandalousness on a daily basis and never freaks out about it;

Michelle Nagler, editor extraordinaire, for pushing me to take my books to a whole other level, and for being amazing to work with;

My mom, as always, for being my biggest inspiration;

My sister, Krissi, for always keeping me amused with her text messages;

Robyn Schneider, Kevin Cregg, Kiersten Loerzel, Rob Kean, Abby McDonald, and Scott Neumyer, for being wonderful friends;

My dad, my grandparents, and my whole extended family for all the amazing support;

Aaron Gorvine, for always listening to me, keeping me sane, and constantly telling me not to blog about him;

And, most of all, everyone who read *Watch Me* and e-mailed me to tell me they liked it, befriended me on MySpace, or left me a blog comment. You guys rock!

courtney | the trip

Day One, 8:07 a.m.

I'm a traitor to my generation. Seriously. All we hear about these days is being strong women and standing up for ourselves, and now look what I've done. I should totally be one of those true life stories in *Seventeen*. "I Built My Life Around a Boy! And Now I Regret It!" Of course, it doesn't pack the emotional punch as some of their previous stories, i.e., "I Got an STD Without Having Sex" but it's important nonetheless.

"You're going to be fine," my mom says, stirring her coffee at the sink. "In fact, you're acting a little bit ridiculous."

"I'm ridiculous? I'm ridiculous?" How can she say that? Has she lost her mind? It's so completely *not* ridiculous to be upset about going on a trip with your ex-boyfriend, when said ex-boyfriend broke your heart and left you stranded for some Internet slut. Although I really can't say I know for a fact that she's a slut. But I'm pretty sure she is. I mean, scamming on guys on the Internet? I thought that was only for forty-year-old divorcées who Photoshop their pictures in an effort to appear younger and thinner. Not to mention what was HE thinking? An eighteen-year-old guy who could have any girl he wanted, having to resort to Internet dating? But maybe that's the problem with guys who can have any girl they want. One is never enough.

"I didn't say you *were* ridiculous," my mom says. "I said you're *acting* ridiculous."

"There's really no difference," I tell her. "It's like if someone says 'You're acting like a cheater,' it's because you're cheating. Which means you're a cheater." Like Jordan. Although I suppose technically he isn't a cheater, because he broke up with me before he started dating the Internet girl. In my mind, I still think of him as being a cheater. Otherwise, he just met some girl he liked better, and it's not as dramatic.

"Courtney, you begged and begged to go on this trip," my mom says.

"So?" That's her big justification for calling me ridiculous? Is she kidding? Teenagers beg and beg for stuff all the time—nose rings, tattoos that say "Badass." Never a good idea. My parents are supposed to be the voices of reason, steering me on the right path at all times. They're obviously insane to have agreed to this plan in the first place. I mean, what was I thinking? Making plans to drive over a thousand miles to college with a boy months before we were supposed to go? Everyone knows the average high school relationship is shorter than an episode of *American Idol.* "You're the mother," I say. "You should have known this was a horrible idea." I'm hoping to lay a guilt trip on her, but she's not having it.

"Oh, please," she says, rolling her eyes. "How was I supposed to know he was going to break up with you? I'm not psychic. Nor do I know the habits of Internet chat rooms."

"It wasn't a CHAT ROOM," I say. "It was Facebook." No one hangs out in chat rooms anymore. Although why some girl would want to date Jordan based on his Facebook page is beyond me. The song he chose for his profile is "Let's All Get Drunk Tonight" by Afroman.

"Right," my mom says, taking a sip of her coffee. My parents are trying to teach me some kind of lesson. They don't think it's right that they would have to pay more than five hundred dollars for a last-minute plane ticket from Florida to Massachusetts, when I'm the one who convinced them to let me go on this trip. Plus, my mom thinks this whole thing is typical teen angst, one of those situations portrayed on a teen sitcom that's resolved in a half hour of laughs and mishaps. You know, where the girl gets dumped, but then realizes by the end of the show that she's better off without him, and then hooks up with some other hottie who's much better for her, while the guy who broke her heart ends up all alone, wishing he had her back. That is definitely not happening. In fact, it's kind of the other way around. Jordan is having tons of fun with his Facebook girl, while I'm the one sitting around, wishing I had *him* back.

I sigh and stare out the kitchen window, looking for Jordan's TrailBlazer. It's 8:07, and he was supposed to be here at eight, which makes me think that:

a) he's late
b) he's acting like an asshole and blowing me off
or
c) he's gotten into a horrible car crash that's left him dead.

The most likely answer is A. (We went to the prom together, and the limo had to wait in his driveway for half an hour. At the end of the night, we got charged for an extra hour. He—read: his parents—paid for it, but still.) Although I'm all about option C. Okay, maybe not the dead part. Just, like, a broken leg or something. I mean, his parents have always been really nice to me and I would feel horrible if they lost their youngest child. Even if he is a liar and a cheat.

"Do you want some coffee?" my mom asks, which is ridiculous because she knows I don't drink coffee. Coffee stunts your growth. I'm only five-foot-two, and I'm still holding out hope that I'll grow another few inches. Plus I'm tense enough. Getting me all hyped up on caffeine is definitely not a good idea.

"No thanks," I say, looking out the window again. I feel a lump rising in my throat, and I ignore it. He wouldn't blow me off, would he? I mean, that's so screwed up. Although if he did, that means I wouldn't have to go with him. Which would be great. If he stood me up, my parents would have no choice but to let me book a flight and take it to Boston. Which is what they should have let me do in the first place.

I take a deep breath. It's only three days. I can get through that, right? Three days is nothing. Three days is . . . I wrack my brain, trying to think of something that only lasts three days. Christmas vacation! Christmas vacation lasts ten days and it always seems to go by so fast. Three days is only a *third* of that.

Plus, I have the whole thing planned out in minute detail. The trip, I mean. So that every single second, we'll be doing something.

Of course, Christmas vacation is fun. And this is going to be excruciating.

My dad walks into the kitchen, wearing a gray suit and drinking a protein shake. He's humming a Shakira song. My dad loves pop music. Which is weird. Because he's almost fifty. Although I think my dad may be having a bit of a midlife crisis, since lately he's taken to buying weird clothes. And I suspect he's been using self-tanner, because he definitely looks a little orange.

"Good morning," he says, heading over to where my mom is sitting at the kitchen table and planting a kiss on

11

her head. He opens the cupboard and pulls down a box of cereal.

"Morning," I mumble, not sure what's so good about it.

"All set for school?" he asks, smiling.

"Yeah, I guess," I say, trying not to sound like too much of a brat. My dad has been way cooler about this whole breakup thing than my mom. He's spent hours trying to cheer me up by telling me I'd meet someone better, there's more fish in the sea, he never liked Jordan, etc. Plus he bought me a new iPod and tons of new clothes for school. He also slipped me a copy of *He's Just Not That Into You*, which I guess he thought was empowering. It actually kind of *is* empowering, because it talks about how you shouldn't settle for a guy who doesn't want to be with you. On the other hand, realizing the guy you like "just isn't that into you" is not very good for one's self-esteem. Plus I was reading parts of it to my friend Jocelyn one time, and she interrupted me to say, "Actually, if you need a book like that to tell you he's just not that into you, you're probably not the type that's going to actually be able to let go." She wasn't trying to say it about me, exactly, but still.

"Jordan here yet?" my dad asks, pouring milk over his cereal.

"Of course not," I say. "Hey, if he doesn't show up, then what?"

"You think he won't show up?" my dad asks, glancing up. "Why wouldn't he?"

"I don't know." I say. "But what if he doesn't?" Hope starts to rise up inside me. There's no way either one of my parents can or want to drive me. I won't even feel bad about the money they'll have to spend on a last-minute plane ticket, since they're the psychos who are making me go on this trip in the first place. "Then what?" I persist.

But no one has to answer that, because the sound of gravel crunching on the driveway outside comes through the window. I look out, and the light shines off the windshield of Jordan's TrailBlazer and hits my eyes.

Some kind of ridiculous rap music is blasting from the car, which makes me even more annoyed than I already am. I hate rap music. He doesn't even listen to normal rap, like Jay Z or Nelly. He listens to "hardcore" rap. (His word, not mine. I've never used the word "hardcore" in my life. Well, until right now, and then only to quote Jordan.)

I ignore the weird feeling in my stomach and run outside so I can yell at him for being late. "Where have you been?" I demand as he gets out of the car.

"Nice to see you, too." He smiles. He's wearing baggie tan shorts and a navy blue Abercrombie T-shirt. His dark hair is wet, which means he probably just got out of the shower, which means he probably just woke up. "I'm sorry, I was packing my stuff, and then I was trying to find my parents so I could say good-bye to them."

Packing his stuff? Who waits until the day they're leaving for college to start packing their stuff? My stuff's been packed for a week, neatly stacked outside my bedroom door until I moved it into the kitchen this morning. I mean, the housing office sent us a packing list. Of stuff to bring. I'll bet Jordan doesn't have any of it. Not like I care. If he wants to sleep on an empty, disgusting, stained mattress because he forgot to purchase extra-long sheets, that's fine with me. I'm so over him. This is me, being over him. La, la, la.

"Didn't you get my e-mail?" I ask him. Three days ago I e-mailed him a copy of our trip itinerary. It was really short, with a subject line that simply said "Schedule" and read, "Jordan, Attached, please find a copy of the schedule for our trip. Best, Courtney." I was really proud of it. The e-mail, I mean. Because it was so short and cold. Of course, it took me and my friend Jocelyn about two hours to come up with the perfect wording, but Jordan doesn't know that. He just must think I'm too important to compose long e-mail messages with him, or get ensconsed in a back-and-forth e-mail exchange. Not that he ever e-mailed me back. But it was obviously because I was so cold.

"The one about the trip?" He frowns. "Yeah, I think so."

"You think so?" I ask.

"Court, you can't plan everything to the minute," he says. "There are going to be setbacks." He takes the sunglasses that are on his head and slides them down over his eyes.

"Well, whatever," I say. Luckily I have three copies of the trip itinerary, along with specific Google Maps instructions all printed out and paper-clipped together. I'll give him one to reference. I start to walk into the house, and Jordan hesitates.

"Are you going to help me with my stuff or not?" I ask.

"Oh, yeah, sure." I raise my eyebrows. "Of course," he repeats more forcefully.

He follows me into the house, and I can tell he's staring at my ass. Pervert.

"Jordan," my dad says, nodding. Jordan nods back but doesn't say anything. I hope he's scared of my dad. If he isn't, he should be. My dad's kind of a big guy. Not that Jordan's scrawny or anything. In fact, just the opposite. He has these really amazing arms that—Ugh. I will not think about any part of Jordan's lying, cheating, never-on-time body, arms or otherwise.

"Excited to be going to school?" my mom asks politely. Her tone is guarded, which makes me happy. When Jordan and I were together, she was always supernice to him. She might be making me go on this trip, but it's obvious where her loyalties lie. I hope Jordan is uncomfortable. I hope he's squirming. I hope he's—

"Yes, ma'am," he says. Which is total bullshit. He could care less, obviously. I mean, he didn't even follow the packing list.

"Whatever," I say, putting my hands on my temples like I can't take it anymore. "Can you start loading up the car? I don't want to be any later than we already are." I give Jordan a pointed look, which he ignores, and then point him in the direction of my stuff, which is packed neatly and piled on the kitchen floor.

"Jesus, Court," he says, looking at the mound. "You know you're only going for four years, right?" I ignore him and pull a copy of the schedule out of my pocket.

"We are way behind," I say, frowning. We were supposed to have left twenty minutes ago. Although maybe if we don't stop for lunch and just drive straight through, we can make up the time that way. Still, it's not good to be starting off late. I've budgeted for traffic and unforeseen circumstances of course, but still. This should not count as an unforeseen circumstance. An unforeseen circumstance is something that you can't avoid. And this could definitely have been avoided.

Jordan reaches down and picks up one of the bags that's on the ground near my feet, and it brushes against my toe.

"Ow!" I say, jumping back. "Watch it. I'm wearing sandals."

He smiles. "Sorry, honey." He turns and heads out to the car before I can reply. I take a deep breath. I will not start fighting with him. There's no way. If I start fighting with him, he's going to know that he's getting to me, and I can't let that happen. The last thing I need is for him to think I'm upset about him breaking up with me. I've spent the past two weeks determined to show him I don't care, and I'm not going to screw it all up now. Of course, it's much easier to pretend you don't care about someone when they're not around you, but I can do it. I just have to gather all my self-control. Disengage and detach is my new motto.

I realize my heart is beating at a ridiculously abnormal rate, and I take another deep breath. I can do this, I tell myself. I start thinking of all the hot guys I'm going to meet in college. Guys who read philosophy books and drink coffee. Guys who listen to real music, like Mozart and Andrea Bocelli and maybe even Gavin DeGraw. Anything but rap music. It makes me feel better, but only for a second. Because, let's face it—no matter how much you tell yourself you're over someone, your heart knows the truth.

the trip ▷ jordan

Day One, 8:37 a.m.

I can't figure out why Courtney is wearing such tight clothing. Do girls normally wear short pink cotton skirts and tight
tank tops while going on a road trip? I've seen that ridiculous
Britney Spears movie *Crossroads*, and I definitely don't remember the girls in that movie wearing such slutty clothes. T-shirts
and track pants is what they wore. Is she doing it in an effort to
drive me insane? And is she going to act like a bitch the whole
time? It's not my fault I was late. I had to pack my stuff, which
you would think would be easy—just throw your clothes, computer, and CDs into a suitcase, right? Wrong. It took fucking
forever. But I was trying to hurry—I didn't even gel my hair,
which was a pretty big sacrifice. When it finally dries I'm
going to look like Seth Cohen or some shit.

My cell phone rings as I'm loading Courtney's stuff
into the back of my truck and trying not to think about
the next three days.

I answer it without checking the caller ID.

"Yeah," I say, lifting a pink bag with long straps into the back. What the hell does she have in here? It feels like weights.

"Yo," my best friend, B. J. Cartwright, says, sounding wide awake, which is surprising. B. J. never sounds wide awake. Especially since he's usually either hungover, drunk, or getting ready to get drunk.

"Yo," I say, sitting down on my open truck bed. "What's up?"

"Breaking news, dude," he says, sounding nervous. B. J. always has breaking news. It used to always involve some girl he wanted to bang, but for the past few months, he's been going out with Courtney's friend Jocelyn. He's still the biggest gossip I know, and one of his deepest secrets is that he subscribes to *Us Weekly*.

"Is that why you're up so early?"

"Huh? Oh, no, I haven't been to sleep yet," he says.

"You've been up all night?" I ask, glancing at my watch. "It's nine o'clock in the morning."

"Dude, the party went until four this morning," he says. "And then we all went to breakfast. You missed a great fucking time."

Last night's party was kind of a last hurrah, a sendoff before everyone left for school, which most people are doing this weekend. I was there for a while, but I took off before things got really crazy. I knew I had to be up early this morning so I wouldn't piss Courtney off by being late. Look how well that turned out.

"So what's the breaking news?" I ask.

"It's about Courtney," he says, and I feel my stomach drop.

"What about her?" I say.

"She's hooking up with Lloyd," he says, and I swallow hard. Figures. Lloyd is Courtney's best friend, this total tool who Court's been in love with since like seventh grade. Well, until she met me. Supposedly as soon as we started dating, she lost all her feelings for him. Or so she said.

"How do you know?" I ask, not sure I want to hear about this.

"Heard it from Julianna Fields, who heard it from Lloyd."

"When?"

"Not sure," B. J. says. "She was talking about it last night. After the party, really late. And then, um, Lloyd left Courtney a Facebook comment last night."

"Well, whatever," I say. I stand up, load the rest of the bags into the back of my truck, and slam it shut. "Courtney can do whatever the hell she wants."

"You okay?"

"I'm fine," I lie. "Thanks for letting me know."

"Cool," B. J. says. "Call me later."

I click off my cell phone and take a deep breath. Whatever. This isn't a big deal. I mean, *I* broke up with *her*. All I have to do is get through the next three days. Three days is nothing. Three days is half of spring break. Spring break flew by in two seconds this year. Thinking about spring break makes me start thinking about vacations, which makes me start thinking about Courtney and me in Miami, and the bathing suit she was wearing, and what happened on the beach. . . . Stop. I tell myself. It's over.

I take another deep breath, and when I turn around Courtney's dad is standing there, holding his briefcase in one hand and a cup of coffee in the other.

"All packed up?" he says, smiling. I do my best to smile back, and resist the urge to punch him.

"Looks like it," I say. I feel my fists clench at my side, and I will myself to unclench them.

"We're clear on everything, right, Jordan?" he says. He leans in close to me, and I can smell his aftershave. "I would hate for this trip to end in a bad way, with Courtney getting distracted before her first day of school."

"I wouldn't want Courtney to get upset either," I say, which is true. What I don't add is that if her father wasn't such an asshole, there'd be no chance of Courtney finding out anything that would upset her in the first place.

"Great," he says, clapping me on the shoulder like we're old friends. "I'm glad we're on the same page." He studies me for a minute, but I don't break my gaze. "I *am* going to tell her, you know."

"Of course," I say, even though he's been feeding me the same bullshit line for the past three months.

21

He hesitates for a minute, like he wants to say something else, or is waiting for me to reassure him that I'm not going to talk. But I'm not going to. Reassure him. Or talk. But he doesn't need to know that.

"Have a safe trip," he says finally, and then takes off down the driveway.

Once he's out of sight, I lean my head against the side of my truck and take a deep breath. I've spent the past two weeks driving myself completely crazy with the fact that if it weren't for Courtney's douchebag dad, and one second that changed everything, we'd still be together. But instead, we're not, and Courtney hates me.

And who could blame her? She thinks I dumped her for some girl I met on the Internet. If she knew what really happened, she'd probably hate me even more. Because the truth is, Courtney and I broke up for a really fucked-up reason that she doesn't know about, and hopefully never will. There is no Internet girl. I made her up.

jordan ⬅ before

I pull my TrailBlazer into my friend B. J.'s driveway and lay on the horn. B. J.'s real name is Brian Joseph Cartwright, but in seventh grade everyone started calling him B. J. We'd all just found out about the term "blow job," and we thought the nickname was super witty and cool. After a few years, it got old to everyone except B. J. He still loves the name and refuses to answer to anything else, even from teachers.

B. J. comes out of the house wearing a green bodysuit, green booties, and a leprechaun hat. I'm less concerned with what he's wearing, and more concerned about the fact that he's moving about as fast as a dial-up connection. We're on our way to Connor Mitchell's party, and I don't want to miss a second of it.

He opens the door (slowly) and launches himself into the passenger seat of my truck.

"Whaddup, kid?" he asks. He slams the door shut and readjusts the green beanie on his head.

"What the fuck is this?" I ask.

"What the fuck is what?" He's confused.

"This whole leprechaun thing," I say, rolling my eyes. I readjust my sideview mirror and back out of his driveway.

"I am not a leprechaun!" he says, offended. "I'm a midget."

"You're a midget?" I ask, incredulous. "You're dressed like a leprechaun. And they don't call them midgets anymore, they call them 'little people.'" I pull my eyes away from the road and glance at him quickly. Is it possible he's drunk already?

"I'm a little person, then," he says, sounding like he doesn't give a shit. "But really, who cares? I'm going to be so wasted it isn't going to matter."

"The only reason it's kind of weird," I say slowly, not wanting to upset him, "is because it's not a costume party. So I don't understand why you'd be dressed up."

"It's not a costume party?" he asks, sounding confused again. "I thought Madison said something about going as a cheerleader." He rolls down his window, which makes no sense, because the air conditioner is on. I don't understand why people have to roll down their windows when the air conditioner is on, since it's obviously hotter outside than it is in the car.

"No," I say, "Madison *is* a cheerleader. Why would she go to a costume party dressed as one?"

"She said she was going to!"

"She said she might not have time to change after the game, and might need to wear her uniform to the party." Madison Allesio is this blonde sophomore who's in study hall with B. J. and me. She's also the reason I'm going to this party tonight. Well, kind of. I probably would have gone anyway, since Connor Mitchell is known to throw some insane parties. Last year half the freshman class was topless in his pool. But Madison's been flirting with me hardcore for the past month, and yesterday she was all, "Are you going to Connor's party?" But she said it in a "Are you going to Connor's party so I can go home with you and get it on?" kind of way.

"I don't give a shit," B. J. says, grinning. "I'm going to be so fucked up I won't even care. And I'm a leprechaun, and you know leprechauns are always gettin' lucky! Woot woot!" He pumps his hands in the air in a "raise the roof" gesture. B. J. is always talking about how much play he's going to get, when in reality, he gets none.

We hear the party before we get there, a mix of what sounds like mainstream rap. Jay Z, 50 Cent, that kind of stuff. Posers. I like my rap hard and dirty, none of this "top forty" bullshit. But once I get a few beers in me, and a few girls on me, I'm sure I'll be fine. I maneuver my car into a parking spot on the street and follow B. J. up the walk and into the house.

Half an hour later, I'm starting to think this party might

actually blow. B. J. was entertaining me for a while, but now he's disappeared into the throng of people somewhere after doing a keg stand, and I have no idea where he is.

I'm sitting in Connor's living room, deciding whether or not to get up and get another beer, when I feel a pair of hands across my eyes.

"Hey," a female voice says behind me. "Guess who?" She's leaning over me now, and I catch a whiff of perfume. I can tell it's Madison from how she smells—good, and like you'd want to get her naked immediately.

"I don't know," I say, playing dumb. "Jessica?" I don't even know any Jessicas. I'm such a stud.

"No," she says, trying to sound hurt.

"Jennifer? Jamie?"

"Not a *J* name," she says. She's closer now, and I can feel her chest pushing into the back of my head.

"I give up," I say, reaching up to pull her hands off my eyes.

Madison pouts her lips and puts a hand on her hips. "It's Madison!" she says, puffing out her lip. She's wearing a short white skirt and a pink halter top. I was kind of hoping she'd be in her cheerleader uniform, but she looks hot anyway. Her long blond hair falls in waves down her back. It's all I can do not to pick her up and take her back to my truck with me.

"Ahhh, Madison," I say. "I was looking for you."

"You were not," she says, sighing. "You didn't even know it was me."

This is what confuses me about girls like Madison. They're hot, they could have any guy they want, and yet they spend most of their time trying to get guys to *tell* them they're hot. It doesn't make sense. It's like they don't want to believe they're good-looking. Or maybe they just get off on having guys tell them over and over.

(Another note about girls like Madison: They're good for hookups, but are not girlfriend material. Inevitably, you get tired of listening to them whine about whether or not you think they're hot, and they have to go. Plus, if you date a girl like Madison, you run the risk of actually starting to like her, and then she will eventually end up dumping you for some new guy who tells her how beautiful she is, because she's sick of hearing it from you. The trick is to play into their egos enough to keep them around, but not so much that they become bored. Luckily, I am a master at this.)

"I was looking for you," I repeat. I try to look disinterested and take a sip of my drink. "You look hot." I scan the crowd behind her, still not looking at her.

"Really?" she asks, looking pleased. She does a little twirl, and her skirt fans out around her legs. Which are really, really tan. And really, really long. I try not to stare, knowing that if I let myself get too worked up, I won't be able to continue playing the game. Hormones are such a bitch.

"So you never responded to my Facebook message," I say, and her face flushes. My last Facebook message was about how hot her lips looked, and how I couldn't wait to kiss her.

"I never got it," she says, but I can tell she's lying. She looks over to where her friends are standing on the other side of the room. "This party is so lame." She glances at me out of the corner of her eye, and I know that's my signal.

"You want to get out of here?" I ask. "I have my truck."

She shrugs, like she doesn't care. "I guess. Just let me go tell my friends."

Madison walks away, and I try to find some way to distract myself. I can't be waiting for her when she comes back. I have to make her work for it a little. I know it sounds mean and fucked up, but it really isn't. It's just how things work. I look around for some situation that has to be taken care of, or some girl I know that I can later claim came up to me, not vice versa. And that's when I see B. J. attached to Courtney McSweeney's leg.

courtney ← before

125 Days Before the Trip, 9:43 p.m.

Tonight I'm going to tell my friend Lloyd that I'm in love with him. Important things about Lloyd:

1. He's been my best friend since the seventh grade, when we got seated near each other in every single class because of our last names. It seemed like every teacher was doing it alphabetically, so since I'm McSweeney and he's McPeak, we were always together. When we got to high school and ended up being able to choose our own seats, we still sat together. It was like a rule.

2. Ever since the first day of seventh grade, I've been in love with him. My friend Jocelyn says that you can't be in love with someone if:

   a) they don't know it
   b) they don't feel the same way
   c) you've never kissed them, held hands with them, or done anything more than be friends with them.

But that makes no sense to me whatsoever, because, hello, it's called unrequited love. Look at people in movies. They're always saying "I'm in love with you" when they haven't done anything physical with the other person. Physical is just physical, it doesn't *mean* anything.

Besides, I *am* going to tell Lloyd how I feel. The reason I haven't up until this point is because I don't want to ruin the friendship (i.e., I'm deathly afraid of rejection). But lately, there have been signs. Lloyd has been calling me every single night—definitely more than usual—and talking on the phone with me for hours. And he helps me with my math homework, even when I get totally confused and it takes us twenty minutes to do one problem. He never gets impatient with me.

I have to make my move soon, though, because Lloyd is going to school in North Carolina and I'm going to school in Boston, so we're going to need to be dating for a few months before we leave for college. That way we'll be all set up for a long-distance relationship. Which is why I plan on telling him. Tonight. After the party. That I want to be more than friends.

I'm even wearing my "I'm going to tell Lloyd I want him" outfit, which consists of a very short jean skirt and a tight white shirt. Which is not the kind of thing I usually wear. But I need to get Lloyd to stop thinking of me as a friend and start thinking of me as someone he wants to date.

So far, the night is not going as planned. First, Lloyd said he would be at this party, and so far, I have not seen him. Second, my friend Jocelyn (who I drove here with), is off talking to this junior guy she has a crush on and has left me standing here by myself. This is not her fault, because I told her I would be fine, since I thought Lloyd would be here soon, and I would be so busy seducing him that I wouldn't need Jocelyn to hang out with me anyway. Third, and definitely the most upsetting, is that right at this moment, there is a guy dressed like a leprechaun with his arms wrapped around my legs. I'm scandalized by this, but I'm trying to be nice, because I think he's drunk.

"Oh, um, hi," I say, trying to push him away gently. "You're, um, a leprechaun." This is why I don't go to parties. Because stuff like this always happens to me. I'm always the one standing in some corner, by myself, with a guy dressed like a leprechaun drooling on my leg.

"I am not," he says, looking up at me. "I'm a midget." I get a good look at his face and realize it's B. J. Cartwright. Great. The craziest guy in the senior class is wrapped around my leg. B. J.'s done some pretty insane stuff, including burning our class name and year into the lawn outside the front doors of our school. He almost got expelled for it, but the school board relented since no one got hurt. B. J. put condoms in all the teachers' mailboxes on Safe Sex Awareness Day, rigged the school penny contest so that our class would win, and showed up on Halloween as Hannah Baker, a girl in our class who got arrested over the summer for prostitution. He wore balloon boobs and everything.

"A midget," I say, trying to disentangle myself from him again, but he has a viselike grip on my leg. "That's, erhm, interesting."

"You've always wanted to do it with a midget, haven't you, Britney?" he asks, licking his lips at me. Oh, my God.

"My name's not Britney," I say, hoping maybe he's looking for someone specific, and once he realizes I'm not her, he'll take off.

"I know it's not," he says, rolling his eyes. "But you look like her."

"Like Britney?" I ask, confused. His hands feel sticky against my bare leg, and I curse myself for wearing a skirt.

"Yes," he slurs, leering at me. "You look like Britney Spears."

"Really?" I ask, pleased in spite of myself. Then it occurs to me that Britney's gone through several stages of attractiveness, and I wonder if he means I look like Hot Britney, or Not So Hot Britney, I consider asking him to clarify but I'm not sure I could handle the answer.

Still, no one has told me I look like a celebrity before. In fact, one time Jocelyn tried to set me up with this guy online, and the first thing he asked me was who my celebrity lookalike was. And I told him "No one, I look like myself," which, you know, was definitely kind of lame. Because even if I DON'T have a celebrity lookalike, I could have made something up, or just given a vague idea, like, "Well, I have long dark hair like Rachel Bilson," or something. Not that it would have worked out anyway. The relationship with the online guy, I mean. He told me his celebrity lookalike was Jake Gyllenhaal, and I hadn't even asked him for the information. He just volunteered it. Which meant that he was dying for me to know, which meant that he was totally conceited. I can't deal with conceited. (Actually, I probably could deal with a little conceit, but I think I was just scared because there's no way I'd feel comfortable going out with a guy who looks like Jake Gyllenhaal. That would not be good for my self-esteem.)

"Yes," B. J. says. "You look just like Britney." He reaches up and pokes me in the stomach. "Except for her abs. You don't have her abs." His face falls. All right then.

"Um, Britney's had kids," I say. "And so her abs, I'm sure, are shot." He considers this, nods, and then licks my leg. Gross.

"Okay, you need to knock that off." I stick my leg out and try to shake him off, but it's harder than it looks. Even though he's dressed like a midget, and has been walking around on his knees all night, B. J. is six-foot-four and probably weighs close to two hundred pounds. He's *heavy*. I look around for Jocelyn, but I can't find her anywhere. Typical. She begs me to come to this party, and then leaves me right at the crucial moment, i.e., when I have a midget-leprechaun attached to my leg. "Stop!" I command, wondering if I can stick the heel of my shoe into his stomach without really hurting him.

"Why?" he asks. "I'm helping you with your midget fetish." He licks my leg again. Oh, *eww.*

"I do NOT have a midget fetish!" I say, louder this time, hoping that my change of volume will help him get the message.

"Not yet." He grins up at me, and I'm about to stick my heel right into his stomach, not caring if it causes permanent damage or not, when Jordan Richman appears out of the crowd and picks B. J. up by his elbows.

"All right, Lucky," he says, removing B. J. from my leg, swinging him around, and placing him a safe few feet away. Oh, thank God. Jordan must be really strong to be able to pick up B. J. like that. Although, once he set him down, B. J. went limp and fell to the ground, so maybe he was so drunk that it didn't matter how big he was. Kind of like when you're in water, your weight doesn't matter. Maybe it's the same when you're drunk. "I think that's enough."

"Whaddup, kid?" B. J. asks Jordan. He grins at him and readjusts the green beanie on his head.

"Nothing," Jordan says, looking slightly amused, "but you can't just go around humping people's legs." He rolls his eyes.

"I wasn't humping her!" B. J. says, offended. "I'm a midget."

"You're not a midget," I say, before I can stop myself. "You're dressed like a leprechaun. And they don't call them midgets anymore, they call them 'little people.'" Jordan grins at me.

34

"I'm a little person, then," he says, sounding cheerful. "But, really, who cares? I'm so wasted it doesn't matter."

"It's not a costume party," I point out.

"I know," B. J. says sadly. "But Madison said she might wear her cheerleading uniform."

"But she didn't," Jordan says.

I don't understand what Madison's cheerleading uniform has to do with it being a costume party, but I know enough to realize they're talking about Madison Allesio. It figures Jordan would be friends with her. There's this rumor going around that she likes to do this oral sex thing with Kool-Aid. Something to do with, uh, different flavors for different guys. Totally disgusting, which seems kind of like Jordan's type. Not that I know him all that well. We're in the same math class, and that's about it. But one time I heard him in the hall before class, arguing with a girl. Something about how she needed to stop following him around. And then she said he shouldn't have hooked up with her if he didn't want a girlfriend. It was actually kind of a math class scandal, because the whole class could hear everything that was going on. Finally, I think he just walked into the classroom while she was screaming. I couldn't see the girl, but later on I found out it was this freshman named Katie Shaw, and then I really didn't feel so bad about the whole thing, because I know for a fact she messes around with a lot of guys—including Lloyd, who she went to third base with in a movie theater. Anyway, the point is, I'm not surprised

Jordan's friends with Madison. He apparently likes girls who thrive on hookups and drama.

"I don't give a shit." B. J. shrugs. "I'm a leprechaun. And leprechauns. Get. Lucky." He pumps his hands in the air in a "raise the roof" gesture. "Besides," he continues, grinning, "Britney liked it." He grins at me again and then waddles off on his knees.

"Sorry about that," Jordan says, smiling sheepishly. "He gets crazy when he's drunk. But he wouldn't have done anything."

"It's okay," I say, feeling stupid.

"Here," he says, pulling a tissue out of his pocket and handing it to me.

"Thanks." I wipe B. J.'s saliva off my leg and check my skin to make sure it's not broken, all the while scanning my brain for diseases that can be transferred by bites. I can't think of any. Lyme disease, maybe? But I don't think you can get that from other people, just from ticks. They should totally concentrate on communicable bite diseases in health class, since apparently I have more of a chance of getting bitten than I do of losing my virginity.

"Anyway, it's Courtney, right?"

"Yeah," I say, surprised that he's asking. He should know my name. We've been in the same advanced math class for four years.

He smiles at me, his eyes shining. "Sorry, that was lame. I know your name. I was just trying to be smooth."

I laugh and so does he.

"Are you here by yourself?" he asks, looking around.

"No," I say quickly, so he doesn't think I'm a total loser. "My friend Jocelyn is here somewhere, but I lost track of her."

"Yeah," he says. "I try to keep an eye on B. J. when he starts drinking, but it's hard with this many people here."

"I can imagine," I say, trying to think of something cool to say. Not that I'm interested in him or anything. I mean, he's cute enough, but that's not why I can't think of anything cool to say. I just have a hard time with small talk. My friend Jocelyn says I'm too quiet. But I'm really not quiet. I just tend to come across that way to new people because I don't like to talk first. What if the other person doesn't want to be bothered? I wonder if I should ask Jordan if he knows what kind of diseases can be transmitted through saliva.

"Anyway, you wanna dance?" he asks, gesturing to one side of the party, where everyone is dancing to a top forty remix.

"Oh, no thanks," I say, trying not to look horrified. There's no way I'm dancing at this party. If he'd ever seen me dance, he would know why. I am not a good dancer. I *like* to dance, I'm just not very good at it. I like to keep my dancing confined to my room, where I can pretend to be Christina or Rhianna without anyone watching.

"Oh," he says, looking confused. Probably no girls have

ever turned him down to dance before. He looks at me, and I realize he's waiting for an explanation, some kind of reason why I can't dance.

"I would," I say quickly, hoping he doesn't think I'm a dork and/or leave. It's not that I'm loving talking to him or anything, but I don't want to be the only loser at the party talking to no one. That's how I got accosted by a leprechaun. "But my leg kind of hurts." This is a total lie. Besides the fact that every time I think of what just happened, my leg feels kind of slimy, I actually feel fine. I mean, B. J. didn't bite me or anything. He just sort of slobbered on me. Which was, you know, unpleasant and everything, but didn't hurt.

"Oh, I'm sorry," Jordan says, looking genuinely concerned. Which makes me feel bad. But I would much rather deal with the guilt of lying about a medical condition than the humiliation of having to dance in front of everyone here. "Do you think you need to go to the doctor or anything?"

"Oh, no, I don't think it's that bad," I say, "but I probably shouldn't, uh, dance on it or anything."

"Okay," he agrees. He keeps looking over his shoulder for something (someone? B. J.?), which is kind of distracting.

There's a pause, and I take a sip of my soda in an effort to appear busy. I finally spot Jocelyn across the room, where she's sitting on an oversized leather couch, talking to a different guy than the one she originally left me for. She gives me a look and raises her eyebrows, like, "What's the deal?" I try to telegraph back, "Absolutely nothing!" But she gives me a

"Yeah, right" look back. I know she's thinking about Lloyd.

"Hey," Jordan says, looking around again. What is he looking for? Maybe he lost something. Or maybe someone stole something from him, and now he's looking for whoever took it. Or maybe he wants to make sure his midget friend is okay. "How does your leg feel now?"

"Fine, thanks," I say without thinking. "Much better."

"Great," he says. "Miraculous recovery." He takes the drink I'm holding out of my hand and sets it down on the table next to us. "Then you can dance."

"Oh, no," I say, panicked. "I don't think I'm ready for that." Putting on an iTunes mix and rocking out in your room while pretending to be Beyoncé is one thing. Actually dancing in front of people from school is another thing. Plus, what if I get all sweaty or fall or something? And then later, Lloyd is like, "You know what, Courtney? I would have gone out with you, except since tonight I saw you looking like a sweaty, clumsy mess. I'm going to have to pass." I don't think I'm ready to risk my chance of happiness with Lloyd over one dance.

"Come on," Jordan says, taking my hand. "You'll be fine." He looks at me and smiles, and I hesitate.

"I don't dance," I admit, going for the truth.

"I'll be gentle," he promises, and before I can protest, he's dragging me out onto the dance floor.

the trip ▷ courtney

Day One, 9:12 a.m.

"So," I say, putting on my seat belt and settling in to the car. "Now that we're completely late and are going to miss orientation . . ." I trail off, hoping he realizes the error of his ways. The error of his ways being, you know, that we'll miss orientation and end up failing out of college because of it. Who knows what could happen if we don't get oriented? It could be bad. We could end up lost and out of it for four years, wrecking our future because we missed some vital information that was given out exclusively during orientation.

"We're not going to miss orientation," he says, pulling down the rearview mirror and checking his reflection.

"Hello? Could you spend less time grooming yourself and more time, like, actually driving?" His hair is a mess. Rumpled, like he just got out of bed. It's actually kind of cute. But I'm not going to miss college just because he didn't have time to do his hair. Or because he's cute. I've lost enough of my self-respect.

"Like, okay," he says, doing a pretty good impression of my voice. He smiles and pulls the sunglasses on his head back down over his eyes. He starts the car. It sputters and stops, and I look at him in alarm.

"Just kidding," he says. He winks and starts the car. Ugh. What an ass. How can he joke at a time like this? I mean, even if he's not concerned about the fact that we're going to miss our orientation, he should still be upset that we're going on this trip and are broken up.

There's silence for a few minutes as he pulls out of my driveway. I reach into my bag and pull out my book, determined to ignore him. I'm reading *The Catcher in the Rye* for the millionth time, figuring it's

a) funny
b) about a kid who goes crazy, so I won't feel so bad about myself, and
c) I won't have to worry about comprehending it, since I've already read it a million times.

I reach down and push my seat back.

"Whatcha readin'?" Jordan asks politely.

"Like you care." I snort. I don't think I've ever seen Jordan pick up a book in his life. I reach over and turn down the car CD player, which is playing some kind of ridiculous rap music. "I can't concentrate on my book."

He shrugs.

"Hey," I say, realizing he's not headed the right way. "You're not going the right way."

"Oh," he says. "Yeah, I know. I thought we could grab some breakfast." He says this like he doesn't know it will upset me, which upsets me even more than if he had been apologetic.

"But I have a schedule," I say, trying not to start a fight this early in the game. The last thing I want is to set him off. "And we're already behind."

"But I'm hungry."

"Well, you should have eaten before you left," I say. If he wasn't eating breakfast, then what was he doing?

"I told you," he says, "I was packing my stuff."

"Well, whatever," I say. "You should have planned properly."

"Look, we can stop really quick at Johni's Diner," he says. "We can pick up the highway right there, and it won't be that much out of our way."

"Yes, but we're already behind schedule," I say, waving the itinerary in front of his face. "So we should actually be trying to make up time, not get further behind."

"Look, if we don't stop now, we're just going to have to—" The sound of his cell phone rings, cutting him off. He has it programmed to play Sir Mix-a-Lot's "Baby Got Back," which is so corny, because that song is so 1999. And he doesn't even like big butts. I don't think. Unless I have a huge ass and don't know it.

He checks the caller ID briefly and then slides the phone open. Of course. His parents buy him everything.

"Hey," he says into the headpiece, glancing at me out of the corner of his eye. He catches me looking at him, and I turn away, reaching into the backseat. I rummage around in one of my bags for the CD I burned last night.

"No, we're on our way," Jordan says, sounding strained. It's probably his Facebook girl. I don't exactly know her name, or anything about her, but that's not from lack of trying. I searched his Facebook profile obsessively but I couldn't find anything. You'd think she would have left him a comment or something, right? But then I thought maybe he figured I would have searched, so he told her not to. Or deleted them. And then, just when I was starting to really obsess, he switched the age of his profile to "14" so that no one could look at it. Facebook has this rule where if you're fourteen or younger, your profile automatically gets set to private, and only the people you have friended can view it. So Jordan switched his age and then took me off his friends list! Which was really a horrible thing to do when you think about it, because it was, like, an actual act of aggression. I mean, it's one thing to dump me for another girl, but to actually block me on Facebook? That's just rude. He blocked me on instant messenger, too. And I couldn't even go through and make up a fake screen name, because he had everyone who wasn't on his buddy list blocked.

But I know she's from Tampa (the new girl, I mean), and that she's going to Boston College. Which is supposedly how she found him. She was searching Facebook profiles for people who were going to college in Boston. I'm surprised he didn't offer her a ride.

How I imagine Jordan's new girlfriend (A Psychotic Delusion by Courtney Elizabeth McSweeney):

1. She's blonde. I have dark hair and fair skin. (Even though I live in Florida, I tend to burn when I sit out in the sun, which sucks, because everyone at school is always tan. At least in Boston, I won't have to worry about that.) She also has blue eyes and dark skin. She looks like one of those girls on Laguna Beach. I have no idea why I think this, because one time we were watching Laguna Beach together, and Jordan told me he thought all the girls on that show looked alike. I guess it's because I figure he would leave me for someone who was completely my opposite, and that includes physically.

2. She has a tattoo of a butterfly or some sort of pink design on her lower back. She wears lots of low-rise jeans.

3. She likes pop music, and she loves to go dancing. In my deluded fantasies, her and Jordan are always going clubbing. She's also one of the worst kind of girls, the kind that all the guys want and drool all over, but is completely trustworthy and never does anything behind her boyfriend's back.

4. She's rich.

5. She's not a virgin, and her and Jordan do it all over the place. In fact,
   she wants to do it so much that Jordan can't even keep up with her.
   He's tired all the time. She's always tearing off her clothes and throwing herself at him.

I find the CD in my bag and rustle around some more, trying to make it out like I'm looking for something else. The last thing I want is for him to think I'm listening to his conversation with Mercedes (that's what I imagine her name to be), even though that's totally what I'm doing.

"Okay, cool," he says. He snaps the phone shut and drops it onto the console between our seats. I rustle around some more, wondering what a good amount of time is to come back up without being obvious. At least he didn't say "I love you" when they hung up. Although maybe they usually do, but he didn't want to say it in front of me, since he was afraid I'd go psychotic on him or something. Which I wouldn't have done. Gone psychotic, I mean. At least not out loud.

"What are you looking for?" he asks. Although it may be a little too early for them to be saying "I love you" to each other, right? I mean, they've only been together two weeks. The thought of Jordan saying "I love you" to another girl makes me feel like I want to throw up. I sit back up quickly, holding the CD.

"This," I tell him.

Then *my* phone starts ringing, and I ignore it, because:

a) I think it's rude to talk on cell phones when you're in the car
   with someone, and since I want to reserve the right to give
   Jordan shit about it in the future, I don't think I should be
   hypocritical now.
b) It's probably Jocelyn, calling to ask me if I'm okay, and
   she's going to ask a million questions, and I won't be able to
   really talk to her, because I'll only be able to give one-word
   answers, like "yes" and "no" and Jordan will obviously know
   that we're talking about him, otherwise why would I be
   giving one-word answers?

"I Will Survive" by Gloria Gaynor comes from my phone, and I curse myself for not changing my ringtone before this trip. How ridiculously lame. I search through my bag, looking for the phone, but by the time I find it, it stops ringing. And then starts again.

"Are you going to answer it or what?" Jordan asks, sounding annoyed.

"Yeah," I say, "as a matter of fact, I am." Which makes no sense, because five seconds ago I wasn't going to answer it, but that was before "I Will Survive" came out of my phone, and now I want Jordan to think I'm fine, and that I just really like seventies disco music. And I know answering my phone will annoy him, which I really, really want to do.

This trip is making me mentally exhausted already, and we haven't even crossed state lines.

"Hello!" I say brightly, without checking the caller ID.

"Courtney?" Lloyd asks, sounding like he just woke up.

"Hey," I say, my heart sinking. Lloyd is going to ask even more questions than Jocelyn would have, and there's no way he's going to let me get away with "yes" or "no" answers. It's not that Lloyd is nosey by nature or anything. It's just that he's going to be superconcerned about what's going on with me and Jordan.

"I thought you were going to call me before you left," he says, yawning.

"I was," I say, "but it was so early, I thought I'd let you sleep."

"So how's it going?" he asks. "Are you in the car?" I push the volume down button on my phone, so Jordan won't be able to overhear any of Lloyd's side of the conversation. Who knows what kind of embarrassing things he'll be prone to say.

"Um, yup," I say, "I am." I glance at Jordan out of the corner of my eye. He's staring straight ahead, his hands gripping the steering wheel.

"Is he acting like an asshole?" Lloyd asks.

"Uh, no, not really," I say, as Jordan reaches over and ups the volume on the CD player by about five notches, making it extremely hard to hear Lloyd over the rap music.

"It's probably kind of hard for you to talk right now, huh? With him there and everything?" Ya think?

"Yeah, sort of."

"Okay, well, call me back later. When you're at a rest stop or something."

"I will," I promise.

Lloyd hesitates, like he wants to say something else, but then clicks off.

"Can you please knock it off with the rap?" I say, snapping my cell phone shut and sliding it back into my bag.

"Was that Lloyd?" Jordan asks, trying to sound nonchalant. He's never liked Lloyd, mostly because in the spirit of total relationship honesty, I once made the mistake of telling Jordan about the huge crush I used to have on Lloyd. Have. Had. Shit. The thing is, the first night Jordan and I hung out, I was all set to tell Lloyd that I'd been lusting after him since junior high. And then some, uh, circumstances got in the way, and things didn't work out exactly according to plan.

But then Jordan had to go and dump me for that stupid Internet girl, and Lloyd was being so supportive about the whole thing, and then last night when Lloyd and Jocelyn came over to say good-bye, I was getting all nostalgic, and I started thinking how things would have turned out if I'd never met Jordan. You know, like if Lloyd and I had ended up together. Which was a really stupid thing to start thinking about, since you should never start thinking about "what might have been," and you should also never start thinking about another boy when you're heartbroken over someone else. Although Jocelyn says the only way to get over someone is to get under someone else. So I started thinking maybe that was true, and maybe I needed to date just to get the one "jerk" out of my system, because, let's face it, Jordan was my first real boyfriend, and who ends up with their first real boyfriend? Yeah, no one.

Anyway, to make a long story short, I was feeling nostalgic and Jocelyn left early because she had to have her mom's car home by eleven, and then it was just Lloyd and me, and right before he left he gave me a hug good-bye, and I kissed him. I know. And then, instead of pulling away, he kissed me back, and it turned into this whole big make-out session, and when he left, I started crying, because it turned out that:

a) making out with Lloyd was just weird, and not at all like I thought it would be
b) I should have made out with him sooner, because maybe then I would have gotten over him way before
c) turns out the best way to get over someone is NOT to get under someone else, because after Lloyd left, I missed Jordan more than ever.

Anyway, now it's totally weird, because I don't know what happens next. Especially since Jordan and I are supposed to be stopping in North Carolina tomorrow to visit Lloyd (he's taking a flight to NC later today), and Jordan's brother, Adam, who also goes to school at Middleton. I suppose at some point Lloyd and I are going to have to talk about our hookup, which is going to be awkward. Or maybe we'll just never mention it again. Stuff like that happens all the time, right? People hook up, and then realize it was a mistake, and since it would be way too awkward to talk about, they just don't.

"What's Lloyd doing up so early?" Jordan asks, smirking.

"Nothing," I snap. I push the eject button on the stereo and pull out the CD that's in the player, which has "Jordan's Gangsta Mix" written on it in black Sharpie. I roll my eyes and replace it with my CD. "Wide Open Spaces" by the Dixie Chicks fills the car, and Jordan rolls his eyes.

"Get used to it," I say, turning back to my book. "We're listening to country."

"Half and half," he says, grinning. "The music on this trip will be fifty-fifty."

"Riiight," I say. "Just like our relationship, right?"

He doesn't say anything, but when we pass the diner, he keeps on driving.

jordan ← before

Courtney McSweeney is grinding on me like she's in a number-one music video. I reach around and pull her close to me, our bodies swaying to the music. She looks surprised, but pushes her body harder against mine. She's always so quiet in math. And she definitely doesn't dress like this in school. I catch Madison's eye across the room and quickly look away, as if I've forgotten who she is. I'm not being a dick. Well, okay, maybe I am, but it's only as a means to the end. The end, of course, being getting Madison to hook up with me.

"Hey," I say, pulling away from Courtney. "You want a drink?" She pushes her hair back from her face and smiles.

"Sure." She heads over to where the coolers are and I follow her. Seriously, she really does not dress like this at school. I'm having a very hard time not staring at her ass.

"What do you want to drink?" I ask, rooting through

one of the coolers. The ice makes my hands cold. "There's soda, beer . . . that's it."

"I'll take a beer," she says, sounding unsure. I twist the top off a Corona and hand it to her. She takes a sip.

"So," I say. The music is kind of loud, and I suddenly realize I'm going to now have to be witty and charming so that Courtney looks like she's having a good time, therefore making Madison think I'm flirting with her.

"So," she says. She fiddles with the rim of her beer and looks down at her shoes. Great. So outgoing, this girl.

"Have you started the math assignment yet?" I ask her, figuring it's a safe subject.

"Yeah, I'm actually done with it," she says. I raise my eyebrows and she rushes on. "Just because that's the one grade I'm worried about."

"Really?" I frown. "How come?"

"Calculus is tripping me up for some reason," she says. "So I try to get my stuff done early, and then I have my friend Lloyd look it over. He's this total math genius."

"Sounds like it, with a name like Lloyd." I snort. I'm not trying to be mean, just funny, but she looks hurt. "Whoa," I say. "Just kidding."

"It's okay," she says, looking away. I catch the look on her face, though, which makes me think she's probably sleeping with him. Or wishes she were. "Anyway," she goes on, "I have to keep my math grade up, so I make sure I get the assignments done early so that my friend has time to look them over."

"What's the big deal?" I ask. "Are you wait-listed or something?" Everyone knows the grades we're getting now really have no effect on what happens to us. By now, college applications are finished and sent, and you're either in or you're not. It's a wonder anyone goes to class. I take another sip of my beer and try to pretend I don't notice Madison watching me.

"No," she says. "I'm going to Boston University."

"No shit," I say. "Me, too." Suddenly I have an awful thought. "Are they checking grades for our senior year?"

"I don't know," she says. "I'm just nervous because of that whole thing with the kid from UNC." I give her a blank look. She sighs. "That kid from UNC, you didn't hear about this? He got accepted and then totally blew off all his classes. They withdrew his acceptance since his grades had taken such a turn for the worse."

"I'm sure they were just trying to make an example of him," I say. "I mean, seriously. They're not going to kick you out of BU just because your math grade is bad." I'm not sure if it's true or not, but she strikes me as being the type to worry about every little thing. And I can't have her getting upset. I need to look happy and like I'm this close to getting into her pants, which will therefore make me that much closer to my main goal, which is Madison.

"Anyway," I say, deciding it's time to start making my move. "You're way too cute. All you'd have to do is send them a picture, and I'm sure they wouldn't care if you failed calc." She blushes and I reach out and touch her arm. Out of the corner of my eye, I see Madison set her drink down and start approaching us. Yes. Mission accomplished.

Before she gets there, though, a guy wearing a striped polo shirt—does anyone really wear polo shirts anymore?— approaches Courtney.

"Hey," he says, touching her elbow. "What's goin' on?"

"Hey, Lloyd," she says, her face lighting up. Ah, the infamous Lloyd. He looks like he'd be good in math. But what is he doing here? I mean, besides the obvious partying. Madison picks her drink back up and pretends not to be looking at me. Shit.

"Who's this?" Lloyd asks, sizing me up.

"This is Jordan," Courtney says. "He's in my math class." He's in my math class? How about "I was just grinding on him like I hadn't gotten any in months"? Nice to know where her loyalties are. I take another sip of my beer.

"Hey," Lloyd says, eyeing me. "What's up?"

"Not much, man," I say, wondering when he's going to leave. He's screwing up the plan. I try to look bored in an effort to make him go away. It doesn't work.

"You're still riding home with me, right?" he asks Courtney, watching me out of the corner of his eye. What's with this guy? He looks like he's about one second away from taking a baseball bat to my knees. Or wanting to. I wonder if this is how serial killers start out. Wasn't the Unabomber really good at math?

"Right," Courtney says, glancing at me, too. I take another sip of my Corona. Hey, they don't have to worry about me. The last thing I need is her expecting me to take her home. Like I said, she's cute enough, and her body is smokin', but I have my sights set on something else.

"So, George, are you a junior?" Lloyd asks, and I roll my eyes. What a tool. I know guys like him. Guys who keep a bunch of girls around, dangling themselves in front of them, but never really hooking up with them. Yet they get pissed if someone else tries to make a move. Which I'm not trying to do. But when he calls me George, I almost kind of want to, since I know he knows my name. A not-so-subtle dig. Nice, Lloyd.

"I'm a senior," I say, and leave it at that. There's an awkward silence.

"So, listen," I say, watching Madison out of the corner of my eye. "I need to get back to my friends, but it was nice dancing with you, Court."

"You, too," she says, and for a second, I almost don't do what I'm about to do. Because she seems like a nice girl. But then I see Lloyd giving me the look of death, and I can tell Madison is watching me, so I go for it. Whatever, if I'm going to hell, it will be for hooking up with Kendra Carlson at her brother's graduation party last summer and then never calling her back.

"So, can I get your number?" I say, trying to sound sheepish, like I'm not sure she's going to give it to me. She looks shocked for a minute, so I quickly add, "Oh, I'm sorry, are you two . . ." I look from her to Lloyd, even though I know there's no way they're together. Lloyd's eyes darken. That's what you get for calling me George, Polo Boy.

"Um, no," Courtney says, looking even more flustered.

"No, I can't have your number?" I say, grinning at her again.

"No, we're not together," she says, more forcefully this time. "And yes, you can have my number." Lloyd's eyebrows shoot up in surprise. Did he really think she was going to say no just because of him? It's obvious she wants him, but please. She's not that hard up. Any girl who dances the way she does is not going to sit around waiting for a guy named Lloyd.

Courtney takes a pen and paper out of the small bag slung around her waist and writes her number down. I make a big show out of putting it in my wallet, even though I have no intention of using it. It's mostly so Madison will see me doing it, although later I'll tell her Courtney and I got paired up for a project at school, I was just dancing with her to be nice, and I got her number so we could work on the assignment. She won't know whether it's true or not, but again, that's part of the fun.

"Nice to meet you, Lloyd," I say, looking right at him. "And I'll give ya a call," I say to Courtney.

"Later," she says, and I think briefly about what's going to happen at school on Monday when I blow her off.

Thankfully, she sits on the other side of the room in math class. And she doesn't seem psychotic, which is always a plus. Psychotic girls are a pain in my ass. Last year I kissed this freshman girl at a pool party and she wouldn't get off my nuts for six months. Which is why my policy is now no psychotics, and no freshmen. The freshmen thing is obviously easy to avoid, while the psychotics pose a bit more of a problem. It's not like girls walk around with "I'm crazy" stamped on their chests.

I decide to head around the party the long way, and then sneak up on Madison from behind. How cute would that be, me doing to her the same trick she pulled earlier? But when I make my way through the crowd to where Madison and her friends were standing, the only one there is B. J. His leprechaun hat is stained with beer and he's sitting on the ground, looking dejected.

"Dude," I say, crouching down next to him. "You okay?"

"Yeah," he says mournfully. "I'm okay. I'm just drunk."

"Sucks."

"Yeah," he agrees.

"Hey, you didn't happen to notice where Madison Allesio and her friends went, did you?"

"I'm not sure," he says, looking thoughtful. He frowns, pulls his leprechaun hat off his head, and twists it in his hands. "I think they said something about going to Jeremy Norfolk's house." Shit. Jeremy Norfolk was also having a party tonight, and apparently Madison and her friends took off while they were supposed to be waiting for me. I'm impressed in spite of myself, and a little bit turned on. Any girl who ditches me while I'm in the process of trying to make her jealous is hot.

"You want to head over to Jeremy's?" I ask B. J. He looks at me, his eyes glazed over and the front of his leprechaun outfit soaked in beer.

"Yes." He nods.

"Dude, you're shot," I say. "You're not going anywhere but home. Come on." I try to help B. J. up without actually getting too close to him. No way I want to kick it to Madison smelling like drunk leprechaun.

Twenty minutes later, after getting B. J. some drive-thru coffee and bringing him home, I decide to stop at my house to reapply my cologne and kill some time. I can't have Madison thinking I took off after her as soon as I realized she was gone.

There's an unfamiliar car in my driveway. My dad's out of town, so I'm assuming it's one of my mom's clients—she's a lawyer, and sometimes when she's in the middle of a big case, she'll have clients over to the house. I open the glove compartment and take a piece of gum out, popping it into my mouth just in case I smell like alcohol. I only had a couple of beers, but the last thing I need is to look drunk and disorderly in front of my mom and one of her clients.

"Mom!" I call, moving through the foyer, and trying to calculate how long my mom might be up and working.

She's a heavy sleeper, and our house is big enough that if my mom's asleep, I could totally bring Madison back here with me later on. "I'm home."

I hear some scuffling and whispers coming from the living room. I turn the corner, and that's when I see it. My mom. On the couch, with her shirt unbuttoned. There's some guy next to her, with his shirt OFF. And it's not my dad. For a second, I just stand there.

"Jordan," my mom says, smoothing her hair. She pulls her shirt closed. "I didn't think you'd be home until much later."

"Obviously," I say, sizing up the guy she's with. He doesn't look embarrassed. Instead, he looks almost pleased. No one moves. We all just wait, not saying anything.

"It's okay," I finally say. I turn around and head back toward the door. "I was actually going back out anyway, so . . ." I trail off, not really sure what I'm supposed to say.

"You don't have to," the guy says. He stands up from the couch. "I was just leaving anyway."

"I know I don't HAVE to," I say, turning back around. "I live here."

"Jordan—" my mom starts, but I turn on my heel and head out to my car. I slam the door of my truck and turn the music up. Loud. I sit there for a second, expecting my mom to come rushing out after me, to explain, to tell me it was some weird misunderstanding. But she doesn't.

After a few minutes, I turn the music down and back out of the driveway. I have no idea where I'm going or what I'm going to do. I'm so not in the mood to chase Madison anymore, and B. J.'s definitely done for the night. And all my other friends are probably at Jeremy's party. I drive around aimlessly for a few minutes, and then I remember Courtney McSweeney's number, written on a piece of paper in my wallet.

courtney ⬅ before

125 Days Before the Trip, 11:37 p.m.

So I chickened out. About telling Lloyd, I mean. But it wasn't really my fault, because while we were leaving the party, we ran into Olivia Meacham outside, and she was all over Lloyd in one of those "I'm making it clear you can have sex with me if you want" kind of ways. Which I could never figure out. How girls can do that, I mean. I'm always terrified of giving a guy any idea I might like him, so I overcompensate by acting like I don't. Like tonight, for example. I totally wanted to dance with Jordan. But I hesitated because:

> a) I thought I would look stupid. Which I probably did, but hopefully everyone was too drunk to notice.
>
> b) I didn't want him to think I wanted him. Because I don't. I want Lloyd. But the point is, no matter who it is, a guy I don't like or a guy I do, I don't want them to think I like them.

Anyway. There was Olivia Meacham, wearing a frayed denim skirt that I'd tried on once in Hollister with Jocelyn and then vetoed because it was way too short, and a blue halter top that showed off her stomach. It's taken me, oh, I don't know, five years to get up the courage to even *think* about telling Lloyd I like him. Olivia transferred into our school around Christmas, and three months later she's practically going down on him at this party.

Anyway, Lloyd starting flirting with Olivia, and the next thing I knew, she was in the car with us, and Lloyd was giving us both a ride home. And Lloyd dropped me off first. Which was kind of weird, since he made that whole production out of making sure I was riding home with him, when that wasn't even the plan to begin with. But I'm not stupid. I know you always drop the third wheel off first.

So here I am, at home, by myself, and it's kind of this big letdown. I really did want to tell him. And I can't even bitch about it to Jocelyn, because she's not answering her phone or replying to my text messages.

And of course no one's on instant messenger, because everyone's either sleeping or out. I download a few songs from iTunes, and then decide to see if Jordan has Facebook. Not because I like him or anything. But because I'm curious.

"Jordan Richman," I type into the search bar, and his profile pops up on the screen. The song he's chosen is "Let's All Get Drunk Tonight" by Afroman. Charming. I scroll through his pics. One of him at school, hanging out in the quad, one of him with his brother, Adam, who I recognize because he was a senior when we were freshman. And a bunch of Jordan with girls. Seriously, he has like ten pics of him with girls. Don't the girls get mad? I wonder. That they're on his page with a bunch of other girl pics?

I hit the back button and check out his friends. 789 friends. Quite the popular one, that Jordan. I have 117.

I scroll through the comments.

Seems like he and "Mad Madd Madison" have quite the Facebook flirtation going on. I go back and forth between their profiles, reading them. "What are you wearing?" Jordan asked her. "Why don't you come over and I'll show you," Madison wrote back. Gag. They couldn't come up with anything better than that? How lame.

My cell phone rings, and I reach for it, figuring it's Jocelyn calling me back. But the caller ID shows a number I don't recognize.

"Hello?"

"Court?"

"This is Courtney," I say, cradling the phone between my shoulder and chin and scrolling through Madison's pictures, most of which show her pouting for the camera, and wearing bathing suits. Seriously, bathing suits. And she's not in the beach or by the pool in any of them.

"Hey," the voice says, sounding nervous. "It's Jordan."

"Oh," I say. "Um, hi." I close out the browser, wondering

if he somehow saw I was on his profile, and is now calling to tell me to stop stalking him.

"You weren't sleeping, were you?"

"No, not at all," I say. "I just got home a little while ago."

"Cool," he says, and there's a pause.

"So, uh, what are you doing? Home from the party?" Oh, yeah, that was really great. Obviously he's home from the party, or he wouldn't be calling me. This is why I've never had a boyfriend. Because while other girls are wearing halter tops and leaving flirtatious messages on people's Facebook profiles, I'm coming up with such gems as "So, uh, what are you doing?"

"Driving around," he says. "I dropped B. J. off and then I was going to hit this other party, but I'm not really in the mood."

"Cool," I say. "But why are you driving around at"—I glance at the clock—"midnight?"

"I'm not sure," he says, sounding confused. "Just seemed fitting."

"Um, okay," I say.

"So," he says. "Where do you live?"

"Where do I live?" I say, flopping down on my bed. "Jordan, I can't tell you that! Technically, you're a stranger."

"I'm not a stranger," he says. "And besides, if I don't know where you live, I can't pick you up."

"Pick me up?" I say, swallowing.

"Yeah," he says. "So you can come to breakfast with me."

"How do you know I'm hungry?" I ask, thinking about his Facebook profile pics, and wondering if all those girls were invited to breakfast, too. I wonder if it's one of those weird competitions guys have. Like this one thing I read about guys in college who made up this game to see who could sleep with the biggest girl. It was really, really mean. Disgusting. Maybe Jordan and his friends have some sort of twisted Facebook pics competition. If he thinks he's getting a pic of us together, he's wrong.

"Well, are you?"

"Starved, actually." I *am* hungry. But that doesn't mean I'm going to breakfast with him. I mean, hello? Isn't this how people get stalked and killed? They sneak out in the middle of the night to meet some guy they know nothing about, and the next thing you know, no one ever hears from them again.

"So it's all settled," he says. "Where do you live?"

I hesitate.

"Courtney?" he says. "Please?" And there's something in the way he says my name that makes me think he really, really wants me to come.

I sigh and reach for the jeans lying on my floor. "Twelve thirty-five Whickam Way," I say. "And you better be buying."

"That was so good," I say an hour later, pushing my plate away. "I can't believe I ate all that at one in the morning. Definitely not a good idea."

"Ahh, it's fine," he says. He reaches over and uses his fork to cut a piece of the pancake that's left on my plate. He pops it in his mouth.

"How can you possibly want to eat any more?" I say. He's had three of his own pancakes, piled high with strawberries and whipped cream, three pieces of bacon, three sausages, home fries, and now he's eating what's left of mine.

"I'm hungry." He shrugs and picks up the check, which the waitress has left on our table. He pulls out a twenty from his wallet.

"How much do I owe?" I ask. I reach into my bag and rummage for my wallet.

"Nah," he says. "Don't worry about it."

"No," I say. "Absolutely not. I'm not letting you pay."

"Why not?" he asks, cutting himself another piece of pancake. "I forced you out of your house at midnight, it's the least I can do."

"You didn't force me," I say.

He shrugs. "Well, whatever. I'm paying."

"Thanks," I say, sliding my wallet back into my bag, and suddenly feeling awkward. I know I joked with him on the phone about him paying, but still. Does this mean it's a date? Who goes on a date at midnight with some guy she met at a party? It's very weird. Is this how things work? Do girls just pick up guys randomly and then go on dates with them? I guess so, since Olivia Meacham hooked Lloyd tonight in about two seconds. Although technically, Jordan picked me up, not the other way around.

"So," Jordan says, standing up. "What do you want to do now?"

"What do I want to do now? Um, in case you haven't noticed, it's one in the morning."

"So?" he says, grinning. "It's early. Oh, unless your parents need to have you home or something."

"Oh, no," I say. "It's nothing like that." The truth is, my parents would probably be thrilled that I'm out. My dad, especially. He's always trying to get me to go out more, instead of just sitting at home, doing homework or playing around on my computer. "My parents totally trust me," I tell Jordan. I reach over and take a sip of my hot chocolate, then grab two sugars from the container on the table and dump them into my cup. "It comes from being such a Goody Two-shoes for the first eighteen years of my life. They refuse to believe that I could do anything wrong, so they pretty much let me do whatever I want."

"So you've built their trust to a point where they wouldn't even consider the idea that their daughter could be text messaging when she's supposed to be learning about cosines, right?"

I almost spit out my coffee. "Hey," I say, "how did you know about that?" I spend almost all of math class texting to Jocelyn, since she has unstructured that period. I usually have a handle on the math stuff from reading the chapters the night before, and plus Lloyd goes over all my work, so it's not like I'm really missing out on anything. But how does Jordan know this?

"I'm at the perfect angle to see you pull out your phone," he says, grinning. "You do it all covert, hiding it under the pocket of your hoodie. Which, by the way, you always put on right before calc, so that you can text."

"Everyone texts in class," I say, shrugging my shoulders. It feels weird knowing he was watching me, that he knows something about me. Thank God he doesn't know exactly what I'm texting Jocelyn about, because trust me, he would flip out. Let's just say the words "Lloyd" and "sex" are used a lot. Not that I'm having sex with Lloyd. Or want to. I just like to talk about it. A lot.

"Anyway," I say, as the waitress comes by and drops the change onto our table, "thanks for breakfast." Jordan leaves $5 on the table and puts the rest of the money back in his wallet. So he's a big tipper. That's hot.

"So what do you want to do now?" Jordan asks, standing up.

"What do I want to do now?" I say. I check my watch. "Well, seeing as we're under twenty-one, I'm thinking our choices are home or home."

"Super Walmart is open," Jordan says, holding open the door for me. "And I heard they're having a sale on hoodies. You could get another one. You know, to help you in math."

"Oh, yeah, great plan," I say. "Our first date you take me out to breakfast at one a.m., and then to Super Walmart. How romantic." He looks uncomfortable for a second. "Not that this is a date or anything," I add quickly. "I was just messing around." Oh, my God, could I have been any dumber? Who says that? Refers to a random call from a guy she doesn't even know at one in the morning as a date? It's so not a date. Dates are when the guy calls you days in advance to set something up, and shows up at your house, meets your parents, and then takes you somewhere. And everyone knows that you're not supposed to even accept a date for the weekend after a Wednesday, because then you supposedly look desperate, right? Or is it Thursday? Whatever; the point is, this is so not a date. In fact, I'm not sure what it is. If I didn't know any better, I'd say it was a booty call. Booty calls always happen at one in the morning. But with booty calls, aren't you supposed to get right to it? Like, the point of the booty call is to get naked right away, not mess around with formalities like dinner and dates. Unless this is a booty call, and I just don't know it. And Jordan is trying to trick me into getting naked by taking me out to breakfast first, so then later, when I'm like, "That was a booty call!" he can be like, "No, it wasn't, we had breakfast." Like a modified booty call. It's probably the new trend in dating.

"So," Jordan says once we're on the road. "You really have to go home?"

"Yeah," I say, thinking about the Facebook comments

him and Mad Maddy exchanged less than twenty-four hours ago. "I should really get home." For a second, I expect that he's going to try to convince me to come back to his place, or worse, park the car in the Super Walmart parking lot so we can mess around. I mean, why else would he invite me out? Like I said, it's not a date, and if it's not a booty call, then what the hell?

He pulls into my driveway. "Are you sure you live here?" he asks, sliding the car into park, but leaving the engine running.

"I'm pretty sure," I say. I pull my keys out of my purse. "I have a key and everything."

"It's just that the mailbox says 'Brewster,' and your last name is McSweeney. So I need to make sure you're not involved in any illegal activity, where I might be implicated since we hung out tonight."

"What sort of illegal activity?" I ask. "Breaking into people's houses to sleep?"

"Well, it could be anything," he says, leaning back in his seat and pretending to look thoughtful. "This could be the headquarters for your drug trafficking posse. And all that texting you do in math is business related, and must be done during eighth period because of the time difference in certain South American countries."

"Yeah, I'm a total drug trafficker," I say, rolling my eyes. "I'm surprised your friend B. J. hasn't told you about me—he's my biggest client."

"Touché," Jordan says, grinning.

"No, but seriously, the truth isn't anything all that shady," I say, looking away for a second. "I have a different last name than my parents."

"Oh," he says. "I'm somewhat disappointed that it's something so normal."

"Maybe I'll tell you about it sometime," I say, opening the door. Although if you want to know the truth, I don't really want to leave. Which is crazy. I mean, this is Jordan Richman. He is totally not my type. Actually, I'm not his type. He likes girls like Olivia and Madison, girls that are super confident around guys and have the hookup list to back it up. My hookup list reads like this:

1. Kissed Jocelyn's cousin Justin during her seventh-grade birthday party during a game of spin the bottle. He had greasy lips. No tongue was involved.

2. Ninth grade—went on two dates with Paul Gilmore (once to the movies and once to dinner at the restaurant his dad owns, which I'm not sure really counts, since he didn't have to pay). Made out (kissing with tongue) during each date, which was slightly awkward since once we were in a movie theater, and once we were in the kitchen of his dad's restaurant.

3. Spent some of last year hooking up with Blake Letkowski, even though he was never really my boyfriend. He smoked. He was bad news. But he was a really good kisser.

Jordan unbuckles his seat belt and turns off the car. "Let me walk you to the door," he says.

"Oh, no, that's okay," I say, hopping out before he can protest. The last thing I want is some random awkward moment at my door, where he's trying to weasel his way into my house so he can attempt to devirginize me. I turn around and look back at him in the car. "Thanks again for breakfast, Jordan."

"My pleasure," he says.

"So, um, see you in school on Monday," I say, realizing it's true. I will see him in school on Monday. Which is weird. Thinking about seeing him in school, I mean.

"See you," he says, and I slam the car door. He waits until I'm safely inside before starting his car back up and pulling out of my driveway. I watch him from my living room window, wondering what the hell just happened, and how I ended up going out to breakfast with Jordan Richman.

courtney the trip

Day One, 11:56 a.m.

We haven't said a word to each other for the past two hours.
I'm starving, but I can't really admit it now, since I pitched
such a fit about not wanting to eat before. But really, I could
go for a burger. A huge one, dripping with mayonnaise and
ketchup. I've been turning pages of *The Catcher in the Rye*
for the past two hours without actually reading any of it. I
know, how lame. The good thing is that since I've read the
book so many times, it doesn't matter, because I already
know what's going on.

My mix CD is still playing. This is the third time it's
repeated, and even I'm getting sick of the songs. But I figure if Jordan's making an effort to be nice, I'm not going to
turn it off. I mean, it's either listening to these over and over
or putting rap on, and that's so not going to happen.

It's kind of strange, being in the car and not saying anything to each other. It's like some kind of suspense movie.

Or like being in an alternate universe, where we're not really Jordan and Courtney, but some other people who don't talk to each other.

My stomach grumbles really loudly, and I see Jordan smirk. But not in a mean way. More in a "isn't that cute" kind of way. For a second, I feel a pang in my stomach, almost like I'm going to cry, but then I start to get a little mad. He doesn't have the right to make a "isn't she so cute" face at me.

"Whatever," I say. "Like your stomach never grumbled."

"It's just funny," he says.

"I don't see why."

"Because you're obviously hungry, and yet you haven't said anything because you're afraid to not stick to the itinerary, because if we go off it even a little bit, you'll think you'll have 'lost' or something. And you hate to lose."

"That's not true," I say, even though it totally is. Well, sort of. It's not that I think I'll have lost, it's just I don't want to give him the satisfaction of thinking he was right. Besides, the itinerary says we're going to stop in another hour and a half, and I can certainly wait until then. I just won't think about it. La, la, la. Not thinking about burgers.

"It is true," he says matter-of-factly. "You'd rather starve than give me the satisfaction."

"Whatever," I say. "I'm not hungry at all."

Two minutes later, he pulls into a rest stop. "There," he

says, putting the car in park. "Now technically you didn't give in, and yet we can still eat." He smiles, his brown eyes sparkling. "And I'm hungry, too."

I'm about to protest, but instead I just pull my seat belt off and slide out of the car. I feel like I want to cry again, which is so, so, ridiculous. I mean, it's not like we were even together that long. Four months is nothing. Four months is like, less than a lot of those reality TV shows. And those people live together. And then probably never talk again. Plus, what about people who get divorced? Like people who are married for ten or fifteen years, and then never speak again? Some of them even go on to get married to other people. And then someone's like, "Hey, whatever happened to your first husband, Harry?" And they're like, "Oh, Harry, yeah, I forgot about him. I'm not sure. I think he might be running a casino in Vegas." People come and go, in and out of each other's lives like it's nothing. So I don't know how/why this should be a big deal.

I follow Jordan into the rest stop, which is really quite awkward. I can't walk next to him, because that's very, you know, couple like, but walking behind him is weird, too, because then it's like I'm not walking next to him on purpose, which may lead him to believe that he's actually affecting me, which I definitely don't want. For him to be affecting me, I mean. Or, for him to think that. Because he obviously *is* affecting me.

When we get inside, he heads to the Burger King line, and I go to Sbarro. I actually wanted Burger King, too, but there's no way I was going to stand in that wicked long line with him while we tried to make conversation. Or worse, just stood there in silence. I brought my book in with me, so hopefully while we're eating, I can read and he can just eat and look at the ground.

I order a sausage calzone before I realize that I should probably get the grilled chicken salad, since now that I have no boyfriend, I need to make sure I don't get really fat. I've been eating a lot lately, and with the freshman fifteen probably a given, I need to make sure I at least make some kind of effort to eat healthy. If I didn't know better, I would have started to think I was pregnant, what with all the food I've been eating. But I know I'm not, because Jordan and I never actually did it. The only time we came close was in Miami, right before we broke up. Thinking about that night makes me feel sick, and I almost throw my sausage calzone into a nearby trash can on my way to pick a table. But then I realize that if I don't have any food, Jordan's going to wonder why, and then what will I say? "Because I'm too upset about you dumping me to eat." I don't think so.

Despite the long Burger King line, Jordan's already sitting at a table when I get there, and so I slide in across from him.

"Hey," he says, unwrapping his Whopper. "What'd you get?"

"Sausage calzone," I say, putting the straw into my diet Coke. I reach into my bag and pull out my book.

"You're kidding, right?" Jordan says, raising his eyebrows.

"No," I say. "I really did get a sausage calzone." Why would I kid about that?

"I mean the book," he says. He takes a bite of his burger and licks his lips. I look away quickly, because a wave of heat has started between my legs and is now moving its way up my body. How ridiculous. That I'm getting turned on just from watching him lick his lips. Especially since he's such an asshole.

"What about it?"

"You're going to read your book at lunch?"

"Yeah, that was the plan," I say.

"Lame," he says, shrugging. He takes the top off his soda and takes a big drink. Jordan never uses a straw. He says it's because he can't get enough soda that way. I used to think it was cute. Apparently I still do, because I'm still getting hot just looking at him.

"Why is it lame?" I ask, frowning.

"It's just kind of rude." He shrugs again.

"Yeah, I don't think we should get into a conversation about what's rude and what isn't," I say. "Or who's ruder. Because I have a feeling I'd win that argument." He shifts in his chair uncomfortably. Good. I cut a piece of my calzone and pop it into my mouth. I look down at my book and try to concentrate on the words.

Suddenly Jordan's cell phone starts playing "Baby Got Back" again. He checks the caller ID, frowns, and then sends it to voice mail without answering it.

"Don't not answer it on account of me," I say. "It doesn't bother me at all."

"I thought it did," he says. "In the car, you acted like it did."

"Well, it doesn't here," I say, chewing and swallowing, even though the calzone tastes funny in my mouth. "In the car, you shouldn't talk on your phone, but here, it's okay. Besides, I'm reading." I force down another bite of calzone, and turn a page in my book.

"It wasn't important," he says.

"Whatever." I shrug.

"If it was, I would have answered it," he says. He takes another bite of his burger. And licks his lips again. My stomach does a flip.

"Good," I say. "Because I would hope that you wouldn't not answer a call from your girlfriend just because of me." Shit. Shit, shit, shit. Why would I say that? Why would I bring up the dreaded *G* word? It reverberates around us, like an echo. Girlfriend, girlfriend, girlfriend. We've never talked about his new girlfriend. Actually, since we broke up, we haven't really talked at all. Okay, stay calm. La, la, la, pretending I didn't say anything.

"It wasn't my girlfriend," he says, looking right at me. I practice making my face a complete blank. Like I'm in one of those poker tournaments and there's a million dollars on the line, and if my face betrays my emotions, then I'll lose it all. I look straight ahead. Think of things that don't make me emotional. Um. Spanish tests. Baseball. Pink shoes. Actually, I love pink shoes.

"Oh," I say, because someone has to say something. "I just want you to know that you don't have to not answer it because of me. If, you know, she does end up calling." I am so smooth.

"Thanks," he says, looking confused. "Aren't you hungry?" He looks at my sausage calzone, and since I don't want him to think I've lost my appetite from thinking about his skanky girlfriend, I down the whole thing even though it tastes disgusting. The sausage is rubbery, and the cheese tastes like plastic.

"Wow," Jordan says. "You really were hungry."

"Yup," I say, taking a big sip of my drink. "Good calzone." Not.

And then I do something that is so totally ridiculous, but I can't stop myself. It's one of those things that you know you shouldn't do, but you have to. Kind of like at the prom, when I had spent fifty dollars to get my nails done (those really cute acrylics that look real if you get the expensive kind), and while Jocelyn and I were in the bathroom reapplying our lipstick, one of my nails seemed a little loose, so I pried it off with a nail file. It was a really stupid idea, because I had to go around for the rest of the week with one nail missing. But I couldn't stop myself. And that's how it is right now.

"So," I say, "how are things going? You know, with, um,

your girlfriend?" I try to say it like I'm asking because I want him to be happy, but I'm afraid it comes out more like I'm prying. Since I just downed my whole calzone, I take a sip of my soda so I'll appear nonchalant.

"Fine," he says, shifting in his seat.

"Good," I say. "I'm glad." My stomach lurches, and I don't know if it's all the greasy food or the fact that I'm thinking about Jordan with another girl.

"Yeah," Jordan says. "And, uh, I guess, you and Lloyd?"

"What?" I say.

"You and Lloyd," he says. "You guys are like a thing now?"

"Yeah," I say, "we're a thing now." Oh. My. God. I cannot believe I just said that. Me and Lloyd are so not a thing. Well, I guess we're as much of a thing as you can be when you make out with someone in your room. Oh, my God. Am I slut? I think I'm a slut. I mean, who lets some random guy go up their shirt when they're in love with someone else? Not that Lloyd is really all that random. I mean, I've known him forever. And lusted after him for just as long. So maybe it was good that I got it out of my system. Because like I said, hooking up with Lloyd was . . . strange. But maybe that's just because we weren't used to each other. I don't really have much to compare it to, except for Jordan. And the first night he and I hooked up was weird, because it was so random. But then it got better. The hooking up, I mean. Because we got used to each other. Maybe Lloyd and I just have to get used to each other?

"Wait," I say. "How'd you know that Lloyd and I were a thing?"

"B. J. told me," he says.

"How does B. J. know?" I ask, rubbing my temples with my fingers. I'm starting to feel light-headed. Is this how celebrities feel, having their secrets splashed across the tabloids and wondering how the hell everyone found out?

"I guess Lloyd left some kind of comment on your Facebook profile," Jordan says, shrugging, "that led B. J. to believe you two were a thing."

I haven't checked my Facebook since last night, before I let Lloyd grope me. Although it wasn't really groping. It was more like . . . I dunno, stroking? Eww, that sounds so nasty. And it wasn't. Nasty, I mean. It just wasn't amazing, like it is with Jordan. Lloyd was kind of tentative, like he wasn't sure what he was doing. Not like I do. Know what I'm doing, exactly. Besides, you'd think that Lloyd would have taken the lead, since I know for a fact he's not a virgin and I am. Although not by my choice. I start thinking about that night in Miami with Jordan again and I really do feel dizzy.

"What did it say?" I ask, trying to make the room stop spinning.

"What did what say?" Jordan asks, frowning. He takes the last bite of his burger and licks his lips again. Can he STOP DOING THAT? Really, how much can one person lick his lips?

"What did the Facebook comment say?" I take a small sip of soda in an effort to calm my stomach down. Isn't that what soda is supposed to do? Make your stomach calm down? Actually, I think that's just ginger ale. Flat ginger ale.

"You don't know?"

"I haven't been online since last night," I say. "My laptop was already packed." I mean it to come out as kind of a dig, like I was all packed up and he wasn't, but it comes out like I'm panicked.

"I'm not sure." Jordan shrugs, and balls up the paper that his Whopper was wrapped in. He's not sure? He's not sure? That's ridiculous. How can he not be sure? As soon as B. J. was like, "Lloyd left Courtney a Facebook comment and I think they're a thing," Jordan should have been like, "Why, what did it say?" That's what I would have done.

"Oh." My stomach is on fire now, but I'm ignoring it. "Well," I say, standing up. I stretch my arms over my head like I don't have a care in the world. "I'm going to the bathroom, and then we'll get back on the road, sound good?"

"Sure." He stands up and starts to gather the trash from our table and put it on the tray. I walk toward the rest rooms, but as soon as I'm out of Jordan's sight, I pull out my cell and dial Jocelyn.

"Hello," she says, sounding groggy.

"Hi!" I say. "It's me."

"Oh," she says. There's a muffled noise on the line, like she's rolling over.

"Are you sleeping?" I say.

"Yes," she mumbles.

"Oh," I say. "Well, listen, I need you to do something for me."

"What?"

"You need to check my Facebook page for me." I look over my shoulder, fearful Jordan might head for the bathrooms when he's done picking up the garbage and see me standing outside, talking on my cell. I walk quickly toward the bathrooms just in case, figuring I can talk as easily in there and not arouse suspicion.

"Now?" Jocelyn asks, sighing. "Honey, no one has left you any comments this morning, trust me. It's too early for that." She yawns.

"It was last night," I say. "Lloyd left me a comment last night."

"What?!" she screeches, sounding fully awake. I hear another mumbled noise, and then the sound of her computer booting up. "What does it say?"

"I don't know," I say, trying not to become exasperated with her, since she's my one link to the Internet. "That's why I'm asking you to check." There's a line at the bathroom that stretches out the door and into the hallway, and I fall into it, behind a woman and her baby. She has a pink streak in her hair. The woman, not the baby.

"How do you know he left you a comment?" she asks gleefully. "Court, this is so hot, what do you think it says?"

"I don't know," I say. My stomach starts churning again. "Probably just like, 'Hey, had fun hanging out with you tonight,' or something like that."

"Maybe it has to do with you going to see him tomorrow," she says. "What time does his flight leave today?"

"I think one this afternoon," I say. "He was supposed to get to Middleton at around three or four."

"Just fyi, I think it's kind of corny that you guys are stopping to visit him," she says. "I mean, he'll have been at college for one day. Could you be any more desperate?"

"I'm not going just to see him," I say. "Jordan is going to see his brother, and Lloyd just happened to find out about it, and decided it would be cool to meet up." Jordan's brother, Adam, is going to be a senior at the University of Middleton, and he stayed in North Carolina this summer to do an internship. When Lloyd found out we were stopping on our way to Boston, he thought it would be cool if we could get together so I'd have a chance to see where he was going to school.

"But he invited you before you guys hooked up, right?" Jocelyn asks. "So it was like a friend thing."

"Oh, my God," I say. "Maybe Lloyd realizes hooking up was a huge mistake, and he doesn't want me to come anymore. Maybe his Facebook comment says something like, 'Wow, I can't believe I was so horny that that happened tonight, but I hope you didn't read anything into it. Maybe it's not a great idea for you to come visit after all.'"

"No," Jocelyn says, her voice low and even, like she's talking to some kind of mental patient. "Because B. J. told Jordan that Lloyd's comment made it seem like you guys were a thing."

Oh. Right. I take a deep breath.

"Okay," Jocelyn says. "It's loading. Hold on, I'm typing your page in." The sound of keystrokes comes over the line. "Okay, let's see . . . Oh, here it is."

"What does it say?" I almost scream. The old woman two people ahead of me in line turns around and gives me a dirty look.

"Don't freak out," she says, which is never good, because if someone has to preface what they're saying with "Don't freak out," you're probably going to freak out.

"Just. Read. It," I say.

"Okay." She clears her throat like she's about to give an oral presentation. "It says, 'Hey, beautiful. I had the best time with you tonight—seriously, it was amazing. I can't wait to see you tomorrow and talk about what this means. Thank goodness for frequent flyer miles, right? Sleep well, Courtney Elizabeth.'"

For a moment, I can't speak. Lloyd obviously does think we're a thing. Which we most certainly aren't. Which means that tomorrow, I am going to have to tell him we're *not* a thing, while trying to make it out to

Jordan that we *are* a thing, since I just told him we were.

"Court?" Jocelyn's saying. "Are you there?"

"Yeah, I'm here," I say. And then, before I can get into the bathroom, I throw up all over the floor.

courtney ⬅ before

"No," Jocelyn says, taking a sip of her chocolate milk and regarding me over the cafeteria table. "That's not going to happen."

"What isn't?" I ask, trying to sound innocent. I've just finished telling Jocelyn about my night with Jordan, and she's acting like it's this huge, bad idea. Which it probably is. But only if I like him. Which I don't.

"You are not going to start pining away for Jordan Richman," she says. "I won't let it happen."

"I'm not pining away for him!" I say. I open up the packet of blue cheese dressing that came with my salad and pour it over the lettuce on my plate. I'm not even really that hungry, but I need something to keep myself busy, so that I don't betray the way I'm feeling, which is that I may have a crush on Jordan. Which is insane. Because Jocelyn is right. That's just ridiculous.

"Good," Jocelyn says, looking satisfied. She takes another sip of her soda, then reaches over and grabs a cucumber off my salad. She pops it into her mouth. "But it is a little weird that he called you like that." She frowns. "Although it's even weirder that he didn't try anything."

"What do you mean?" I ask.

"Well, it's just that if a guy calls you late at night like that, usually it means he wants something physical. So for him not to try anything is kind of weird, you know?"

"Unless he thought he wanted to hook up with me, and then when he sobered up, he found me repulsive and decided not to."

"Was he drinking?"

"Not really."

Jocelyn rolls her eyes. "Then that makes no sense. Anyway, why are we still talking about this?"

"I have no idea." Because I can't stop thinking about him, and was a little disappointed when he didn't call me yesterday. Okay, even I can see that's pretty ridiculous. I mean, he's not my boyfriend. He's not even a guy I'm dating. So to be disappointed that he didn't call me on Sunday is just stupid. I think I should chalk it up to a random thing, one of those freak occurrences that no one can really explain. Like crop circles. Or that lady who got hit by a foul ball at a Yankees game, and then when she went to get it checked out, it turned out they found a tumor, and if she hadn't gotten it checked out, she would have died.

"Good," Jocelyn says, sounding satisfied.

"But . . ." I say slowly, twirling a piece of lettuce around on my fork.

"But what?" Jocelyn screeches. "There are no buts!" She grabs my hand and stops me from twirling. "Honey, no," she instructs. "He's bad news. He's not right for you."

"I know," I say. "You're right. Definitely." I frown. The thing is, when we were hanging out, he *did* seem right for me. Nothing like I really thought he was. But maybe that's just a ploy, something he does to make girls want him. It makes sense when you think about it—he must be doing *something* to get all these girls to fall in love with him. It must have to do with sweet-talking them and making them think he's a good guy. But I will not fall for that. I will be strong and not give in to his psychotic, mind game–playing ways.

"Don't talk to him anymore," Jocelyn says. "Don't look at him, don't call him, don't online stalk him."

"I won't," I say, not mentioning the fact that I checked his Facebook profile about three hundred times yesterday, and was secretly very pleased to see that Madison Allesio left him a comment, which he never replied to.

"I mean it, Courtney," she says. "Don't go getting all psychotic over something that's not even a thing."

"You're totally right," I say. And she is. Getting all worked up over some guy who is definitely not a thing is really stupid. Especially since I'm already all worked up over Lloyd, who is also not a thing, and is even hooking up with the girl he met at Connor's party. Unlike Jordan, Lloyd did call me yesterday, to tell me about how he felt up Olivia in the backseat of his car. Things in my love life are not going well.

"Besides, what about Lloyd?" Jocelyn asks, like she's reading my mind. She picks a cherry tomato off my plate and puts it in her mouth. I wordlessly hand her my fork, and she spears a forkful of my salad. Jocelyn is one of those people who is always trying to lose weight by not eating and then makes up for it by eating off everyone else's plate.

"He's hooking up with Olivia."

"Lame," Jocelyn says, rolling her eyes. "I give it a couple weeks."

"Yeah, maybe," I say. Madison Allesio goes walking by, flanked on both sides by girls from her cheerleading squad. I swallow hard.

"I have a scandal going on," Jocelyn announces.

"Oh, God," I say. "Do I even want to know?"

"Yes," Jocelyn says. "You want to know." She bites her lip. "But you can't get mad at me for not telling you sooner." Jocelyn likes to sit on her scandals. As in, she likes to wait a few days before telling anyone what's going on. Last year when she broke up with Kevin Scott, who she'd been dating for two years, she didn't tell me for a week. I just thought they were in a big fight, since I didn't see them hanging around each other in school. I've learned not to take it too personally. It's just how she is.

"I won't," I say. I wonder if the fact that Jordan Richman called me out of nowhere on the same night I was supposed to tell Lloyd I wanted him is some kind of sign. That Jordan and I are supposed to be together. Or that Lloyd and I aren't. Or that I really am supposed to be with Lloyd. That last one makes no sense, though, because why would Lloyd hooking up with Olivia mean he and I are supposed to be together? This is why believing in signs is never a good idea. They're so damn confusing.

"Okay," she says. "You know how on Saturday night you tried calling me really late, but I didn't answer?"

"Yes," I say. Unlike Jocelyn, I like to dissect and analyze any drama I'm involved in immediately. As soon as I got home from hanging out with Jordan on Saturday night, I called her.

"And you know how I didn't answer?" she says.

"Yes."

"And you know how I didn't call you back until four in the morning?"

"Yes," I say.

"And you know how you said you were sleeping, but we talked anyway, because—"

"Jocelyn! Yes, I know, I was there, now spill."

"Well," she says slowly. She twirls a strand of her light brown hair around her finger. "It was because I was hooking up with someone."

"Really?" I say. "Was it Mark?"

"No," she says.

I wait. Silence.

"Okay," I say. "Are you going to tell me who it was?"

"I don't know," she says.

"Jocelyn!"

"It's embarrassing!" she says. She pulls my plate closer to her and takes another bite of my salad.

"Why?" I say. "I mean, how bad can it be?"

"It's pretty bad," she says, sounding pained.

"It can't be as bad as the Blake Letkowski debacle," I say. Blake Letkowski is this kid who I ended up making out with last year when we were working together on a science project. He was bad, bad news. He smoked, he drank, he made racist comments . . . but I loved kissing him. Whoever Jocelyn hooked up with cannot be as bad as Blake Letkowski.

Silence. "Jocelyn?"

"Yeah?"

"Is it?" I pull my math book out of the messenger bag by my feet, hoping feigning nonchalance will get her to spill.

"Is it what?" she asks, frowning.

"Is it better than the Blake Letkowski debacle?"

"Yes. Definitely better."

"Better meaning more of a scandal, or better meaning it isn't as bad?" I say.

"I guess that depends on how you look at it," Jocelyn says slowly. She takes a sip of her chocolate milk. Jocelyn always drinks chocolate milk at lunch. Special, low-carb chocolate milk in single-serving containers that she buys before school each morning at the Mobil on the corner.

"What do you mean?" I say. You'd think I'd be getting bored of this conversation, since she's so obviously jerking me around, but surprisingly, I'm not. I want to know who she hooked up with.

"I mean, do you think it's good that I've hooked up with someone worse than Blake Letkowski, or are you going to be sympathetic?"

"So whoever it is, IS worse than Blake."

"Courtney!"

"WHAT?"

She takes a deep breath. "Never mind, I'm not telling you."

"Fine." I pretend to be engrossed in my math problem. After a few seconds, I can tell she's getting antsy, but I break first. "Just tell me!"

"No!"

"I'll find out."

"No one will find out."

"Why not?"

"Because I'm not going to tell anyone."

"What if *he* tells someone?"

"He won't."

"Why not?"

"Because we both said we wouldn't tell anyone."

"Oh, okay, cause that always works out. Guys who say

they won't tell anyone you hooked up always keep their mouths shut." She's silent. "But whatever," I say, shrugging and turning back to my math book. "If you don't want to tell your best friend in the whole world who you hooked up with, well, then . . ." I trail off.

"It's not that I don't want to tell you," she says. "It's just that I don't want to be judged."

"When have I ever judged you?" I say, rolling my eyes. "I am the least judgmental person ever."

"Well," she says, looking thoughtful. She takes another bite of salad. "When I joined newspaper last year because Dan Carlio was on the paper, you kind of judged me."

"That was different," I say. "He was brainwashing you." At the end of junior year, Jocelyn got wrapped up in this ridiculous guy who was one of those activist, literary types. He was always trying to use the school newspaper to further his political beliefs. Jocelyn started skipping school to go to environmental protests and almost lost her credits because of all the time she missed. Plus Dan was really creepy, and he referred to Jocelyn as his "little soldier." Weird.

"He was not!" Jocelyn says. She's horrified.

"Jocelyn, he made you join the Green Party."

"So?"

"So, do you even know what the Green Party is?"

"It has to do with Ralph Nader," she says, proud of herself.

"Whatever."

Silence.

"So tell me."

"Okay."

"Waiting."

"You can't laugh."

"I won't."

"You can't say anything."

"I *won't*."

"B. J. Cartwright."

Silence.

"Say something!" she shrieks.

"You told me not to!" I say. "So I wasn't." B. J. Cartwright. Yikes. That's . . . "disturbing" is really the only word I can come up with, but I can't tell Jocelyn that. Because I told her I wouldn't judge. Besides, Jocelyn takes attacks on people she's hooking up with as a personal attack on herself. So if I were to say to her, "Wow, Jocelyn, that's disturbing," she would take it as meaning, "Wow, Jocelyn, you are disturbed." Which may or may not be true, but still.

"Well, by not saying anything, you're saying a lot."

I think carefully. "Well," I say slowly. "Why don't you tell me how it happened?"

"Okay," she says eagerly. She pushes the empty salad plate away from her. "Well, you know how I was trying to flirt with Mark, right?"

"Right."

"Well, B. J. was hanging out sort of near him, and we started talking."

I try to figure out how I can ask her if this was before or after B. J. clamped onto my leg like some kind of dog in heat, without actually saying, "Hey, Jocelyn, was this before or after B. J. clamped onto my leg like some kind of dog in heat?"

"So we started talking, and then later he called me and invited me to go to Jeremy's party, and then . . . I don't know, really. We ended up back at his house." She stops. "Making out," she adds, in case I missed it.

"Okay," I say slowly. "So what now?"

"Duh," she says. "Now I avoid him."

"Good plan." Pause. "Why, again?"

"Because, hello, it's B. J. Cartwright! Although," she says thoughtfully, "he was a really good kisser."

Ewww.

The bell rings, signaling the end of lunch, and we throw our trays away and head down the hall, me to AP Bio, her to Creative Writing.

"Now," she says, as we stop at her locker on the way. "We're clear on this whole Jordan thing, right?" She twirls the dial to the right.

"What do you mean?" I ask.

"Don't try to talk to him or anything like that," she says. "Ignore him. He's bad news, Courtney."

"Totally," I say. "But what if he says hi to me first?"

"No," she says. "Well, if he says hi first, you can say hi to him. But that's all." She grabs me by the shoulders and looks me straight in the eye, like I'm going off to do battle. "Clear?"

"Totally clear."

before jordan

123 Days Before the Trip, 2:18 p.m.

Courtney McSweeney is acting like I don't exist. We're sitting in math class, and I'm watching her text on her phone through her pink Abercrombie hoodie, and I'm starting to get a little annoyed. Not one word. She hasn't even looked at me.

I raise my hand while Mrs. Novak is going over the homework.

"Yes, Jordan?" she asks.

"I had a question on number nineteen," I say, which isn't true. I don't even know what number nineteen is, but whatever. Mrs. Novak doesn't know that, and hopefully it will get Courtney to look at me. But she doesn't. She just keeps texting. I realize I'm really, really annoyed, which is weird. I don't get annoyed when girls blow me off, especially if I have no interest in them.

"What's your question, Jordan?" Mrs. Novak asks, looking

at me suspiciously. I usually don't raise my hand in math. I usually don't raise my hand in any class. It's not that I don't know the answers. I just find it unnecessary.

"Can we go over the whole problem?" I ask. "Courtney and I were actually discussing how this assignment was a little tricky."

"Sure," Mrs. Novak says, and starts going over the problem Courtney keeps texting, still not looking at me. What the hell is her problem? Actually, what the hell is *my* problem?

I even made sure I came into the classroom right as the bell was ringing, just in case she had any ideas about us talking. One time sophomore year, I hooked up with this girl (a freshman, figures) who was in five of my classes. It was a nightmare. Every time I'd walk into class, she'd be sitting at my desk, waiting for me, so we could "chat" before the bell rang. That's what she called it—"chatting."

"I just want to chat," she'd say, only her idea of "chatting" involved her asking me ridiculous questions like "Don't you ever get bored with shoes? Since you're a guy and you don't have many choices?"

I learned that if you're in a class with a girl you don't want to talk to, you sneak in just as the bell rings. That way, you avoid having to interact with her. But Courtney hasn't even looked at me. Not once. Even when I mentioned her name.

So when the bell rings signaling the end of the period

and the end of the school day, I wait until she walks out of the classroom, and then walk up behind her, pulling on her hood.

"Hey," I say, when she turns around.

"Oh," she says, looking surprised. "Hey." She shifts her bag to her other shoulder. "What's up?"

"Not much," I say, trying to keep it light. "So is this how you usually treat guys who buy you a meal?"

She smiles. "What do you mean?"

"By ignoring them." I smile back, to show her I'm not bothered by it.

"I wasn't ignoring you," she says, holding up her phone. "I was busy texting."

"Well, I wouldn't want to interrupt whatever secret business it is you were working on."

We've reached her locker now, and she starts to turn the combination dial. She's biting her lip while she does it, and I suddenly have the urge to reach over and bite it for her. Her lip. Not her locker. God, I'm losing it.

"So," she says, sliding some books into her bag. When she does that, it reminds me that the school day is over, and that I might actually have to go home now. Which sends me into a mild panic. After I left Courtney's house on Saturday night, I drove around for a while (okay, a long while), and by the time I got home, it was four in the morning, the rogue car was gone, and my mom was asleep. I slept until around seven (well, tossed around in my bed), and then grabbed breakfast at Dunkin' Donuts and started driving. And driving. And driving. I drove until eleven, called B. J., and spent the day at his house, helping him nurse his hangover and playing Xbox. I ended up crashing at his house, and this morning stopped at my house only when I knew my mom had already gone to work to take a quick shower and change my clothes.

The day, so far, has been a normal Monday at school, but I'm shot. I feel exhausted, but for once, I'm not looking forward to getting home and taking my Monday afternoon nap. I don't want to go home. Now. Or ever. The other thing I realize is that I want to hang out with Courtney. Right now.

"Hey," I say, leaning against her locker and giving her my most charming smile. "What are you doing now?"

"Going home," she says, sliding her backpack over her shoulders and slamming her locker door.

"You want to hang out for a little while, get something to eat or something?"

A look of surprise crosses her face, and she frowns. "I can't," she says firmly. She turns on her heel and starts walking away from me. Which, of course, just makes me want to chase after her. I grab her backpack and pull her around.

"Why not?" I grin.

"Why?" she says.

"No," I say, sighing. "Why not?" What is it with this girl?

"I mean, why do you want to go get something to eat with me?" She puts her hand on her hip, like she's challenging me. She's wearing a small silver chain bracelet and it slides down her wrist.

"Because I'm hungry?" I say. Obviously the best answer isn't "Because I caught my mom having an affair and I don't want to go home." Besides, it's not like I'm lying. I am hungry. And I do want to hang out with her. Plus, why is she challenging me? Who says shit like this?

She turns and starts walking away again. "Courtney!" I'm literally chasing her now, making my way down the hall and through the throng of people leaving for the day.

"Yeah?" She turns around.

"What is your problem? If you don't want to go, just say it."

"I don't want to go." She crosses her arms in front of her.

"Fine," I say. "Then that's all you had to say." I turn on my heel and start walking down the hall.

"Jordan!" she calls after me, and I almost don't stop. But she says my name again, and I turn around.

"Look," she says, "I'm sorry. It's just been a weird day, that's all." She bites her lip. "If you still want to go . . ."

"Don't feel like you have to do me any favors," I say, still a little pissed. "It's not a big deal. If you don't want to go, you don't want to go."

"No," she says, pushing her hair away from her face. "I do want to go. But I'm buying."

"Fine," I say, shrugging. "Then let's go."

* * *

Half an hour later, we're sitting in my truck, eating drive-thru food from Taco Bell. I wanted to go to a real place, but she was adamant that we go for fast food. This chick is really strange, because then she wouldn't even let me take her INTO the restaurant, and instead insisted on eating in my car.

"So," I say, "thanks for ignoring me today."

"I wasn't ignoring you," she says, looking uncomfortable. She shifts in her seat. "I was just paying attention."

"Right," I say. I take a bite of my Taco Supreme and look over at her. She's barely touched her food. Plus, she keeps giving me all these one-word answers. I grope for something to say that will force her to engage in conversation with me.

"So," I say. "Tell me about your parents."

"My parents?" she asks.

"Yeah. Why you don't have the same last name as them, if and how they're involved in the whole drug trafficking scheme, any neuroses they may have, if you hate them, etc."

"It's really not that scandalous," she says. "So if I tell you, it may ruin the whole thing. Maybe I should keep it a secret, so you'll think I'm mysterious and engaging."

"I already think you're mysterious and engaging," I say, taking a sip of my soda.

"You do?" She turns to me, and the sun shining through my windshield hits her hair and illuminates her face. She smiles. "Why?"

"Why what?" I say. Suddenly I feel weird. For the first

time, I realize I'm in a car with a girl. Not only that, but it's just hit me that Courtney's fucking hot. Not hot in the way Madison is, with her revealing clothes and huge amounts of lipstick, but hot in the sense of . . . I don't know. Just hot. An overall package of hotness.

"Why am I mysterious and engaging?" she asks, sounding exasperated.

"Oh," I say. "Because you ignored me in math today. And no one ever ignores me."

She rolls her eyes. "Right. No one ever ignores you."

"Well," I say, looking at her out of the corner of my eye. "Sometimes girls do ignore me. But it's only because they want me to think they're ignoring me, so that I'll want them."

"Maybe they're ignoring you because they don't want you." She shrugs. "Maybe they're just weirded out by the fact that you've basically ignored them for four years of high school, and then started randomly taking them to drive-thrus and diners at weird times."

"Except I don't usually take girls to random drive-thrus and diners at weird times."

"Where do you usually take them?" She's smiling at me now, and I smile back.

"The backseat," I joke, and the smile vanishes from her face. "Whoa," I say, "just kidding." This girl is such a hardass. "Lighten up, Court."

She takes a small bite of her taco and stares out the window.

"So," I say. "Your parents? What's the deal?"

"My dad isn't my biological father," she says, shrugging. "He adopted me last year, but I just decided to keep my last name. Didn't want to have to go through the hassle of changing it, but I might at some point."

"That's cool," I say, hoping she doesn't ask about my parents and what the deal is with them. No way we need to get into the fact that my mom is screwing around on my dad. "Is your dad a good guy?"

"Yeah," she says. "He's great. He's been married to my mom since I was three, so I don't really know anything else, you know?"

"Cool." I take the last bite of my taco and throw the balled-up wrapper back into the empty bag. "So what should we do now, Court?"

"Why do you keep calling me 'Court'?" she asks.

"Because," I say, shrugging. "It's my new pet name for you."

"As opposed to your old pet name?"

"Yeah, my old pet name," I say, miming that I'm texting someone on a phone. "'Weird Text Girl.'" It's a gamble, but it pays off. She reaches over and pushes me playfully, and I block her hand. I realize again how good she smells, and I swallow. No way I'm going to start hooking up with Courtney McSweeney. That's just insane.

"Are you flirting with me?" I ask.

"No." She looks shocked and moves back to her side of the car. "Not even."

"You totally were."

"Sweetie," she says, turning to look at me. "If I was flirting with you, you'd know it."

She raises her eyebrows at me, and I realize she's probably telling the truth. If she were flirting with me, I'd probably know it. I'm also really, really turned on.

An hour later, we're in the DVD section at Barnes & Noble, debating whether or not *Laguna Beach* is a good TV show. I somehow conned her into coming into the bookstore with me, which wasn't that hard since it's right next door to Taco Bell.

"They're like talking mannequins," Courtney says, shaking her head. "I have no idea how you could remotely be interested in this show."

"I didn't say I was interested in it," I say, rolling my eyes. This is a lie. I watch it all the time.

"What night of the week is it on?" she asks, raising her eyebrows.

"Wednesday," I recite without thinking. She smiles smugly.

"That doesn't mean anything!" I protest. She slides the DVD of *Laguna* back onto the shelf and turns around.

"Whatever." She shrugs and starts walking toward the Action/Adventure movies.

"Everyone knows *Laguna Beach* is on Wednesday nights! All you have to do is turn on MTV for half a second. There's commercials on all the time."

"Fine," she says again, shrugging.

"And so what if I watch it?" I say, "It is what it is."

"*Ridiculous* is what it is. They're like pod people."

"Okay," I say, switching tactics. "Did you watch *The OC*?"

"Totally different," she says.

"Oh my God, not even!" I say. "It's the same thing. Only one is written for television, and one is reality TV."

"*The OC* is completely different," she says. "Because even though the characters are rich and materialistic, they at least have intelligent conversations. They have issues. Dilemmas. Debates!"

Hmm. She has a point. I'm trying to think of a good *Laguna* debate that didn't involve the Kristin Cavallari/Nick Lachey situation in the media. My cell phone rings before I can think of one, and I pull it out of my pocket.

It's B. J. I hesitate. It's probably rude to answer it, but Courtney's not going to want to hang out with me forever, so it's a good bet that at some point, I'm going to need to head over to B. J.'s to avoid going home. In which case answering the phone is going to be in my best interest.

"Do you mind if I take this?" I ask. "It's kind of important."

"No problem," she says, turning back to the movies. She kneels down to get a look at something on the bottom shelf, and the back of her shirt rises up, showing her back. I swallow.

"Whaddup?" I say, flipping my phone open and walking a few feet away from Courtney.

"Dude, shit is going down," B. J. says, sounding like shit really is going down.

"What is it?"

"So I just got out of the gym, right?" B. J. stays after with the football team every day to work out, so I'm assuming that's what he's referring to.

"Yeah," I say.

"So when I leave the school, there's Jocelyn, in the parking lot with Krista Crause and Tia Biddlecome."

"Okay," I say, already starting to become bored with this story. I'm a little bitter about B. J.'s whole hookup with Jocelyn, since after I got him coffee the other night and drove him home, he ended up going to Jeremy's party anyway. So while I was catching my mom cheating on my dad and acting insane about Courtney McSweeney, B. J. was out partying without me. I try to catch a glimpse of Courtney's bare back again by glancing around the display of *Star Wars* DVDs. She's still leaning. She has a nice ass. I wonder what kind of underwear she wears, if it's a thong, or maybe those boy shorts. Something lacy, maybe.

"And she ignores me!" B. J. says. Courtney leans over farther. Her shirt slides farther up her back. I try to figure out how close I need to be to get the best view without her actually hearing my conversation. Is it insane to be having these thoughts about her? Probably. I mean, I'm supposed to be kicking it to Madison. It's just that Courtney's fun to be around. She takes my mind off all the shit that's going on at home. Which is good.

"Hello?!" B. J. asks on the other end of the phone.

"Yeah," I say, swallowing. "Jocelyn ignored you."

"I can't believe it!" he says. "That's fucked up, dude."

"Girls are fucked up," I say, shrugging. "Do you like her?"

"Not anymore," he says, not sounding like he means it. "Not if she's going to act like a shit."

"She's messing with you," I say. "Just ignore her right back."

"But I don't want to fucking ignore her," B. J. says. "I want to hook up with her again!"

"I know," I say, sighing. "But if she's going to play it all cool, the last thing you want is to come off as Psycho Obsessed Asshole."

A Barnes & Noble employee, a young guy in a green apron with pierced ears almost bumps into me. "Sorry," I say.

"Where are you?" B. J. asks suspiciously.

"At the bookstore."

"The bookstore? What the fuck for?"

"I'm, uh, looking at books," I say. "And I should get back to it. Let me call you later."

"Who are you with?" B. J. asks.

Fuck. "What do you mean?" I ask, trying to infuse my voice with as much innocence as possible. He sighs.

"Who. Are. You. There. With."

"I'm by myself," I lie. Why did I just lie? I hate lying.

I don't believe in lying. Lying only gets you in trouble. Manipulating situations is one thing, but lying is another. My theory (especially with girls), is that if you don't lie, you can't be held responsible for anything bad that goes down.

Case in point: When I hooked up with Jana Freeze last summer. I told her I didn't want a girlfriend, and that I was going to be hooking up with other people. She got all pissed off when I kissed Michelle Tessiro the weekend after. But really, it wasn't my fault. Because she knew the deal, and she chose to put herself in that situation.

I know I sound like a slut. But I'm really not.

"You're by yourself?" B. J. asks incredulously. "What the fuck for?"

"I told you," I say, trying not to lose my patience, since it's really my fault for lying to him. "I'm looking at books."

"Dude, that's some fucked-up shit," he says.

"Fine," I say. "I'm with Courtney McSweeney."

"Courtney McSweeney?" B. J. asks, as if I've just announced I'm out on a date with Mischa Barton. "What the fuck for?"

"I don't know," I say, realizing it's true.

"Whatever," B. J. says. "Can you maybe ask her about Jocelyn for me?"

"Ask her what about Jocelyn?"

"Ask her what the deal is. They're friends." He sighs as if he can't believe my obvious ridiculousness at not getting the plan. Which is really worrisome to me, because if B. J.

is saying something I'm not understanding, that means my head is completely fucked up.

"Okay," I agree.

"But don't let her know I want to know," he instructs.

"Of course not." I don't point out that expecting me to ask a girl I hardly know about how her friend feels about B. J. without actually telling her why I want to know is going to be a pretty hard thing to do.

"Lata." B. J. clicks off before I can make plans with him for later. Shit.

Courtney comes around the corner, carrying *Laguna Beach* Season One on DVD. She holds it up and smiles at me. "Maybe I'll give it a second chance."

"You should," I say, grabbing the blue DVD case out of her hand and checking out the back. What's not to like about this show? Hot girls. Hookups. Who needs intelligent conversations and debates? It all boils down to wanting one another, anyway. So people should just hook up and get it over with.

"So . . ." she says, taking it back from me. "I should probably get home."

"Oh," I say, kind of surprised. Girls don't usually end dates with me. Not that this is really a date. It's more like a hang out. I follow her up to the cash register, where she purchases the *Laguna Beach* DVDs. Definitely not a date. Because if it were a date, I'd be paying. And we'd be hooking up. And that is definitely not going to happen.

Half an hour later, we're kissing in my car.

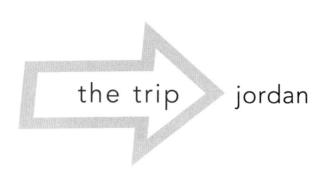

the trip ▶ jordan

Day One, 12:36 p.m.

I'm heading toward the bathroom to see what's taking Courtney so long when I see her lean over and throw up all over the floor. It's pretty nasty, a bunch of brown chunks and green liquid. I knew that sausage calzone didn't look right.

"Court," I say, rushing over to her. "Are you okay?"

She looks up at me, her eyes bloodshot, and then leans over and heaves again. I take her cell phone out of her hand, hang up on whoever it is she was talking to without bothering to say anything, and lead Courtney past the line of waiting women (who are all staring—have they never seen anyone upchuck before?) and into the women's bathroom.

"Jordan," she says, leaning against my shoulder. "You can't come into the girls' bathroom."

Four women at the sink are gaping at me openly. "It's okay," I say to them. "I'm just helping my friend. She's not feeling so well."

"We're not friends," Courtney says, and then throws up again into one of the sinks against the wall. It's not the best move, saying the guy who's taking care of you isn't your friend, but I let it slide since she's obviously in distress. I pull her hair back from her face.

"Do you have a hair tie?" I ask her, ignoring the stares of the woman at the sinks. What is their problem? Do they not see that she's sick? You'd think they'd be rallying around me, excited I was so obviously concerned that I would risk a trip into the women's bathroom. Maybe it's a new kind of crime, guys pretending they're friends with random girls who get sick at rest stops, so that they can sneak into women's bathrooms and get a peek at . . . I look around. At middle-aged women washing their hands.

Courtney hands me her bag, and I riffle through it, looking for a hair tie. Makeup, notebook, mirror . . . why do girls need so much stuff? I pull Courtney's hair back from her face, trying to gather it in a ponytail. Her skin feels smooth against my hands.

"Let me do it," Courtney says, taking the hair tie away from me. Her fingers brush against mine, and my heart rate speeds up again. God, I want her so bad.

She pulls her hair back, then leans over the sink again and gives one final, silent heave. I rub her back until her body stops shaking.

"You okay?" I say.

"Yeah," she says. She's gripping the sides of the sink so

hard that her knuckles are turning white. "I'm okay. I just hate throwing up."

"Will you be okay in here for a second by yourself? I'll go get you a bottle of water."

"Okay," she says, not really sounding like she means it. I look around the bathroom. The floors are dirty and there are random paper towels and toilet paper strewn around the floor. It smells like exactly what you'd think a thruway rest stop bathroom would smell like.

"Actually," I say. "Why don't you just come with me? We'll get you some water, and then you can sit in the back of my truck. Some air might make you feel better."

"Okay," she agrees, and starts walking shakily toward the door of the restroom. I go to put my arm around her like before, but she shrugs me off. "I'm fine."

Ten minutes later, she's sitting with her feet hanging over the side of my open truck back, sipping water slowly, and looking a little bit better, although really pale.

"I should call Jocelyn back," she says. "I was talking to her when I started throwing up."

I feel relieved that she wasn't talking to Lloyd, which is completely ridiculous. Courtney and I are over, and no matter how much I still want to be with her, it's not going to happen. And she deserves someone who's going to make her happy. If Lloyd does that for her, I really am cool with it.

My phone starts ringing in my pocket, and I check the

caller ID. Courtney's dad. The fucker will not leave me alone. Every five minutes with him.

"I'm gonna take this," I tell Court. "Are you going to be okay for a few minutes?"

"Yeah," she says. "I'll call Jocelyn back so she doesn't worry."

I walk safely out of Courtney's earshot, and then open my phone. "What?" I say. He may have gotten me to break up with Courtney, but as far as I'm concerned, the power he has over me stops there. Well, that's not exactly true. Because he keeps calling me.

"That's not a nice way to answer the phone, Jordan," he says, sounding cheerful.

"Yeah, well, I'm not in exactly the nicest mood right now," I say.

"Oh, and why's that?" he asks, sounding amused.

"Because you keep calling me."

"I just wanted to make sure everything was going okay," he says. "That the trip was proceeding safely."

"Yeah, everything's fine," I say, not mentioning the fact that Courtney just spent ten minutes throwing up into a sink.

"Jordan, you know I'm not trying to be a dick about this," he says, sighing.

"Yeah, spare me," I say, watching Courtney from where I'm standing. She looks really small and really pale.

"I'm not," Mr. Brewster says. "I just want Courtney to be happy, and I really think this is the best way to go about it.

And Jordan, I think you know that telling Courtney what happened really isn't going to serve any real purpose."

Other than to make her hate me, I think to myself. And it's true. If I told Courtney what I knew, she would hate me even more than she does now. And having her hate me because she thinks I dumped her for another girl is much better than having her hate me because of what I know.

"Well, you don't have to worry," I say, swallowing hard. "I'm not going to say anything."

"Thanks," Mr. Brewster says. "I really do appreciate it, Jordan. And I *am* going to tell Courtney. But on my own time."

"Whatever," I say. I snap my phone shut and take a deep breath. After a few seconds, I turn back around and head back to the truck. I cannot wait until this trip is over.

courtney | the trip

Day One, 1:47 p.m.

I'm going to throw up again. "I'm going to throw up again," I tell Jordan, feeling it rising up in my throat. We're back on the highway now, and he signals and pulls over quickly to the side of the road. I open the door and lean out, throwing up onto the pavement. This is so disgusting. Seriously. I hate throwing up. I have this really bad phobic fear of it. I go to great lengths not to throw up, and until today, I hadn't thrown up since the fourth grade. Fourth grade! That's like eight years. It's a real phobia, too. Throwing up, I mean. I know no one likes to throw up, but it's proven that some people are really scared of it. Like me. And some celebrities. Matthew McConaughey, I think.

"You okay?" Jordan asks, and I feel his hand on my back.

"Yeah, I'm okay," I lie, wiping my mouth on the back of my hand. Gross, gross, gross. I'll bet his Facebook girl never throws up all over herself when they're together. I'll bet they're too busy having sex to eat anything that might cause her stomach to get all sketch.

"You sure?" Jordan asks. "You don't look okay."

"Gee, thanks," I say, slamming the door shut.

Jordan hands me a napkin. "Uh, here," he says, "you might want to wipe your mouth."

I take the napkin from him and turn away, wiping the drool off my mouth. Have I mentioned this is really disgusting?

I throw the napkin into the ashtray and push the seat back again, reclining all the way back. It's actually very easy to trick yourself into not throwing up. You just lay back, perfectly still and straight, close your eyes, and try not to move.

"Hey, Court?"

"Yes?" I ask, trying not to move my mouth in case it sets off some kind of motion wave to my stomach.

"Listen, I think maybe we should check into a hotel somewhere," he says, sounding hesitant, like he doesn't want to piss me off. "You're obviously sick, and you need to rest."

"I'm fine," I say. "And besides, it would mess up the schedule." Is he crazy? We're already way behind thanks to his lollygagging this morning. Plus the traffic. Plus the long bathroom lines at the rest stop. Plus my throwing up.

"Are you sure?" he says, "Because I saw a sign a few miles back for a Days Inn coming up."

"It. Would. Mess. Up. The. Schedule."

"Okay," he says, looking at me out of the corner of his eye. "Are you sure?"

"YES." Of course I'm sure. I'm not going to let throwing up stop me from getting to college on time.

Two miles later, after we've had to pull over three more times so I can throw up, he pulls off at the next exit and follows the sign that says DAYS INN. I don't stop him.

So this is really awkward. Jordan's checking into the Days Inn, which is a completely and totally unscheduled stop, and the front desk clerk has assumed we want one room. This place is kind of sketch (the clerk asked us for how long we wanted the room, and I think he meant in hours), and there are some very scantily dressed girls standing outside. Which is weird, because it's four in the afternoon. Definitely not late enough for prostitution. Although maybe I've been conditioned by the media to think prostitutes only come out after midnight. Like this one special I saw once about hookers who frequent truckstops. They call them "lot lizards" and they only come out at night.

"Yes," Jordan says. "We'll take the one room."

"No," I say. "We'll take two."

The guy looks nervously between the two of us. "No, we won't," Jordan says, turning out to look at me. I'm sprawled in one of the chairs in the "lobby," which is really a foyer. I have vomit on my shirt, my hair is coming out of my ponytail, and on the way in here, I almost fell over and Jordan had to take my bag. "Court, you're sick. I'm not leaving you by yourself."

"Fine," I say. "But two beds."

"Of course," Jordan says, rolling his eyes.

Of course two beds. I forgot for a moment that Jordan has a girlfriend. One who he obviously loves enough to leave me for, which means there's no way the thought of sharing a bed with me would have crossed his mind. For the first time, I wonder what his girlfriend thinks of the fact that Jordan is here, on a trip with me. She's probably one of those super-secure girls who is all confident in her relationship. How annoying.

Conversations About Me Jordan Had with His Girlfriend (A Deluded Fantasy by Courtney Elizabeth McSweeney):

Jordan: So I'm stuck going on this trip with Courtney.

Mercedes: Okay.

Jordan: Just so you know, nothing's going to happen.

Mercedes (starts taking her clothes off so she and Jordan can have sex): I know.

Jordan: You want to have sex again? We just finished two hours ago.

Mercedes (climbs on top of him): Yes. **(Pauses.)** This Courtney girl or whatever her name is, she's not cute, is she?

Jordan: No.

Mercedes: Cool.

Jordan picks up our bags and starts down the hall. "Room 103," he says, reading off the card the front desk guy gave him. I'm concentrating on making it down the hall without passing out, since the floor seems to be spinning. I'm watching my feet (which are cased in very cute purple sandals) as I move one in front of the other, trying not to lose it. One. Two. Step. Step. Ha, like that song by Ciara. "I love it when you one, two step." Although I don't think Ciara was trying to keep herself upright while walking down a hotel room hallway with her ex-boyfriend who she was still in love with when she wrote that song. I think Ciara was having dance parties and fun and all sorts of really good things that had nothing to do with nausea or horrible road trips.

I lean against the door frame as Jordan slides the plastic card into the electronic sensor that will let us into our room. A green light flashes and he holds the door open for me. I push by him, and as I do, my chest brushes against his, and for a second, I lose my breath, but then I'm past him and it's over. I slide onto one of the beds and drop my bag onto the floor.

Whoever was in the room before left the air conditioner on full-blast, and it feels good. I'm hot. I lean back on the bed and close my eyes.

"You okay?" Jordan asks, plopping himself down on the other bed.

"Yeah," I say. "I'm fine."

He picks the remote off the floor and turns on the TV. The sounds of ESPN come blaring out of the speakers.

I pick my suitcase up off the floor and head to the bathroom without telling him where I'm going. I take a long, cool shower, then change into a pair of soft pink pajama shorts and a black spaghetti-strapped tank top. I feel much better. I pull my cell out of my purse. Three missed calls. My dad. Jocelyn. And Lloyd.

Shit. Lloyd. I almost forgot about him.

Whatever, I'm not going to think about that now. La, la, la. Just going to call Jocelyn back. I dial her cell number.

"Hey," I say when she answers. "Did you call?"

"Yeah," she says. "I wanted to see how you were feeling."

I hear the sound of car horns honking in the background.

"Uh, Joce?" I ask. "What are you doing?"

"I'm tailing B. J. to McDonald's," she says, sounding satisfied.

"Tailing B. J. to McDonald's?" I repeat dumbly. She can't be serious. Who does that outside of Veronica Mars?

"Yeah," she says. "I'm following him to see if he goes to Katelyn's."

"Who?"

"Katelyn Masters. Who he hooked up with freshman year?"

"Why would he be going to see Katelyn Masters?" I ask, confused.

"Because she left him a Facebook message that was semiflirty, and then today he was very vague about what he was doing. So I headed over to his house and waited outside until he left. And now he's at McDonald's, and I'm following him to see where else he's going." Facebook is seriously going to be responsible for everyone losing their minds.

"Aren't you afraid he's going to see you?"

"No, not at all," she says. "I'm staying far enough behind him, and besides, I'm in my mom's car."

"Why are you in your mom's car?" Jocelyn has a perfectly good car, a black Honda Civic, which her parents bought her a few months ago as an early graduation present.

"Duh," she says. "Because I don't want him to figure out I'm following him."

"Hey, Joce?" I say, trying to sound gentle. "Wouldn't it be easier just to ask him where exactly he's going?"

"Courtney," she says, sighing in exasperation. "I can't ask him! He'll think I don't trust him."

"You obviously don't."

"Asshole!" Jocelyn screams. "Sorry, some guy tried to cut me off while turning in to Home Depot. What were you saying?"

"I don't remember," I say, scared by Jocelyn's sudden road rage.

"Oh, right, about B. J. and me. How I don't trust him."

"Why would you want to be with someone you don't trust?"

"I wouldn't. But what if I confront him on it and it turns out not to be true, and he breaks up with me because he thinks I don't trust him?"

"But you don't!"

"True." She considers this. "But it could be all my own psychosis."

"Probably."

More car horns honking. "I gotta go—I think B. J.'s coming out of the drive-thru, and I don't want to lose him."

"I'll call ya later," I say, clicking off.

I look at the phone and consider calling Lloyd, but then I slide it back into my bag. I'll deal with it later.

When I get back to the room, Jordan's sitting on the bed, flipping between a poker tournament and a baseball game.

"Hey," he says. "You okay?"

"Yeah," I tell him. "I'm fine." The truth is, I don't know if I'm fine or not. Suddenly, I feel totally exhausted, like I can't even move. I haul myself up onto the second bed, pull the covers down, and grab one of the pillows from the top of the bed. I move it to the bottom. I like to sleep upside down on beds. Plus, the way the room is set up, the TV is closer to the bottom of the bed, so it makes sense. Not that I care about watching poker. But I wouldn't mind watching the baseball game.

"Who's playing?" I ask Jordan. My eyes feel really heavy, and my throat feels scratchy from throwing up so much.

"The Tampa Bay Rays and the Yankees," he says softly, looking at me. I meet his eye for a second, and then look away. Jordan and I spent almost every night this summer watching the Rays on TV. And on one of our very first dates, we went to a game. Whatever. Not thinking about it. "Do you want to watch something else?" he asks.

"No," I say, my eyes closing. "I'm really, really tired."

"Yeah," he says. "You should probably get some rest."

"Probably," I say. I must have fallen asleep in about two minutes, because the next thing I know, I open my eyes, and the clock says it's four in the morning. Which means I've slept for like fifteen hours. My stomach feels hollow and tired, like it's been through an ordeal. Which I guess it has. I let my eyes adjust to the darkness of the room. And then I realize Jordan's next to me, sleeping, his arms wrapped around me, our legs tangled together under the blanket.

before ⟵ jordan

123 Days Before the Trip, 4:30 p.m.

I'm trying to kiss Courtney McSweeney. If you had asked me six months ago if I would ever be making out with Courtney McSweeney, I would have said no, absofuckinglutely not. But here I am, trying to get her to kiss me. We're parked in front of her house, sitting in my car, and somehow I pulled her close to me before she could get out of the car. Which she let me do. But then, when I went to kiss her, she turned her head.

"Not gonna happen," she says, her voice muffled against my chest.

"Why not?" I ask, wondering if I've underestimated her. Maybe she's a game player, one of those girls who makes you work for it. The weird thing is, I'm usually into that, but thinking about Courtney messing with my head is disappointing for some reason.

"Because," she says. "Once you cross that line with someone, you can never take it back."

126

"What do you mean?" I ask. Why would she want to take it back? I'm a very good kisser. Or so I've been told.

"I mean that once you kiss someone, all this other stuff comes into it, whether you want it to or not."

"Not necessarily," I say. I'm stroking her hair now, and all she would have to do is move her face about two inches and tilt it up, and we'd be kissing.

"It does," she says. "It brings all kinds of drama you never have to deal with if you just stay friends."

"Not true." I try to pull her closer, which doesn't really work, because she's already as close as she's going to get. "I've had hookups that haven't resulted in any kind of drama."

"None whatsoever?"

"Nope."

"No broken hearts?"

"Nope."

"No psychotic prank phone calls?"

"Nope."

"No feeling like you wanted to throw up and/or kill her new boyfriend?"

"Nope."

"Name one girl you hooked up with that you're still friends with."

"Nope."

"That's what I thought," she says smugly. Although being smug really makes no sense here, because I think she really

127

does want to kiss me. Otherwise why would she be leaning against me like that?

"You tricked me," I say.

"So do it, then. Name one girl you hooked up with that you're still friends with."

"It doesn't have to be dramatic," I say, ignoring her request. "It can just be about . . . the moment."

"I'm not good with the moment," she says. "I'm always worried about what's going to happen next."

"You should stop worrying," I say. And then I reach down and tilt her face up toward mine, and I kiss her. She doesn't pull away. Her mouth is on mine, and our tongues are together, and my hands are on her face. And it's really, really nice. She pulls away first, and we lean our heads together.

"That was nice," I say, smiling.

"That was such a mistake," she says, smiling back. And then she gets out of my car and heads into her house without looking back.

When I get to my house fifteen minutes later, my mom is sitting at the kitchen table. So much for waiting it out and hiding until I got up the courage to confront her. She's wearing a purple sweater set and a cream-colored skirt. Which is weird. Because she looks . . . normal. Not like she was just fucking some random dude on the couch that her and my dad picked out for their anniversary.

"Jordan," she says, standing up and smoothing down

her skirt. Her eyes glance at me nervously and I look away. "Listen, we should talk."

"I don't know if we have anything to talk about," I say simply. I'm trying to figure out the best way to work this to my advantage. I'm pissed.

"We have to," she says. "Sit down."

I pull out a chair from the kitchen table and plop down across from her.

"What do you want to talk about?" I look at her, and suddenly, I'm really, really scared. It's something on her face. Because here's the thing—up until this point, I figured it was just a random thing. Maybe her and a client were working late and got carried away. They started kissing, I came in, and she sent him home after she came to her senses. That's how these things usually work, don't they? I curse myself for watching *Laguna Beach* instead of learning valuable life lessons on *The OC*.

"I think we need to talk about what went on here the other night." She bites her lip again and looks around nervously.

"What about it?"

"Jordan, I really, really, need for you not to tell your father about what happened until I have a chance to talk with him."

"You can't be serious," I say. "There's no way I'm not going to tell Dad about this." She must be delusional. Does she really think I would keep this kind of huge secret from my dad? How can she even expect me to do that?

"Jordan," she says, "I have the right to be able to tell him on my own time, on my own grounds." She tugs on the hem of her skirt nervously. "That's the only way we're going to be able to work it out."

"Whatever," I say, heading to the refrigerator and grabbing a Coke out of the side door. "I'm staying out of it. In fact, I'm totally over it."

I leave her standing in the kitchen and head up to my room, where I spend the next two hours listening to rap music on my iPod and thinking about how it felt to kiss Courtney McSweeney.

courtney the trip

Day Two, 4:07 a.m.

I lay there for a second, not really sure what I'm supposed
to do. I mean, Jordan is in the same bed with me. Wrapped
around me. A part of me wants to scream, to push him off, to
flip out, and possibly kick him in the balls. But it feels good.
To be close to him. And I realize that I'm probably never
going to be this close to him again. Ever. So maybe I should
just give in to it for a little while, hold on to this last thing.

I can feel his chest moving next to me, up and down
with his breathing, and his arms feel strong around me.
My stomach grumbles, probably because it's empty. What a
pain in the ass. I know I can't eat anything, because if I do,
I'm going to end up sick again.

I push Jordan's hand off my shoulder. It bumps my
head. Great. Why is he in this bed with me? Is it possible I
got into some kind of weird delusional state because of my
apparent food poisoning and then grabbed him and pulled

him into bed with me? Maybe it was a fugue. We learned about those in psych class. I'm horrified.

I push his arm up and over my head, trying not to wake him up. The last thing I want is for him to be aware of the fact that we're in this position. Maybe it happened naturally. Like in movies, when guys and girls are always falling asleep and not realizing they're getting wrapped around each other. Maybe it's our bodies' way of telling us we were meant to be. Or maybe I, like, cuddle raped him or something.

I need to get out of this bed. Out of this hotel. Out of this trip. It's definitely not good for my mental state. I grab my phone off the nightstand by the bed, extract myself quickly from the tangle that is Jordan, and head to the bathroom. I check my missed calls. Four of them. They're all Lloyd. Lovely.

I wonder if four in the morning is too late/early to call him. Actually, it could be the perfect time, because there's no way he's going to be awake. So I can leave him a quick message, a "Thanks for calling me, but I was sick and sleeping," kind of message, so that I won't actually have to talk to him. I'm so brilliant.

I push the button in my phone book next to his name and listen while it rings. Ring . . . Ring . . .

"Hello?" he says, sounding tired.

Great. What kind of fool answers their phone at four in the morning? On the day they get to school, nonetheless!

Doesn't he have orientation? Whatever. This is so ridiculous. I mean, I hooked up with him, it's not the end of the world. People hook up all the time. And then you just deal with it. You talk about it. You work it out. This is Lloyd. He's my friend. He's not psychotic. He's Lloyd. I take a deep breath.

"Oh, hi," I say.

"I miss you."

"Oh." It's the only thing I can think of to say. I don't have to say it back, right? I mean, it's not like when someone says "I love you," and you're kind of obligated to say it back, even if you don't mean it. And I do miss him. Kind of. Although I don't really know how you can miss someone you just saw one night ago. I mean, normally, we don't see each other every day. So it's kind of weird for him to say he's missing me, since even though we're both going to be away at school, nothing's really changed yet.

"What time is it?" I hear the sound of him moving around in his bed.

"Um, four in the morning," I say.

"I'm so glad you called me back," he says. "I was worried about you."

"Yeah," I say. Silence. "So, listen, I can't really talk for that long, because I'm in the bathroom and I don't want to wake Jordan up."

"Why would you wake Jordan up?" he asks, sounding confused.

"Because he might hear me talking, and then he would wake up. And having to deal with him while he's awake during normal hours is enough of a trial for me." I'm assuming Lloyd will like the fact that I'm saying something bad about Jordan, but my statement has the opposite effect. Lloyd flips out.

"You guys are staying in the same room?" he asks. Suddenly he sounds wide awake, and there's more noise on the other end of the line, like he's sitting up and taking notice. Suddenly, I feel like I'm in some really weird episode of *The Twilight Zone*, where Lloyd wants me and I don't want him, Jordan broke up with me, I'm in bad hotel room lighting, and it's four in the morning. But it's not. It's real life. So weird.

"Yeah, we're staying in the same room," I say, trying to sound breezy. "But there's two beds, and it was only because there was only one room left." I'm now lying to Lloyd. I'm a liar.

"There was only one room?" Lloyd asks incredulously. Apparently a very bad liar.

"Yup," I say.

"I'm sorry, Court," he says. "Are you okay? Having to stay in the same room with him like that?"

"Yeah, it's fine," I say. "I'm holding up."

"Good."

"Yup," I say. "So, anyway, you sound really tired, so I should let you go. I'll call you tomorrow, though, before we get there and let you know when—"

"Today," Lloyd says.

"Today what?" I ask. My head is starting to hurt, and I'm not sure if it's because I'm getting over some sort of whacked-out food poisoning thing, or if it's because of the stress of this trip.

"You'll be here today, technically," Lloyd says. "Because it's four in the morning?"

"Oh," I say. "Right." Silence.

"Are you sure everything's okay?" Lloyd asks.

"Yeah," I say. "It's fine."

"Is it Jordan? Has he tried anything?"

"Uh, no," I say. "He hasn't. Tried anything, I mean. He has a girlfriend." I don't mention the fact that I just woke up with Jordan's arms wrapped around me. Because that was obviously some sort of weird mistake, something that happened while we were sleeping.

"Like that's going to stop him." Lloyd snorts. No, really, he snorts. The guy I made out with last night is snorting. "You guys were together when he started hooking up with his new girlfriend, so I wouldn't put anything past him, Courtney."

I want to point out that (allegedly) Jordan didn't cheat on me, but really, what's the point? Lloyd is going to believe what he believes. And whatever, he's probably right. Jordan probably did cheat on me. I feel myself starting to get upset, and I take a deep breath.

"Okay, well, I'm going to go back to sleep," I say to

135

Lloyd. "I'll give you a call tomorrow and let you know how we're progressing."

"Okay," Lloyd says. "I miss you, Courtney, and I can't wait to see you."

"Yeah, you too," I say, and then hang up before he can say anything else. I slide my cell phone back into my bag and creep back into the room. I climb into the other bed, the one Jordan's not in, close my eyes, and try to fall asleep.

courtney ⟵ before

"Stop hooking up with him," Jocelyn says. "It's going to get bad."

"What do you mean?" I ask, frowning.

"Just what I said. You like him, Court. And that's not good."

"I don't like him," I say, rolling my eyes. "We're just, you know, hanging out." It's been a couple of weeks since I first kissed Jordan, and after a couple of days of me trying to blow him off, and him being very persistent, we've been hanging out a lot lately. And by a lot, I mean, um, a lot. As in, like, every second that we're not at school, we're together. And even when we're in school, we're texting. Or hanging out at lunch or during our unstructureds in the library. Or passing notes in math. It's really not that bad, though. I mean, school is almost over. So it's not like we have a ton of work we should be concentrating on or anything.

137

"You like him," Jocelyn says. "I can tell from the way you talk to him. And it's not good. When people start liking people, that's when someone has the ability to get hurt."

"I'm not going to get hurt," I say, shrugging. We're sitting in Jocelyn's living room, watching my DVD set of *Laguna Beach* and talking about nothing.

"Just be careful, that's all I'm saying."

"You should talk," I say, picking up a pillow from my side of the couch and throwing it at her.

"Totally different," she says. "I'm not nearly as emotionally attached to B. J. as you are to Jordan."

"I'm not emotionally attached to Jordan," I lie. The truth is, I kind of am. Emotionally attached to him, I mean. At first, it was just fun. I liked kissing him, and being around him, and holding his hand. But then it turned into something different. I talk to him. I tell him things I've never really told anyone, like about how I'm afraid once I get to college everything will be different, and I won't be smart anymore, and I'll end up flunking out and my parents will disown me.

"Well, whatever," Jocelyn says. She grabs the remote and turns up the volume on the TV. "Just be careful, Courtney. Because he is most definitely not emotionally attached to you."

jordan ⬅ before

99 Days Before the Trip, 6:07 p.m.

I think I'm emotionally attached to Courtney McSweeney.
This is not a good plan for a few reasons. I make it a point
to never get emotionally attached to anyone. Emotional
attachments are messy. They end with broken hearts and
stalking. Not that I've ever been on that end of it, i.e., been
the one who was stalking or getting brokenhearted. But I've
seen plenty of girls get emotionally attached to me, and it's
never a good situation. Emotional attachments are for really
stupid people, or people who are much, much older and can
deal with messy things like emotional attachments.

Also, Madison Allesio is now stalking me. When I say
stalking, I mean it in relative terms. She's dropped the hard-
to-get act, and is now making it pretty clear she wants to
hook up. She's doing this by leaving me Facebook messages
and texts that say "I want to hook up." The weird thing
is, this shouldn't really be a problem. Because I don't even

really want to hook up with her anymore. Which is why I probably should. Because if I don't, it means I'm emotionally attached to Courtney. And I can't have that.

This is what I'm thinking about as I'm driving to Courtney's house to do the math assignment. We usually do our math homework together in her room, which entails us doing a problem and then making out for a few minutes. Then she stops and says, "Jordan, we really have to do our work," and then we do two more problems and make out again for a while. It takes a lot longer to do the assignment this way, and yet the time seems to go by much faster.

The other thing that worries me about the Courtney situation is that I'm obviously spending so much time over there in an effort to avoid what's going on at my house. My strategy, as with most things, has been denial and avoidance. I just deny and avoid. The weird thing is, my parents don't seem to notice.

"What's up?" Courtney asks when I get to her house.

"Not much," I say. She leans into me as I pass by her on the way into the house, and I inhale her scent. She smells so good. Like . . . I don't know, exactly. Like Courtney.

Two hours later, we're making out on her bed. Our math books are on the floor. My hands are in her hair, and on her face, and under her shirt on her back. Her tongue is in my mouth, and I want her so bad.

"Wait," she says, pulling away. She pushes her hair away from her face and looks at me seriously. "I don't know what's going on here." She sits up and smoothes down her shirt.

Uh-oh. This is not good. This sounds like it's going to be a talk. Talks, as a rule, are not good. They usually mean something bad is going to happen. When bad things happen, I just like them to happen. Why waste time talking about them? Or about the possibility that they *could* happen? Again, denial and avoidance is really a great strategy, and saves everyone a lot of trouble.

"What do you mean?" I ask. I kiss her neck in an effort to distract her. "Your skin is so soft."

"Jordan," she says, pushing me away. "Stop. Seriously." Whoa. Okay. I pull away from her and back up against the wall behind her bed.

"I just . . ." she trails off. "I don't want to be a typical girl, but I need to know what's going on."

"Okay," I say slowly, not sure what to say. Not because I'm being forced to confront the issue, but because I really don't know what to tell her. I've been in this situation a lot before. Usually, girls aren't so vocal about it. You can just kind of tell they're getting to the point where they're going to press you for an answer about what's going on. They want you to be their boyfriend, not just a hookup. Which is fine, I can't blame them. I'm kind of a catch. Usually, I tell them I'm just not up for it. Sometimes they hate me. Sometimes we keep hooking up (although it's never the same). But this time, I realize I don't want to tell Courtney that I don't want to be her boyfriend. In fact, I do want to be her boyfriend. If that's even what she's saying.

"What are you saying?" I ask.

"I don't know," she says slowly. She looks down at the bed and traces her finger around a blue flower on her comforter. "It's just, I mean, I don't need you to be my boyfriend or anything." Oh. "But I just . . . I mean, what exactly is going on here?"

"Well," I say, running my hand through my hair. "I don't know. I love spending time with you, and I love being around you." I realize she's two feet away from me, and that makes me nervous. I reach out and touch her hand, and start drawing little circles with my index finger against her palm. I try to pull her close to me, but she resists.

"It just feels kind of weird to be spending all this time together and doing all the stuff we're doing without figuring out exactly what this is." She bites her lip. I lean over and kiss her. "Jordan, seriously," she says, pushing me away.

"Okay," I say, backing away. "Sorry. So, what do you want? Let's be together. Me and you." I kiss her again. I can't help it. "Be my girlfriend."

"Jordan, I'm being serious," she says. She rolls her eyes and pushes me away.

"So am I." I pull her close and look into her eyes. "Let's be together."

She leans her head against mine. "Is that really what you want?" she asks. She tilts her head up toward mine.

"Yes," I say.

"Because you shouldn't say it unless, you know, you really mean it. I don't want you to think you have to."

"I don't feel like I have to do anything," I say. I inch my lips closer to hers.

"Okay," she says. "So . . ."

I kiss her then, and she finally stops talking.

Three hours later, we're finally done with our math assignment. It was ten problems. Ten problems took us three hours. It's ten at night. I'm going to have no time to finish the rest of my homework. I hope having a girlfriend doesn't mess with my ability to keep my grades up. Ha.

"I should go," I say, trying to disentangle myself from Courtney's body. We're laying in her bed, kissing, and I can't stop. It's like I'm physically unable to be away from her.

"Okay," she says, not moving. She closes her eyes for a second, and I try to memorize the way she looks, her hair spread out around the pillow, her lips slightly parted. She sighs and pulls herself out of bed, then holds her hand out, and pulls me up. I pull her close to me and kiss her again.

"I'll walk you to the door," she says when she pulls away.

"'Kay." I gather my stuff, shove it all into my black messenger bag, and walk with Courtney down the stairs.

As we're walking into the kitchen, the back door opens.

"Dad?" Courtney asks. Shit. Courtney's dad has been on a business trip for the past few weeks, so I haven't had to meet him. I hate meeting dads. Dads, as a rule, don't like me. They think I'm a punk who's trying to deflower their precious daughter. Which is usually the case. But not in this instance. Although I wouldn't mind deflowering Courtney, I'm content with the whole making-out thing. Maybe it wouldn't even be a deflowering. We haven't had the whole "Are you a virgin?" talk yet.

The back door opens and Courtney's dad walks in.

"You're home!" She flings herself at him and grabs him in a hug. This is going to be doubly disastrous, because Courtney and her dad are superclose. Which means getting his approval is key to our relationship. I use their reunion time to smooth my clothes and run my fingers through my hair. I hope I don't look like I've just been making out with his daughter.

"Jordan," Courtney says. "Come meet my dad." She pulls back, still holding his hand.

"Nice to meet you, sir," I say, holding out my hand. I get my first good look at him, and then stop. Because Courtney's dad is the guy my mom was making out with on the couch.

"Let me get this straight," B. J. says a couple hours later, leaning back in the booth. We're in Denny's, having a late-night snack, and I've just finished telling him the whole sordid tale. Everything. My mom. Courtney. Her dad. Everything. "Courtney is now your girlfriend."

"Right."

"And two hours after you two crazy kids came to the conclusion that you're soul mates, you figured out your mom was fucking her dad."

"Right." I don't even wince at B. J.'s crude language. I'm beyond that.

"Dude, that shit is FUCKED UP." He takes a fry and drags it through some ketchup. "What are you doing to do?"

"I have to tell her," I say. Silence. "Right?"

"Right," B. J. says, sounding uncertain.

"Why do you sound uncertain?"

"I don't," he says, sounding even more uncertain than before.

"Yes, you do!"

"Well, it's just one of those things that sounds good in theory, but might not really be necessary." He takes the straw out of his drink and throws it on the table, then takes a long gulp of his soda right from the cup. On cue, the waitress comes over and replaces his old soda with a new one.

"Thanks," B. J. says, grinning at her.

"You're welcome," she says, looking at me. "Do you need anything else?"

"No, I'm fine," I say, slightly annoyed that she's interrupting.

"You sure?" she persists. "Dessert? Coffee?"

"Nah, I'm good," I say, looking away and hoping she'll get the message.

"Oooh, you know what?" B. J. says, looking excited. "I'll have a piece of that strawberry thing, the one with all the whipped cream?" I resist the urge to hurl myself across the table and strangle him.

"Okay," she agrees. "Vanilla ice cream?"

"Sure," B. J. says. He shrugs. "Do it up."

"I'll bring two spoons." As soon as she clears the area, B. J. takes another gulp of his soda. He leans back in his chair and lets out a huge burp.

"Anyway," I say, trying not to freak out. "Can you please tell me why I shouldn't tell her?"

"Dude," B. J. says. He pulls an ice cube into his mouth and starts crunching it.

"Dude what?"

"Hold on," he says. "I'm trying to think of how to phrase this." Great. We'll be here all day.

"Don't try to think about how to phrase it," I say. "Just say it."

"You sure?"

"Yes!"

"You probably won't be with her for that long." He shrugs. "So there's really no point in telling her."

"Geez, tell me how you really feel."

"You said to just say it!"

"I know, I know," I say. I lean over the table and rub my temples with my fingers. Maybe B. J.'s right. Maybe I don't have to tell her. Maybe I can wait a little while until

I figure out how I feel about her and then I can decide whether or not to tell her. I do like Courtney, I like her a lot, I don't want to hang out with anyone else, but I am fickle. What if I tell her and it wrecks her life? What if she's not supposed to know about this, and not only do I tell her, but otherwise, she never would have found out? It's not like my mom is planning on marrying her dad. I don't think, anyway.

"Dude, are you stressin' about this?" B. J. asks. "Don't freak me out."

"Why would that freak you out?"

"Because you never stress."

The waitress returns with a huge plate of strawberry pie, ice cream, and whipped cream. She sets down two spoons.

"I made a double portion," she says, smiling. She licks her lips and smoothes her hands across her tight apron. Lovely. My world is falling apart, and some random waitress is making threesome jokes. She walks away, swinging her hips from side to side. If I wasn't so fucked up right now, I'd probably be turned on.

"Dude," B. J. whispers, leaning across the table. "Does she want to have a threesome with us?"

"Probably."

"Whoa." His eyes widen. "Not that I ever would. No offense, bro, but that would be way too fucked up." He takes a bite of strawberry pie. "That is some good shit. Try it."

"No, thanks," I say. I'm suddenly not very hungry, and

the cheeseburger and fries I just devoured feel heavy in my stomach.

"You need to chill," B. J. says. He has whipped cream all over his mouth. I reach across the table and wordlessly hand him a napkin. He smiles sheepishly and wipes his mouth. "For now, you can't worry about it. The last thing you want to do is get Courtney all freaked out for nothing. And if you do decide it's going to turn into something serious, you can always tell her later."

"What if she asks why I didn't tell her before?"

"You can tell her the truth. That you wanted to make sure you knew what was going on between you guys, and between your parents, before you did anything psychotic." I stare at B. J. in disbelief. How is it that someone who is so idiotic most of the time can somehow be able to give such good insight? Maybe it's because he thinks on such a simple level most of the time that he doesn't get bogged down by things like emotion and manipulation. He just figures out the best way to handle a situation, and then he does it.

"Good idea," I say. "Thanks."

"No problem." He grins at me through a mouthful of strawberries.

"Anything else I can get you two?" the waitress says, appearing at our table.

"Just the check," I say. "Thanks."

She rips it off the pad slowly and places it down in front

of me. "If you need anything else, I can always add it." She smiles again, turns on her heel, and walks away.

"You could so do her," B. J. says.

I pick up the check. $15.65. "Carrie," it says on the bottom. "Call me, cutie! 555-0181." Followed by a smiley face.

I throw a twenty down on the table and leave the check where it is.

the trip ▷ jordan

I'm probably going to get into a fight with Lloyd when we get to Middleton. That bitch has had it coming for a long time, and I couldn't be blamed for fucking him up. He never took the relationship I had with Courtney seriously. Even when we were together all the time, he'd still make little digs. Case in point: One night, when Lloyd, Court, me, B. J., Jocelyn, and a few other people were hanging out, Courtney decided she wanted to order food. And Lloyd was all, "Oh, Courtney, you always have to order food while we're watching baseball." Which may have been true. But it was the way he said it that pissed me off. It was like he was talking about food, but he basically was saying, "Jordan, I know Courtney better than you, and I could fuck her if I wanted to."

Anyway, we're in the car on our way to see my brother, Adam, and Lloyd at Middleton, and Courtney's acting like it's the night before Christmas. She's practically taking her clothes off already. I'm not stupid. I know some of it is an act, something she's probably doing to piss me off, but still. They hooked up. There has to be something there, or else she's one hell of an actress.

So far, she's asked me how her hair looks about five million times. She's wearing a black flippy skirt and a black tank top. Her hair is in pigtails, which you think would be kind of silly, but on her looks really cute. I've hardly ever seen Courtney dressed like this. She usually isn't so, uh . . . revealing.

"Does my hair look okay?" she asks again, flipping down the visor and checking herself out in the mirror.

"Yes," I say through gritted teeth. "Your hair looks fine."

"Sorry if I'm being annoying," she says, pulling a lip gloss out of her bag and lining her lips. "I'm just nervous."

"Understandable," I say, watching her out of the corner of my eye. She has the best mouth. I stare straight ahead again, keeping my eyes on the road.

"I'm starving," she announces. "Are we going to stop for breakfast or something?"

"Do you think that's smart, with your stomach and everything?" The last thing I need is Courtney throwing up all over my car again. Not that I really cared yesterday. I actually liked taking care of her. But things are different now. Yesterday she was cute and vulnerable. She wrapped her legs around me in bed, and pulled me close to her during the night. Now she's dressed like a tramp and thinking about having sex with Lloyd. So forgive me if I'm not rushing to hold her hair back. Let Lloyd do that shit if she's so into him.

"I'm hungry." She shrugs and pulls out the CD in the player and tosses it into the backseat. She pushes the button for the satellite radio and turns it to the country station.

"Feel free," I say, rolling my eyes. My phone starts vibrating in my pocket, and I do my best to ignore it.

"Your phone's ringing," Courtney says helpfully.

"Thanks," I say.

"You should answer it." She starts humming along to the song on the radio, something about someone's last days on earth and taking advantage of them. I'm about to go crazy listening to this country radio bullshit. Country is so depressing. There's too many slow songs. Why am I putting up with this shit? It's my car. I'm driving. I should be able to listen to whatever the fuck I want. Especially now that she's banging Lloyd. Let him put up with her country music bullshit, and her throwing up.

"Fine," I say. "I will." I pull my phone out of my pocket and make a big show of answering it.

"Hello?" I say, sounding upbeat, and like I'm happy to be on the phone. I decide to pretend it's my imaginary girlfriend. Fuck pretending to be nice.

"Yo," B. J. says.

"What's going on, honey?" I say, trying to glance at

Courtney out of the corner of my eye without her noticing that that's what I'm doing. She's going through her bag, probably looking for more makeup, so she can make herself look good for Lloyd.

"Honey?" B. J. asks. "Jordy, I had no idea you felt that way about me. I have to warn you, though, I happen to be in a very committed relationship."

"Yeah, I miss you, too." Courtney starts flipping through the satellite radio stations. Good. I hope she's rattled. I hope she realizes that if she weren't hooking up with Lloyd, I would let her pick any song she wanted to listen to. And that I would not be pretending to talk to my fake girlfriend.

"I'm guessing I'm your fake girlfriend?" B. J. asks, sighing. It's a miracle that he figured it out. He's not usually the best with things that aren't spelled out for him.

"Of course, sweetie," I say. I try not to think about the fact that I'm talking to B. J. like we're in love. B. J. is six-foot-four and 220 pounds. Not someone you want to think about being intimate with. Out of the corner of my eye, I see Courtney pull her iPod out of her bag and shove the headphones into her ears. I'm not buying it. I know she doesn't have the thing on. No way she doesn't want to hear me talk to my new girlfriend.

"Listen, I'm sorry to bother you when you're obviously busy with, uh, important things," B. J. says. He sounds sarcastic. "But you remember a few months ago, when we scored that pot for Brian Turner?"

"Sort of," I say, wondering if it would be going too far to call B. J. "pookie" or "schmooper." I want Courtney to be jealous, but I also don't want her thinking I'm a pussy. Which is really fucked up, since, you know, *I'm* the one that broke up with *her*.

"We paid for that, right?"

"Yeah," I say. A couple months ago we bought some pot for Brian Turner's party. It was this long, drawn-out procedure, since the first guy we were supposed to get it from wasn't where he was supposed to be, and then this guy named Gray Poplaski, who somehow ended up coming along even though he's kind of a tool, said he knew this other guy who could probably get us some. Which annoyed me, because I don't even like pot that much. Anyway, we finally met up with some very shady-looking guys and got it, but the whole experience was weird.

"Do you think anyone found out about that?" B. J. asks, sounding nervous.

"Found out about what?" I ask, trying to imagine why I would say that to my fake girlfriend. Maybe if she asked "Do you think anyone found out about that?" meaning, "Do you think anyone found out about us having sex in my parents' bed?" or something. I hope Courtney is smart enough to infer that that's what is probably going on. I wonder if it would be going too far to actually come out and say, "You mean about the doggie-style we had?"

"Found out about the pot we bought!" B. J. says, sounding exasperated. He's been sounding exasperated with me a lot lately. Which, like I said before, really worries me. Because if B. J. thinks you can't keep up, it probably means you're in deep shit.

"Like who?"

"I don't know," he says, lowering his voice. *"Like their posse."*

"Like whose posse?" I realize I probably won't be able to keep up pretending that I'm talking to my fake girlfriend for long, so I fake a call waiting beep. "I have to go," I say to B. J., a.k.a. my fake girlfriend (M.F.G.). "I have a beep." I pretend to mess around with the phone for a minute. "Hello? Oh, hi, B. J." I glance over at Courtney, hoping she now thinks that I was on the phone with my fake girlfriend until B. J. beeped in.

"Are you done?" B. J. asks, sounding annoyed.

"I think so."

"Anyway, their posse," B. J. says. "Could be after me."

"Whose posse?" I repeat, hoping Courtney doesn't notice that I appear to be having the same conversation with B. J. that I was just having with my fake girlfriend.

"Those thugs we bought it from!" B. J. says.

I'm starting to get a headache. "I'm starting to get a headache," I say.

"Look, I think someone's been following me," B. J. says. "And the only thing I can think of is that it might have something to do with that pot we bought."

"Someone's following you?" I ask. "Where are you?" I merge onto the freeway, and try to fight myself through the traffic. I really should put my phone on speaker, but I obviously can't, because then Court will know I've been talking to B. J. and not M.F.G. I have a headset in the glove compartment, but that would involve reaching over Courtney. Or asking her to pass it to me.

"I'm driving to the gym," he says. "And there's a car behind me, weaving in and out of traffic. I think I saw it yesterday, too."

"You're being paranoid." A red Jetta on my left side veers into my lane, and I swerve to avoid hitting it. My cell phone drops to the floor. Shit. I grope around on the ground while trying to get my car back into its lane. This is extremely dangerous.

"—and shoots me or something," B. J. is saying by the time I get the phone back to my ear.

"What?"

"What the fuck is going on over there? My shit is about to get BLOWN UP, and you're playing some kind of fucking game!" he says.

"Hold on one second." I put the phone into my lap. "Courtney," I say sweetly. "Can you reach into the glove compartment and hand me my cell phone headset?"

She ignores me and pretends to be listening to her iPod.

"Court?" I say, raising my voice. From the depths of the cell phone in my lap, I can faintly hear B. J. saying "Hello?

Are you there? Jooorrrddaannn!" I flip the cell phone over, to muffle B. J.'s voice.

"COURTNEY!"

"Someee hearts just get luucccky sometimesss," she sings, her voice totally off-key. I'm in the midst of three lanes of high-speed traffic, have a friend on my cell phone who is obviously losing his mind, am faking phone calls, and am listening to my ex-girlfriend, who I'm still in love with, sing country songs. I really, really need to get off of this trip.

"Court." I poke her. She ignores me. I poke her harder.

"WHAT?!" she screeches, pulling her earphones out of her ears. "What do you want?"

"Can you reach into the glove compartment and hand me my cell phone headset, please?" I ask.

From my cell phone comes the faint sound of B. J. screaming. I pick it up and reduce the volume. Courtney sighs and reaches into the glove compartment like it's some huge imposition. She makes a big show of rummaging through the stuff until she locates the headset. Such a drama queen.

She hands it to me. "Thanks, honey," I say, and give her a wink. She rolls her eyes and puts the earphones of her iPod back into her ears. Like she's really listening to it.

"THIS SHIT IS FUCKED UP!" B. J. is screaming once I get the headset in.

"Sorry, I'm here," I say.

"What were you doing?"

157

"I was getting my headset so I could talk to you," I say. "Now, what's going on?"

"I. Am. Being. Followed. Like I said before."

"Are you sure?" I ask.

"Yes," he says. "There is a car following me. It followed me yesterday, too. It's those thugs from the drug deal, probably. Or maybe those fuckers we beat from Westhill."

"Maybe you should call the police," I say.

"I will not," he replies indignantly. "I'm not afraid of a gang. Or some shitty football team. I'll call my boys."

"Okay," I say uncertainly.

"Call ya back," he says and then disconnects.

"What's going on?" Courtney asks from the passenger seat. Oh, now she's concerned.

"Nothing," I say. "B. J. thinks he was being followed."

She looks startled. "Oh," she says. "Uh, by who?"

"Not sure."

"What's he going to do?"

"Call the police, I guess," I say, shrugging. No way I'm telling her about the gang violence and the fact that we bought drugs. She'd flip out, especially since we were together at the time. A worried look crosses her face, but she doesn't say anything.

"Can we PLEASE stop and get some food?" she asks five minutes later. "I'm starving."

I want to make a snide comment about how she wants to eat so she'll have energy for her and Lloyd's impending sex-a-thon, but I don't. I also want to point out that the schedule doesn't call for this kind of stop, but whatever.

"Geez, Jordan," she says. She pulls her lip gloss out of her bag and starts relining her lips. "Could you be a worse driver?"

I clutch the steering wheel and concentrate on not losing my temper. I've decided passive aggressive is my new tactic. But five minutes later, when Courtney looks at me pointedly as we come up on the next exit, I put on my signal and pull off the highway.

before → jordan

77 Days Before the Trip, 6:07 p.m.

Courtney's dad is onto me. We're having dinner out at a Greek restaurant, and I can tell he wants to kill me. Okay, so he doesn't want to kill me, but he knows I know he's banging my mom.

"You have to try the souvlaki," Courtney says, reaching across the table and taking my hand. I hold her hand, trying not to freak out. Jesus, this is awkward. Definitely on my top ten list of things I don't ever want to do. "Number Three: Have dinner with your girlfriend and her dad, when said dad is having an extramarital affair with your mom, which your girlfriend doesn't know about." It really should be some sort of list on *Letterman*. "Top Ten Things You Never Thought About Happening, But Should Try to Avoid at All Costs."

"That sounds good," I say. I have no fucking idea what souvlaki is. It sounds disgusting. But I'll try it, because

Courtney's dad is here, and he's from Greece, and I'm trying to make a good impression.

"I hope you're hungry, Jordan," he says, smiling at me across the table. That's the other weird thing. He's acting like nothing is wrong. I wonder if maybe he has no idea who I am. But that would be impossible. He knows my last name. And he saw me the night I came in and found him feeling up my mom. Maybe he doesn't know my mom's last name. And maybe that night he was just so intent on banging her that he doesn't really remember what I look like. Maybe they haven't talked since. Maybe they broke it off.

"I am hungry, sir," I say. Courtney rolls her eyes next to me. Of course I'm going to "sir" him. I have to kiss his ass for many reasons, not the least of which is that even though I haven't told her yet, I think I'm in love with his daughter.

Courtney's dad ("Call me Frank," he said when we got here—Frank! Ha, fat chance!) motions the waiter over and starts talking to him in Greek. I wonder if they're talking about taking me outside and doing away with me. I don't think the mob is in Greece, though. The Sopranos are definitely Italian.

"He's ordering appetizers," Courtney says, as if she's reading my mind. She's wearing a black skirt and a long-sleeved pink shirt, and when she leans in close to me, I can see the black bra she's wearing underneath it. Despite all the stress, I feel myself starting to get turned on.

The waiter turns to me and asks me in a thick Greek accent what I'd like. I order the souvlaki since Courtney recommended it, and since she said it, I already know how to pronounce it.

"Salad?" the waiter asks, smiling. He's about twenty-two and he looks like he's in pretty good shape, but I know I could take him. If it came down to that.

"Yes, please," I say, figuring salad is safe. Salad is good. Salad is just lettuce. With dressing. Although maybe it's some kind of funky Greek salad. Even so, Greek lettuce is better than some unknown shit. I've never thought of myself as a picky eater before, but now I realize it's basically because I subsist on hamburgers and pizza most of the time. I'm probably going to die before I'm thirty.

"Whachu leek feetaumbla dreez?" the waiter says. At least, that's what it sounds like he says. Who the fuck can tell with his accent? Courtney and her father look at me expectantly. Fuck.

"What kind of dressing do you have?" I ask, proud of myself for inferring that was probably the question he asked.

"No," Courtney says, squeezing my hand and trying not to smile. "He asked if you want feta cheese. On your salad. They only have one kind of dressing here, the Greek house dressing."

"Oh," I say, shrugging. "Sure, I'll take the feta." I have no idea what feta cheese is.

Courtney and her dad give their orders, and the waiter clears the menus and leaves.

"So," Courtney's dad says. He picks up a piece of pita bread and dips it in some kind of cream that's sitting next to it. He pops it in his mouth and chews. I have no idea how the dude can be so calm, given what's going on right now. "I hear you're going to BU, Jordan."

"Yes, sir," I say. I wonder who he heard it from—Courtney or my mom. Although I'm not sure how comfortable my mom should feel talking about my life right now, since I haven't talked to her in weeks. For all she knows, I've scrapped this BU idea and have decided to head to Vegas and become a professional poker player. "That's wonderful," Frank says, smiling like it's anything but. He hates me.

The waiter sets our salads down in front of us, and I realize very quickly that the whole feta cheese thing was a horrible mistake. It looks gross and it smells gross, like old socks. And it's in chunks. I don't like anything that's in chunks. Chunks remind me of unpleasant things. Like vomit.

"Jordan's majoring in accounting," Courtney says in an effort to make me look good. In actuality, I'm going in undeclared, but I'm leaning toward accounting. I have no idea why, other than my dad is an accountant, and I feel like I need to do something to make him happy now that it turns out my mom is cheating on him.

"Nice," Frank says. He takes a bite of his salad, including a piece of feta. "This cheese is unbelievable. How's your salad, Jordan?"

"It's really good, thanks," I say. And it is really good. Except for the cheese. And except for the fact that I have no appetite.

"You're not eating the cheese," Frank says accusingly.

And you're fucking my mom, I want to say back. But I don't. I take a bite of the cheese. It falls apart in my mouth. I try to swallow it without tasting it, like a pill, and almost choke.

"You okay?" Courtney asks, handing me my water.

"Yeah," I say. "I'm fine."

"So tell me more about this Miami trip," he says, looking right at me. "Courtney says you two are planning to go next month."

"Yes, sir," I say, trying to convey in those two words that we are going to hang out only, not to have sex ever. Which is true. I'm not expecting sex at all. Not even a little bit. Okay, so I'd be happy if it happened, but I'm not planning on it. Courtney's a virgin. As far as I know, she wants to stay a virgin. At least for a little while, anyway.

"And where will you be staying?" he asks, looking at me closely.

"My dad's best friend from college has a house there," I say, wondering if he's going to give me shit about the fact that there will be no parental supervision. "And he goes to

Europe for the summer, and lets me use the house whenever I want."

"How generous of him. It sounds like it's going to be a fun trip," he says, shooting me a look over the table that basically means, "If you put a hand on my daughter, I will shoot you." Which really isn't fair, since he's feeling free to feel up my mom at any opportunity.

"Yes, sir," I say. I sound like a broken record.

"I'll be right back," Courtney says. She pushes her chair back from the table and stands up.

"Where are you going?" I ask, suddenly panicked. Why would she leave me alone with her father? Is Courtney insane?

"To the bathroom," she says. She kisses me on the forehead and then disappears.

Once she's cleared the area, Frank looks at me like I'm a piece of gum on his shoe.

"Listen, Jordan," he says. "This situation is only as difficult as you decide to make it."

"What do you mean?" I ask. Who does he think he is? Some kind of threatening hit man? Or Dr. Phil, warning me that I have my fate in my hands? I push the feta cheese around my salad with my fork, resisting the urge to throw it at him.

"I mean that this doesn't have to be an issue," he says. He wipes his lips with his napkin and sets it on the table. "I have no problem with you, Jordan. I have no problem with

165

you seeing my daughter. The only problem we're going to have is if you decide not to be discreet."

Decide not to be discreet? Is this guy for real? The word "discreet" sounds so gross, like some kind of ad for hookers. I might not be pleased with my mom right now, but she's definitely not a hooker.

"I don't know what you're talking about," I say, just to be a dick. I start taking the feta cheese off my salad and dropping it onto my bread plate.

"Yes, you do," he says easily. "And I want you to know that I'm going to be the one to tell Courtney and her mom what's going on. Not you."

"You seem really sure of that," I say, continuing to throw the feta cheese onto the bread plate, spearing each piece and pretending it's Frank's head.

"I am," he says. "Because if Courtney finds out from you, I'll make sure you never see her again. Hell, I won't have to make sure of it. She'll hate you for keeping it a secret from her for this long."

I don't say anything because I know he's right. I had my chance to tell Courtney when I first found out her dad was the one who was having an affair with my mom, and I didn't. And now, because she had this preconceived notion that I was kind of a dick, if I tell her now, it's going to come off like I *am* a dick. But maybe . . . maybe if I keep my mouth shut, if I don't tell her I knew, if her dad does eventually tell her, we can deal with it together. We can help each other through it.

"Whatever," I say. "I'm not going to tell her."

"Good," Frank says. He takes a bite of his salad and licks the dressing off his lips. "I really do think that's the best way."

"Hey," Courtney says, returning to the table. "What'd I miss?"

before jordan

76 Days Before the Trip, 10:10 a.m.

"I think I might be in love with her," I tell B. J. in unstructured on Thursday morning. It's the last day of school, and we're sitting in the library, going over the review sheet for our AP Bio final.

"You are not in love with her," B. J. says. He leans back in his chair and rubs his temples.

"I am," I say. "I'm in love with her. I haven't told her yet, but I've been thinking it." It's true, too. Over the past two months we've gotten really close, and in the past month, I've started to think it. There have even been a couple times, especially when we're getting off the phone at night, or when I'm leaving her house that I want to say it. But I haven't yet, because I'm not sure if she feels the same way, and I don't want to freak her out.

"That is insane," B. J. says. "You can't be in love with her."

"Why not?"

"A myriad of reasons," B. J. says. I try to keep in mind this is the same guy who was dressed as a leprechaun the night he first hooked up with his girlfriend.

"Such as?"

"You haven't had sex."

"So?"

"So, sex is very important to a relationship," he says. "How do you know you love her if you haven't had sex with her?"

"Not even dignifying that with a response," I say. The weird thing is, even though Courtney and I haven't had sex, I haven't thought that much about it. I mean, I have thought about having sex with her, of course, and I definitely want to, but I haven't thought much about the fact that we're not having it. It's just something I figure will happen when it happens. Courtney's a virgin, so obviously I'm not going to rush it.

"Okay," B. J. says. He leans back in his chair and stretches his arms behind him. "How about the fact that you weren't supposed to get attached to her? Dude, her dad is banging your mom. If she finds out you kept that from her, you are so fucked."

"I'm sure she'll understand," I say, a knot of uneasiness starting in my stomach. She won't understand. Courtney has this thing about trust. And if she knows I lied to her, she'll break up with me immediately.

"Dude, you have to tell her," B. J. says. "I would never keep something like that from Jocelyn."

I resist the urge to roll my eyes. B. J. and Jocelyn hooked up more or less around the same time Courtney and I did, but for some reason, I get super annoyed when he tries to imply that the relationships are the same. From what I can tell, he and Jocelyn have sex a lot. As in, every single day. Sometimes multiple times. They spend a lot of time together, but they don't really do anything. Except have sex. I've never even really seen them talk. Unless they're setting a time to meet up later so they can have sex.

The bell rings and we file out of the library and into the hall. "I know I have to tell her," I say. "But her dad is freaking me the fuck out."

"Don't be afraid of that shit-sucker," B. J. declares. "You need me to have a talk with him?"

"Nah," I say. "I'll figure it out." But as I leave B. J. in the hall and walk in to take my English final, I have no idea how I'm going to do that.

courtney ◁ before

"You had sex with him?" I say to Jocelyn, trying not to spit out my Sprite. Why she would wait until I took a drink to announce she had sex with B. J. is beyond me. Maybe because it's the last day of school. So she feels the need to start the summer with a huge confession.

"When did this happen?"

"You mean when was the first time?" she asks, frowning.

"There's been more than one time?" Is it possible she means more than one time in one night? Don't boys need time to, uh, recharge? Not that I would really know much about that. The recharging, I mean. Or the sex in general.

"Yes," she says, then leans in conspiratorially, since we're in the cafeteria and all. "I think I might be a little addicted to it."

Great. My best friend is a sex addict. And not only that, she's addicted to doing it with B. J. Which is a mental

171

picture I'm really trying to keep out of my head. Not that B. J. is ugly or anything, but still. It's B. J.

"Well," I say. "I'm going to have sex with Jordan."

"Courtney!" Jocelyn exclaims. Her eyes widen and she puts down her fork, which she's been using to eat french fries off my tray. I have no idea why she doesn't just pick them up and eat them, but she won't. She spears them with a fork and then dips them in the little cup of ketchup that came with my lunch.

"What?" I ask.

"You cannot have sex with Jordan."

"Why not?" I ask. "I actually can. I mean, my body is capable of doing it." I think it is, anyway. Although I do remember reading somewhere that if you don't have sex for a while, your virginity actually grows back, and it can be hard for you to do it again. Not that that's my situation, since I haven't had sex before. But maybe if you wait too long, it gets harder to do it. But that's insane, right? Besides, I'm seventeen, not thirty.

"Well, of course your body is capable of doing it," Jocelyn says, rolling her eyes. She flips her hair over her shoulder and studies me seriously. "Courtney, you can't undo this. It's not like buying a new shirt."

"I know that," I say, rolling my eyes right back. "And the thing is, it doesn't scare me." It doesn't. I want to be with him. I love him.

"Oh, my God," Jocelyn says. "You love him."

"No, I don't," I say, as if the thought of me being in love with someone is so totally ludicrous. Which, in a way, it kind of is. Here's the weird thing—before I met Jordan, I kind of thought I would never be in love. Like, ever. It just seemed totally far-fetched that I would find a guy who would fall in love with me and take care of me and every- thing. But I did. I'm in love with him.

"You do!" Jocelyn says. "You love him. If you didn't, you wouldn't even be considering sleeping with him." Damn. That's what happens when you have a friend who knows you really, really well. You can't get away with pretending to be someone you're not.

"Does he love you?" she asks.

"I don't know," I say slowly, thinking about it. "I think he does."

"Think is not good enough, Court," she says. "Do you really want to sleep with someone if you don't know they love you?"

"It's not like that," I say, frowning. "I love him. Isn't that enough?"

"Not really," she says. "This is a huge decision, Courtney. You have to make totally sure this is what you want. Because it's something that's forever."

"What about you and B. J.?" I ask. "How come it's okay for you guys?" This sounds like a sex double stan- dard. How come she's allowed to do it and I'm not? I'm not going to say anything, but sometimes I wonder if her and B. J. even really like each other. They never do any-thing except drink and make out. And now, apparently, have sex.

"Different situation," she says. She pulls a tube of lip gloss out of her purse and lines her lips. "Want some?" she asks, extending the tube to me. "It would be really cute on you."

I take it and dab a little on my lips, marveling at the fact that she can intersperse talking about sex with talk-ing about lip gloss. How can she be so cavalier? Is this what happens after you have sex? You just talk about it like it's nothing? That makes me nervous for some reason, to think that something that's such a big deal now could end up being nothing in the future. Although I guess it's to be expected. Like, look at the girls on *Sex and the City*. They did it all the time.

"How is it a different situation?" I roll the lip gloss around my lips, wondering if it makes me kissable.

"Because we're different people," she says. "I don't know if you can separate the emotional from the physical."

"Why would I want to do that?" I ask, frowning. Who does that? Separates the emotional from the physical? I guess sociopaths, maybe. And I guess Jocelyn is now claiming to do it, too, although I never pegged her for a sociopath.

"Because if you don't, you could end up getting really, really hurt," she says. "Listen, I'm not trying to discourage you. But you just have to make sure this is what you want to do."

"It is," I say. And I really do feel like it is. I want to have sex with Jordan. And when we go to Miami next month, I'm going to.

the trip ⮞ courtney

Day Two, 1:31 p.m.

"Did you not hear me?" I hiss into the phone. "He's starting to talk law enforcement."

"I don't understand how this could have happened!" Jocelyn's annoyed. "I've been so careful."

"Well, apparently you haven't, because he told Jordan someone's been following him since yesterday, and that he was going to call the police." I'm sitting in Jordan's TrailBlazer at a Burger King right off our route. Jordan's inside using the bathroom and getting us food. I told him I wanted to wait in the car since it's raining, but really I wanted to call Jocelyn and warn her about B. J.'s revelation.

"You have to stop," I say. I look out the back window to see if Jordan is coming out of the restaurant yet, but I don't see him. "Stop right now."

"I can't stop yet!" Jocelyn says. "It's too early. Maybe I could borrow my sister's car . . . Did he say how he figured out someone was following him? Maybe I just have to change my technique."

"I don't know how he figured it out."

"Can you ask him?"

"Ask who?"

"Jordan!"

"No, I can't ask him! What would I say? 'Can you tell me how B. J. found out he was being followed, because it was Jocelyn and she wants to know if she needs to switch cars or just change her stalking technique?'" Oh, my God. Jocelyn is delusional. This is exactly why hooking up with people is not a good idea. Once you've crossed that line it just makes you insane. You start doing things normal people would never, ever do. Where the hell is Jordan with the food? I'm hungry again. Which is weird. Is it possible that since I was throwing up all day yesterday, I'm trying to eat enough food for two days? Hmm.

"Maybe there's nothing going on," I say. "Maybe B. J. really is just going to the places he says he is."

"Courtney!" Jocelyn gasps. "Please tell me you are not that deluded! Guys are never doing exactly what they say they're doing."

"Why not?" I say. "Maybe some are doing exactly what they say they're doing."

She snorts. "Listen, do what you can," she says. "And let me know if B. J. calls back."

I hang up the phone and lean my head against the headrest.

We're about two hours away from Middleton and Lloyd, which is making me nervous. I'm trying to play it off to Jordan like I'm wicked excited, while inside I feel like I'm going to explode. I have no idea how this is going to go down.

The driver's-side door opens and Jordan gets into the car, juggling a drink carrier and two bags of food. I take one of the bags out of his hand.

"Thanks," he says. He sets the other bag down carefully between us, pulls my soda out of the carrier, and hands it to me.

"You needed two bags?" I ask incredulously. I peek inside and inhale the scent of the food. It smells good. And greasy. I love grease. Grease makes me happy. I am only going to eat half of my food, though. Just half. So that my stomach doesn't get all sketched out.

"No, but there was a mix-up and somehow I got someone else's order, too."

He shrugs and pulls out a container of fries.

"Did you tell them?" I ask without thinking.

"Of course I told them," he says, rolling his eyes. "They let me keep it." Right. I'll bet Mercedes or whatever the hell her name is doesn't question Jordan's morals when it comes to fast food that's been given to him.

"Cool," I say nonchalantly, shrugging my shoulders. Jordan's cell phone starts playing "Baby Got Back" again, and he ignores it.

"Going to answer that?" I ask.

"Nope," he says cheerfully. He opens a container of chicken tenders and pulls open the packet of honey mustard that comes with them. I hate honey mustard. It seems like such a bad idea. Honey and mustard together. Who could like that?

"You don't have to feel weird about answering it," I say. "I told you."

"I don't," he says. He takes a chicken tender and dunks it into the honey mustard. Something about that makes me sad. Because all the little things about him, like the way he loves honey mustard and the way he always forgets the cheese on my burger, aren't mine anymore. It's weird that everything can be the same, that he can go on liking honey mustard, and yet everything is different.

"So, uh, the whole B. J. thing," I say, trying to distract myself from my impending condiment sadness. Honey mustard is so not a good reason to be upset. Orphans in Africa, drunk drivers killing innocent people, even not getting into your safety school (for me it was Florida State) are all good reasons to get upset. Chicken tenders sauces are definitely not. I try not to think about it, and instead focus on the fact that Jocelyn is insane.

"What B. J. thing?" He reaches into the bag and pulls out a napkin. He wipes his hand with it and sets it on his lap.

"With him calling the police or whatever. Do you think he's really going to do that?"

"I dunno." His phone starts going off again, and my

sadness over the honey mustard is suddenly annoyance that he won't answer the call. Why won't he answer it? It's either because he's trying to look cool by not or he's trying to protect my feelings. Does he really think I'm that upset by the whole breakup? I mean, I am, but I've given him no reason to think I would be. Have I? I wrack my brain, trying to determine if there's any way he could know how upset I am.

"Would you answer your phone?" I snap.

He reaches in his pocket, pulls it out, and makes a big show of turning it off.

I roll my eyes. "Whatever. Listen, we need to talk about the schedule." Our schedule is now completely screwed up. We were supposed to be in North Carolina by now.

"What about it?"

"It's all screwed up. We need to reevaluate it."

"It's not that screwed up." He shrugs. "We'll be at Middleton by tonight, and we'll leave tomorrow. Obviously we won't be able to visit for that long, but we won't be that far off the schedule."

Suddenly, I'm struck with a brilliant idea. Maybe I can convince Jordan that we can't stop at Middleton, because IT WILL MAKE US LATE FOR ORIENTATION. That would be perfect. I could call Lloyd, tell him that we can't make it because we're way behind schedule, and then I wouldn't have to deal with the whole thing.

"Well," I say slowly, pretending that I'm thinking about it. "Maybe we shouldn't stop."

"What?" Jordan asks, frowning. He takes another tender and dips it in the honey mustard. I resist the urge to reach over and take it out of his hands and throw it out the window. Honey mustard is obviously not good for my mental state.

"I just mean with the schedule the way it is and everything, it might be better if we just drove straight through."

"But it's not going to throw us off that much. If we don't stop, we'll actually be ahead of schedule."

God, why is he being such an ass? And since when is he such an expert on the schedule? He didn't even read the damn thing. Does he really need to contradict everything I say?

"Besides," he goes on, "I thought you'd be happy to see Lloyd."

Right. "I am," I say. "But we need to stick to the schedule, too." This should be a perfectly reasonable explanation. I mean, he knows I'm totally anal retentive.

My phone rings before I can come up with a better response, and I check the caller ID. Lloyd. Lovely.

"Aren't you going to answer that?" Jordan asks, grinning.

"Of course," I say, rolling my eyes.

"Hey," I say into the phone. "What's up?" I think "What's up?" is a very good, neutral phrase to be saying to Lloyd under the circumstances. Like, I could totally see myself saying it to a boyfriend, so Jordan will be convinced that something really is going on with Lloyd, but at the same time, it's also something you can say to a friend, so Lloyd won't be all, "Oh, wow, Courtney must be in love with me."

"Hey," Lloyd says. "I've been trying to call you for a while."

"Really?" I say, trying to sound innocent. I know he's been calling. I just turned my phone off.

"Yeah," he says. "It kept going right to voice mail."

"I don't know why," I say, still trying to sound innocent. "It's raining here, so . . ."

"It's raining where?" he says, sounding confused.

"Where we are," I say, trying to sound deliberately vague.

"What does that have to do with anything?"

"It may have been messing with my cell reception."

"I don't think that has anything to do with it, Courtney," he says. Well, duh. Why would rain be messing up my cell reception?

"I don't know," I say again. Jordan shifts on the seat next to me and takes a loud sip of his soda.

"You don't sound right," Lloyd says. "Is Jordan giving you a hard time?"

"Uh, no," I say, "He's not."

Jordan stops with a fry halfway to his mouth. "I'm not what?" he asks, frowning.

I shake my head at him and hold up my hand, trying to act like it's not important. Which, true to what's been going on, makes him just want to know more. "What did he say?" Jordan demands. He reaches over and turns off the radio.

"Nothing," I mouth at him, and turn it back on. He turns it off. I turn it on. "Quit it," I say.

"What's going on?" Lloyd asks again through my phone.

"Nothing," I say to Lloyd. "We're just having a little problem with the radio. You know, because of the storm."

"You guys are listening to the radio?"

"Well, not right now," I say, which is true. Jordan's turned it off again, and now he's maneuvering his body, trying to get closer to me so that he can hear what Lloyd is saying.

"Not right now what?" Lloyd asks.

"We're not listening to the radio right now," I say. "Because we're having problems with it because of the storm. Jordan has satellite."

"Figures." Lloyd snorts. Lloyd hates the fact that Jordan is kind of spoiled. Which really makes no sense, because Lloyd himself is quite spoiled. In fact, his parents just bought him a brand-new Mustang for graduation. Which he can't even use, since he can't have a car at school. So now his brand-new car is just sitting in the garage, probably getting used by no one. I wonder if Lloyd would let Jocelyn drive his car. There's no way B. J. would recognize it.

"Anyway," I say. "I'm going to let you go now, but I'll call you when we get close."

Jordan, seeing that the conversation is about to end anyway, reaches over and moves the volume up to almost full blast. Rap music comes blaring out of the speakers.

I reach over and very calmly turn off the radio. "Jordan," I say, "would you please refrain from turning up the music like that when I'm on the phone? I'd really appreciate it."

"HELLO?" Lloyd says much too loudly, now that the radio is off.

"Yeah," I say. "Sorry about that."

"I don't understand why you guys are listening to music," Lloyd says.

"What do you mean?"

"I thought you were dreading this trip," he says.

"I was," I say. What does that have to do with listening to music?

"*Was* as in past tense?" Lloyd asks, sounding quite like a jealous boyfriend. I'm not stupid. I know Lloyd isn't jealous about me, per se, but more about the fact that I'm with Jordan.

"No," I say. "I am not having a fun time on this trip." I am still dreading it, although that really makes no sense, because there's nothing to dread anymore, since I'm in the middle of actually taking part in it.

"You're not having a good time?" Jordan asks, sounding surprised.

"Why does he sound surprised?" Lloyd asks.

"I am having a horrible time on this trip," I say to Lloyd. Which isn't exactly a lie. I mean, I've spend a good part of it with food poisoning, listening to Jordan talk to his new girlfriend, dealing with the fact that Jocelyn is possibly going to get a restraining order taken out against her, and listening to rap music. It's been bad. "Now I will call you when I get close."

"I can't wait to see you, Court," Lloyd says, his voice softening.

"I'm excited to see you, too," I say, a twinge of guilt rising up in me as I realize this might not exactly be the truth. But I don't know if it's exactly a lie, either. After all, even if this whole hooking-up thing doesn't work out, Lloyd has always been my friend. So it will be nice to see him and hang out. I click off my phone.

"You're having a horrible time?" Jordan asks, looking hurt.

"Can we not talk?" I say. I open the bag my food is in and pull out a french fry.

"Why not?" he asks, sounding hurt again. "Now we can't even talk?"

"No." I take a bite of my fry, which is now cold. Surprisingly, for some reason this makes it taste better. I love fast food. I take a sip of my diet Coke and eat another fry.

"We can't talk, ever, for the rest of this trip?"

"Yes, we can talk for the rest of this trip, I'm not stupid. I know it would be impossible to not talk for the rest of this trip."

"So what you're saying is we can talk, but we can't?"

"Look, it's not that hard to figure out," I say. "We can talk about normal things, like the route we're taking, the schedule, toll money, etc. But no, like, chatting." These fries are so good. I take out a packet of ketchup and look for somewhere to squeeze it. I hate ketchup directly on my fries. I'm definitely more of a dipper. Jordan hands me his empty chicken tender container wordlessly, and I squeeze the packet of ketchup into it.

"Thanks," I say.

"So thanking me is allowed?" he asks.

"Jordan, stop. You know what I mean."

"Oh, I'm sorry," he says. He sounds pissed. Why is he pissed?

"Why are you pissed?" I ask.

"I'm not pissed."

"Well, you look pissed. And you sound pissed."

"Well, I'm not."

"Okay," I say, knowing that he is. Jordan can never admit when he's pissed. I don't know why. It's like this thing, where if he admits to you that he's angry, he's lost or something. Although I think he's just that way with me. Or maybe with girls. I wonder if he's like that with his new girlfriend.

"I just don't think you should be listening to every little thing Lloyd tells you to do," he says.

"I'm not," I say.

"Okay," he says, not sounding like he means it.

"Seriously, I'm not. I just think it would be better if we don't talk much." I shrug.

"Because of Lloyd."

"Can you get off the Lloyd thing?"

"Why?"

"Because I already told you, it has nothing to do with Lloyd."

"Well, it's a little weird that you were fine until you talked to Lloyd, and now all of a sudden you don't want to talk to me."

I snort. Does he really think we were fine this whole time? Has he not noticed the fact that there is this very weird tension between us, due to the fact that he dumped me two weeks ago for some other girl?

"What?" he demands.

"Nothing," I say. "I think it's just kind of funny that you think we're fine."

"I don't see why we can't be," he says. "People break up and stay friends, Court."

"True," I say. "But I don't really want to be your friend." It's true. I don't want to be his friend. I want to be his girl-friend or nothing. I feel a lump rising in my throat and I take a sip of my soda in an effort to push it back down. I can feel Jordan watching me, so I open up the fast food bag and take out my Whopper. I peel off the paper and take a bite of the burger. He remembered the cheese this time. I look at the burger and promptly burst into tears.

the trip ▶ jordan

Day Two, 1:50 p.m.

"Dude, it's Jocelyn," I say, looking over my shoulder nervously, just waiting for Courtney to get out of the Burger King. Could this trip be any more fucked up? Seriously. Courtney bursts into tears, something about cheese on her burger (which I know I remembered, because I knew if I didn't, she was going to flip the fuck out). She ran into Burger King crying, and I stood outside the bathroom, yelling in to her and looking like a freak. She kept telling me to go away, so finally I did, and now I'm waiting in the car for her to come out. The weird thing is, all I can think about is that song by Digital Underground, the one with the lyric "I once got busy in a Burger King bathroom." I think I have it on a mix CD in here somewhere.

"This isn't Jocelyn," B. J. says, sighing. "It's Jordan. Dude, try to play a better trick than that. You sound nothing like her. Plus your number came up on my caller ID."

188

"No," I say, feeling like I'm living in some sort of weird alternate reality. "Jocelyn is the one who's following you."

"Why would Jocelyn be the one who's following me?" B. J. asks, sounding thoroughly confused. Again, I'm struck by his ability to be very insightful and smart about some things and then totally clueless about others. Maybe he's one of those idiot savants.

"Because she wants to know where you're going, obviously," I say. I crane my neck to get a look at the Burger King. Still no sign of Courtney. I'm giving her five more minutes, and then I'm going back in there. What is it with me and the women's bathroom?

"Why would she want to know where I'm going?" B. J. asks, sounding even more confused. "Wait, how do you even know this?"

"Because Courtney was asking all these questions about who was following you, and about how I should try to convince you not to call the police because it was probably nothing."

"So?"

"So obviously she was saying that because it's Jocelyn, and they don't want you calling the police and getting her in trouble, and/or finding out it's her."

"Did you just say 'and/or'?"

I don't respond.

"Why would Jocelyn be following me, though?" B. J. asks again. "She knows where I'm going. I tell her every second where I'm going to be. I check in."

"Maybe she doesn't believe you," I say. "Maybe she's following you because she wants to make sure you really are where you say you are."

"That's ridiculous," B. J. says. "Why would I lie about where I'm going?"

"She doesn't trust you," I tell him. "I have to go."

"Why wouldn't she trust me?" he demands. "I'm totally trustworthy."

I try not to point out that not only does B. J. tend to get caught doing things and then lie about them, he also has an extremely impulsive personality, which makes him do things spur of the moment. Like dress up as a midget. Or cheat on his girlfriend. Not that B. J. has ever cheated on Jocelyn. Not that I know of, anyway.

"Listen," I say, "I gotta go. But it's definitely Jocelyn. You should talk to her."

"Hmm," B. J. says, sounding unsure. I want to be a good friend, but I really can't deal with this right now. I slap my phone shut and head inside to rescue Courtney from a women's bathroom for the second time in twenty-four hours.

courtney ◁ before

33 Days Before the Trip, 6:57 p.m.

"This house," I say, "is amazing." I take a soda out of the refrigerator, pop the top, and pour half of it into my glass. I can't believe I'm in Miami. It feels exotic for some reason, just saying that.

"It is pretty awesome," Jordan says, sitting down next to me at the bar. I hand him my glass and he takes a sip of my drink.

"So what's this place like tonight?" I ask. Jordan, B. J., Jocelyn, and I are going to the beach, then out to dinner, and I want to make sure I'm dressed appropriately.

"What do you mean?" Jordan asks. He hands me back my soda.

"I mean, is it dress up or what?" I bought this amazing black dress that I can't wait for Jordan to see me in. It has a flowing, crinkly skirt and a low back.

"You don't have to dress up," he says. "But you can if you want."

"And what about after?" I say, leaning in close to him. "What are we going to do after?"

"What do you mean?" he asks, grinning. He shifts in his chair and moves closer to me.

"I mean are we going out to a club or anything?"

"A club?" Jordan throws his head back and laughs. "You want to go to a club?"

"Of course," I say. "Why wouldn't I?"

"Um, because you don't dance?"

Hmm. This is true. But I feel like dancing tonight. "We're in Miami," I say. "Isn't that what people do in Miami? Besides, I do so dance."

He raises his eyebrows.

"It's my new thing," I say. "Dancing is my new thing."

"Oh, really?" He leans in close to me and puts his forehead against mine. "Since when?"

"Jordan," I say, "are you trying to say I'm a bad dancer?"

"No," he says. "Of course not."

"Good," I say. "Need I remind you that my dancing was the thing that attracted you to me in the first place?"

He tilts his head to the side, then kisses me lightly on the lips. "That is true," he says. "You're a very hot dancer."

"I know," I say. "And tonight I'm going to be a dancing machine."

"Okay," he says, kissing me again. "But you have to

promise you're not going to dance with anyone else."

"No one else?" I say. I cock my head to the side, pretending to consider. "But what if some really cute guy asks me to?"

"No," he says. He kisses me again, a little more forcefully again. "I want you all to myself."

"What about girls?" I ask, smiling. "Can I dance with girls?"

"Only if I can watch," he says, grinning.

"Eww," I say. "You're dirty." I push him playfully, but he grabs my arms, and this time, I kiss him. He kisses me back, and his hands are in my hair and on my face.

"We have to stop," he says, after a few minutes, pulling away. But I can't help but think about what would happen if we didn't stop, if we just kept on kissing, if we just kept going and didn't stop.

"I don't want to," I say, trying to pull him close to me again.

"We have to," he says, giving me another light kiss on the lips.

"We don't *have* to do anything," I say.

He laughs. "We're supposed to be going to the beach," he says. "With B. J. and Jocelyn, remember?"

"Yeah," I say, sighing.

"And if we don't go, they'll probably end up killing each other."

"True," I say. "I don't want to be responsible for the deaths of our friends."

"Then come on," he says. He holds his hand out, and I slide my palm into his. "But later," he whispers huskily, "you're mine."

You have no idea, I think. I follow him happily up the stairs to where Jocelyn and B. J. are waiting.

jordan ← before

33 Days Before the Trip, 7:07 p.m.

"Seriously, they do have naked beaches here," B. J. says, grinning. He's wearing camouflage shorts and a T-shirt that reads "Hi! You'll do."

"Perfect," Jocelyn says, pulling off the pink tank top she's wearing and exposing the top of her white bikini. "So you'll have no problem if I go topless."

"No problem at all," B. J. says, grinning again.

"Great," Jocelyn says. "So you'll have no problem with all the guys on the beach staring at me." She crosses her arms across her chest with a satisfied expression on her face. B. J. frowns, and Courtney and I look at each other nervously.

B. J. and Jocelyn are, at their best, volatile. They have this weirdness between them that tends to come out at horrible times. On prom night, they got in this huge fight in the limo about Katelyn Masters, a girl B. J. used to hook up with freshman year. In the midst of the fight, B. J. went to change the radio station, and Jocelyn screamed, "If you touch that music I'll break your fucking fingers!" I'm beginning to think that Jocelyn is quite crazy, although Courtney assures me it's just something B. J. brings out in Jocelyn, that she's usually sane.

"You're not going to be exposing your boobs to every guy on the beach," B. J. says. We're all in Miami, at my dad's friend's house, standing in the room Courtney and I are sharing. We were getting ready to go out to the beach, and then B. J. made the remark about boobs, which has obviously put a kink in the plan.

"Why not?" Jocelyn asks. "You're so intent on seeing everyone else's boobs, and you're all excited about the naked beaches."

"So?" B. J. asks. He takes the baseball cap he's wearing off his head and throws it onto the bed, which is not a good sign. In my experience, when B. J. starts removing any kind of clothing, it can only lead to bad things.

"Actually," I say, "it's private beach property outside, so there probably won't be that many people around."

"So let's go! Do you have your sunscreen?" Courtney asks brightly. She pulls a bottle of Coppertone out of her bag and squirts some into her hand.

"I don't!" I say. "I don't have my sunscreen!" I'm almost shouting it. I sound like a tool, but it's what needs to be done if we want to save the situation. Otherwise, Jocelyn and B. J. are going to be fighting all night and ruining our good time.

"Jocelyn?" Courtney asks, holding up the bottle. "Do you need some sunscreen?"

"Yes," Jocelyn says calmly. "Actually, I do." Oh, thank God. Situation diffused. Score one for Jordan and Courtney.

"Here you go," Courtney says, holding out the bottle. Jocelyn takes it, then reaches behind her back, unhooks her bikini top, and starts slathering the lotion on her bare boobs.

"Jesus!" B. J. screams. "What the fuck are you doing?"

Courtney looks at me, and I quickly look away from Jocelyn's boobs.

"I'm getting ready for the beach!" Jocelyn says. I move to the other side of the bed and sit down facing the wall. The last thing I need is seeing my girlfriend's best friend's bare boobs. That can definitely not be good, especially since she's also my best friend's girlfriend. This whole thing is getting very incestuous, what with Courtney's dad banging my mom and everything.

"Um, I think we should go," Courtney whispers in my ear.

"Probably a good idea," I say.

"So, we're going to go," Courtney announces, as B. J. screams, "PUT THAT BACK ON IMMEDIATELY!"

We walk out of the room (OUR room, I might add— B. J. and Jocelyn have their own room, but of course they elected to start their naked fight in ours) and onto the beach.

Once we're settled into the sand, Courtney and I look at each other and start laughing.

"They are so fucked up," I say, leaning back on my towel. The sun is starting to set, which means there probably wasn't too much reason for sunscreen. "Good diversionary tactic with the sunscreen," I say.

"Thanks," she says, smiling. She's wearing a purple bikini and black sunglasses, and I reach over and pull her sunglasses off her eyes. "Come here," I say, pulling her close to me.

"I'm so glad we're not them," Courtney says, snuggling into my arm.

"Ya think?" I say, kissing the top of her head.

"They're so crazy," she says. "They're not honest with each other at all. It's like they almost get off on messing with the other person's head."

There's a sick feeling in my stomach when she says the word "honest" and I try to ignore it.

"Yeah," I say. "They're all screwed up."

"Not like us," she says, pushing me down on the sand. She gets on top of me and starts kissing my neck.

"Whoa, whoa," I say, turning away. Her long hair slides across my chest. "You want to make out on the beach?"

"There's no one around," she says, and I pop my head up and look down the beach. She's right. Way down, there's an old guy walking his dog, but they're moving in the opposite direction from us.

She starts kissing me again, on the mouth this time, and

my hands are in her hair and on her face. Every so often she pulls away and looks at me, and her eyes are the most beautiful thing I've ever seen. Then suddenly, she's looking at me intently and whispering something, and I'm so caught up in her that I don't hear what it is.

"What did you say?" I murmur into her hair. She slides her body off mine and settles in next to me.

"I said I want to be with you," she says into my chest.

"You are with me," I say.

"No, I mean, I want to make love to you," she says, and my eyes spring open. Whoa.

"Whoa," I say. I prop myself up on my elbow and look at her. "Court, that's . . ."

"I know," she says, smiling. "I know it's a big deal and all that. And Jordan, I've thought about it, I really have." I believe her, too. She's definitely an analytical sort of girl, and I know she wouldn't take something like this lightly.

"Are you sure?" I ask, dumbfounded. It's not that I don't want to. Believe me, I do. There are times when Courtney and I are doing our math homework and making out that I feel like I'm going to go insane from wanting her so bad. But anytime we've even talked about it, she's made it pretty clear that she wasn't ready.

"Yes," she says. "I'm sure." She frowns. "You don't want to?'

"Of course I want to," I say truthfully.

"Good." She starts kissing me again, and her tongue is

in my mouth and she tastes and feels so good, and I can feel her body pressing against mine and I'm so turned on that I almost lose my head.

"Wait," I say. "You want to do it right here?" How is this happening? Somewhere along the line, Courtney has become sex crazed, and now wants to have sex on the beach.

"If you want to," she says.

"You don't want your first time to be on a beach," I say.

"I don't care, as long as it's with you," she says, her face flushed. She starts kissing my neck. "Hey, Jordan?" She pulls away and looks right at me.

"Yeah?"

"I love you." She's looking in my eyes, and she's waiting for me to say it back, and I want to. I feel it. I do love her. But then I start thinking about her dad, and how I'm lying to her, and suddenly, I know I can't say it. I shouldn't say it.

"Thanks," I say, swallowing. A look of confusion crosses her face, and for a second, I don't think I'm going to be able to do it. But I look away from her before I can get caught up in the moment. "We should go inside." She climbs off me, and I still don't look at her, because I know I won't be able to take the look on her face. "And check on Jocelyn and B. J." I stand up and brush the sand off my shorts and start walking toward the house. And after a second, I can hear Courtney following me.

courtney the trip

I'm having a breakdown in a random Burger King bathroom. This is upsetting for a few reasons, not the least
of which is that it's happening in a bathroom. I mean, a
breakdown at any time is not something that one should
be excited about, but to have one in a public rest room
is definitely doubly upsetting. And it's not even like one
of those nice public bathrooms that you see on TV, with
attendants and breath mints and real monogrammed
towels. It's a Burger King bathroom. And not a particularly clean one, either.

I take a wad of toilet paper off the roll and blow my
nose loudly. The most disgusting part of this whole thing is
that I'm sitting on the toilet while I do this. Because there's
no top to the toilets. So I'm actually sitting on the toilet. Without my pants down, of course. Who knows what
kind of disgusting germs are transferring themselves onto

my skirt. I'm probably going to have to burn it after this. Which is horrible, because I've never even worn it before. In fact, the only reason I'm even wearing it now is because I wanted Jordan to think I was dressing up for Lloyd. Which is really screwed up. I don't know when I lost my sanity, but it's not a good feeling.

I throw the toilet paper with my snot on it into the toilet and flush. I just need to take a deep breath. The trip is half over. That should make me feel better, but really, it doesn't. It makes me feel worse, because the past couple of days have seemed like a lifetime.

I head out of the stall and start washing my hands at the sink. The bathroom is deserted, which is good because it would be embarrassing for someone to see me looking like this—eyes red from crying, ketchup stain on my cute new shirt, and my hair a mess from when I kept running my hands through it in the stall in an effort not to touch anything germ infested.

"Court?" Jordan's voice comes from outside the bathroom.

"What?" I say, trying to make it out like I didn't just go running from his car crying and into the bathroom.

"You okay?"

"Yeah," I say. "I'm fine."

"Okay," he says. There's a pause. "Was it . . . Are you upset about the food? We can go somewhere else?"

He thinks I started crying over fast-food burgers. He

can't be that stupid, can he? He obviously knows I'm upset about him, and he's just trying to be nice. Great, pity. Just what I need.

"No, the food was fine," I say. "I think I'm just a little upset about seeing Lloyd."

"Why would you be upset about that?" he asks, sounding confused. Good question.

"Not upset about seeing him," I say. I wet a paper towel and use it to wipe my face off. It feels scratchy and kind of gross, but I put up with the momentary discomfort so that I can look human again. "Upset because I haven't seen him for a while."

"You just saw him two days ago," he says.

I throw the paper towel away, pull my shirt down a little bit so that the ketchup stain is less noticeable, and emerge from the bathroom. He's leaning against the wall, his hair wet from the rain, and he looks really, really, cute. And really, really worried about me. I will NOT start crying again.

"Yeah, well, when you're in love with someone, two days can seem like an eternity." I toss my hair defiantly over my shoulder and start walking toward the door. My attempt at haughtiness is overshadowed by the fact that the shoes I'm wearing (cute sparkly purple flip-flops with butterflies on them) are drenched from the rain, and so every time I stomp, my shoes squish.

"So, wait, now you guys are in love?" Jordan asks, sounding confused.

"Yes," I say definitively. "And since you really care about your new girlfriend, I'm sure you understand how two days without seeing someone can really seem like a long time."

"Yeah," he says, not sounding sure. "But Court, I really doubt you're in love with Lloyd."

"Whatever, Jordan," I say. "Not to sound like a brat or anything, but you don't really know me anymore. I'm a new woman."

We're in the parking lot now, and I open the door to his TrailBlazer and pull myself into the passenger seat. He gets in and starts the car. I pull my seat belt on and decide it's time for a new attitude. No more crying.

"Let's go to Middleton," I say. "I can't freakin' wait to get there."

Jocelyn calls two hours later, while we're stuck in traffic. I'm looking through a magazine that I bought at a rest stop and reading an article about what to do if you get dumped. It's actually not helping me much, because I'm pretty sure it's satire. The article, not the magazine. It basically says that once a guy dumps you, you should cease worrying about what he thinks of you, and that you shouldn't try denying your psychotic urges, because it's not natural. It says that if you feel like you want to stalk him, you totally should. If you want to break into his e-mail account, do it. Drive-bys? Harassing his new girlfriend? Totally allowed. It's quite scary, actually. The article, I mean.

I flip open my phone. "Whaddup?" I say, tossing my

magazine onto the floor. I'm totally over my nervous break-down. You'd think I'd feel good about this, but I don't. For some reason, it makes me uneasy, like the fact that I got over it so quickly just means that something worse is going to come. It's like I'm in some sort of denial mode.

"So he wasn't hanging out with Katelyn," Jocelyn says, sounding smug. Which makes no sense, because in order to sound smug, you have to be right about something. And since Jocelyn thought that B. J. was cheating on her, and now she's found out that he isn't, she shouldn't sound smug. She should sound sheepish.

"How do you know?" I ask.

"He caught me stalking him," she says breezily.

"He caught you?" I ask, wondering why she's not more upset. I feel Jordan shift in his seat next to me. I look at him suspiciously and when he catches my eye, he nervously adjusts the rearview mirror.

"Yes, he caught me." Jocelyn sighs. I hear the sound of splashing in the background, and music. Loud music.

"Where are you?" I ask.

"At a pool party," she says.

"Hold on," I say, pushing the volume up on my phone in an effort to hear her over the background noise. "How did you end up at a pool party?"

"Hailie Roseman invited me," she says simply. "So B. J. drove us here."

"No," I say. Is she drunk? "I mean, how did you get

from stalking B. J., to getting caught, to ending up at Hailie Roseman's pool party?" I don't even think Jocelyn is friends with Hailie Roseman, a junior who I always suspected Jordan of hooking up with, even though he constantly denies it.

"Oh," Jocelyn says. "That's actually why I'm calling." Duh. "See, B. J. found out I was stalking him because Jordan told him it was me."

"Oh, really?" I say. "He told him it was you?" Jordan shifts in his seat again, then reaches over and starts flipping through the satellite stations. He clears his throat.

"Yes," Jocelyn repeats. "Jordan told him."

"And how did Jordan know?"

"I guess he figured it out because you were telling him to tell B. J. not to call the police."

"Really," I say, contemplating this revelation.

"Mm-hmm," Jocelyn says. More splashing. "But listen, that's not the best part."

"What's the best part?" I ask, not really seeing what was so good about the first part. Jordan looks over at me curiously. Ha. Like I'm really going to clue him in on what's going on. I like making him squirm. Also, since the traffic isn't moving, it isn't really like he can do anything about the fact that I'm making him uncomfortable. He just has to sit there.

"So after B. J. caught me and I confessed, we had this really long talk," Jocelyn says. Her voice sounds kind of slurred, like she's been drinking. More splashing and music in the background. I love the fact that my friends are off having an end-of-summer party with drinks and swimming and music and I'm stuck on the road trip from hell. So not fair.

"That's great, Joce," I say, meaning it. "You and B. J. *should* be able to talk about things more openly. I think it'll really help you to feel more comfortable with the situation."

"So, listen," she says, sounding kind of nervous. "I have to tell you something that he told me. He told me so that I'd feel more like I could trust him."

"You mean like a secret?"

"Yeah," she says, sounding nervous again. "Exactly like a secret." I wrack my brain for what kind of secrets B. J. could possibly have. A criminal record? No, he wouldn't keep that a secret. When he burned our class year into the school lawn and almost didn't graduate, he bragged about it to anyone who would listen, including two girls he'd never met that happened to overhear us talking about it one night at a random ice cream stand. An STD? Nah, Jocelyn would be freaking out. And she doesn't sound freaked out.

"Okay," I say, wondering how she could possibly think it's a good idea to put a start to her new, trusting relationship with her boyfriend by telling me a secret he told her not to tell. But I don't tell her this, because I kind of want to know the secret.

"Now, I know it's probably not the best idea to tell you, you know, since we're now having an open, honest, communication based on mutual trust and respect," she says, sounding kind of like Dr. Phil. It's hard to take her seriously, though, because even though she's talking like she understands the psychobabble she's spewing, I can still hear the sounds of the party in the background, including a male voice that's yelling, "LET'S GET FUCKED UP!" over and over again. This is being met by cheers of "Woooo!"

"Then why are you?" I ask.

"Hold on," she says. "I'm going inside the house, it's getting loud out here."

"Okay," I agree. I roll down my window.

"What are you doing?" Jordan asks. "The AC is on."

"I want some air," I tell him.

"How can you possibly want some air?" he asks, frowning. "The AC is on. It's hotter outside than it is in here."

"I didn't say I was hot," I say. "I said I needed some air." The guy in the car next to us is apparently so fed up with the traffic that he's gotten out of his car and is rummaging around in his trunk. He emerges with what looks like travel Scrabble, and looking satisfied, slams his trunk shut.

"I can't believe we forgot to bring our travel games," Jordan says, I guess thinking he's funny.

"Hello!" I yell into the phone. No response. How long does it take to get into someone's house? I can still hear the sounds of the party in the background, so I know she didn't hang up. Maybe she dropped her phone. "Helllloo!" I yell again, thinking maybe she'll hear me and come back.

"Why are you yelling?" Jordan asks.

"Because Jocelyn put me on hold and she hasn't come back yet."

"Well, there's another person in this car. So try not to yell."

"Oh, I'm sorry," I say. "Is my yelling bothering you?"

"Well, yes," he says. "Besides, it's not like you're in a big rush to get her back on the phone, right? You're not doing anything important. We're sitting in traffic."

"Wow," I say. "You're so astute, Jordan. I love how totally insightful and good you are at reading situations."

He looks away then, and I yell, "HELLLOOO!" into the phone once more.

"Oh, hi," Jocelyn says, sounding breathless. "Sorry about that. I couldn't figure out how to open the back door, so I had to walk all the way around the house, and it took a while." I want to ask her why she didn't just talk to me while she walked, or at least pick up the phone to give me a status report, but I don't.

"Anyway," I say.

"Yeah, anyway, I'm inside now."

"Good."

"Yup."

"So . . ."

"Oh right! The secret. Okay, so I know I probably shouldn't be telling you."

"Probably not," I agree. "But before we get into it, who was that yelling 'Let's get fucked up!' like that over and over? Just out of curiosity, I mean."

"Oh, that was B. J.," she says. "He's getting drunk tonight." I think it's a great sign that they're celebrating their newfound, trusting relationship by getting drunk and blabbing each other's secrets, but I don't say this. I'm not one to pass judgment on anyone's relationships.

"Oh, okay."

"Anyway, I know I shouldn't tell you, but the reason I am is because it's kind of about you. Well, indirectly anyway. And I do want to be loyal to B. J., I really do, but you're my best friend, and if you found out from someone else, and then you found out I knew and didn't tell you, you'd probably be pissed. And chicks over dicks, you know?"

"Okay," I say, starting to get worried. I don't like Jocelyn finding secrets out that have to do with me from B. J., because inevitably they're going to involve Jordan. And the fact that I just had a breakdown in a public rest room makes me very nervous about my mental state.

"Okay," she says. "B. J. told me that Jordan made up the Facebook girl."

"What do you mean?" I ask. My heart is beating really fast all of a sudden, and I wonder if Jordan can hear it.

"The girl he supposedly met on Facebook? That he dumped you for? He didn't dump you for her. He made her up."

"Why would he do that?" I ask.

"I have no idea," she says, but even as she's saying it, I know the answer. He did it as an excuse to break up with me. He knew it would be easier if he had a reason, something concrete that would at least give me some sort of answer. And this whole time, I've been making myself feel better by thinking up horrible attributes to Jordan's new girlfriend, telling myself she's a slut, and someday he'll realize what a huge mistake he's made.

The truth is, he just doesn't love me.

the trip > jordan

Courtney is making me extremely nervous. Whatever the fuck is going on in her phone conversation cannot be good. I've already figured out that she knows I tipped B. J. off to the whole Jocelyn thing, which makes me slightly annoyed. When I told him, it was so she wouldn't get in trouble, not so he could go and tell her how he found out. He had to know she was going to come back and tell Courtney. What was he thinking?

The traffic inches slowly forward, and Courtney sits next to me in silence. When we get to Middleton twenty minutes later, the vibe in the car is not any better. I wish Courtney would just talk to me and tell me how pissed off she is, but that's obviously not going to happen.

Add that to the fact that I have four missed calls on my phone, all from Courtney's dad, who I have most definitely decided is the craziest motherfucker that I know. Seriously, his shit is whacked. I used to think maybe B. J. was the craziest person I know, but now I realize that B. J. only does crazy things, and that there is a definite difference between acting crazy and being crazy. And Courtney's dad is the latter.

Since we've been stuck in traffic, and Courtney's been giving me the silent treatment, I've come up with a great plan for our time in North Carolina. It consists of one part: Stay away from Courtney and Lloyd, and hang out with my brother only. This is going to be slightly problematic, since I'm not sure how Courtney is going to feel about me just dropping her off at the gates of Middleton. If they even have gates.

I pull the car into the visitor parking lot and switch off the car. "Well," I say. "I guess this is it."

"What do you mean?" she asks, frowning.

"I mean, I guess this is it. This is where we part ways."

"Part ways?" she asks, and it could be my imagination, but for some reason she looks almost panicked.

"Yeah, you know," I say. "Part ways, leave each other, go in different directions."

"Why would we do that?" She bites her lip and looks out the car window.

"Why wouldn't we? I'm sure you want time alone with Lloyd, and really, I don't want to be around that shit." Whoops. Shouldn't have said that out loud. Last thing I need is for her thinking I want her back. Even though I do. Actually, not true. I never wanted to break up with her. But whatever. Semantics. "Lloyd and I aren't exactly BFFs, if you know what I mean."

She nods. She's probably thinking about the time Lloyd and I almost got into a fistfight.

"So!" I say cheerfully. I pull the keys out of the ignition. "I'll open the back so you can get your stuff."

"Great!" she says. She pulls out her cell phone and makes a big production of turning it on silent. I guess so her and Lloyd won't get interrupted while they're hooking up.

"Just make sure you close the truck when you're finished," I say. I grab my black duffle from the back and sling it over my shoulder.

"That's all you have?" she asks. "I mean, that's all your bringing? For the overnight."

"Yeah, that's all I'm bringing for the overnight," I say.

"Well, I have a lot more than you," she says pointedly. If she thinks I'm going to help her carry her stuff, she's definitely mistaken. I like to consider myself a nice guy, but I draw the line at helping my ex-girlfriend bring her stuff up to some guy's dorm room. That's insane. Especially since it's pretty obvious that she's planning on sleeping with him.

"Of course you have a lot more than me," I say. "You're a girl. But take your time getting whatever you need. Just make sure you close the back when you're done. I'll meet you here tomorrow at eight, and we'll get back on the road, all right?"

"Yeah, okay," she says, not sounding okay with it at all.

A look of hurt passes across her face briefly as I turn away, and it's almost enough to make me turn around, but then I think about Lloyd and the Facebook comment, and I keep on walking.

My brother, Adam, lives in a single room in Gluster Hall, where he's an RA. We're not super close, and I'm not sure why that is. I think it might have something to do with the fact that we were so spoiled growing up, that it made it easy not to have to interact. My parents bought us everything—video game systems, DVDs, cell phones, toys, whatever we wanted. Which means there wasn't a lot of time spent sitting around, reading books or hanging out, making forts and trying to amuse ourselves with imaginary games.

I knock on his door and he opens it wearing a pair of boxers and a T-shirt.

"Dude," Adam says, squinting at me. "Are you fucking kidding me?" If you knew my brother, you'd know this isn't really strange. He talks like this a lot, in random questions that make no sense. "Are you fucking kidding me?" is actually one of his favorites.

"What's up, bro?" I ask, and contemplate pulling him into a hug. We're not usually very touchy-feely, but he is my brother and I haven't seen him in a while. Before I can decide if this would be appropriate, I catch a whiff of pot coming from his room. I look at him again. His eyes are bloodshot and he has a half-grin on his face. That's just great. The asshole is high.

"Dude, are you fucking kidding me? Right now?" he repeats.

"Uh, no," I say. "I guess not. But it's, uh, good to see you." I realize he's blocking the door, so I take a step closer to him, in an effort to show my intent to actually get into his room. Although I'm sure once I get in there, I'm going to start getting a pot buzz by default.

He still doesn't move out of the way, and I bump into him awkwardly. For the first time, I realize he's not wearing any shoes. I know this because I step on his foot.

"You're not coming in," he says, putting his hand up.

"What do you mean?" I ask, confused.

"Why didn't you tell me about Mom?" he asks, and I realize he's not only high but pissed. Psychotically, scary pissed. His eyes are rimmed in red out of anger, not just from pot. I thought pot was supposed to make you mellow.

"What do you mean, 'tell you about Mom?'" I ask, automatically reverting to avoid-and-deny mode.

"About Mom having an affair, about how she's leaving Dad for someone else," he says, and this time he bangs his fist against the door. I take a step back.

"I didn't know," I say quietly, which is only a half lie. I knew she was having an affair, but I didn't know she was going to leave my dad. Suddenly, I feel like someone's punched me in the stomach.

"That's bullshit," he says, leaning against the door frame. "That's bullshit and you know it. She told me you knew. She told me you caught them."

"I did," I say, "But I didn't know she was going to leave Dad because of it. She acted like it wasn't a big deal, like it was a random thing that was going to stop." In reality, I knew this wasn't true. My mom had said that to me, but it was pretty obvious that's not what was going on. I figured maybe she just needed time to end it—I mean, let's face it. Courtney's dad is one fucked-up motherfucker. I didn't know exactly what was going on, but I knew there was a chance he could have been making it difficult for my mom the way he was making my life difficult.

"So that made it okay not to tell me? Jesus, Jordan!" He runs his fingers through his hair and looks at me like he can't believe my obvious stupidity.

"It wasn't mine to tell," I say. "It was up to her to tell Dad, it wasn't my place."

"You're right," he says. "At first. But this shit has been going on for months, Jordan. Were you ever going to tell anyone?" Suddenly, he seems very coherent and not like he's been smoking pot at all, which scares me. My brother is quite a bit bigger than me, but it's not like I think he wants to fight me. We've been in fistfights before. Nothing major, just little scrapes that started out over something dumb and then escalated to the point where we would rough each other up a bit. But now, he doesn't even seem

217

like his words are motivated by anger. It's something else—almost like a hatred.

"I don't know if I was going to tell anyone," I say.

"That's great," Adam says and then slams the door in my face. I stand there for a minute, staring at the door and trying to calm down. Then I pick up my stuff and head back out to my car. When I get there, Courtney and her bags are gone.

courtney the trip

Day Two, 5:19 p.m.

I can do this. I can pretend I like Lloyd. I've been in school plays before. Well, not since junior high, and even then it was just a bit part that was akin to being in the chorus. I didn't have any actual lines or anything. But still. I had to act through my facial expressions.

I've been standing outside Lloyd's dorm for about ten minutes, my pink duffle bag slung over my shoulder and my cell phone in my hand. I want to call him, really I do, but for some reason, I can't. Technically, I can't get into the building unless he comes down to get me, since they have some sort of swipe card system to get in the dorms. I guess it's for security reasons, although there have already been two helpful students who have offered to swipe me in. So much for secure dorms.

"Courtney?" I turn around and there's Lloyd, standing behind me.

"Oh!" I say. "Hi! I was just about to call you." I hold up my cell phone, to prove my point. It's not like I'm lying. I really was about to call him. Or at least, I was about to *try* to call him. And effort should count for something.

"I came down, just in case you couldn't find the dorm." He wraps his arms around me and I lean into his body. "I'm so glad you're here," he murmurs into my hair. I bury my face into his neck and try to make myself feel something, anything for him. I wrack my brain for all the things I loved about him while I lusted after him for the past six years. His arms, which I always thought were really buff, now just feel . . . I don't know, hard. Okay, not the arms, not the arms. Hmm. I used to spend a lot of time thinking about kissing him. But now that I've actually kissed him, I can't really think about what it would be like anymore, because I've already done that. And it wasn't bad exactly, but it wasn't great either. Nothing like kissing Jordan.

"I'm glad I'm here, too," I say, sort of meaning it. I don't know what's going to happen with Lloyd and I, but being out of that car can only be a good thing.

"Let's get your stuff inside," Lloyd says. He takes my pink duffle bag, and I follow him into the dorm.

Two hours later, I feel like I might want to kill myself. It all started when I got a glimpse of Lloyd's closet. For some weird reason, Lloyd must have decided that when he unpacked all his stuff, it would be a good idea to start with his clothes. Actually, not all his clothes, but just his polo shirts. So now his room is pretty bare, but his closet, which is open, has all these polo shirts hanging in it. For some reason, this seems weird to me. I keep thinking about this one time when Jordan called Lloyd "Polo Boy" by accident in front of me.

I was on the phone with Jordan, and I clicked over to the other line, and when I came back, Jordan was like, "Was that Polo Boy?"

And I was all, "Who?"

And Jordan was like, "Nothing."

Apparently he and B. J. call Lloyd "Polo Boy" and he accidentally let it slip. He thought I'd be pissed, but I wasn't. At the time, I actually found it really, really funny. But now, looking at all the shirts hanging up in Lloyd's closet, something about it is kind of . . . disturbing. Does he not like any other shirts? Does he even have any other shirts? I think I saw him in a T-shirt once. When we were in the same gym class.

"So I see you unpacked all your clothes," I say, running my hands down the line of shirts in the closet.

"Yup," he says. He's sitting on the bed, and I know I'm supposed to probably go sit down next to him, but I'm afraid if I do, he might start trying to kiss me or something, and I really, really don't want that to happen. I'm hoping that maybe if I hang out with him a little longer, I'll start feeling more comfortable. This is, after all, the very first time we've hung out since we hooked up. And hooking up with him couldn't have been that bad. I mean, it went on for a while. We were making out for at least an hour or two, and I can't see myself doing that if it was really, really bad.

"Cool," I say. For some reason, I can't stop looking at his shirts. Or touching them. I'm, like, stroking his shirts right now. Over and over, like some sort of shirt pervert.

"Come sit down," Lloyd says, patting the spot on the bed next to him.

"Okay," I say uncertainly. I sit down next to him.

"So what do you want to do tonight?' He takes my hand in his, and interlaces his fingers with mine. I don't know what to do. I have no plan. I figured Jordan would be hanging out with us, at least for a little while, and that I would have to pretend to be interested in Lloyd when I really wasn't. But now, I realize that was the most ridiculous thing I've ever thought in my life. Jordan and Lloyd don't like each other. Why would we all hang out?

"Uh, I don't know," I say, looking around the room. I realize I'm supposed to sleep here tonight, and suddenly, I feel like I'm going to throw up.

"Maybe just hang out here," Lloyd says. His index finger is now making circles on the back of my hand. I try to slide out of his grip without him noticing, but I think he thinks I'm stroking his hand, because he grabs it. Hard. Normally, I like a guy who knows what he's doing, but this feels, um, kind of weird.

"Or maybe we could go somewhere," I say. "Like to a movie." Actually, wait, bad idea. Visions of dark movie theaters and Lloyd rubbing my hand definitely does not make me feel comfortable.

"A movie sounds good," he says. His mouth is against my neck now, and I can feel his breath while he's talking. Which you think would feel good, but for some reason, I'm now thinking of Lloyd as being Polo Boy, defined only by his polo shirts, and therefore, his breath has now become polo breath. I am definitely about to have another breakdown.

"Or!" I say. "You could show me the campus." A walking tour sounds good. A walking tour sounds very safe, something high school kids do with their parents. Something that we'd have to be standing up to do. Although I suppose people do kiss and make out (and have sex?) standing up. But it would be in public. So it would be limited.

"You really want to see the campus right now?" Lloyd asks. He turns my head toward his and kisses me. He's kissing me. Right now, his tongue is in my mouth. I'm kissing him back. It doesn't feel horrible, but it doesn't feel right either. It's like we have no kissing chemistry or something.

"Lloyd," I say, breaking away. "I think we should go somewhere, I mean, we have the whole night to . . ." I'm trying to figure out a way to say "hook up" without actually saying "hook up" when I suddenly realize that I don't have to hook up with him. Jordan is gone. I don't have to pretend to want to hook up with Lloyd.

"I'm sorry," Lloyd says, talking into my neck. "I don't want you to think I just want to mess around."

"Oh, that's okay," I say. In a way, it actually might be better if he does just want to hook up. Because then, when I tell him it can't happen, he won't be that upset. It won't be like there are feelings involved or anything. He'll just be like, "Oh, okay, I'll just find some other girl to hook up with. La, la, la." And then we can go back to being friends. Friends that have kissed. And made out a little. And then visited each other at college, where someone decided they didn't want to hook up anymore. Hmmm.

"Because I really do like you, Courtney," he says. "I never told you this, but when you were with Jordan, it made me realize that I've had feelings for you all this time."

"Oh." Great. I look at Lloyd, and suddenly, I feel like a horrible person. What am I doing? Messing with my best friend's head so that I can make some guy who made up a fake girlfriend jealous? That's completely and totally insane. It's like I don't even realize who I am anymore.

"Lloyd, listen," I say. "I can't stay here."

"What do you mean?" he asks, looking confused. He takes my hand again.

"I just can't stay here," I repeat. I feel like I'm suffocating. I'm thinking about Jordan making up the Facebook girl, and being here with Lloyd, and I just can't take it. I need to get out of there. Immediately.

"What are you talking about?" he says.

"This," I say, gesturing. "I just . . . I can't. I'll call you later." I pick up my bag, sling it over my shoulder. I need to get outside. Fast.

Lloyd calls after me, but I ignore it, and once I get outside, I feel much better. I take a deep breath. That was the right thing to do. I couldn't stay there, especially after he told me that he liked me. That would have been cruel. And horrible. But now I realize I have no plan. I don't know where to go, where to stay, or what to do. I head back to Jordan's car, figuring at least that's sort of a central location. And maybe he'll be hanging out there for some reason, and I'll just be able to weasel my way into spending the night in his brother's room.

But when I get to where Jordan's car was parked, he's not there. And his car is gone.

the trip > jordan

Day Two, 6:43 p.m.

I'm sitting in a motel down the street from Middleton contemplating my life when my cell phone rings. It's B. J., and I want to ignore it, but from what I could tell, he was at some party and he might need help. Not that there's anything much I can do from North Carolina, but still. He could have alcohol poisoning or something. Plus, if he's not in any kind of trouble, I'm going to bitch him out for telling Jocelyn I told him she was the one following him. How is it that I am away from home, and yet I still have all this drama? I've spent the past half an hour on the computer in the lobby, on Courtney's Facebook page, reading the comment Lloyd left her, and then scrolling back through ALL her comments, trying to find some clue of exactly what happened. Did they have sex? I checked his page, too, but she hasn't left any comments for him since they hooked up. Although ominously enough, he's changed his "relationship status" from "single" to "in a relationship," which is slightly suspect. The information age is so psychotic—without the cell phone and Internet, I would be drama free right now.

"Yeah," I say into the phone, hoping my tone conveys the idea that I'm pissed, but will still help him if he's dying.

"'Sup, kid?" B. J. asks. He doesn't sound like he's alcohol poisoned. I kick my shoes off and sit down on the hotel room bed. I hate hotel rooms. There's something unreal about them, and temporary, like you're on borrowed time or something.

"Nothing," I say, making sure to keep it short.

"Listen," B. J. says. "I'm drunk."

"Okay." He's talking, which means he can't be too drunk. So he's probably calling to apologize. I'm upset that he didn't call until he was shit-faced, but I guess a drunken apology is better than no apology at all.

"I have to tell you something," B. J. says, sounding nervous. I consider telling him I already know, but then decide it's more fun to make him squirm for a while.

"Oh, yeah? What's that?" I pick up the remote and turn on the TV. That's another thing about hotel rooms. You have to pay ten dollars to order movies. Movies should come with your hotel room. It should be a perk, like the pool.

"First, let me just say that I'm really, really sorry," B. J. says.

"Mm-hmm," I say. I flip through the channels, wondering if the Devil Rays game will be on TV in North

227

Carolina. I turn to ESPN, but for some reason, they're showing the Cardinals game, which makes no sense, since the Cardinals play in St. Louis, and Tampa is much closer to North Carolina than St. Louis is. I wait for the little bar at the bottom of the screen to show the game update.

"And I want you to know that I wasn't thinking when I did it. It's just that Jocelyn really had me by the balls."

"Okay," I say, sighing. Tampa's losing 4–0 to the Yankees. Fucking Yankees. I'm actually glad that the game isn't being shown now, because if I was watching it, I'd get pissed.

"So," B. J. says. "Uh, the thing is, that I kind of told Jocelyn about the Facebook girl." Pause. "But don't worry, she's not going to tell anyone," he adds quickly.

"You told her what about the Facebook girl?" I ask, sighing. This Facebook girl is really starting to become a pain in my ass. It's impossible to remember what I've told people about her. It wasn't as simple as just telling Courtney I had a new girlfriend. I had to tell other people as well, to get the word out. In fact, the only one who knows the truth about the whole thing is B. J. I didn't plan the Facebook girl well enough—I should have written down all her vital stats, so that I could keep track of who I told what to. I wonder if I should stage a Facebook breakup.

"I told Jocelyn about her," B. J. repeats.

"Yes, B. J.," I say, forcing myself to keep my patience because I know he's drunk. "But what did you tell Jocelyn about the Facebook girl?" Fifty bucks says whatever he told Jocelyn, Courtney already knows. Those two tell each other everything.

"I told her the truth about her. About how you made her up." I'm sure I've misheard him.

"I'm sure I've misheard you," I say, muting the television. B. J. is not that stupid. He wouldn't do something so ridiculously stupid. Would he? I think about all the stupid things B. J. has done in the past, and suddenly, I feel sick.

"Now, don't start freaking out," B. J. says, sounding nervous again, because I'm sure I sound like I'm about to flip the fuck out. "Jocelyn said she wasn't going to tell Courtney."

"And you believed her?" I ask incredulously. "Are you fucking kidding me right now?" I add, borrowing a line from my brother. "They tell each other everything! Every single thing! Courtney probably knows how big your dick is!"

B. J. gasps. I'm not sure if it's because I'm yelling or because Courtney might know how big his dick is. Probably a little bit of both.

"I can't believe you told her!" Suddenly, I'm irate. This uncontrollable anger is coming over me, and I think it's everything—the whole situation with my parents, my brother kicking me out of his dorm, being in this fucking hotel room when the Devil Rays are losing to the Yankees, the whole situation with Courtney and the Facebook girl . . . I'm pissed off. More pissed than I've ever been in my life.

And at that moment, Courtney's dad decides to beep in on my call waiting.

"What!" I say when I get to the other line. I don't even bother telling B. J. to hold on. Either he'll figure it out or think I hung up on him. Either way is fine with me.

"Hey," Frank says. He always acts like we're the best of friends, which could quite possibly be the most annoying thing about him.

"What do you want?"

"I just wanted to check in, see how the trip is going," he says. "I tried Courtney's cell phone, but she's not answering it."

"It's over," I say, not realizing I mean it until the words are out of my mouth.

"What is?" he asks, sounding confused.

"I'm telling her the truth." And with that, I hang up on both B. J. and Courtney's dad, shut my cell phone off, and head out of the motel to find Courtney.

courtney   the trip

I don't know what else to do, so I head over to Jordan's brother Adam's dorm. Maybe I could tell them Lloyd and I are fighting? Or that he proposed to me, and when I said I wasn't ready to get married, he kicked me out of the room. Hmm. It's going to be challenging, trying to come up with an explanation that makes sense as to why I have nowhere to sleep tonight.

Adam's building has the same swipe card system as Lloyd's did, but for some reason, there are no people coming in and out. Maybe Lloyd's building is like, the party building, where people are just coming and going all the time. And Adam's building is the studious building, and all the kids are in their rooms studying.

A girl in a pink tank top and tons of eyeliner walks up the steps, and I try to follow her into the building, but she turns around and gives me a death glare. I am a master at the death glare (I perfected it even more just for this trip), but this girl is really, really good.

"You can't come in without your card," she says.

"I forgot my card," I say.

"You forgot it?" She tosses her hair over her shoulder.

"Yeah," I say. "I forgot it in my room."

"Not my problem," she says and starts shutting the door. "Go to the student center and get a temporary." And then she shuts the door in my face. God, I hope she's not leading the prospective student tours around this place. Who would want to go to school here? So far, I know three people here. Lloyd, Adam, and Pink Shirt. Lloyd is currently pissed off at me because I won't hook up with him, Pink Shirt was just a bitch to me, and one time, Jordan's brother told him he should break up with me because I had no tits. This place is so great.

I pull out my cell phone, which for some reason is on silent. Oh. From when I made that big show about putting it on silent when Jordan dropped me off here. So that Lloyd and I could hook up. I take a deep breath and contemplate what I'm going to say. Something to make it look like I ditched Lloyd? But then I realize that this whole time, this whole game I've been playing about the Lloyd thing is kind of pointless. Because I was hoping to make Jordan jealous by using Lloyd to make him come to his senses—i.e., realize Facebook Mercedes was a total slut, while I, on the other hand, was so obviously desired and cool that I was moving on at the speed of light. But now that I know the Facebook girl is made up, it kind of ruins it. He just doesn't like me. Or love me. So it doesn't matter if I have a boyfriend or not, because he doesn't care.

I feel like I'm going to cry, so instead of calling Jordan, I follow the signs to the student union and order a pink lemonade, which I drink while sitting on a bench outside and trying to figure out how long I have until it gets really dark and I'm forced to do something. My cell phone rings. It's my dad.

"Hey," I say, trying to sound like everything's fine. Must not sound like I am stuck with no place to spend the night after getting attacked in Lloyd's dorm room. Okay, not really attacked. More like accosted. But still. I can't let my dad know I have nowhere to sleep.

"Hey, honey," he says, and something in his voice makes me nervous.

"What's wrong?" I ask.

"Listen, Courtney," he says. "I have something that I need to tell you."

before ← jordan

17 Days Before the Trip, 6:23 p.m.

"I'm breaking up with her tonight," I tell B. J. We're on the phone, and I'm waiting for Courtney to come over to my house. "I can't keep doing this. It's ridiculous."

"Okay," B. J. says uncertainly. "But I don't understand why you can't just tell her."

"I could just tell her," I say. "But the thing is, B. J., what if she's never supposed to find out? What if this thing with her dad and my mom runs its course, and what she doesn't know isn't going to hurt her unless I tell her?"

"Well," B. J. says, "if she's never going to find out, then why would you break up with her? It's not going to hurt anyone. Especially if she's going to start giving it up. Don't give up a piece of ass just to spite your face." He sounds smug.

"I'm not even going to address that," I say, leaning back in my chair and running my fingers through my hair. "This is going to be bad."

"Damn straight," B. J. says. "I hope she doesn't go psycho."

"Thanks," I say sarcastically. "You're such a good friend."

"Hey, I'm here for you, bro," he says. "But I think you're making a mistake."

"She loves me," I say. "And I can't be with someone who loves me when I'm lying to her. I'd rather have her hate me for thinking I'm a typical male asshole than by keeping something so important from her."

"Does she know it's going to happen?" B. J. asks.

"I told her we needed to talk tonight," I say, swallowing around the lump in my throat. "So I think so."

"You're a better man than I am, dude," B. J. says. "And may the force be with you." He clicks off, and I stare at my phone incredulously, partly because the fact that my conversation with B. J. is over means I'm going to have to deal with this whole Courtney thing, and partly because my best friend is quoting *Star Wars* when I'm in the middle of the biggest romantic crisis of my life.

Five minutes later, Courtney knocks on the door to my room. "Come in," I say, putting up an away message on my instant messenger that simply says "Away."

"Hey," she says. She's wearing a pair of red-and-white-checked shorts and a strappy red tank top. I can see the straps of her bra peeking through, and her hair is up in one of those sloppy ponytail/bun things girls always wear. She looks sexy.

235

"Hi," I say, not moving from my computer chair. She sits down on my bed and looks at me expectantly. Things with Courtney and I have not been the same since we got back from Miami. I've been slightly avoidant of her, and she's been standoffish with me, too. Once I didn't say "I love you" back to her, and once she made it clear she was ready to sleep with me and I didn't act on it, it's been awkward between us.

"Listen," she says. "I don't know what's going on with us, but I'm starting to feel really horrible about it." She bites her lip, and I look away from her. If I have to look at her, I'm not going to be able to do this. And it needs to be done.

"I don't want you to feel horrible, Court," I say truthfully. "And I don't want things to be weird between us."

"I'm sorry about Miami," she says. "I shouldn't have put pressure on you to have sex with me, and I shouldn't have told you I love you. I'm just . . . I just . . . I just got caught up in the moment, and I'm sorry."

I want so badly to take her in my arms and tell her it's okay, that I love her, too, but I can't. I look away, and don't say anything.

"But it doesn't have to change anything," she rushes on. "It's not a big deal. I mean, I don't need you to feel that way about me. Everything can go back to the way it was before, it doesn't have to be different. It doesn't have to change."

"It does change things, though, Courtney," I say, still not looking at her. "It does."

"It only does if we decide it does," she says. A note of worry has crept into her voice, like she knows this is something that can't be fixed, but it's for a different reason than she thinks, and it's killing me. "It doesn't matter to me, Jordan, really. I just want to go back to the way things were before."

"I can't," I say simply. "Courtney, on the beach I realized that I don't want to be tied down right now. I want to be able to be young and date other people." Oh, my God. I sound like a really old, annoying uncle who's trying to convince someone they should date while they can.

"You want to date other people?" she asks, her voice cracking a little bit.

"I'm not a relationship person," I say, shrugging. I still can't look at her, because I know if I do, I'll lose it.

There's a moment of silence, a pause, and I expect her to start screaming, or maybe to beg me to change my mind, or to start crying or something. But instead, she gets up from my bed and walks out my door. In a way, it's almost worse than a big scene. Because now she's probably never going to want to talk to me again. I wait until I hear the front door of my house shut before I give in to it and start to cry.

the trip ▶ jordan

Day Two, 8:03 p.m.

"Where's Courtney?" I ask when Lloyd opens the door, not bothering with any pleasantries. I knew I was going to get into a fight with Lloyd at some point on this trip. It was inevitable. I thought maybe I'd be able to avoid it if I didn't see him, but now, when he answers the door to his room with a shit-eating grin on his face, I want to rip it off. His face, I mean.

"Well, well, well," Lloyd says, leaning against the door frame. "What's up, Jordy?" Lloyd is such a tool that he actually sometimes thinks he's cooler than me. Which is ridiculous. Especially since he's wearing a polo shirt. You cannot be cooler than anyone, especially not me, when you're wearing a polo shirt.

"Where's Courtney?" I repeat.

"Why?" he asks suspiciously, narrowing his eyes. "If you're here to do one of those last-minute things where you rush in and save her, you're a little too late." He smiles. He actually fucking smiles at me. I'm done with this dude.

I push him out of the way and walk right into his room. She's not there.

"She's not here," I say.

"Good work, Captain Obvious," he says. He crosses the room and sits down at his desk.

"Where. Is. She?" I ask. I wonder what will happen if I punch him. I'm so pissed off at everyone right now, the thought of getting into a fight with Lloyd actually scares me. I don't know if I could stop at just punching him. We'd probably get into it pretty good, and campus security would come and arrest me.

"I don't know," Lloyd says, shrugging. "I assume she's out looking for you."

"Why would she be out looking for me?"

"Because she left, and since she doesn't know anyone else here, I would assume she's looking for you," he says, rolling his eyes. Is this kid for real?

"You just let her leave?" I ask. "Why would you do that?"

"I don't know," he says. "She freaked out a little bit, and I figured she needed her space."

"You're an asshole," I say, pushing past him and outside. I pull my cell phone out of my pocket and dial her number, but she's not answering. Fuck. Where would she go? I head back toward the truck and dial her cell phone number on the way, hoping maybe she's turned it back on.

239

And then suddenly, I see her. She's sitting on a bench near where I parked my car. She's holding her cell phone in her hand, just looking at it. Which is weird, because I'm trying to call her. Her cell phone is ringing in her hand, and she's just ignoring it.

"Court!" I yell. I start walking toward her and she looks up. Her blue eyes meet mine, and suddenly, I stop. Because I can tell she knows.

"Hey," I say, walking toward her. She looks up, and the look she gives me is horrible. There are tears in her eyes. "Courtney," I say. "Let me explain."

"Let you explain?" She throws her head back and laughs at the absurdity of it. "Yeah, great, this should be interesting. Go ahead and explain."

"I didn't do it to lie to you," I say. "I wanted to protect you. I didn't know it was your dad, I didn't—"

"Great job of protecting me, Jordan," she says, cutting me off. "Do I look like you spared my feelings?" She picks up her bag and slings it over her shoulder, like she's going to leave. I reach up and grab her arm.

"Don't touch me!" she says, wrenching away from me.

"Court, please, listen—" I start to say.

"No," she says, standing up. "I'm done."

She starts walking away.

"Court!" I yell after her. "Where are you going?"

But she doesn't answer.

jordan ⟵ before

13 Days Before the Trip, 3:30 p.m.

I'm walking out of the mall when I see Courtney's dad walking in. I try to get out of the way to avoid him, but he's already seen me, and I don't want to give him the satisfaction of seeing me turn around.

"Mr. Brewster!" I say cheerfully.

"Jordan," he says, nodding at me. "Looks like you've had a successful trip to the mall." The way he says it implies I've been on a silly little shopping trip, while he's been hard at work all day. Which is probably true. I've been in Abercrombie for more than an hour, and I've spent over four hundred dollars. All on my mom's credit card. Serves her right.

"I *have* had a successful trip," I agree.

"Abercrombie," he says, reading it off the bag in the same tone he used before. Sue me if I need retail therapy. This whole Courtney breakup is driving me insane, and shopping makes me feel better. I'm turning into a girl. Plus I love the feeling I get when my mom's credit card runs through the machine.

"Yup," I say. "You look like you could use a trip there yourself." It's meant to be an insult, like he has no sense of fashion, but he doesn't get it.

"Oh, not today," he says. "I'm here to upgrade my cell phone plan, and then I have to get back to the office."

"Good for you," I say, resisting the urge to hit him. "Good luck with that." I move past him into the parking lot, but he calls after me.

"I heard you and Courtney broke up," he says. "I'm sorry to hear that."

"I'm sure you are," I say sarcastically.

"Now, Jordan, that's not fair. I never wanted to cause you or Courtney any pain."

"It's not a big deal," I lie. "Courtney and I didn't break up because of you. We broke up because I met someone else." The last thing I want is to give Courtney's dad the satisfaction of thinking he broke the two of us up. Besides, this whole breakup with Courtney has spun out of control—I've made up a new girlfriend. A fake girlfriend, someone I supposedly met on Facebook. I got sick of everyone asking why we broke up, and I figured having a fake girlfriend is a better reason than "I don't know." Plus, it helps me when I get tempted to call Courtney and beg her to take me back.

"Well, that's great," Mr. Brewster says. He looks at his

watch and glances over my shoulder into the mall. "I should get going."

"Sure," I say. Asshole.

"I hope it won't be that big of a deal to you to drive to school without Courtney. Perhaps your new girlfriend could make the trip with you? It's an awful long way to go alone."

"What do you mean?" I ask, frowning. Court and I had planned to drive up to Boston together for school, and I figured it was still on. Actually, that's not true. I was hoping it was still on, but I was afraid to approach her about it since a) she won't talk to me, and b) if I brought it up, she might tell me it's canceled.

"Well, I assumed you wouldn't still be going on the trip. I haven't talked to Courtney about it yet, but—"

"Oh, no," I say. "We're still going."

"Really?" His eyebrows shoot up in surprise. "Does Courtney know this?"

"I haven't talked to her," I say. "But we're going." Suddenly I realize just how badly I want to go on this trip. That it could be my last chance to spend time with Courtney. And that since it's already planned, it won't look that suspicious if we still go.

"Jordan, I'm not sure that's the best idea," he says. "Courtney's already going through a lot with the breakup and—"

"We're going," I say. "You'll tell her she's still going. And if you don't, well . . ." I trail off, and I see a flash of panic cross his face. Because now that Courtney and I are broken up, he has no power over me. I could tell her everything if I wanted to. And with that, I turn around, head to my car, and drive home with my four hundred dollars' worth of Abercrombie merchandise in the trunk and the Beastie Boys on the radio.

courtney ⬅ before

13 Days Before the Trip, 6:00 p.m.

"They're fucking making me go!" I scream into the phone. As a rule, I don't usually say the f-word, but this definitely warrants it.

"Um, okay," Jocelyn says, sounding confused. "You want to back up a little bit?"

"No, not really," I say. I throw myself down on my bed and reach over and crank up the AC that's in my window. I like my room frigid. My parents are always complaining about the electricity bill, but whatever. If they're going to make me suffer, I can totally make them suffer right back.

"Then I can't help you," Jocelyn says simply. I hear voices in the background.

"Where are you?" I ask.

"At the beach," she says. "With B. J. You wanna come down?"

"No thank you," I say. Why, why, why would my parents

do something like this? Why would they make me still go on this trip? I can kind of understand it from my mom, but my dad? He hates Jordan! I even offered to pay for the plane ticket myself, out of my graduation money, but nooo. The irony of all this is that B. J. and Jocelyn, who should be the poster children for dysfunctional relationships, are going strong. They're hanging out, cuddling, probably having sex on a beach, while Jordan and I, who NEVER EVEN FOUGHT, are done.

"So what are your parents making you do?" Jocelyn asks.

"They're making me go on the trip with Jordan! They said it's too late to get a ticket, and that I need to learn to take responsibility for my actions, and since I planned this trip, I should go." Saying the words out loud makes me so mad that I start punching the up button on the air conditioner, even though it's already as high as it can go.

"Are you serious?" Jocelyn says. "Courtney, I'm so sorry."

"We'll probably end up killing each other," I say, still hitting the air conditioner. Bang. Bang. My finger is starting to get a little sore, but for some reason, it's making me feel better. Maybe just because no more cool air is coming out doesn't mean the power isn't going up, therefore making the electricity bill get higher, therefore screwing my parents over.

"Yeah," Jocelyn says. "You probably will."

"Thanks a lot," I say. "I can't believe they would do something like this to me. I'm only seventeen! Since when am I supposed to take responsibility for my actions?"

"I dunno," Jocelyn says. "It sucks, but hey, you'll probably learn a lot."

"Learn a lot!" I shriek, abandoning the air conditioner and burying my head in my pillow. "Don't get all deep on me now, Jocelyn."

"I'm just saying," she says. "Usually the hard stuff you're forced to do makes you learn a lot."

"I don't want to learn a lot," I say. "I already know enough."

"Sometimes you don't have a choice," Jocelyn says, and there's something in her tone of voice that makes me uncomfortable.

the trip ▷ courtney

Day Two, 8:45 p.m.

I have never been so pissed off in my life. My heart is pumping at three million beats a second, and I'm consumed with rage.

And right now, I'm taking it out on the guy at the front desk of the Bellevue Motel who's trying to tell me you can't check in unless you have I.D. stating you're eighteen.

"But I just told you," I say, trying to keep my voice calm. "My I.D. was stolen. All I have is the cash I just happen to have in my pocket, which I can use to pay for the room." I wave around the emergency money my dad gave me just in case something went wrong on the trip. If this doesn't constitute something going wrong, I don't know what does.

"I understand that, ma'am," he says. "But it's motel policy."

"Well, that's just great!" I screech like some kind of crazy person. "I'll just sleep outside then, while I wait for my family to come get me. And while I'm out there, I'll call up some local newspeople and tell them what kind of establishment you're running here." I glance at his name tag. "Sound good, Scott?"

He looks nervous for a second, probably not because of my threat to call the media, but because I think he's getting the idea that I might be a bit unstable. He probably thinks I'm about two seconds away from coming back here and blowing the place up. "Let me see if there's any way the computer can circumvent the I.D. check," he says, tapping some buttons. Five minutes later, I'm on my way up to room 205.

I hate my dad, I hate Jordan, I even hate myself, because Jocelyn warned me he was bad news. I *knew* he was bad news. And I did it anyway. Which is so not like me. I don't get caught up in the moment. I analyze everything to death. I play it safe. And the first time I take a risk, look what happens. I end up wandering around a college campus in North Carolina, brokenhearted and with nowhere to go.

I pull out my cell phone and delete past the screen that says I have eighteen missed calls. Most of them are from my dad, who I hung up on when he told me he'd been cheating on my mom for the past six months.

"I have something to tell you, Courtney," he'd said, and I'd sat down on the bench, thinking maybe he was going to tell me he was sick, or my mom was sick, or that something bad happened to my grandma. Because he had that tone in his voice, the tone people get when they know they have to tell you something bad and they're dreading it.

"What is it?" I said, my heart in my stomach and my stomach in my throat.

"I'm having an affair," he'd said, and for a brief second, I thought he meant he was throwing a party or something. Like those people on that MTV show *My Super Sweet 16*. They're always referring to birthday parties as affairs. So I thought maybe my dad was planning a party, or that maybe he was even throwing one for me. But then I remembered that I'd already had a graduation party, a pretty big one actually, and that if my dad was going to throw a party, he definitely wouldn't sound so serious.

"An affair?" I asked.

"Yes," he said. "I've been cheating on your mother for the past six months." I couldn't believe the way he was saying it—it almost seemed kind of like a joke. He was using such horrible words. "Affair." "Cheat." It was like if it had been true, he would have tried to soften the blow a little bit.

"Okay," I said, not sure what I was supposed to do with this information.

"I'm so sorry to be telling you this now," he said, sounding like he meant it. "I didn't want to have to burden you with this while you're getting ready to start school." He sighed. "I know it's the last thing you should have to deal with, and I'm sorry for that, Courtney."

"Why are you telling me now?" I asked.

"Because Jordan said he was going to tell you if I

didn't," he said. "And I knew you had to hear it from me."
My heart skipped in my chest.

"How does Jordan know about it?" I asked, wondering when Jordan would have heard such a thing. How had he found out about this? We'd been on this trip for the past couple of days. Had he gotten a phone call from someone who found out?

"Jordan's known for a while, Courtney," my dad said. "He caught me with his mom a few months ago."

"You're having an affair with Jordan's mom?" I'm surprised, because Jordan's mom is so . . . I don't know. She's like this high-powered lawyer, totally the opposite of my mom, who's more glam. But maybe that's the problem.

"Yes," my dad said, sighing. And then I hang up the phone. On my dad. I hit the red button on my phone, like I'd just had a normal conversation that ended with "See you soon, love ya!" or some other pleasant sign-off.

Have I mentioned I'm pissed? I'm pissed at my dad, for thinking he could keep something like this from us. I'm angry that he thought I couldn't handle it, that he thought I would fall apart. I'm pissed that he was so selfish that he felt the need to keep things from me, just so he wouldn't have to deal with me being pissed off or upset. But most of all, I'm mad at Jordan. I'm mad that he didn't tell me what he knew, that he never felt he could be completely honest with me. I'm mad that he felt he needed to protect me, when I never gave him any indication I was weak.

I feel like I'm on that reality show *Joe Schmo*, where it turned out all the participants except one were paid actors. I feel like Joe Schmo. Courtney Schmo, whom everyone is lying to. I take a shower and change into my pajamas, then spend the next seven hours in my hotel room, watching celebrity countdowns on E! I'm starting to feel a little better, except for a moment during the countdown for the twenty-five hottest blondes, when I realize that some of the people featured on the countdown aren't natural blondes. Which feels like they're cheating. And being LIARS. CHEATING, LYING, BLONDES.

At four in the morning, I call Jordan's phone.

"Hello?" he says, sounding wide awake. I hear the sound of the TV in the background, so I know he's not sleeping in his car. I try to think of the worst place possible that would have a TV. Jail? A serial killer's basement? I try to wish him there.

"Oh, hello," I say, as if it's perfectly normal for me to be calling him at four in the morning.

"I've been trying to call you," he says. I've just turned my phone on, and as he's saying it, I hear the notification of my missed calls beeping in my ear. Fifty-six missed calls from Jordan. Ten from my dad. Six from Jocelyn. None from Lloyd. What an asshole. Although I'm not sure what's worse. Not calling at all, or calling fifty-six times.

"Really?" I say. "I must not have heard my phone."

"Courtney, where are you? Let me come and get you. We need to talk about this."

"I'm not telling you, and we don't need to talk about it," I say, trying to sound like a bitch. "I was just calling to make sure you still plan on driving the rest of the way to school with me tomorrow." I've thought about this a little bit, and I've decided I have two options:

1. Drive to school with Jordan, getting there on time. Once at school, follow previous plan of ignoring him and meeting fabulous college boyfriend.

2. Don't tell Jordan where I am, and find other way from North Carolina to Boston, which would most likely entail calling my dad to find out how I can get a plane ticket or a train or something. This actually might not be that bad, except I have a bad feeling my dad might hightail it to North Carolina and insist on escorting me to Boston himself. Either way, I would be late to school. And I have not gone through all of this to be late to orientation.

"Courtney, stop," Jordan says. "You're acting like a crazy person. Now tell me where you are, I'll come and get you, and we can talk. We can even start driving again, if you want."

"I'm not acting like a crazy person," I say, even though I totally am. Although I guess it's all relative. Finding out your dad is cheating on your mom with your ex-boyfriend's mother, and that your ex-boyfriend knew about it and didn't want to tell you so bad that he made up a Facebook girl is pretty traumatic. So calling someone at four in the morning probably isn't the worst thing I could be doing to deal with it. "And besides," I say. "Why would we start driving at four in the morning?" Jordan's driving is questionable at best on a good day, one where the sun is shining and there's no traffic.

"Because I know you're worried about getting there on time," he says, sounding like it's obvious.

"We're still going to get there on time," I say, a panicky feeling starting in my stomach. "We only have twelve hours to go."

"I know," he agrees. "We will still get there on time, but I just thought it might make you feel better if we left now. Since we're behind schedule."

"But we're not behind schedule," I say, exasperated. "We planned on staying in North Carolina until tomorrow." I glance at the clock. "Well, technically today, since it's four in the morning."

"Oh," he says.

"Which you would have known if you'd read the damn itinerary I gave you."

"I lost it," he says.

"Of course you did," I say.

"What's that supposed to mean?"

"Just what I said! That I'm not surprised you lost the

itinerary, since you had no interest in any kind of schedule for this trip!"

"Well, maybe now I do," he says, sounding indignant.

"Maybe now you do what?" I ask. He's watching ESPN in the background. I can hear the SportsCenter music through the phone. I wonder if serial killers have cable. Probably. Lots of serial killers are totally normal people, with jobs and friends and all the pay channels.

"Maybe now I care about the schedule for the trip," he says, his voice sounding firm.

"Well, whatever," I say breezily. "Listen, I didn't call to fight with you." Which is kind of a lie. I did kind of call to fight with him. Or at least to wake him up, which obviously didn't work, since he was up at four in the morning like some kind of psychopath. Although I'm up at four in the morning as well, so I guess if I'm using that argument, I'm a psychopath, too. But we already knew that.

"So then why did you call?"

"I called," I say, sighing, "to make sure that you're still going to give me a ride to school tomorrow."

"Why wouldn't I be?" he asks.

"I don't know," I say. "Because there have been some weird events going on today, and so I thought if you'd decided to kick me off this trip, it would behoove you to let me know, so that I can make alternate arrangements." I just used the word "behoove" in a sentence. This is definitely not good. I'm finally cracking up.

"I'm not kicking you off the trip," he says.

"Good."

"In fact, I'd like to get back started on the trip right now," he says. "So tell me where you are and I'll come pick you up, and we'll get back on the road."

"No," I say. "I'm tired. And if you had your trip itinerary, you'd know that we're not scheduled to leave until eight o'clock. And it's only four. So we have four more hours of sleep."

"But we're not sleeping," he points out.

"Well, I would be," I say, "if you would let me off the phone." Which is obviously a lie.

"Fine," he says.

"Fine," I say.

"Wait!"

"What now?!"

"Court?"

I don't say anything.

"Are you there?"

"Yes, I'm here," I say. "What is it?"

"I love you." And then he hangs up the phone.

jordan | the trip

Day Three, 7:56 a.m.

"Dude, I'm sorry," B. J. says. "It's all my fault."

"It isn't your fault, really," I say, sighing. "It's mine. I set up the situation, so I can't be pissed at you when I have to deal with the fallout." I'm in my hotel room, on the phone with B. J., and I just finished recounting the night's activities.

"Well, look on the bright side," he says. "At least now you don't have to worry about her finding out. She already knows."

"Yeah, that makes me feel much better," I say sarcastically, looking around the room to make sure I haven't forgotten anything. Courtney and I are supposed to get back on the road soon. Although she hasn't called me since this morning's four a.m. phone call, so who knows.

"I just mean," B. J. persists, "that maybe now you can make things right."

"What do you mean?" I ask, sitting down on the bed. To make matters worse, I have developed a horrible headache, and was forced to buy a travel pack of aspirin at the front desk, which cost me five bucks.

"I mean you have nothing to lose now," B. J. says. "You can try to get her back without worrying about her dad and all that shit. You guys can really deal with what's going on, instead of some fucked-up fake shit."

"Yeah," I say, sighing. "Maybe. But she was pretty rip-shit last night." My call waiting beeps. "That's her," I say.

"Good luck," B. J. says. I click over.

"Are you going to tell me where you are now?" I ask. I open the packet of aspirin and step into the bathroom to fill a glass of water. I feel hung over, even though I'm not.

"Are you leaving to come and get me immediately?" she asks, all bossy like.

"Yes, Courtney, I'm leaving immediately," I tell her, sighing. It's hard to balance a glass of water, the aspirin, and my phone in this tiny hotel bathroom. "Now can you tell me where you are?"

"Let me hear you actually leaving," she demands. "I'm not telling you where I am until you actually leave."

"How the hell are you supposed to know that I'm actually leaving?" I ask. I drop one of the aspirin into the sink. "Shit," I swear, grabbing it before it makes it down the drain.

"What's going on?" Courtney asks.

"Nothing," I say. "Now will you tell me where you are?"

I look at the aspirin and wonder how many germs are on it and if I'll die just from putting it in my mouth. I wonder what's worse—having a headache or eating this bad aspirin.

"I want to hear you leaving," she says.

"Again, how can you hear me leaving?" I definitely need this aspirin if she's going to be acting like this all day.

"I want to hear the door close behind you."

I slam the bathroom door shut. "There," I say. "Now tell me."

"How do I know that wasn't just the bathroom door?" she asks suspiciously.

"You don't," I say. "But you were the one who came up with the criteria of how to know I was actually leaving, so don't get mad if your method isn't foolproof." I turn on the water and rinse my aspirin off, figuring an aspirin that's been rinsed off is better than an aspirin that hasn't. Besides, if it weren't for Courtney, I probably wouldn't even have thought twice about the germs. She has this uncanny need for germ-free environments and I think it's rubbed off on me.

"I can hear you running water!" Courtney says. "Unbelievable! Although I can't say I'm surprised, since you have proved yourself to be totally untrustworthy."

"Hey, do you know anything about germs in sinks?" I look at the aspirin questioningly. I really, really want that aspirin.

"What do you mean?" she asks.

"I dropped some aspirin in the sink and I want to know if it's okay to take it."

"Why can't you just throw it out and take another?" she asks, exasperated.

"Because I bought one of those travel packs that only has two pills in it," I say, still looking at the offending aspirin. Whatever. I pop it in my mouth with a copious amount of water.

"Just buy another travel pack," she says. "I wouldn't take it. It probably has sperm on it."

"Why would it have SPERM on it?" I ask, horrified. I open my mouth and look in the mirror, but it's too late. I've already swallowed it.

"Because I saw an exposé once on *20/20* about hotel rooms, and they're all covered in sperm," she says.

"Fine," I lie. "I'll buy another travel pack. Now I really am leaving, so tell me where you are."

"I'm at the Bellevue Motel," she says. "It's—"

"I know where it is," I say, sighing. We were at the same fucking motel. This whole time, we were in the same building. "I'll meet you outside in two minutes." I slide my cell phone shut and look at myself in the mirror, wondering what's more likely—me, dying from hotel bathroom germs, or Courtney ever forgiving me.

courtney | the trip

Day Three, 11:13 a.m.

I can't believe he swallowed that disgusting pill. (Like it wasn't totally obvious.) I can't believe he was in the same hotel as me. I can't believe he told me he loved me. I can't believe I'm still on this trip.

We're in Jordan's car, on the road, and we haven't spoken for three hours. The vibe in the car isn't exactly bad. It's almost a relief, like a bunch of tension has been released, and now we can just drive.

"I have to go to the bathroom," I announce.

"Okay," Jordan says. Half an hour later, we pull into a rest stop. I'm beginning to hate rest stops. I feel like I spend half my life in a rest stop. Or in a rest stop bathroom.

I use the bathroom quickly, and try not to think about how gross it is that I've been using public bathrooms way too much lately. Although if Jordan took that aspirin, he should definitely be more concerned about his germiness than I should. And good luck getting anyone to kiss him at college. I'm going to tell everyone he took a random, germ-infested sperm pill. Disgusting.

I wash my hands and dry them with a roll of suspect-looking paper towels, figuring drying my hands with gross paper towels is better than not drying them at all.

My phone rings. Jocelyn.

"Hey," I say, balancing the phone against my shoulder and tossing the paper towel into the overflowing garbage can.

"Courtney, B. J. just told me what happened," she says. "I am so, so sorry. Are you okay?"

"I'm okay," I say, sighing. I look at myself in the mirror over the sink. My eyes are a little bloodshot and my hair's a little messy, but other than that, I don't look like someone whose world is falling apart.

"Do you want to talk about it?"

"I'm sure I will, at some point," I say. "But right now, I just want to get off this trip and away from Jordan. I'm so mad, Joce."

"Yeah," she says. "I understand, but it's . . ." she trails off.

"But it's what?" I ask. "Don't even tell me you're taking his side." What a traitor.

"No, I'm not taking his side," she says. "I'm just saying, you have to remember that things aren't always completely black and white, Court."

"Yeah, well, it's black and white that he lied to me." I

feel myself starting to get mad again. I pull a brush out of my purse and start fixing my hair. Now that I'm single again, I need to look hot. So that hot, honest college guys will want me.

"Did you know he's the one that insisted you guys still go on the trip?" Jocelyn asks.

I stop brushing. "He did?"

"Yeah," Jocelyn says. "Your dad didn't want you to. But Jordan convinced him."

"How do you know that?" I ask softly.

"B. J. told me."

"But why would Jordan do that?"

"Because he wanted to spend time with you." I don't say anything. "Listen," she says. "I'm not saying what he did was right, Court. I'm just saying don't turn your back on things just because you're hurting. Try to at least think about his side of it." She hangs up, and I slide my phone back into my purse.

When I walk out of the bathroom, I almost bump into Jordan, who's standing against the soda machine.

"Watch it," I say, rolling my eyes. "I almost bumped into you."

"Courtney," he says, taking my hand. I pull away. "I want to talk about this."

"We're not talking about anything," I say, walking toward the exit. "We've talked about it enough."

"We haven't talked about it at all," he says, following me.

"And that's enough," I say. And it is. I don't want to talk about it. I don't want to deal with it. My phone starts ringing again, and I check the caller ID. It's my dad.

"Ignore it," Jordan says. We're in the parking lot now, standing near his car. I look at him. "Ignore it," he says again.

"I'm supposed to ignore *him*, but you expect me to talk to *you*?" I say, crossing my arms. That makes no sense. One of them is just as bad as the other.

"Yes," he says.

"Why?" I ask.

"Because he's your dad, and he's always going to be in your life, so it can wait," he says. "But if you and I don't deal with this now, we might end up getting into a situation that can't be repaired."

"It already can't be repaired," I say, feeling myself starting to tear up. This is why I didn't want to talk about it. Because I don't want to have to deal with this right now. I don't want to cry. I don't want to get upset. I'm enjoying the very numb, very comfortable, very avoidant feeling that I'm having right now.

"It can," he says. "Courtney, I love you."

"Don't say things like that," I say, turning around and trying to open the door to his truck. But it's locked. "It's not fair."

"What isn't?" he asks, studying me. "What's not fair? Telling you how I feel?"

"Open the door for me," I say, determined not to break down.

"No," he says. "I want to talk about this."

I don't say anything, because I know if I do, I'm going to start crying. And I don't want to give him the satisfaction of seeing me cry. We stand there for a minute, me in front of the passenger door of his truck, my back to him, him standing behind me, holding the keys. Finally, he opens the door.

"Thank you," I say, launching myself into the car. Only twelve more hours and then this trip will be over. I lay my head against the back of the seat and pray I can fall asleep.

the trip > jordan

Day Three, 7:45 p.m.

Courtney doesn't say one word to me for the rest of the trip. We drive almost straight through to Boston, only stopping to go to the bathroom and grab snacks at a gas station. For the last six hours or so, she sleeps, probably because she didn't last night. Neither did I, but crazily enough, I don't feel tired.

"Court," I say when we finally pull into the front parking lot of school. "We're here."

"Mmmm," she says, opening her eyes slowly. I'm half hoping she doesn't wake up so that I'll have an excuse to touch her, to gently shake her awake, but she rubs her eyes and sits up.

There's a throng of people milling around, parents, students, all trying to find their dorm rooms. Jesus Christ. It looks like fucking Grand Central Station. I figured getting here so late would spare us most of the craziness, but apparently not.

266

"How was your nap?" I ask. She looks cute, her hair rumpled from sleep, her cheek red from where it was pressed against the seat.

"Can you help me with my stuff?" Courtney asks, ignoring my question. She reaches into the backseat, grabs her sweatshirt, and pulls it on.

"Yes," I say. "Court, listen, I don't—"

"Jordan," she says, holding her hand up. "I can't deal with this right now."

"But if we don't—"

She opens the car door and jumps down into the parking lot. After a second, I pop open the back of my truck, and then follow her around to the back of the car.

A perky blond girl holding a clipboard and wearing a maroon polo shirt emerges from the crowd before we have a chance to start unloading any of the stuff. "Hello!" she says. "I'm Jessica, part of your welcome orientation committee. Do you need help finding your dorm?"

"No, thanks," Courtney says. "I know where my dorm is. I mapped it all out during my tour in the fall."

Jessica's face falls, but she recovers quickly. She turns to me. "What about you?" She gives me a dazzling smile.

"No, thanks," I say. "I'm cool." I open the back of my truck, sending Jessica the silent message to go away. I want to be able to talk to Courtney before we go our separate ways, and Jessica's screwing up the plan.

"Well," she says, acting like we've made some sort of huge

mistake by not taking her help. "Here are your welcome packets, map, etc." She hands us each a huge stack of papers. Courtney and I take them obediently, even though I know I'm going to lose half this shit by tomorrow. "Do you have any questions?"

"No," Courtney says. She starts tapping her foot.

"No," I say.

"Then let me explain a little bit to you about how our meal plan works. You won't have to worry about it tonight of course, because—"

"Listen," Court starts. "We said we didn't want to hear any of this." She takes a step toward Jessica. Whoa. She must be really pissed off if she's cutting off the orientation committee chick. Wasn't her whole thing about getting oriented?

"Um, Jessica, listen," I say, deciding to step in before anything can get out of hand. I can't have Courtney fighting some girl in the parking lot, no matter how hot that would be. "We've had a really long drive, we're both tired and cranky"—Courtney raises her eyebrows—"and we just want to get to our rooms. So, thanks, really, for all your help, but we'll come and find you if we need anything."

"Okay," Jessica says, still sounding uncertain. She opens her mouth like she's about to say something else, glances at Courtney, and then changes her mind. She turns around and disappears back into the crowd.

Courtney reaches up and pulls a blue suitcase out of the truck and sets it down on the pavement.

"'Thank you, Jordan, for saving me from the scary orientation girl,'" I recite.

She ignores me and continues to unload her stuff. Okay, so apparently, trying to lighten the mood isn't the way to go. Check.

I decide to try and make normal conversation. "You have a lot of stuff," I try. "Seriously." I set a huge box down in the parking lot. "What do you have in here?"

"My books," she says. She reaches up and gathers her hair into a ponytail, then slides a hair tie around it with her other hand.

"Why would you bring books to college?" I ask her. "You know they give you books, right?" I mean it as a joke, but she gives me one of those looks, one of those "You'll never understand me" looks, so I decide it might be better to keep my mouth shut until we're done unloading everything. We spend the next half hour making trips back and forth to her dorm room. I was kind of hoping she'd want to start setting stuff up, maybe let me hang around for a while, but she just deposits stuff in a pile on her floor, presumably to deal with later. By herself.

I realize that once we're done unloading the stuff, I'm going to have to leave. So I take my time, but there's only so much and finally, all of it is in Courtney's room.

"Thanks," she says. She's standing in the doorway of her room, and I'm in the hall, and she starts to shut the door.

"Court, are we going to talk about this?" I ask, putting

my hand on the door so that she can't shut it. Well, she can shut it. Just not without breaking my hand. Hmm. On second thought, I drop my hand.

"No," she says. "We're not."

"I understand you're mad," I say. "But I want to talk about it, make you understand."

"I already understand," she says simply. She shrugs.

"You're upset now," I say, starting to become frantic. "I know that. But you need to just take a breather, I think. Take a break from me and from the trip. You're tired." I realize once I leave this room, I won't have anything to look forward to. No trip with Courtney. No seeing her every day in math. It's over. We're at college now. "Let's have breakfast tomorrow. Before orientation. I know you don't want to miss it." I smile at her then, to let her know it's okay, that I'm making a joke.

"Jordan," she says. "Please leave."

And then she shuts the door.

courtney   after

One Day After the Trip, 9:03 a.m.

The first full day of college is overcast and gray, which is not a good omen. Bad starts and all that. I'm a big believer in the fact that the weather of the day can totally dictate how the day is going to go. So far (at least for today), this theory has been proven true.

First, I had eighteen new messages waiting for me on my voice mail when I woke up this morning. Jocelyn ("I'm worried about you, call me when you're ready."), my mom ("Courtney, honey, I want you to call me when you get this."), my dad ("Call me, we need to talk about this."), Lloyd ("It was kind of weird the way you left like that, Courtney, and I'm mad and worried."), and finally, Jordan ("Courtney, please call me, I love you."). I deleted all of them, then realized that was a horrible plan, as all it did was clear out my voice mail and leave me available to receive new messages.

Second, my roommate hasn't arrived yet, so I was stuck walking to the orientation breakfast by myself. The whole way over, all I saw were groups of twos, threes, fives, eights. It seemed like everyone had friends but me. Which was bad enough. But now that I'm here, I realize I don't know *anyone*. Not one single person. Well, except Jordan, but I'm really, really hoping I don't run into him today. Or ever again. In my life.

I grab a plate off the pile at the end of the buffet table and load it high with eggs, pancakes, and fruit. I figure if I'm not going to be talking to anyone, then I'm going to have to keep myself busy by eating. A lot. I wish I'd brought my book. But then wouldn't I look like the loser who has to bring a book to the first day of college? If I'd known that navigating the social landscape of college was going to be so crazy, I never would have been in such a hurry to get here.

I grab an orange juice off the table of beverages, and very carefully make my way to the end of an empty table.

But once I set my stuff down, I'm stopped by a boy wearing a black T-shirt and a pair of jeans.

"Uh-oh," he says, shaking his head. He looks visibly upset, like someone's just told him his dog is sick, or that he failed a test.

"What's wrong?" I ask.

"It's just that . . ." He sighs. "You're sitting at the table where the orientation committee is supposed to sit."

"Oh," I say. "I'm sorry." I grab my plate and start to

stand up. Leave it to me to sit in the one spot I'm not supposed to. I turn around and scan the dining room, but the tables have filled up fast, and there's not another empty one. Which means I'm going to have to sit with someone else. A stranger. I try to decide between a table full of girls who look like they walked off the cover of a magazine, or two girls sitting by themselves with about twenty piercings between the two of them. The pierced girls would probably be nicer, although the magazine girls look like they could have an in on the cool things to do around here. Although, God could be trying to play a trick on me for judging people on their appearances, and it could be the other way around.

"I'm afraid it's not that easy," the orientation guy says. He sighs again and runs his fingers through his short blond hair.

"What isn't?" I ask. A girl wearing a blue sequined tank top sits down with the magazine girls, nailing the last seat. Crap.

"It's just that if you sit at a table you're not supposed to during orientation, that's a disciplinary infraction." He starts flipping through the papers on his clipboard.

"What do you mean, a disciplinary infraction?" I ask, swallowing hard. This is just great. My first day of school—actually not even official school, just orientation—and I'm already in trouble. I wonder how many disciplinary infractions you can get before you get kicked out. And if it's going to go on my permanent record. I thought at college you were supposed to have more freedom. Apparently not, if you can get in trouble just for sitting at the wrong table.

"What's your name?" the guy asks.

"Courtney," I say. "Courtney McSweeney."

"I'm Ben," he says. He holds out his hand. "Nice to meet you." He winks.

"Hold on," I say, my eyes narrowing. "Am I really in trouble?"

"No," he says, laughing. "You're not in trouble."

"So you were just messing with me?"

"Yes," he says. "But only because I wanted to know your name." He smiles, and now that I'm not worried about disciplinary infractions, I realize for the first time how cute he is. Tall, blond hair, green eyes, and a really nice smile.

"Okay," I say. "So now you know my name."

"I do," he says, nodding. "And you know mine." He leans in closer to me. "Now, I'm not really supposed to do this, but, do you want to have breakfast with me? Usually we don't let the freshmen sit at the orientation table, but I've taken up all this time talking to you, and now there're hardly any seats left." He gestures toward the crowded dining area.

"Sure," I say. "I'll sit with you." He pulls out a chair for me, but I hesitate. "Hey, Ben?" I ask.

"Yeah?"

"Do you listen to rap music?"

"Rap music?" he asks, looking confused. "No. Alternative rock. How come?"

"No reason," I say. I sit down in the chair he's offered and Ben sits down next to me.

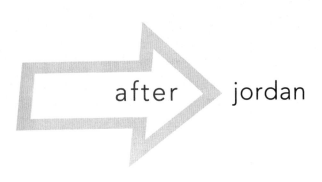

after jordan

One Day After the Trip, 9:23 a.m.

Courtney is sitting with a guy. Some dude who's on the orientation committee. How skeezy is that? Hitting on freshmen when you're on the orientation committee. It's like hitting on students when you're a teacher. Definitely not cool.

"Hey," I say, turning to my roommate, a guy from Queens named Ricardo. Ricardo's a cool dude, one of those guys who you can tell is always going to know what's going on. Which means at some point this semester, we'll probably get in some trouble, but, hey, that's the price you pay. "What's the deal with tonight?"

"It's gonna be sick," Ricardo says. He takes a piece of toast and dips it into his over-easy eggs. There weren't over-easy eggs on the buffet, but Ricardo conned one of the dining room workers into making him one. "There're no upperclassmen on campus yet except for the orientation committee, which means it's going to be all freshmen." He smiles at me and gives me a knowing look. I pretend like I know what he means, even though I really have no idea. Does Ricardo have some knowledge of statistics pertaining to freshmen girls giving it up?

I glance over at Courtney, where she now appears to be writing her phone number down on the back of a napkin for the guy.

"Define 'sick,'" I say.

"Tons of chicks, tons of booze," he says. "It's like the official kickoff to partying in college. And the girls here," he adds, looking around the dining room, "are unfuckingbelievable."

He's right, too. The girls here are amazing. Much hotter than the ones in high school. And there's a lot more of them to choose from.

I step away from the table for a second, pull out my cell, and dial Courtney's number.

"Hey," I say into the phone. "I just wanted to tell you that I'm done. I don't want anything to do with you, so you don't have to worry about it. I'm not going to call you anymore." I snap my phone shut with a satisfied click and start thinking about what I'm going to wear to the party.

"So these girls are going to head over there with us," Ricardo says later that night. He's standing in front of the mirror, gelling his hair. From what I can tell, Ricardo spends a lot of time in front of the mirror. "You, my friend," he says to his own reflection, "are spades."

"What girls?" I ask. I'm riffling through my suitcase, trying to find a clean shirt to wear to the party. One of the problems with packing my shit so late was that I didn't have time to worry about if my clothes were clean or not. Therefore, I have a lot of dirty clothes in my suitcase, which is why I haven't bothered to put them in my dresser or hang them up. Why fold them when I'm just going to have to wash them anyway?

"These chicks I met at one of the orientation icebreakers," he says. The whole freshman class spent the afternoon playing lame icebreaker games, like "three truths and a lie" in an effort for everyone to get to know each other.

"Hot?" I pull a black button-up out of my suitcase and give it the smell test. Definitely not. I throw it back in.

"Smokin'," he says. "They're roommates, friends from high school. It's always good when the girls are friends." Ricardo picks up a bottle of cologne from his dresser and gives himself a spray.

"Jesus, that shit's strong," I say, backing away.

"It's Diddy's new cologne," he says. "It's a total pussy magnet."

"Oh."

"Anyway," he says, giving himself another spray. "I figure we can head over with Chelsea and Krista, lay the groundwork. And then if it doesn't work out, we can ditch them when we get there."

This guy's good. I hold a long-sleeved blue shirt up to my

nose. Not the best, but it'll do. I pull it over my head, slide my feet into my Timberlands, and sit down on the bed.

"What time's this thing start?" It's already eleven.

"Usually things don't get going until around eleven," Ricardo says. He's making weird faces at himself in the mirror, pushing his lips out like a fish.

"What are you doing?" I ask him.

"Getting ready."

"What's that thing with your lips?"

"I read about it in some magazine. It supposedly gets your pheromones racing, so chicks want you."

"Cool." My roommate is an insane person. I don't have too much time to think about this, though, because there's a knock on the door.

"The girls," Ricardo says, opening the door. "Come in, come in." He ushers them into the room. For an insane person, Ricardo definitely knows his women. They're both blonde with big boobs. One's wearing the shortest skirt I've ever seen, and the other one is wearing a top that exposes her midriff. I realize I haven't hooked up with anyone since I've been with Courtney. And now that Courtney and I are broken up, I can hook up with one of these girls. Maybe both of them. I feel myself starting to get turned on.

"I'm Jordan," I say.

"Chelsea," one says.

"Krista," the other one says. I'm never going to be able to tell them apart.

We head over to the party, and Ricardo makes it easy for me by latching on to the taller one (Krista, I think), and so I drop back and start talking to Chelsea. I'm starting to think that for all of Ricardo's weirdness, he and I might get along just fine. Unlike B. J., he has play. Ricardo obviously knows the first rule of the double hookup, which is that when two guys are out with two girls, you immediately pair off in an effort to let the girls know a hookup is definitely expected.

Chelsea and I do the required small talk on the way to the party. I find out she's from Boston, an elementary education major, and really, really likes to party. I know this because she says, "Do you like to party?" and I say, "Yeah, I guess," and she says, "Well, I really, really like to party."

By the time we get to the frat house, the festivities are in full swing. There are people all over the place—outside, inside, on the porch, on the lawn. It seems like the whole freshman class is here.

I grab two cups of beer from the keg and take them over to where Chelsea's waiting for me by the door.

"Here," I say.

"Thanks." She takes a few huge gulps. Whoa. This girl doesn't fuck around.

"So what dorm are you in?" I ask.

"I live off campus," she tells me, and then smiles. The strap of her bra is showing. Red. Hot.

"No shit," I say. "How'd you manage that?"

"My parents pay for everything," she says. "They feel

guilty that they're never around, so they make up for it by trying to give me everything I want."

"That sounds sweet," I say, wondering if she'll give me pointers on how I can finagle that situation for myself. My parents already give me pretty much whatever I want, but making my mom feel guilty is very appealing.

We talk for a little longer, and drink even more, and half an hour later, I've got quite the buzz going on. I can't stop looking at her bra strap. This girl is seriously hot. I wonder if it's because she's a college girl. But that really makes no sense, since until a few months ago, she wasn't in college, and it's unlikely that she's morphed into a hottie in just a few months.

"Hey," she says, leaning into me. "We can probably get out of here now, if you want."

Her lips are a few inches from mine, and I can feel my body responding to hers. She smells like beer and perfume and something sexy. "Yeah," I say, leaning back into her. "What did you have in mind?"

"We could go back to my place," she says.

"Go back to your place?" I ask.

"Yeah," she says. "And watch movies. I have a flatscreen and tons of DVDs." For some reason, Courtney's face flickers across my brain, but I push it away. Fuck Courtney, I think. This chick is hot. The thing with Courtney is over. I take another sip of my drink, figuring if I can just get a little more buzzed, I'll be fine.

"That sounds cool," I say. "Just let me tell Ricardo."

I start making my way through the crowd, and finally find Ricardo standing by the keg with his arm around a brunette. I'm impressed. Anyone who comes to a party and then hooks up with a different girl than the one he brought, has to have serious game.

"I'm leaving," I say. "I'm going back to Chelsea's apartment."

"Sweet," he says. "Nice one, bro. I'll catch you later."

But when I turn back around, I see Courtney in the corner, talking to that guy she was with at orientation. She's leaning against the wall, and he leans in to whisper something in her ear. She throws her head back and laughs, her hair falling down around her face. My stomach feels like it's in my throat, and then someone walks in front of me, blocking my view.

"Hey," Chelsea says, grabbing my arm. "There you are. I was wondering what was taking you so long." She leans into me again. "Are you ready to go?" I can feel her breath against my ear, and her chest against my shoulder.

"I'm sorry," I say to Chelsea. "I . . . I can't go with you."

And then I walk out of the party, down the street, and back to my dorm.

courtney after →

Two Days After the Trip, 1:53 a.m.

I get home from my first college party to find a voice mail from Jordan on my cell. He left it earlier this morning, but I left my cell phone in my room all day, in an effort to not have to deal with anyone. "I'm done," the message says. "I don't want anything to do with you, so you don't have to worry about it."

Good, I think. I don't have to worry about you. In fact, I was just at a party with Ben, the guy I met at orientation. The *sophomore* I met at orientation. The older guy who doesn't listen to rap music, and who went out for pizza with me afterwards.

Although, his friends were kind of obnoxious. One spilled beer on his hand and then wiped it on my sweater. And I think Ben might have laughed. But I'm sure it was about something else. And then, at the pizza place, I had to pay. But whatever. I'm not materialistic or anything. I don't need guys to pay for me. And besides, it wasn't even that much money. Although Ben and his friends all got extra cheese without even asking me, which was two dollars more. But whatever. The point is, I went to a college party. And I'm meeting guys. Better, mature guys. I don't need Jordan anymore.

My newfound freedom should make me feel good, but instead, I am starting to get angry. What is he talking about, he's done? *I'm* the one who's done with *him*. I'm the one who decided never to talk to him again. Not the other way around.

The door to my room opens and a girl with shoulder-length brown hair walks in. She's wearing a cute jean skirt and a navy blue zip-up hoodie. "Hey!" she says. "You must be Courtney. I'm Emma." She holds her hand out, and I take it. "I got here late," she says. "My flight was delayed."

"Oh," I say, looking around the room. I was so caught up in Jordan's ridiculous voice mail that I didn't even notice there's someone else's stuff in the room. There are clothes in the other closet, a computer on the other desk, and the other bed is made up.

"I'm sorry, was it okay to leave all my stuff?" Emma asks, looking worried. "I didn't have a chance to completely unpack because I didn't want to miss orientation, and I tried to move it out of the way, but—"

"Oh, no, it's fine," I say. "It wasn't in the way."

"Oh, okay," she says, looking confused.

"I'm sorry," I say, realizing I'm not being the most friendly roommate. "My psycho ex-boyfriend just left me a message, which really pissed me off."

"Really?" she says, looking interested. She plops down on her bed, and lays upside down, with her feet on the pillow. "What's the deal?"

"He did something really mean to me," I say. "And I told him to screw off." Emma nods. "And then . . . Then he leaves me a message saying 'I won't be contacting you again.'"

"Okay . . ." Emma looks confused. My roommate thinks I'm crazy.

"Like it was his idea that we don't talk anymore! That's ridiculous! That's insane! That's . . ." I feel myself starting to get madder and madder. "Do you have your student directory?" I ask her.

She reaches over and pulls it out of her night table. "Thanks." I open it to the *R*s and slide my finger down the list until I get to Jordan's name. Good, he's not that far from here. "I'll be back in a few minutes," I say.

"Okay," Emma says again, still sounding uncertain.

I march down the hallway and out into the night. I don't care that it's two in the morning. I don't care that his roommate might be sleeping. It's about time someone let Jordan know he can't just treat girls like this, constantly using them for his own agenda. I need to stand up for myself.

When I get to his dorm room, I can hear music coming from inside. Rap. Of course. I knock on the door. Loudly. I hope he gets a noise complaint, and his RA throws him out of school.

"Jordan!" I say. "I need to talk to you."

I hear a rustling sound in the room, and for a second, I lose a little steam. What if he has a girl over? What if he left me that message to make himself feel better, to make it known to me that it was over, so that he wouldn't have to feel bad if he thought he was cheating on me? What if he thinks I'm the psycho one? I guess showing up at his room at two in the morning isn't the best way to combat that, but whatever.

I knock on the door louder. "I know you're in there!" I'm practically screaming.

He opens the door. "Hey," he says.

"Are you alone?"

"Yeah, why?"

"I don't know," I say. I cross my arms. "First night of college and all. Figured you'd want to christen the room."

"Yeah, well, I figured I'd take the night off, *slowly* settle into college. Unlike you." He looks pissed.

"What's that supposed to mean?"

A door opens across the hall, and a guy in a pair of gray boxers pokes his head out into the hall. "Hey," he says. "Could you keep it down? I'm trying to sleep."

"Sorry," Jordan says. He motions to me as if to say "Psycho girls, what can you do about them?"

"Don't even," I say. "This is your fault, and you know it."

"What's my fault?" he asks. "And if you're going to be yelling at me, would you like to come in? I don't think my neighbors want to listen to this."

"No," I say, throwing up my hands in exasperation. "I do not want to come in."

"Then why did you come over here?" he asks, crossing his arms. He's wearing a white T-shirt and a pair of red-and-black mesh shorts. He looks like he was laying around in bed. Must. Not. Let. Hotness. Distract. Me.

"I came over here," I say, "because of that ridiculous message you left on my voice mail."

"What was so ridiculous about it?" he asks. "That's what you wanted, right? For me to leave you alone."

"Yes," I say. "I did."

"Did? Or do?"

"Do!" I say. "I don't want anything to do with you."

"Then why did you come over here?"

"Because!" I say, throwing my hands up at his obvious stupidity. "Because I want to make sure you know that it's my decision."

"What is?" He frowns.

"The decision to not talk anymore. It my decision." I cross my arms and tap my foot.

"Sure," he says. "Whatever you say."

"It is."

"Fine."

"Fine!"

I turn on my heel and start walking down the hall, but he yells after me, "Be careful about Upperclass Joe, there."

"Who?"

"The guy you've been all over all day."

I swallow. How does he know about that? "How do you know about that?" I ask. "And I haven't been all over him all day."

"Well, whatever," he says. "Just be careful."

The door across the hall opens again, and the same guy pops his head out. "Seriously," he says, sounding really annoyed.

"Sorry, dude, " Jordan repeats, not really sounding it. He looks at me. "Look, do you want to come in? Because for someone who's not talking to me, you certainly seem to have a lot to say."

"You do," the guy across the hall agrees. "And you should go in and talk about it. Otherwise I'm not going to get any sleep."

"Fine," I say. I push past Jordan and into his room. He shuts the door behind me. His room is a little smaller than mine, and he still hasn't unpacked his stuff. His comforter is thrown over his bed, and it looks like he was laying on top of it. Probably because he didn't pack extra-long sheets.

He sits down on the bed. "Do you want to sit down?" he asks, motioning to his desk chair.

"No," I say. I stand in the middle of the room. Neither of us say anything.

Finally, he sighs. "You can't keep running away from things, Court."

"I'm not," I say. "Just because I don't want to deal with you, doesn't mean I'm running away from things."

"Oh, really?" he says. "Have you talked to your dad?"

"No."

"Lloyd?"

"No."

He raises his eyebrows at me.

"That doesn't mean I'm running away from things," I say. "It just means that I don't want to talk to anyone right now."

"You're talking to me," he says. I don't say anything. "Courtney, I need to know if there's a chance. If you can forgive me, if there's . . ." he trails off, and I look at him. He's looking at me with this genuine expression on his face, and I can hear in his voice that he really means it. Just like the first night he called me and wanted to hang out and it made no sense to me, but I could still hear in his voice that he really wanted to.

"I can't," I say, shaking my head. "You lied to me, Jordan. If you loved me, you wouldn't have done that."

"It's not always that black and white, Courtney," he says, running his fingers through his hair. "It's not."

"It is to me," I say. My heart's beating fast now, and I can feel the adrenaline racing through my body. "I would never have done what you did to me."

"Maybe not," he says. "And I'm not trying to say that

what I did was right. But I freaked out. I'm in love with you. I thought you were going to hate me. I thought you were going to blame me for not telling you. I had just found out my mom was cheating on my dad. It was fucked up, Court."

He looks at me then, and I feel something soften inside me.

"You didn't handle it the right way," I say, and I can tell I'm going to start crying.

"I know that now," he says. He takes a step closer to me, and this time, I don't pull back. "And I wish I would have handled it differently. I wish I could have seen through all the insanity and just talked to you. But I don't want to make that mistake again. I want to talk about this." He's close to me now, and he reaches out and puts his arms around me.

"I'm really upset right now, Jordan," I tell him, being honest for the first time. "You really upset me. With everything. Breaking up with me, keeping things from me."

"I know," he says. "And I'm sorry. I didn't do it on purpose, Court. I couldn't stand the thought of you hating me, so I just chose not to deal with it. But I'm not going to do it anymore. I'm going to deal with it. *We* have to deal with it."

"How?" I ask, and his arms are around me now, and I'm crying and my eyes are making wet spots on his shirt but he's not pulling away.

"By doing whatever it takes," he says simply.

"Do you know . . . I mean, do you know what they're going to do? About things? My dad and your mom?" I pull away for a second and look at him, knowing that whatever the answer is, it won't be good.

"I'm not sure," he says. He hesitates. "My mom told my brother she was leaving my dad, but I'm not sure if she's really thought it through, or if she'll really do it."

I nod.

"We'll get through it," he says, pulling me close again.

"I don't know," I say. "I don't know if it's going to ever be the same."

"That's okay," he says. "That you don't know, I mean. But if there's even a chance, then I want to try."

I look at him then, and I see how hurt he is. I think about how awful it must have been for him to find out his mom was cheating on his dad, and even more awful that he felt he couldn't tell me. I think about how people make mistakes, and how I lied to him about the Lloyd thing, and how emotions and heartbreak and love can really screw with your head. Most of all, I think about how it is to be with him, and how if there's even a chance we can be together, I can't be afraid to find out.

He kisses me then, softly on the lips, and I lean into his body. "You're going to be okay, Court," he whispers into my ear, and I know he's talking about the stuff with my family, not with him and I.

"I know," I say. "And I wish you had known that, too.

You can't always protect me from everything. I can be strong, too, you know."

"I know that now," he says. "And isn't that what matters?" He looks at me then, and we're kissing and his hands are on my body. We fall onto his bed, and he pulls away for a second to look at me. "I love you, Court," he says.

"I love you, too."

And then he holds me until I fall asleep.

courtney after →

"Hey," my roommate says the next morning when I get back to our room. She's sitting at her computer, messing around on Facebook. "I take it things either went really, really well or really, really bad."

"What do you mean?" I ask.

"Well, you never came home last night. Which means you either made up with your boyfriend, or you didn't make up with him, and spent the rest of the night trolling around the streets, looking for mischief. Or holed up with some other random guy. Or crying your eyes out in an alley."

I giggle. "It went . . . well, let's just say I'm being cautiously optimistic."

"Good," she says, smiling. "Cautiously optimistic is good."

"Hey," I say. "I'm sorry about last night. I'm not crazy, I swear. I just have a lot of stuff going on."

"Not a big deal," she says. She shuts down her computer and picks up her purse. "I'm heading over to the financial aid office, because they screwed something up with my forms." She rolls her eyes. "But do you want to have breakfast together? We could meet at around eleven? You can tell me about last night."

"Sure," I say. "I have some phone calls to make now, so that works out perfect."

"Cool." She smiles.

Once the door shuts behind her, I pick up my cell phone and take a deep breath. I have to call Lloyd. I have to call my mom, my dad, and Jocelyn. I told Jordan he had to stop protecting me, and now I have to stop protecting myself. I decide to go for it, to jump right into things, to make the hardest call first. I dial my dad's number at work. The sun is shining through the window, casting stripes of light on the floor. "Hey," I say when he answers. "It's me."

right of way

For Michelle Nagler, who took a chance on me
and my writing, and made my dreams come true

ACKNOWLEDGMENTS

Thank you so, so much to:

Jennifer Klonsky, Alyssa Eisner Henkin, and everyone at Simon & Schuster for all their hard work on my behalf;

Krissi, Kelsey, Jodi, Kevin, and my mom for all their support;

My husband, Aaron, for everything;

Everyone who read *Two-way Street* and took the time to write me and tell me you loved it—I appreciate it more than you know!

peyton the trip

I'm a traitor to my generation. Seriously. All we hear about these days is how we're supposed to be strong women and not depend on anyone else and blah blah blah. And now look what I've done.

"Are you sure there's no way you can come?" I say into my phone. I'm crouching behind some bushes outside the Siesta Key Yacht Club, which is not comfortable. At all. The bushes are prickly, there are bees floating around, and the ground is kind of wet. Which makes no sense. I thought it never rained in Florida. Isn't it called the Sunshine State?

"I'm sorry," my best friend, Brooklyn, says on the other end of the line. "I'm so sorry, but there's no way I can come now. My parents found out, and they're freaking out. And honestly, Peyton, I kind of think you should just forget the whole thing. I mean, what if my parents call your parents?"

My heart leaps into my throat. "Are they going to?"

"I don't know. My mom said she wouldn't as long as I talked you out of it, but you never know what my mom's going to do. She's a loose cannon." It's true. Brooklyn's mom really is a loose cannon. One time last year she came down to our school screaming about women's equality on the wrestling team. It was pretty ridiculous, since Brooklyn is totally unathletic, and no girls were even trying out for the wrestling team. But her mom had read some article about Title Nine that had gotten her all riled up.

"But what am I supposed to do?" I ask. "My parents already left. I can't call and tell them I don't have a way to get back to Connecticut. They'll be pissed."

Brooklyn and I had this whole thing planned out. She was going to fly down to Florida from Connecticut, and meet me here, in Siesta Key, at my uncle's wedding. Then we were going to rent a car and drive to North Carolina, where we were going to spend the summer. It was a very simple two-part plan. One, she takes a plane down here. Two, we rent a car and go to North Carolina. Leave it to her parents to wreck everything.

"You're going to have to call your mom or something," Brooklyn says. "It'll suck, yeah, but what else are you going to do?"

I don't say anything. My eyes fill with hot tears. There's

a bee buzzing near my face, and I don't even bother to swat it away. I really, really do not want to call my parents. And not just because they're going to be pissed. But because it's going to mean that I have to go home, and I really, really do not want to do that.

Brooklyn sighs.

"Look," she says finally. "Is there any way you can book a flight to North Carolina? And maybe get a ride to the airport?"

"I don't have a credit card. Or any money, really."

"Can you ask Courtney for help?"

"I could ask her, I guess, but I don't know if she has any money either." I stand up and scan the outdoor tables for my cousin. I don't see her dark hair anywhere. I look for her boyfriend, Jordan, but I don't see him either. In fact, I don't see *anyone* I recognize. Most people have already left the brunch and gone home. The wedding was yesterday, and the festivities are over.

I guess I could call Courtney, I think, taking a step back toward the tables that are set up on the lawn of the yacht club. But who knows if she would tell my parents? Or her dad? I mean, I trust her, but—

My eyes stop scanning the crowd as they land on the only person I recognize who's still at the brunch. The only person I don't want to see. Jace Renault. He looks up from the table where he's sitting, talking to some older couple that he probably just met. The old lady is laughing at something Jace is saying. Which isn't surprising. Jace is charming like that. Ugh.

He catches my eye, and I quickly turn away.

"Brooklyn," I say. "Please, can you lend me the money for a plane ticket? I'll pay you back, I promise."

"Peyton, you know I would if I could, but my mom took my credit card away."

"I can't believe this," I say. "I planned so hard so no one would find out, and now—"

There's a tap on my shoulder. I turn around. Jace is standing there, a huge smile on his face. "Hello," he says.

I turn and start to walk away from him. "Who's that?" Brooklyn asks.

"That's no one," I say loudly, hoping that Jace will get the message to go away. But of course he doesn't. He just starts to follow me as I walk through the grass of the club back toward my room. He's doing a good job keeping up, since I'm having a little trouble walking. My shoes keep slipping on the wet grass.

"You really shouldn't be walking through here," he says conversationally. "I don't think the groundskeepers are going to be too thrilled with all the divots you're making."

"Who the hell is that?" Brooklyn asks. "Is that Jace?"

"No," I say.

"Yes, it is."

"No, it isn't."

"Yes, it is!"

"No. It. Isn't."

"No it isn't what?" Jace asks from next to me. He's caught up to me now.

He really is like some kind of gnat that I can't get away from. I knew there would be pests and bugs in Florida; I just didn't expect them to be six foot two and of the human variety.

"I'll call you back," I say to Brooklyn. I hang up the phone and whirl around. "What do you want?" I ask.

He shrugs. "I don't know," he says. "I saw you staring at me, and you looked upset."

"I wasn't staring at you!" I say. "I was looking for Courtney." I smooth down my dress. "And I'm not upset."

"Courtney and Jordan left a little while ago," he says.

"Do you know where they went?" I ask, my heart sinking.

"I'm not sure." He shrugs like it doesn't matter. And I guess to him, it doesn't. He's not the one who's stranded at some wedding in Florida with no way to get to North Carolina. "Why?"

"None of your business." I'm walking again, looking down at my phone, scrolling through my contacts. I wonder if there's someone I can call—someone who might be willing to help me. Why didn't I make more of an effort to get to know someone at the wedding? Why didn't I befriend some nice old lady who would be able to take me somewhere—preferably a senile one who would be too out of it to ask any questions? *Because you were too busy with Jace.*

"Do you need a ride or something?" Jace asks.

I snort.

"What's so funny?"

"I just think it's kind of hilarious that suddenly you're so concerned about my well-being after what you did to me last night."

"Peyton—" he starts, his voice softening. But I'm not in the mood.

"Stop." I hold my hand up. "I don't want to hear it. And I don't need a ride. So just go away."

"Then how are you getting to the airport?"

"I'm not going to the airport." God, he's so annoying. How can he think that after what happened between us last night that I would get into a car with him? Is he crazy?

Although I guess when I really think about it, it's actually not that surprising.

Anyone who is as good-looking as Jace is usually completely out of touch with reality. It's like they think their looks give them the right to just go around saying whatever they want to say, and doing whatever they want to do. As if the fact that they're six foot two and broad-shouldered with dark hair and gorgeous, deep-blue eyes gives them the right to get away with anything.

"If you're not going to the airport, then where are you going?"

I keep ignoring him, continuing through the grass in

these stupid high heels, trying to get back to my room. And he keeps following me, still not having any trouble keeping up. I glance down at his feet. He's wearing sneakers. Of course he is. Jace Renault would never do anything as, you know, *polite* as wearing dress shoes to a wedding. Although technically he's wearing them to the brunch the day after the wedding. But still. Proper attire should be worn. Proper attire that doesn't include sneakers.

I'm so caught up in looking at his feet that I don't realize that my own shoes are sinking farther into the wet grass, and so when I slip, I'm halfway to the ground before I feel his arms grabbing me around the waist.

He's so close that I can feel his breath on my neck as he lifts me up, and it sends delicious little shivers up and down my spine. He looks at me, his eyes right on mine, and I swallow hard. If this were a movie, this would be the moment he'd kiss me, the moment he'd push my hair back from my face and brush his lips softly against mine, telling me he was sorry for everything that happened last night and over the spring, that he had an explanation for the whole thing, that everything was going to be okay. But this isn't a movie. This is my life.

And so instead of kissing me, Jace waits until I'm upright and then he says, "Those shoes are pretty ridiculous."

"These shoes," I say, "cost four hundred dollars."

"Well, you got ripped off."

"I didn't ask you."

He keeps following me, all the way back to my hotel room. What is *wrong* with him? Like it's not enough that he stomped all over my heart? Now he has to keep torturing me with his nearness? When we get to the outside of the suite I'm staying in, I unlock the door and push it open.

"Well, thanks for walking me back to my room," I say, all sarcastic.

But he doesn't seem to notice. In fact, he just peers over my shoulder into the sitting area of my room. "Jesus, Peyton," he says, looking at the mound of bags that are stacked neatly in the middle of the floor. "How long did you plan on staying? A few months? I knew you were high maintenance, but that much luggage is a little crazy, don't you think?"

"I'm not high maintenance!"

He shrugs, as if to say I am high maintenance and everyone knows it, so there's no use denying it. Like he knows anything about me and my high-maintenance ways. (And yes, I am a little bit high maintenance. But not in a bad way. I just like to have things the way I like them.)

"Looks pretty high maintenance to me." He steps into the room, then reaches down and picks up the bottle of water the hotel has left on the desk. He opens it and takes a big drink.

"You owe me four dollars." Plus I wanted that water. But I'm not going to tell him that. Why give him the satisfaction?

"Don't you mean I owe your parents four dollars?"

I narrow my eyes at him then hold out my hand. "Give it to me."

"Fine," he grumbles, reaching into his pocket and pulling out a bunch of crumpled up bills.

"Figures that you don't have a wallet," I say.

"Figures that you would notice something like that, being that you're so high maintenance." He grins at me sweetly.

"I am *not* high maintenance! So stop saying that!"

"Then why do you have a million bags for a weekend trip to a wedding?"

I feel the anger building inside me—he's so damn arrogant I can't even stand it—and before I even know what I'm saying, I'm telling him. "Because," I say, getting ready to savor the look of shock that I know is about to cross his face, "I'm running away."

the trip   jace

Peyton Miller hates me. And for good reason—I've been nothing but an asshole to her since we met. And even though I *knew* she was pissed at me because of what happened last night, even though I *knew* she hated me and probably wanted to beat me senseless with those ridiculous shoes she's wearing, I found myself getting up from my table and walking over to her while she was in the bushes.

I wanted to explain to her what happened last night; I wanted to explain to her all the reasons I had for being such an asshole. But when I got close to her, she started being such a brat that I figured it wasn't the time. Either that, or I just chickened out. Probably a combination of both.

Which is probably for the best, since there are a million

fucking reasons that things are not going to work out between me and Peyton Miller, even before considering the fact that she hates me.

Some of these reasons are:

1. She is beautiful and she doesn't know it. This is a very annoying trait for a girl to have, because it makes you want them, while at the same time you can't even hate them for being conceited because they're not.

2. She is ridiculously smart—so smart that I sometimes cannot believe it. In fact, she is a horrible mix of beautiful and smart. One second she'll be tottering around in those stupid high-heeled shoes she always wears, and the next she'll be debating me over whether or not there should be universal healthcare.

2a. She is way too smart to put up with any of my shit and calls me out on it any chance she gets.

3. Right now she's trying to get rid of me, even though I'm trying to help her.

4. She broke my heart.

Number four is obviously the biggest one. She's the only girl who's ever broken my heart, and it's a very weird, uncomfortable feeling for me. I like to be the one doing the heartbreaking. Well, not really. No one ever *likes* to break someone's heart, but sometimes it has to be done. And if I have a choice between breaking a heart and getting my heart broken, well, call me selfish, but I'll take being the heartbreaker.

"You're running away?" I say now. I move into the room so she can't see the shock on my face, mostly because I know she *wants* to see the shock on my face. She wants to see me freak out like a little girl and ask her all kinds of questions. Which I'm dying to do, let's face it. But I don't want to give her the satisfaction.

Instead I head over to the minibar in the corner and start rustling through the contents until I find a Snickers. I rip open the wrapper and take a bite, then hold it out to her. "Want some?"

She wrinkles up her nose. "It's ten o'clock in the morning."

"So? It's never too early for chocolate."

"I don't share food with people."

"What, are you worried about germs? Because I think it's a little late for that after what happened last night, don't you?" I give her a grin.

"Get out," she commands, pointing toward the door. "Or I'm going to call security."

"Ooooh, good idea," I say. I plop down on her bed and take another bite of my candy bar. "And what will you tell them?"

"That an annoying jerk won't get out of my room."

I roll my eyes at her. "Relax," I say. "I'm going." I polish off the rest of the candy bar and drop the wrapper into the trash. I'm halfway to the door and trying to think of an excuse to stay, when she speaks.

"Wait!" she says. "You need to pay for that."

I reach into my pocket and pull out a few more bills, then drop them onto the desk. "You should be careful," I say, "if you really are running away."

There's no sarcasm in my voice because I really am worried about her. She can't run away. She hardly has any street smarts. And I highly doubt her high heels are going to protect her from any robbers and miscreants that she might encounter out on the road.

"Yeah, well," she says. "You don't have to worry about me."

"Oh, I'm not *worried* about you. I just—"

She gives me a look, silencing me. Then she plops herself down on the bed. She bites her lip and pushes her hair out of her face, and then a second later, she's crying.

Shit. I hate when chicks cry. I never know what to do. You can never tell if they're crying about something that's actually important, of if they're upset because their jeans don't fit.

I move back into the room and sit down next to her on the bed, making sure there's a sliver of space between us. I cannot allow myself to get too close to her. If I'm too close to her, something might happen. Thinking about getting close to her and something happening makes me think about last night, about what did happen, after the wedding, after the champagne, after the two of us were alone. And then, of course, I think about how it ended.

"What's wrong?" I ask her gently.

"What's *wrong*?" Peyton yells and then sits up, grabbing for the tissues that are sitting on the nightstand. "What's *wrong* is that I'm supposed to be running away from home, and my friend, the one who was supposed to help me, she . . . she . . . she got caught and now I'm going to have to call my parents and tell them what happened!"

Wow. She's kind of hysterical.

"Why do you have to call your parents?" I ask.

She looks at me like I'm stupid. "Because!" She jumps up and starts pacing around the room, like she has so much energy that she can't take it. I'm a little disappointed that she's not sitting next to me anymore, but it's most likely for the best. I really have no self-control, and I probably would have tried to kiss her. It's one of my character defects. The lack of self-control, I mean. (Although I guess the fact that I want to kiss a girl who completely broke my heart and who hates me could also be considered a character defect.)

"Because why?"

"Because they thought that Brooklyn was flying into Florida, and that we were going to rent a car and drive to North Carolina, checking out colleges on the way, and then fly home to Connecticut together next week."

"But you were really running away."

"Right." She sniffs. "We were going to spend the summer in North Carolina. Brooklyn knows a boy there, and I . . ." She trails off, then shakes her head, obviously not wanting to tell me the reason she's going.

I shrug. "So why not just call your parents and tell them Brooklyn couldn't come and get you, and that you don't want to go by yourself? Tell them you need a plane ticket home. They might be annoyed, but they're not going to be pissed. It's not your fault she bailed."

She puts her back against the wall and slides down until she's sitting in a heap on the floor. "But then I'll actually have to go home," she says.

"So?"

"So!" She throws her hands up in the air, and I'm reminded of another reason why I don't like her. She's overly dramatic, even for a girl. "I was running away!"

"Yeah, I get it. But that plan's changed now. So call your parents. You can run away some other time."

She snorts. "Whatever," she says. "I should have known better than to expect you to understand."

"What's that supposed to mean?"

"Never mind," she says. "Just get out of here." Whatever it was that made her want to confide in me before is gone, and now she's back to being her old, bratty self. Reason number five things won't work out with us: She runs hot and cold. (Obviously I need to stop listing the reasons things won't work out. It's kind of depressing. And at some point, I'm going to lose count.)

"No, I want to know what you meant by that."

"Just that you've never dealt with anything hard in your life."

"I've dealt with hard things before," I say. But even as I'm saying the words, I know they're kind of a lie. My parents are together—happily in love. They're not rich like Peyton's parents, but they make enough money so that I can shop at Abercrombie once in a while and drive around in a (used) Nissan Sentra. I'm the starting forward on the school basketball team. I've never really had a problem getting girls, and I'm going to be valedictorian at my graduation tomorrow. (I have to give a stupid speech and everything, and my mom's all excited about it. I'm actually kind of dreading the speech. The whole graduation thing just seems so pointless, a big charade that's supposed to make you feel good about yourself, when everyone knows that in reality, high school is just one big sham.)

"Oh yeah?" Peyton asks. "Like what?" She smirks. "I'd love to know all these torturous things you've been dealing with."

"Like I'm really going to tell you." I stand up, because I'm starting to realize that this is pointless. Peyton hates me. And I'm not going to put myself out there for a girl who hates me, and who I don't even like. "Well, good luck."

"Thanks." She's still sitting there, her dress in a pool around her on the floor. She looks small and vulnerable, and I remember what it was like to kiss her last night, how her hair felt in my hands, how soft her skin was. What the fuck is wrong with me? I just said I was done with her, and now I'm thinking about kissing her again? I sigh.

"Listen," I say, kneeling down next to her. "Let me take you home."

She looks up at me, her eyes shining. "What?"

"I'll drive you home."

"You'll drive me *home*? I live in Connecticut."

"I know where you live," I say, rolling my eyes.

"You have your car?" she asks.

I nod. "Yes."

"And you'd drive all that way for me?"

"Not *for* you." I shake my head. "I wanted to check out a college up there anyway. This gives me an excuse." It's a lie, of course. But I can't let her know that I'm desperate to keep her with me, that once I leave this room, once we're apart, I don't know when I'm going to see her again, and that the thought is too much for me to take.

"But I thought you were going to Georgetown in the fall."

"How did you know that?"

"Facebook." She blushes, but points her nose in the air, all haughty. "What?" she asks. "I'm not allowed to look at your Facebook page? It's not like it's private or anything."

"I don't care if you look at my Facebook." I shrug. "And Georgetown's not definite." Another lie.

"So you'll drop me off somewhere along the way?" she asks. She pulls at the bottom of her skirt nervously. "Because like I said, I wasn't really planning on going home."

"No." I shake my head. "I'll drive you home, but that's

it. I'm not getting involved in any kind of weird running-away plan. Your parents would kill me. Not to mention, I'd be kidnapping a minor."

She rolls her eyes, already wiping her tears away, already standing back up and smoothing down her dress. "Fine," she says, biting her lip. "But first I have to change." She crosses to the middle of the room and starts going through her suitcase, pulling out clothes and setting them on the bed until she finds what she wants, and then packing everything back up.

"Do you have to call your parents or anything?" she asks as she walks into the bathroom and shuts the door.

I try not to think about what she's doing in there, mainly taking off her clothes. "Call my parents?"

"Yeah," she yells through the door, "so that you can tell them you're not going to be home for a while."

"Oh, right."

"Are they going to be okay with it?"

"My parents don't run my life," I scoff. "They'll be fine with it."

And the lies just keep on coming.

peyton before →

Here are the reasons I hate going shopping with my mom:

1. She always wants me to buy things I don't like.
2. She's always insisting I show her how the clothes look on me, even when I tell her they're hideous and don't need to be seen outside of the privacy of my dressing room.
3. It makes me feel fat.

"Peyton, please tell me you don't need the size eight," my mom calls from the dressing room across from me. We're in Nordstrom, which is one of the worst stores in which to try on clothes, because they have this whole area where you can come out and twirl around in front of a four-way mirror. That is just wrong.

"I don't need the size eight," I call back. "The six fits just

319

fine." I open the door and hold the dress out to the salesgirl, who gives me a wink as she takes it out of my hand.

"I'll be right back with the eight," she mouths.

"Thank you," I whisper back gratefully. She's just out of sight when my mom emerges from her dressing room.

"What do you think?" she asks. She's clad in a tight black dress that hits just above the knee. It's sleeveless, but classy, with a cowl neck and a sexy zigzag pattern worked into the fabric.

"You look great, Mom," I tell her. And she does. My mom's body is amazing, especially for someone who's had two children. Of course, she works hard at it, with tons of pilates and spinning and Zumba and those crossfit groups that are oh-so-trendy right now. Every morning at five she's out the door, clad in spandex, a towel thrown over her shoulder, a water bottle in her hand, ready to spend the next two hours sweating at the gym. She's always trying to get me to go with her, but I refuse. What kind of crazy person is up at five in the morning? There are worse things in the world than being a size eight.

"But do you think black is too somber for a wedding?" She turns this way and that, inspecting herself in the mirror, admiring the way she looks.

For about the tenth time since we started shopping, I wish my older sister Kira was here. Kira's into fashion, and she always knows what to say to my mom in these situations. Plus Kira makes shopping fun, joining me as we roll our eyes behind my mom's back and sneak the clothes we really want up to the cash register. But Kira's away at college, and so I'm stuck fielding my mom's questions by myself.

I don't really know a ton about the rules of fashion, but I do know that my mom expects me to answer, even if I don't really know what I'm talking about. And I also know enough that, since we're shopping for an outdoor summer wedding, in Florida, black might not be the best choice. "Well," I say slowly, "it *is* a summer wedding, and the ceremony's outside, so maybe you should look for something a little brighter."

Her face falls for a moment, but then she's back to smiling. "You're right!" she says. "Maybe something in tangerine. Although it would be shame not to get this one, too. I can always find somewhere to wear a little black dress!" She laughs like this is some kind of joke, and I giggle along with her, even though it's not really that funny.

The salesgirl reappears holding a size eight of the fluttery grey dress I just tried on. She looks back and forth between my mom and me nervously, like she's worried my mom is going to catch her with the bigger dress. But my mom's already forgotten about what happened a few moments ago.

"Nora," she says, even though the salesgirl's name is Nicole. "Nora, please fetch us some dresses in bright colors. I want tangerine, green, pink, yellow . . . but nothing peach.

It washes my daughter out." She flutters her hand at all the dresses that are littering the floor and bench of the dressing room. "And take these things away. They're all wrong. Wrong, wrong, wrong!" She giggles again.

"Of course," Nicole says, scurrying into the dressing room to gather the clothes.

"I think I'm going to go out and choose some things myself," I yell to my mom. I'm back in my own dressing room now, changing into my jeans and T-shirt. There's silence from the other side of the door, and I can tell I've said the wrong thing.

"Honey, they have people to do that sort of thing for you," she says. "This is Nordstrom, not JCPenney."

"I know," I say, keeping my voice light. "Sometimes I just like to do it myself."

"Okay," she says. But I can hear the disappointment in her voice. The disappointment that means I'm not doing what she wants. The disappointment that seems to be directed at me more and more lately.

I walk out of the stuffy air of the dressing room and back into the store, where Nicole is busy flicking through a rack of pale-green sundresses.

"Sorry about my mom," I say, rolling my eyes. "I wish I could say that's not like her, but it totally is."

Nicole smiles. "Oh, no," she says. "It's no problem at all. I always want to make my customers happy."

I smile back, even though I'm sure it's a completely

canned response and that she secretly wants to throttle us and then start wandering the aisles, looking for something that's both bright and fun and won't make me look like a sausage.

My phone starts vibrating in my purse, and I fish it out. Courtney. My cousin. It's her dad, my mom's brother, who's getting married in a few weeks.

"Hey," I say. "What's up?" Courtney's a year older than me, just finishing up her freshman year at Boston University. Her family lives in Florida, and so we've never gotten the chance to be super close, but we're still pretty good friends. It's never uncomfortable to talk to her, and whenever I see her we always have an amazing time.

"Hey, Peyton," she says. "What's going on?"

"Just out shopping for your dad's wedding," I reply, watching as Nicole disappears into the dressing room holding an armful of outfits that my mom is sure to veto. "What's up with you?"

"Not much," she says. "Are you finding anything good?"

"Not yet," I say. I move a couple of more steps away from the dressing room, just in case my mom can hear. "We're in Nordstrom and my mom's acting like she's in Prada or something. She keeps making the salesgirl go out and fetch things for her."

Courtney laughs. "That sounds like Aunt Michelle."

"Yeah, well, I'm picking out my own stuff, thank you very much."

"Good for you," Courtney says. She clears her throat. "Um, so the reason I'm calling is that I need to talk to you about something."

"Okay," I say. Sure enough, Nicole's coming out of the dressing room, her arms loaded up with the dresses she just brought in there. My mom, I'm sure, sent her right back out, saying that none of them were right without even trying them on. I swear, sometimes I think she does things like that just to be a diva.

"Well," Courtney says, "remember when the invitations came out for my dad's wedding? And you sent me that Facebook message asking me if Jace was coming?"

As soon as she says his name, my heart skips from my stomach up into my throat. "Yes," I say, trying to sound nonchalant. "I remember."

"Well, at the time I said no, because my dad told me that the Renaults were going to be out of town. I guess they'd had some big trip to Europe planned for, like, years. And since my dad's wedding was slightly spur-of-moment, it was really too late for them to cancel."

"Right," I say. "I remember you told me that." I remember everything Courtney told me about Jace's Europe trip, because I remember everything about Jace. The way his hair flopped over his forehead. The way his smile curled up more on one side than on the other. The way he loved to debate me on everything from politics to the difference between McDonald's and Burger King. The way he smelled like peppermint and shaving cream, even though when I was kissing him it always seemed like his face was slightly scruffy.

"Well, it turns out the Renaults are coming after all. Something about the dollar not being strong enough, and figuring out a way to waive the cancellation fees. Or something." Courtney pauses, and my world stops. "Peyton?" she asks. "Are you there?"

"Yes." I lick my suddenly dry lips, and then sit down right there in the middle of the floor.

"Listen," Courtney says. "I'm sorry to spring this on you. I know how it feels to have to see a guy you have a weird thing with. If this same thing had happened to me and Jordan a year ago then I'd—"

"No," I lie, cutting her off. "It's not weird. It's totally fine. And me and Jace are nothing like you and Jordan." This part, at least, is true. Courtney and her boyfriend Jordan were together for like, months before he broke up with her and totally broke her heart. They got back together after that, but to compare what Courtney and Jordan have with what Jace and I have (had? never had? should have had?) is ridiculous. Jace and I have only met once, when I was in Florida over Christmas. And yeah, it was the most intense experience I've ever had with a guy, but still. That isn't saying much, since he lives hundreds of miles away. (And since my experience with guys is pretty limited.)

"Okay," Courtney says, not sounding so sure. "But if you decided you didn't want to come to the wedding, I would totally understand. And my dad would too. I could just tell him that—"

"Oh, no," I say. "It's fine, I promise. I'm still going."

"Okay." She pauses. "Well, I just thought I'd let you know."

"Thanks."

"So what else is new?"

"Not much. I'm just waiting for—"

"Ta-da!" my mom yells, waltzing out into the middle of the store. She's wearing a long yellow dress that's so tight it looks like it might be cutting off her circulation. The bottom flares out, mermaid style. The dress looks amazing on her, but I don't know if it's really appropriate for a wedding.

"Peyton?" Courtney asks.

"Yeah, I'm here," I say. "Can I call you back?"

"Sure."

I hang up the phone and walk slowly over to my mom. "Wow," I say. "It's very . . . different."

"Isn't it?" She's raising her voice now, and I can tell it's because she wants everyone in the store to start looking at her. Which people are. Sort of. And not necessarily in a good way. "Nora, darling, do you think I should wear a hat with this?"

That's when I notice that Nicole is standing behind her, looking a little dazed. "Ummm . . ." She looks at me for guidance, knowing she better give my mom the answer she wants. I nod my head slightly.

"Yes, definitely," Nicole says, smiling. "A hat would set this dress off just beautifully. And it would be perfect for an outdoor wedding."

My mom beams. "Thank you, Noreen," she says. "Can you please go and pick out an assortment of hats for me to try on?"

Nicole scuttles away.

My mom looks at me, finally realizing that I'm not holding any dresses. "Peyton!" she says. "You haven't even picked out one dress!"

I sigh, suddenly feeling defeated. This wedding is turning into kind of a debacle. I mean, let's assess the situation, shall we?

First, if I'm being completely honest, I kind of hate weddings. All those people celebrating a couple that most of them don't even really know that well, and who will probably be divorced in less than ten years. It's more depressing than happy when you really think about it.

Second, I'm going to have to buy some stupid dress that I don't really want, mostly because my mom wants me to have it.

And third, Jace Renault is going to be there. Jace Renault, the only boy I've ever dared to let myself care about. Jace Renault, who I've only seen once in my life, and who still somehow managed to break my heart.

"Mom," I try, "I was thinking, maybe I should stay home while you guys go to Florida. I could watch the house and you wouldn't have to worry about buying me a plane ticket. That way—"

"You most certainly will not stay home!" she says. "This is a big day for your uncle, and I know he would be hurt if you weren't there."

I sigh. "But, Mom," I say, "I'm going to be so bored. And you and Dad—"

"Peyton," she says. "You're going. And that's final."

"Fine," I say. I consider adding, *You'll be sorry,* but I'm old enough to realize that would be pretty immature. Of course, if I thought it would make a difference, I'd say it anyway, immature or not. But it won't. She's made up her mind, and that's that.

So instead, I walk toward another rack of dresses. If I'm going to have to see Jace Renault, I might as well make sure I look amazing.

jace before

I'm hanging out at my friend Evan's house when my phone rings. The caller ID flashes a number I don't recognize, and so I hesitate. Usually I don't pick up numbers I don't recognize. It's almost never a good idea. Bill collectors, girls you don't want to talk to . . . these are the kinds of people who call from blocked numbers.

But since Evan just informed me that he wants to jump off the roof of his house and into the pool, and I don't necessarily feel like dealing with that, I answer it.

"Jace?" a girl's voice asks.

"Who's this?" I ask, deciding it's best not to give too much away just yet.

"Who is it?" Evan asks. He's busy fastening some kind of ramp together on the other side of the pool. I have no idea

329

why he needs a ramp if he's going to be jumping off the roof, but whatever.

"Who is this?" I ask again, motioning for Evan to be quiet. Like it's going to do any good.

"It's Courtney," the girl says.

"Oh," I say, relieved. "Hey, Courtney."

"Courtney!" Evan abandons his ramp and runs over to where I'm sitting on the patio. Cold water drips from his hair onto the pavement. He's wet because he cannonballed into the pool as soon as I got here, so he could "figure out how deep I'll end up."

"Dude," I say, shaking my head at him. "No offense, but you're kind of disgusting."

"Courtney," Evan says, grabbing the phone away from me without even asking. "Do you want to come over? I'm building a ramp and I'm going to either skateboard off it into my pool or possibly jump off the roof, and then I'm going to send the tape into MTV so they can—What? No, this is Evan. . . .Yeah, I know you have a boyfriend, but didn't that douchebag Jordan break up with you?" He snorts. "Right, and you really think he's changed, huh? . . . Well, whatever. If you change your mind, let me know."

He throws the phone back to me and then does another cannonball into the pool. Freezing water splashes into the air and lands all over my shirt.

"Hey," I say to Courtney. "Sorry about that."

"That's okay," she says. I guess you could say Courtney

and I are friends—her parents and my parents have been best friends for like five years. They tried to hook us up once when we were fourteen, but it didn't work out. At all. Mostly because it just wasn't right. Courtney's cute and smart, but we just didn't click in that way. There were no hard feelings, though, and we've always been friendly. But we're not the type of friends who just call each other out of the blue, so there must be something she wants to talk to me about.

"So what's up?" I ask. I stay on the patio but move as far away from the pool as possible. I need to be able to see Evan just in case he needs to be rescued from some sort of calamitous situation.

"So this might be weird," Courtney says, "and I really don't want to come across like I'm being a bitch or getting involved in your business."

"Is your mom still mad about the Christmas party?" I ask, sighing. I really do not want to get all caught up in *that* again.

Courtney's parents got divorced not that long ago, which was this huge scandal, because *my* mom wanted to stay friends with *Courtney's* mom, but then Courtney's mom said she wouldn't be friends with my parents unless they stopped hanging out with Courtney's dad. Everything came to a head when Courtney's dad threw this Christmas party, and my parents went, and Courtney's mom got all mad at them. The whole thing is completely ridiculous, if you ask me. Which, of course, nobody ever does.

"No, no, it's not about that," Courtney says. "It's, um . . . look, I know this is probably none of my business, and you can feel free to tell me to screw off. But Jace, what happened between you and Peyton?"

"Peyton?" I take in a deep breath through my nose. I don't want to think about Peyton. I don't want to talk about Peyton. I don't even want to hear Peyton's name.

"Yeah."

"Nothing happened." I shrug, even though Courtney can't see me. "I hardly even remember her. What's she up to now, anyway?"

"Okkkayy," Courtney says, not sounding convinced. And who would blame her? I'm not even convincing myself.

"Hey!" Evan calls from somewhere over my head. "Up here! Look at me!"

I shade my eyes from the sun with my hand and peer up at the roof. Evan's standing there in a bathing suit and a pair of neon-green goggles, a huge grin on his face. "What the hell are you doing?" I ask. "Are you fucking crazy? Get down from there."

"Go get the camera!" he yells, pointing over to the side of the pool where he's left the camcorder.

"No way." I shake my head. "You're going to split your head open."

"Courtney!" he screams. "This one's for you!" And then he starts pounding his fists against his bare chest like he's Tarzan or some shit.

"What's going on over there?" Courtney asks, sounding worried.

"Nothing," I say, sighing. "It's too much to get into right now. But, um, I kind of have to go. Is there anything else?"

"Yeah," she says. "I just wanted to let you know that Peyton's going to be coming to the wedding."

"Whatever," I say, shrugging again. Apparently this has become my thing. Shrugging without anyone there to see it. I am now shrugging for my own benefit. What will be next? I wonder. Shaking my head no when I want to get a thought out of my head? I try it. But I'm still thinking about Peyton. Her long hair. The way she would bite her lip when she was thinking about something. The way her body was curvy and perfect and made me want to hold her close and protect her. Jesus. All this for a girl I've only met once.

"So it's all good then?" Courtney's asking. "You don't mind that she's coming?"

"Of course I don't mind that she's coming," I lie. "She's your cousin."

And then something occurs to me. If Courtney's calling me to see how I feel about Peyton being at the wedding, she's probably called *Peyton* to see how Peyton feels about *me* being at the wedding. It only makes sense. It's like girl code or whatever. (Which I've never understood, by the way. Girls going around screaming about girl code, when girls are the ones who'll stab each other in the back the first chance they get. Dudes aren't like that. Take Evan, for example. He's up on the roof, shirtless, wearing green goggles and getting ready to possibly kill himself, and what am I doing? I'm sitting here, like a good friend, trying to talk him out of it, while at the same time being willing to film the whole thing if it comes down to it. Now that's what's called being a good friend.)

"Why?" I ask Courtney. "What did Peyton say about me?"

"Nothing."

"Nothing?" From up on the roof, there's the sound of something sloshing around, and then a bunch of water comes sliding down and onto the patio.

"Yes," Courtney says simply. "Nothing."

"Are you sure?" I ask accusingly. "She said *nothing*?"

"She just said she didn't care if you were there."

"She didn't *care* if I was there?"

"That's what she said." I want to ask Courtney what *exactly* Peyton said, but then I realize that hearing Peyton doesn't care is probably enough, especially if I want to protect my mental state.

"Well, whatever," I say. "I'm coming to the wedding. And you don't have to worry about me and Peyton."

"Great," she says, sounding relieved.

We hang up and I look toward the roof warily. Water is still pouring down in rivulets, pooling on the patio in front of me. "Evan?" I call.

"Yes?" He appears at the top of the roof, dripping wet, an empty plastic milk jug in his hand.

"What the *hell* are you doing?"

"I told you," he says. "I'm going to be jumping off this roof and you're going to be filming me."

"But why are you soaking wet? And why are you holding an empty milk jug in your hand?"

"Because," he says, looking at me like I'm the stupid one, "I needed to get my body accustomed to the water by wetting myself with it. I can't just jump in without knowing what I'm getting myself into it. I might get hypothermia or something."

"So you brought a jug of water up and poured it over your head?"

"A jug of pool water," he reports proudly.

"But you were already in the pool," I say. "Why did you have to wet yourself all over again?"

He frowns. "I don't know."

"Listen," I say. "I think you should—"

But before I can stop him, he jumps off the roof and into the water. He does a huge cannonball, and the splash soaks me.

He surfaces at the side of the pool. "Holy shit," he says. "What a rush!" He hoists himself up and onto the patio. "That was just practice, of course."

"Oh, of course." I ring out the bottom of my T-shirt.

"Now you'll film me, right?" He picks up the camera

and shoves it into my hands, then starts heading back to the front of the house so he can get back on the roof.

I flip the camera's power switch to on, and the little red light starts blinking. I sigh. Maybe there's something to that girl code bullshit after all.

peyton | the trip

Saturday, June 26, 10:47 a.m.
Siesta Key, Florida

Jace is so obviously trying not to let me hear the phone call with his mom, but I can still tell that it's not going so well.

The conversation, a summary:

Jace: Oh, hi, Mom, I just wanted to let you know that I'm with Peyton in her hotel room. The thing is—

Jace's mom: What?! You're with a girl in her hotel room? What are you doing in there? Leave at once!

Jace: No, no, it's fine, we're not doing anything. The thing is, Mom, her parents kind of abandoned her here, and so I'm going to be driving her home.

Jace's mom: Oh, okay, honey. That sounds fine. Where does she live?

Jace: Connecticut.

Jace's mom: WHAT?! (Begins to freak out and maybe even swear.)

At this point, Jace leaves the room and walks outside. Of course I can't really be sure of what his mom is saying since I'm hearing it through Jace's cell phone from where I'm changing in the bathroom. So that conversation is pretty much made-up. But still. It's what I imagined, and it's probably scarily accurate.

I look at myself in the huge mirror that's mounted over the double sinks, then run a brush through my hair before changing into a pair of shorts and a soft pink tank top. I take a deep breath, then another and another, trying to calm down and force my heart to stop beating so fast.

It'll be fine, I tell myself. *You'll have Jace drive you where you need to go, and then you can ditch him at a rest stop or something and take a cab to the place you're going to be staying in North Carolina.*

Of course, it's definitely kind of weird to be going without Brooklyn, since I don't know anyone in North Carolina. But there's no way I can go home. Not now. Maybe not ever.

I grab my purse and set it down on the marble countertop, then pull out the brochure from the rental condo that the listing agent sent us a few days ago. The condo was one of the only places that would let you rent if you were under twenty-one, and even then Brooklyn had to sign the rental agreement, since she's eighteen and I'm not.

CREVE COEUR it says on the front of the brochure, and I run my fingers over the letters, over the name of my new building. "Creve Coeur" means broken heart in French. Brooklyn and I both agreed that was a weird name for a condo complex, especially one that's touted as "relaxing and tranquil; only a short drive to the shore!" But whatever. In a way, it was actually pretty fitting. Almost like a sign or something.

When we came up with the plan to go away, Brooklyn had just broken up with her boyfriend, Trevor, who she'd been with for a year and a half. She broke up with him because she said the two of them had nothing to talk about anymore. She cried in her room for two days straight, and I comforted her, although I couldn't figure out how broken her heart could have been when she was the one who broke up with him. If she was so hurt, then why didn't she just call him up and tell him she wanted to get back together?

It wasn't like me and Jace. He had been the one who wanted to end things—not that there was even a thing to end, because it wasn't really like that—so I always felt like my broken heart was a little more serious than Brooklyn's.

Not that I ever told her that. And to her credit, she *had* been with Trevor for a year and a half, while I had only ever seen Jace, um, once. Which is horribly embarrassing when you think about it. That I'd gotten all worked up over a guy I'd only ever spent time with once.

But I read a very smart thing in a self-help book (don't judge—they can actually be very comforting) about how sometimes the people you don't spend that much time with are actually the ones you can end up getting the most hurt by, because you can get attached to the *idea* of them, as opposed to who they really are. You don't get enough time to really get to know them and their flaws, which is why you can sort of create this fantasy of who they are, and therefore indulge all your hopes and dreams of who you wanted them to be.

It was a very smart book.

Anyway, Brooklyn had just broken up with Trevor, and even though I didn't exactly understand how she could be so upset, it ended up working out to my advantage. Because when I came up with the idea of going away for the summer, Brooklyn immediately jumped on it, getting all excited, and even suggesting North Carolina. Which was fine with me. I didn't have a preference about where we went, just as long as it was far away from Connecticut.

Brooklyn knew a boy in North Carolina, a boy she'd met on a vacation to Myrtle Beach a couple years ago, a boy she'd somehow kept in touch with. They'd been talking a little since she broke up with Trevor, and I think she was looking for a rebound.

So North Carolina became the plan, and I let Brooklyn believe I wanted to go just so I could get away from thinking about Jace.

She still has no idea what the real reason is that I wanted to leave home. I thought about telling her, I did. I thought about telling Brooklyn, or my sister, or maybe even my dad. But I didn't. I *couldn't.*

"Peyton?" Jace knocks on the bathroom door.

I shove the Creve Coeur brochure back into my purse. "Yes?" I open the door.

"We're all set!" he says with a smile. "I'm ready to drive you back to Connecticut."

"Are you sure?" I push by him and into the room. "Because it didn't sound like your mom was all that thrilled about it."

"My mom was fine with it."

"Really? Because it sounded like you two were fighting."

"We weren't fighting," he says. "And why were you spying on my phone call?"

"I wasn't eavesdropping on your phone call." I sit down on the bed and then slide my feet into the flip-flops that are sitting on the floor. I really want to wear my sparkly sandals with the low heel, but they're probably not road-trip appropriate. Not to mention I don't want Jace to think I'm trying to impress him. Or that I'm high maintenance.

"If you weren't listening, then how do you know what my mom was saying?" Jace asks.

"I don't know for sure," I say. "But I could hear her voice all the way in the bathroom, so I kind of got the gist."

"I'm a grown man," Jace says, puffing out his chest. "I can take my car wherever I want."

"Really?" I ask. "And who pays for that car?"

Jace glares at me. "Whatever," he says. "Forget it. You can find your own way home."

And that's when I panic. "Hey," I say. "Look, I'm sorry." But he's moving toward the door, and as much as I don't want to, I follow him. I grab his arm just as he's about to walk out, and little sparks zip up my fingers. "Don't go."

He stops, and then, after a beat, he turns around. "Are you going to stop being such a brat?"

"Yes," I say. "I'm sorry." It's not the complete truth. I'm kind of sorry I was a jerk to him, but at the same time, he really does deserve it. On the other hand, just because he broke my heart doesn't mean I should be a bitch to him. I should rise above it, two wrongs don't make a right, you catch more bees with honey or whatever and blah blah blah. Besides, like it or not, right now I need him to take me to North Carolina.

"Truce?" I say, and hold my hand out.

He takes it, his fingers wrapping around mine, making the electricity that's already zinging through me multiply. "Truce," he says.

He holds my hand for a few seconds longer than is really necessary, and we're just standing there, staring at each other, my hand in his, and oh, my God, I want to kiss him so badly it's almost painful.

"Peyton," he says, and he's running his finger over my hand in a little circle, and it's making my body freak out in all the best ways. And for a second, I think he's going to tell me that he's sorry, that he can't believe he ever let me go, that he thinks we should just start over and maybe even be together, that he made a mistake and can I ever forgive him? But then he drops my hand.

"Are you ready to go?" he asks.

I nod, and he moves past me and back into the room, picking up the bags that are sitting on the floor. I feel like a balloon that has been deflated. *Get yourself together, Peyton,* I tell myself as I shoulder my bag and follow Jace out of the room. *Jace Renault is not for you. He's bad news. And thinking anything different, even for a second, is just going to get you hurt.*

the trip jace

Saturday, June 26, 10:59 a.m.
Siesta Key, Florida

Peyton is shady. And not just because she was listening in on my phone call, either. Which, by the way, was none of her business. I'm a grown-ass man. If I want to take my car up to Connecticut, it's none of my mom's business. And it doesn't matter that my mom pays for my car. That's a completely inconsequential fact.

I'm eighteen, and the car is in my name. Which means that if we were in a court of law, she couldn't legally stop me from doing anything I wanted with it. I know my rights. I watch those law shows on TV. (What? They're good. And sometimes there's nothing else on, especially when I'm skipping school.)

Of course, my mom did flip out, mostly because I have graduation tomorrow night and I'm supposed to give a speech since I'm valedictorian. And my mom got all freaked out and started screaming because she thought I wasn't going to be back in time to attend. And so I told her very calmly that I probably wouldn't be. I never wanted to give that stupid graduation speech, anyway. That's when she started screaming some more, and so that's when I hung up on her.

But anyway.

Peyton is shady for lots of reasons, but right now she's shady because she's running away. I don't know much about her family life—she never wanted to let me in on that kind of thing, which is a completely different story—but her mom seems nice enough, if you like those MILF types. Not that I want to bang her mom—cougars aren't really my thing—but I bet Evan would be all over it. So then why is Peyton running away? The summer right before she's supposed to start her senior year? What could be so bad that she can't last at home for one more year before she goes off to college?

I know she has a nice house. I know because I've seen pictures of it—pictures that she sent me. One is of her and her friend Brooklyn, sitting by the fireplace around Christmastime, wearing elf hats, their arms thrown around each other, beaming at the camera. And a couple of, um, more risqué ones she sent me of her in a bathing suit out by her pool. The whole place looked pretty nice.

So then what's her problem? Is she just one of those girls who writes people off without any real reason? Like maybe she and her parents got into some dumb fight about something, and now she's running away?

"Be careful with that one," she instructs as I load one of her suitcases into the trunk of my car. "It has a lot of important things in it."

"Yeah?" I say, tossing it into the trunk. "Like what?"

She glares at me and then starts rearranging all her bags, putting them just so. "Like my computer."

"Oh," I say. "Right. Your computer. We wouldn't want your Twitter log-in getting lost or anything, that's for sure."

"Sorry," she says. "But I don't go on Twitter anymore. Twitter is the new MySpace. I mean, how totally 2011." She wrinkles up her nose, like she's talking about some stupid website for tweens instead of a multibillion dollar website that has become the center of the social media network and changed our culture and the world forever. What a snob.

"Right." I nod and slam the trunk shut. "Well, then, we wouldn't want anyone getting access to any of your personal pictures."

She nods, looking confused for a second. And then understanding dawns on her face. She looks at me in horror. "You better have deleted those."

"Deleted what?" I give her a fake innocent look, which seems to infuriate her.

"You know what I'm talking about." For a second, I think she's going to hold her hand out or something and demand I give them back. Which would be ridiculous. You can't give someone back a digital picture. "Those pictures I texted you."

I pull my phone out and scroll to the one of her in the elf hat. "Oh, you mean this one?" I chuckle and shake my head. "But you look so cute in it!"

She reaches for my phone and I'm so caught off-guard that she's actually able to take it away from me. I'm All-State in basketball, and this chick is actually somehow able to get my phone.

She starts scrolling through the pictures. "I'm deleting the one of me in the elf hat!" she announces.

"Give me that," I say, reaching for it. The thing is, I did delete her stupid bathing suit photos a day after she sent them to me, just like she made me promise. Of course, that was when I was acting like some lovesick schoolboy instead of a grown-ass man who drives his own car wherever he wants.

"No!" she says. "Not until I make sure you deleted those pictures."

I reach for the phone again, but she runs away from me, around toward the front of the car. Now she's standing in front of the hood, and I'm in the back, trying to get at her—it's like some kind of new game, halfway between chicken and freeze tag. An older couple goes walking by and gives us disapproving looks, like they can't believe what the youth of America are up to these days.

"Peyton Miller," I say real loud, "you better give me my

phone back! It's your own fault that you were sexting me inappropriate pictures. If you didn't want me to have them then you shouldn't have sent them."

The older couple looks at us, horrified.

Peyton glares at me and then holds my phone up over her head, like she's going to smash it.

"Put that down!" I yell.

"Ooh, what's wrong?" she says. "Mommy and Daddy won't buy you another one?"

"You can't just go around smashing other people's property!" I say.

The old man and woman are past us now, and I can hear the old man asking his wife what sexting means.

"Take back what you said about me sexting you," Peyton says.

"I take it back." She lowers the phone. "Even though you did."

The phone goes back up over her head.

"Okay, okay," I say, holding my hands up in surrender. "I'm sorry, you're right, you didn't sext me."

She lowers my phone slowly, giving me a chance to take back what I just said. But I don't. "Good," she says. "Because a bathing suit picture hardly counts as a sext." Her face is flushed red, though, and I can tell she's embarrassed thinking about it. I'm a little flushed, too, thinking about it, although not because I'm embarrassed.

I walk around the car toward her and hold my hand

out. But when I get there, she's looking down at the screen.

"Is that her?" She holds it up, and I swallow hard. There's a picture of Kari on the screen, her hair all blond and wild in a ponytail after one of her lacrosse games.

"Yes," I say, taking the phone from her and shoving it in my pocket. "That's Kari."

"She's pretty," Peyton says. For a second, I see the flash of hurt in her eyes, but it's so quick that I wonder if I imagined it.

"Thanks," I say, which makes no sense. Why should I thank her for telling me that Kari is pretty? It's not like I'm responsible for Kari's prettiness.

"Are you ready to go?" Peyton asks. She looks up at me, and my heart catches. I want to explain to her, about what happened last night, about what happened over Christmas, about Kari, about everything. I open my mouth, and she rolls her eyes. "Well?" she demands. "Are you ready or not?"

"Yes," I say. "I'm ready. I just have to get my stuff out of my room. And Hector, too, of course."

She shakes her head. "Hector," she mumbles. "He's probably going to be the only good part of this trip."

before   peyton

So once Courtney called and informed me that Jace was going to be at the wedding after all, I somehow ended up with a very sexy dress. It's this gorgeous turquoise color and it plunges down in the front, making my boobs look bigger than they already are. It's tight and short and has spaghetti straps and it makes my waist seem tiny.

I started grabbing dresses left and right after I hung up the phone, not even looking at prices. Which is why Nicole was ringing us up before I realized that the dress I picked out was eight hundred dollars. Eight hundred dollars. For a dress. My mom's dress was only five hundred. Of course, her hat was another two hundred, so really she ended up spending seven hundred, but still. That's a lot of money for dresses we're probably only going to wear once.

Then, of course, we had to get shoes, and by the time we left the mall, we'd spent close to two thousand dollars.

"Damn," Brooklyn says from my bed as I turn this way and that. It's later that afternoon, and she's come over to inspect my purchases. "That might have been the best eight hundred dollars your mom ever spent."

"You think?" Now that I'm home, I'm starting to feel that this dress might be a little too scandalous for a family wedding. That, and it maybe makes my butt look big.

"Yeah." Brooklyn nods. "You got it going on in that thing."

"Thanks." I run my hands over the shimmery material, not being able to stop myself from wondering what Jace is going to think when he sees me in it. He always told me how much he liked my body. But that could have been a lie. The same way everything else he told me was a lie.

"Uh-oh," Brooklyn says. "You're thinking about him again, aren't you?" She sighs, then reaches over and pinches me hard on the arm.

"Ow!" I say, pulling away from her. "What the hell was that for?"

"That was aversion therapy," she says. "Every time you think of Jace, I'm going to pinch you. And that way, after a while, you won't think about him anymore."

"Either that or I'll just be pissed off at you," I say, rubbing my arm. "And how do you know I was thinking about him?"

"Weren't you?"

"Yes," I admit. I throw myself forlornly down on the bed and stare up at the ceiling. "I was thinking about what he was going to think when he saw me in this dress."

"He's going to think that you look hot and that he made a huge mistake," Brooklyn says. "And he's not going to know what to do with himself."

"Really?" I smile, even though I know in my head that stuff like that only happens in movies and books. More than likely I'll end up at the wedding, looking absolutely phenomenal, and Jace will end up there too, and he'll see me in the dress, but he won't care.

Probably he'll have a new girl with him, or even worse, he'll find another girl at the wedding that he'll dance with all night. She'll be wearing the same dress as me, only hers will fit her even better because she'll be a lot skinnier than me, and it will turn out that Jace doesn't love my body as much as he said. That it was just a ruse to get me to send him a bikini picture.

The two of them will dance all night, and then they'll sneak off into the tropical night air of Florida so that they can—

"I told you that I needed to get a new dress for the wedding!" The sound of my mom's voice comes up the stairs, and I sit up, straining to hear what she's saying. Not like it's hard. She's practically screaming.

"And you couldn't wear one of the millions of dresses you

have in your closet?" my dad yells back. "Christ, Michelle, you spent two hundred dollars on a hat! Two hundred dollars! Do you even understand what money is?"

"Of course I understand what money is!" my mom screams. "How can I not when you keep reminding me of it every single second?"

"Then I don't understand how you could be confused," my dad says, and I hear the sound of them moving toward the back of the house. "If I say it as much as you think I do, then how can you not . . ."

Their voices fade away as my dad follows her around the house. I've seen this dance before. My mom spends money. My dad gets upset with her about it. She knows this, and so sometimes she'll come home and try to hide the stuff she's bought before he sees it. Sometimes he catches her, and then he flips out, following her around the house yelling at her.

The thing is, my parents are technically separated. Well, in the middle of a divorce, really. But they're still living in the same house, mostly because they can't afford to sell it right now—they owe more on the mortgage than it's worth. I'm not sure why my dad doesn't just move out and get an apartment, but I'm pretty sure his lawyer told him not to.

Brooklyn looks at me, her eyes anxious. "You okay?"

"Yeah." I sigh, feeling even more guilty about spending so much on a dress. I reach out and finger the material. "Maybe I should take this back."

Brooklyn stands up and shakes her head. "You know what you need?" she asks. "A burger from McGreedy's."

"No way. I'm not going to start eating a ton of fattening food before the wedding. I need to make sure I look like my most fabulous self."

Brooklyn rolls her eyes. "You've been watching too many Jennifer Hudson Weight Watchers commercials." She picks her purse up off my nightstand. "You already look fabulous. And there's no way you're going to let some guy—no, some *loser*—stop you from eating what might be the world's perfect burger."

I think about it. She is kind of right. I mean, it's not going to matter if I don't eat anything but lettuce from now until the wedding. Jace is probably going to act like a jerk no matter what I do, and then not only will I be all upset about it, but I won't even have been able to enjoy any really good food in the meantime.

"Can we get fries, too?" I ask, perking up.

"Yes."

"And afterward can we go and look at lip glosses?"

"Yes," Brooklyn says. She grins. "Just because you don't care enough about what Jace thinks to change your eating habits doesn't mean we shouldn't use him as an excuse to buy beauty products."

jace ➤ before

Fucking Peyton Miller. Ever since Courtney called me earlier, Peyton is all I can think about. I keep looking at the dumb picture of her that I have in my phone. It's her and her friend Brooklyn sitting in front of the fireplace on Christmas wearing these goofy Santa hats. She has her hair pushed back from her face and she looks so adorable I almost can't take it.

"So then I jumped off the roof," Evan's saying, "and right into the pool."

"You didn't," Kari McAfee says.

"I did." Evan nods. "Jace got it all on video, didn't you, Jace?"

"Unfortunately, yes," I admit. I did get the whole thing on video. If it ever gets out I'll probably get sued or something.

355

Okay, that's going a little too far. But I would definitely get in trouble with Evan's parents.

"Next I want to do a prank." Evan takes a big bite of the hot dog he's eating. We're sitting on the bleachers at our school, watching one of the last baseball games of the season. Actually, I guess it's one of the last baseball games of my whole high school career. The thought should make me sad—I am valedictorian after all—but somehow, it doesn't. "You up for a prank, Jace?"

"What kind of prank?" I ask warily.

"I dunno." Evan shrugs and then shoves the rest of his hot dog into his mouth. "I saw this one on YouTube that had like a million hits. This dude filled his parents' house with bottles of water while they were on vacation. You know, he like, moved all the furniture out, everything. It was hi*lar*ious!"

"That sounds lame," I say. "And besides, your parents never go on vacation."

"We wouldn't have to do that exact one," Evan says, like it should be obvious. "We'd come up with something better."

"I think it sounds cool," Whitney Blue says. She scoots a little closer to Evan on the bleachers, and I tune them out as they start to talk about all the different pranks they might be able to do.

I shove my phone back into my pocket and try to get Peyton out of my thoughts. It's been three months since we've spoken. Three months. Three months is a lifetime.

She could be doing anything right now. She could have a boyfriend. A boyfriend who she's bringing to the wedding. A boyfriend I'll have to see her with. A knot forms in my stomach and I feel my fists clench as I think about having to see some asshole with his hands all over Peyton. Not that I would ever punch someone out. Well, that's not that true. I would if someone was hurting her.

"Penny for your thoughts?" a voice says. I turn to see Kari scooting closer to me on the bleachers. She holds out her container of nachos and I take one.

"Thanks," I say, grateful for the distraction. I drag the chip through the melted orange cheese and pop it in my mouth.

"So what's new?" she asks. Kari and I have been friends ever since sophomore year, when she transferred to our school from New York City. Everyone was afraid of her at first because she showed up wearing black jeans and a black sweater. Yes, we wear black in Florida, but not all black, and not with knee-high boots. Half the school thought she was going to fight them. Well, the girls at least. And maybe some of the boys.

"Not much," I say. "What's new with you?"

"Same old," she says. She flips her head over and gathers her long blond hair up in a ponytail. Kari totally assimilated to Florida, dying her hair blond and ditching the black clothes for the jeans-and-tank-top uniform of the Gulf Coast. She even joined the soccer team.

We lapse back into silence. "What's wrong with you?" she asks.

"Nothing," I say. "Why?"

"Because you're being all quiet," she says. She elbows me playfully in the side.

"I'm fine," I say, and shrug. "Just tired." I look out onto the field as Ian Walker strikes out. Everyone on our side of the bleachers groans. I roll my eyes. Ian Walker is a douche, and everyone knows it.

"Late night last night?" Kari asks.

"Not really," I say. I'm not much of a partier, and Kari knows it, so she's teasing me.

"Well, you should hang out with us tonight," she says. "Me and Whitney are having a slumber party, aren't we, Whit?" She turns and looks over her shoulder to where Whitney and Evan are sitting on the bleachers behind us.

"If you call just the two of us a slumber party," Whitney says.

"Oh, I definitely call that a slumber party," Evan says, raising his eyebrows up and down suggestively.

"You can come too," Whitney says to Evan. "We're having it at my house."

"Oh, really?" Evan licks his lips and rubs his hands together, like there's going to be all kinds of debauchery happening. Which is ridiculous. And kind of creepy.

But Whitney doesn't seem to mind. She giggles. "You

guys can't sleep over, though. We'll just watch movies or something."

Evan looks a little disappointed, like he thought he was going to actually be able to spend the night. Which is stupid for a few reasons, not the least of which is that Evan's mom is the strictest parent I know. I think that's maybe why he's always trying to do crazy stunts—it's like he's rebelling, only instead of doing drugs or alcohol, he takes chances with his safety.

"I'll watch movies," Evan says. "I'll bring some scary ones."

Kari looks at me. "You in?"

"Sure." I shrug. "Why not?" It will give me something to do to get my mind off Peyton. Although with the way I'm feeling right now, that's going to be a tall order. I hope Evan brings a really, really good movie.

"Do I look okay?" Evan asks me as we walk up the driveway of Whitney's house later that night. He's wearing jeans and a black sweater. "I just bought this sweater," he says proudly. "It's Gucci."

I roll my eyes, then reach over and pull the Old Navy tag off the back. "You left the tag on."

"Oh." Evan frowns, then rips it in half and throws it on the ground.

"Jesus," I say, picking it up. "You like this girl and you're disrespecting her property like that?" I shove the tag back into his hand. "Throw it in the garbage when you get inside."

He looks aghast. "No way. What if she sees it?"

"What if she sees it out here?"

"Jace, she's not going to see some random tag out here on the lawn. And if she does, maybe she'll think it blew over from a neighboring house."

"A neighboring house?" I shake my head. "Why are you talking like that?"

"I'm trying to seem more refined." He squares his shoulders. "I think it's important to cultivate a good vocabulary."

We're not even inside yet and this is already turning into a debacle. "Look," I say. "Whitney likes you. Otherwise she wouldn't have invited you here tonight. Now you should just be yourself."

Evan looks horrified. "I would never be myself," he says.

"Why not?"

"Because myself isn't really all that likeable."

"That's not true," I say, even though it kind of is. If I were a chick, I doubt I'd be that interested in Evan. Although all those guys from *Jackass* seem to get a lot of women, so maybe he's onto something. Besides, what the hell do I know?

Up until this Christmas, when I met Peyton, I'd been doing pretty well with the ladies. It seemed like every month I had a new one. (I was starting to get a little worried about myself, honestly, wondering if maybe I was turning into a male slut.)

And then I met Peyton at the Christmas party, and it was like I got sucker punched. Suddenly, I didn't want any other girls. I didn't even want to *look* at another girl or *talk* to another girl, much less hook up with one. It was pretty intense. And then after Peyton and I stopped talking, I never really recovered. I could still appreciate when a girl was good-looking, of course. It just wasn't the same.

"Look," I say to Evan now, "you should just be yourself. Otherwise you're going to get stuck playing a part the whole time you're around her."

He frowns, considering what I've just said. "You think?"

"Absolutely." I reach out and ring the doorbell. "Don't go changing just because of some chick."

"Yeah!" he says, nodding his head. "I'm not going to go around changing for *any* chick."

"Just be honest and be yourself." I meet Evan's outstretched fist with mine for a pound.

"Hey," Whitney says when she opens the door. "Come on in, guys. Kari's in the kitchen ordering pizza."

Evan holds his hand out to Whitney and she looks at him, puzzled. "Can you throw this away?" He uncurls his fingers to reveal the ripped Old Navy tag. "I bought this sweater at Old Navy today in an effort to impress you and I forgot to take the tag off."

"Um, sure," Whitney says, taking it. She looks at me as I brush by her and into the house.

"Don't ask." I shake my head. Maybe that wasn't the best advice, telling Evan to be himself. After all, I was myself with Peyton, and look where that got me.

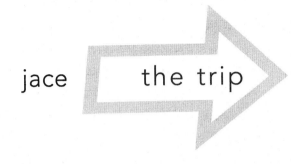

jace · the trip

"Is this car even safe?" Peyton asks as we pull out onto the road.

"Of course it's safe," I say. "I'm very good about upkeep." That's bullshit. I'm good about keeping the inside of my car clean just in case I happen to have a girl in here or something, but other than that, I'm pretty lax. I'm not the best with oil changes. One time I heard from a mechanic that you don't have to have your oil changed more than once every five thousand miles, and if you do, you're just getting ripped off. I took the advice to heart.

"Somehow I doubt that." She scans the backseat, looking for something she can call me out on, some misplaced fast-food wrapper or empty soda can. But there's nothing. The only thing back there is Hector. My dog.

Well, not *my* dog exactly. A few days ago, Evan showed

up at my house with Hector, a golden retriever mix, and somehow conned me into letting the dog stay. Hector was supposed to be a present for Whitney, but it turns out she's allergic. So now Evan's trying to find a new home for him, and since Evan's parents are super strict and wouldn't let the dog stay at their house, I got stuck with him.

And since I couldn't leave Hector at home while my family went to the wedding, he was with me in my hotel room last night. Which means he's now coming on this road trip.

Peyton gives Hector a scratch on the chin, and he licks her hand. "Good boy," she says, all gentle. "You're so beautiful."

I snort.

She glares at me. "Only a jerk hates a dog."

"I don't hate him," I say. "I just don't understand why everyone loves him so much. Yes, he's cute, but looks aren't everything now, are they?"

"I don't know," she says, all snotty. "You tell me."

She leans back in her seat and closes her eyes before I can come up with a witty comeback. I sneak a glance at her. God, she's beautiful. I shake my head, disgusted with myself for having these thoughts, and pull the car down the curving road of the yacht club and toward the exit. When I get through the gate at the end of the winding drive, I pull my car onto the main road and start to coast toward the highway.

"Um, hello?" I say to Peyton.

"What?" she snaps, her eyes still closed. She reaches down and hits the lever on the side of the seat and drops it back. Hector moves forward and rests his chin next to Peyton's head, then gives a happy little sigh. Great. Now it's two against one. Figures.

"Do you have directions?" I ask.

"To where?"

"Um, to Connecticut?"

Her eyes pop open. "No," she says, looking a little panicked. "I don't have directions."

"So then how are we supposed to get there?"

She bites her lip, thinking about it. "Can't we just drive north?" she asks. "Connecticut's north. We're bound to hit it eventually."

"Oh, yeah, that's a really great plan," I say. "Just keep driving north until we 'hit it eventually.'" I shake my head. "For someone who was so worried about the safety of my car, you're not really that prepared."

"Sorry I don't have directions to my house in Connecticut," she says, rummaging around in her purse. "But I thought I was going to North Carolina. And besides, don't you have a GPS?"

"No."

"*No?*"

"No! Why would I have a GPS? Until this morning, I was planning on going home right after brunch, which is a fifteen-minute drive that I know very well, not a fifteen-*hour* drive that is going to take me God knows where."

"Twenty-seven," she says.

"What?"

"Twenty-seven-hour drive."

"It's *twenty-seven hours* to your house?"

She shrugs. "I thought you knew."

"And how would I have—?" I cut myself off. Nothing good is going to come of us arguing the whole time. Besides, it's way too early in the trip for us to be fighting at all. Shouldn't our fights be reserved for later in the day, when things have gone wrong and we're tired and cranky? "Look, never mind," I say, shaking my head. "We need to stop and buy a GPS."

"Hold on," she says. "I think I have one on my cell." She has her phone out, and she's looking down at the screen. "What the hell?" She frowns, then turns it off and then back on again. "My phone's not working."

"Did you drop it or something?" I ask.

She shakes her head.

"Well, I hope you backed up all your pictures," I say. "We wouldn't want you losing any of those now, would we?"

But she's not listening. She's just staring down at her phone, with a look of understanding on her face. "What?" I ask. "What is it? What's wrong?"

"My phone's shut off," she says. "It . . . it's not broken, it just . . ."

"What, you forgot to pay the bill or something?"

"Yeah, or something." She sighs, then rubs her temples with her fingertips. She looks so small just sitting there like that that I start to feel a little bad for her.

"Look, don't worry about it," I say. "We're going to stop and get a GPS. And if you need to use my phone to make calls, you can. It's not a big deal."

She shakes her head slightly, and gets a faraway look in her eyes, and I'm afraid that maybe she's going to start crying again. "Peyton," I say softly. "It's okay. I'm going to take care of everything. Don't worry, all right?"

And after a second, she nods.

When we pull into a parking lot of a Target about fifteen minutes later, Peyton seems to have calmed down a little bit. She slides her sunglasses down over her eyes and walks with me through the parking lot toward the store, still not saying anything.

She grabs a basket when we get inside. "A basket just for a GPS?" I ask.

"I need a few things that I forgot," she says. "Um, shampoo, stuff like that." She doesn't say it bratty, though.

"Okay."

"You might want to get some stuff, too," she says. "You know, just in case we have to spend the night somewhere."

The thought of spending the night with her makes my pulse race. Just the two of us. Alone in a motel room. Maybe there will only be one room left, with one bed. I'll try to sleep on the floor of course, but then in the middle of the night it will be bothering my back too much and I'll have to sneak up—

"Hey!" a voice booms out in front of me. I look up to see a guy standing in front of us. For a second, I can't really place him, but then, when I do, my heart sinks. B.J. "Peyton and Jace! Nice to see you two crazy kids!"

"Nice to see you, too," Peyton says. Which I really wish she wouldn't have done.

B.J. has a screw loose. He's Courtney's boyfriend Jordan's best friend, and he's definitely not all there. Who knows what kind of shenanigans he's up to?

I give him a slight smile, then take Peyton's arm and start trying to steer her past him.

"I'm B.J.!" B.J. says. "Don't act like you don't remember, Jacey! Not after what we talked about last night." He gives me a wink, and I pray to God he doesn't bring up what we were talking about last night. Not in front of Peyton. "We're friends. At least, I thought we were." He opens the box of Twinkies he's holding and pulls one out, breaks it in half, and licks out some of the frosting.

"Yeah," I say. "I know, I remember. That was fun, haha." I try to steer Peyton around him again, but he follows us.

"You want some Twinkie?" He holds it out to Peyton, probably because he can tell there's no way in hell I would take it. He obviously doesn't know Peyton that well, because there's no way in hell she's going to take it, either. She's way too uptight.

"Thanks," Peyton says. She reaches out and grabs the Twinkie half and takes a bite. "I'm starving."

B.J. nods. "Me too," he says. "You know you're allowed to eat food in the store as long as you pay for it when you check out?"

"No," I say, "I didn't know that." Not only is this dude really fucking annoying, he's also kind of disgusting. He has frosting smeared all over his lips, which isn't really the best look for anyone.

"I did," Peyton says. "Whenever I go grocery shopping with my mom I always open up a bag of Oreos."

B.J. nods. "So smart," he says. "It's like I'm always telling Jordan—"

"Yeah, okay," I say. "Sounds good, but we're actually in a bit of a hurry."

"How come?" B.J. asks conversationally.

"It's kind of classified," I say. "Sorry."

"Jace is driving me home to Connecticut," Peyton reports. "My ride totally bailed on me."

"That sucks," B.J. says. He's reaching into the box for another Twinkie. He breaks it in half and hands one piece to Peyton. "Hey, you know that Jordan and Courtney drove from Florida to Boston once, right? It was cool; they ended up getting back together on that trip. Well, not exactly *on* the trip, but—"

"Well, that will definitely not be happening to us," I say, cutting him off. I give him a look, a look that says, "go away and don't you dare bring up what we were talking about last night."

"Definitely not," Peyton agrees.

"But last night—" B.J. starts, sounding confused.

"No," I say, giving him a firm look. And somehow, miraculously, it seems like he gets the message.

He nods. "Yeah," he says. "I guess that makes sense." He turns to Peyton. "You're so cool, Peyton, and Jacey's a little . . ." He trails off, maybe because he realizes that I'm standing right there.

"Can we just get the GPS please and get out of here?" I ask.

"What do you need a GPS for?" B.J. asks, following us.

"Because I don't really know the way home from here," Peyton explains.

I pick up my pace until I'm a few steps ahead of them, listening as they babble about Jordan and Courtney and road trips and a bunch of other nonsense. I'm about to lose my shit when B.J. says, "All right, well, I'll see you guys later. I have to go look at some costumes."

"Costumes?" Peyton asks.

He nods. "Yup. We're going to have a big costume party on the beach tonight. At least, I'm trying to get it to be a costume party. I love costumes." He takes another bite of Twinkie. "They're just so *fun*."

"Okay, well, I hope you have a good time," I say. "See you later." Or not.

Peyton says goodbye to B.J, and then he disappears into the aisles.

"That dude is crazy," I say.

"I like him," Peyton says. "He's different."

I snort. "Yeah, if by different you mean totally out of his tree."

She rolls her eyes. "It figures you would say something like that."

We're in the electronics aisle now, and those moments of vulnerability she had in the car, when she was leaning back with her eyes closed, and then again when she was upset about her phone being turned off are long gone. Now she's back to acting like she's totally in control with a little bit of brattiness thrown in for good measure.

"What's that supposed to mean?" I ask, following her to the display of GPSs.

"Nothing." She shrugs. "Just that you don't like anything that's not cookie-cutter." She surveys the display and then shakes her head. "Why are these things so expensive?"

I follow her around the corner of the aisle while she looks at the rest of the units. "I like things that aren't cookie-cutter," I say, sounding defensive.

"Ha!" She kneels down and starts looking at the GPS units in a glass case. "Name one band you like that they don't play on the radio."

"Guru Steve."

"Guru Steve?" she repeats, tilting her head. "Isn't that . . . isn't that your *friend's* band?"

"Yeah, so what?"

"Oh, my God." She rolls her eyes. "You're hopeless."

"Just because I don't like all kinds of crazy indie music, now I'm hopeless?"

"Yes." She's standing up now, looking around and sighing loudly. "How come I can never find a salesperson when I need one? Someone needs to open this case."

"I'll have you know," I say, "that I am into a lot of things that people aren't into at first. For example, I was the first one out of all my friends to have a Twitter account."

"Only counts if you have your name."

"What?"

"Were you able to score the Twitter user name Jace?"

"Well, no," I say, "that would be impossible. And besides, I wouldn't want that name anyway. Too much pressure."

"Too much pressure?"

"Yeah, like if you don't tweet interesting things all the time, people think you don't deserve the name and that you should give it up to some other, cooler Jace."

"Whatever." She shakes her head. "Are you going to find me a salesperson or not?"

"Fine." I stomp off, wondering if what she said is really true. But there's no way I'm cookie-cutter. And the fact that she said that just proves that Peyton Miller doesn't know anything. I scan the aisles, looking for a salesperson, but of course there aren't any.

I sigh. Peyton's right about one thing: You can never find a salesperson when you need one.

the trip   peyton

Saturday, June 26, 12:07 p.m.
Bradenton, Florida

I cannot believe my phone got turned off. Actually, that's a lie. I *can* believe my phone got turned off, and I know exactly why it got turned off too. Because my mom didn't pay the bill. And I know why she didn't pay the bill. Because she doesn't have any money.

I'm so frustrated that I almost kick at one of the shelves in the electronics section. Which would be a disaster because I definitely don't have the money to pay for those kind of damages. So instead, I punch the air as hard as I can. Just like that, the anger's gone, and for a second, I feel like I'm going to cry. But then *that's* gone, too, and now I just feel really depressed.

I open my purse and look through my wallet. I have three hundred dollars. I figured that would be enough traveling money to get me to North Carolina, since everything was mostly already paid for. Brooklyn was going to use her mom's credit card to pay for the rental car, and I was going to pay her back once we got to North Carolina and I found a job.

But now that I'm going to have a buy a GPS, I'm not sure how much money I'm going to have left over. The cheapest GPS they have here is almost a hundred bucks. And with tax, that's going to leave me barely enough to support myself in North Carolina until I can find a job. Not to mention that at some point I'm going to have to figure out what I'm going to do about my cell phone. I need to get it turned back on, but who knows how much that's going to cost? And what if Jace and I need to get a hotel?

By the time Jace finally returns with the salesperson, I feel like maybe I'm going to have a nervous breakdown.

"I finally found someone," Jace says. "Someone" is a pimply-faced guy who looks like he's around twenty-one, and that the last place he wants to be spending his Saturday morning is here, selling me a GPS.

"Is that the cheapest one you have?" I ask, pointing to some no-name brand GPS that looks like it's definitely going to break in about two weeks. But who cares? If it can last a couple of days, I'll be happy.

"I dunno." The guy shrugs.

"Well, do you sell maps here?" I don't know how to fold a map, much less read one, but desperate times call for desperate measures.

"Hey, don't worry about it," Jace says to me. "I'm paying for the GPS."

I shake my head. I'm no one's charity case. If there's one thing this whole situation with my mom has taught me, it's that I need to stand on my own two feet. Which is one of the reasons I'm running away. Well, that and the horrible thing she did to me. The horrible thing I'll never get over, the horrible thing I'm not going to think about right now, and maybe not ever, thank you very much.

"No way," I say. "You're not buying it."

"Relax," Jace says, rolling his eyes like I'm stupid for thinking he was trying to do something nice for me. "I need one for my car anyway. This way I can keep it after I drop you off. I'm going to have to get home somehow."

"Oh." In that case, I guess it's okay.

I step back while Jace looks through the case. I watch his eyes move over each GPS—watch as he asks a bunch of questions. I think about what happened last night in his hotel room, and close my eyes for a second, wishing I were back there, before Brooklyn bailed on me, before I found out Jace was a big liar after all, before I was dealing with any of this.

After a few minutes, Jace settles on the GPS that he wants, and then we split up. I fill my basket with shampoo (generic), conditioner (generic), and a bottle of water (generic). Then we meet back up at the register, where I pay for my stuff, and Jace pays for the GPS and some bones for Hector. So I guess he's not completely heartless.

As we walk back out to the parking lot, my stomach is in knots. The warm Florida air is helping a little bit, though, and I raise my face to the sun, willing the vitamin D to help my mood.

Jace unlocks the car and I slide into the passenger seat. Hector immediately starts licking my face, glad that we're back, glad that he hasn't been abandoned in the car.

"Good boy," I say, giving him a scratch on his chin and burying my face in his soft fur.

We have a GPS. Now I just have to figure out how I'm going to get Jace to bring me to North Carolina while thinking he's taking me to Connecticut.

before   peyton

Saturday, May 22, 7:07 pm
Greenwich, Connecticut

I'm just about to finish my frozen yogurt when my cell phone rings.

"It's my mom," I tell Brooklyn. "She's probably wondering where I am." I left my house without telling my mom or dad where I was going, mostly because they were still fighting about those stupid dresses when I left, and I didn't want to have to deal with it. Sneaking out was a good decision. The burgers we ate were amazing, and the frozen yogurt we got for dessert is even better.

"Hello?" I say, swirling the rest of my peanut butter cup yogurt around the last piece of Oreo cookie that's in my bowl.

"Peyton!" my mom yells. "Where are you?"

"Getting frozen yogurt with Brooklyn," I say.

"Well, you need to come home immediately." In the background, there's a frantic rustling noise.

"Why?" I ask warily.

"Because we need to take these dresses back! And the shoes! And the hat! Your father is acting ridiculous about it and so now I have to spend my Saturday night back at the mall, returning things!" At the last part of her statement, her voice raises, I'm assuming so that my dad will be able to hear her. Not that it's necessary. I'm sure she already told him all of this while they were fighting.

"Mom," I say, "you're freaking out about nothing. Just wait a little while until this blows over and then I'm sure you'll be able to keep the dresses."

She should know this. It's a total pattern that my parents have. My mom goes out and spends a lot of money, my dad freaks out about it, they get into a fight, then my mom freaks out about it even more and starts ranting and raving about how she's going to just take everything back and can you believe her husband did this to her and blah blah blah. Then my dad relents and shakes his head and says that's why they're getting divorced and then goes into his home office and slams the door and doesn't come out for hours.

"No," my mom says. "We're taking them back. Meet me at the mall in fifteen minutes." The line goes dead.

"What was that all about?" Brooklyn asks.

I sigh, then eat my last spoonful of frozen yogurt. "I have to meet my mom at the mall," I say. "Can you drop me off?"

"Of course." She looks at me across the table sympathetically. Brooklyn's the only one I've ever told about my parents fighting about money the way they do. She's super understanding about it, even though her parents' relationship is, like, as normal as you can get.

But for some reason, I still haven't told her about my parents getting divorced. In fact, I haven't told anyone. I don't know why. Maybe it's because I don't really believe it's really going to happen, since my parents don't ever follow through on anything.

Of course, I could just be in denial.

I push that thought out of my mind, then get up and toss my empty yogurt cup into the trash before following Brooklyn out to the parking lot.

By the time I get to the mall, my mom is all smiles again. "Hello!" she says when she sees me. "I worked it out with your father, and so we get to keep the dresses."

I sigh. "Then, Mom, why did you make me come all the way down here? I was out with Brooklyn, and we were—"

"Because part of the deal was that I would return the hat." I look down to the register kiosk she's standing in front of and see the hat there, thrown haphazardly on the counter.

Nicole comes scampering over. "Can I help you?" she asks brightly, but her smile falters as she realizes it's me and my mom, back to torture her some more.

"Yes," my mom says, wrinkling up her nose. "We need to return this hideous hat."

"Okay." Nicole picks it up and looks at the price tag. "Do you have your receipt?"

"Of course I have my receipt, I just bought it this morning." My mom slides it across the counter toward her, and Nicole gets to work entering the information for the return into the cash register.

"I'm sorry you had to return your hat, Mom," I say.

She waves her hand like it's nothing, even though she was just freaking out about it at home. "It's okay," she says. And then she lowers her voice. "Whatever you do, Peyton, make sure you don't marry for money." She sighs and looks wistfully at the hat. "Because money comes and goes."

I resist the urge to roll my eyes. My mom makes no secret of the fact that she married my dad for his money. My mom is adopted, and she grew up in a house where they didn't have a lot of material things. They weren't poor— just average middle class. They lived in a nice house, but scrimped to be able to afford it and to send my mom to a nice school. My mom was friends with all the popular, rich kids, and she confessed to me once that she always felt like she needed to keep up with them.

And I think—and this is my own idea, not something I've ever heard my mom say—that along the way, my mom somehow took the fact that she was adopted and extrapolated that into the idea that she was meant to be rich. Almost like she thought that her biological family had come from money, and so that was the kind of person she was supposed to be. Never mind that she knew nothing about her birth mom, and never really showed any interest in finding her. (Probably because she was afraid she'd find out she wasn't wealthy after all.)

Anyway, when she graduated college, she became determined to marry a man who had money. Right after she turned twenty-three, she married my dad, who was thirty at the time. He was a real-estate developer, and was making millions flipping properties and investing in commercial buildings.

They had my older sister, Kira, a year later, and my theory is that my mom didn't want to work and thought it would be easier to get away with that if she had a kid. When Kira was five and ready to start kindergarten, my mom had me, and by the time *I* was ready to go to school my mom was thirty-three and had been out of the workforce for ten years and so it was just easier for her to stay home.

Somewhere along the way, I think my dad started resenting her for it. And as the real-estate market started getting progressively worse, and my dad started making less and less money, my mom refused to—or couldn't?—cut back on her spending. And their marriage started falling apart.

Which is why I would never, ever let myself get all worked up about some guy because of his money. I mean, that's really the last thing my mom needs to be worrying about. In fact, if there's one thing this whole thing with Jace has taught me, it's that guys in general shouldn't be your focus. Ever.

"Come on," my mom says as Nicole hands her the slip showing her credit card has been refunded for the cost of the hat. "Let's go have dinner."

"Do you think that's a good idea?" I ask. I'm not sure we should really be spending more money, but I'm not going to come right out and say that because I know that's not what my mom wants to hear.

"Of course," she says, and rolls her eyes. "We're not destitute, Peyton." From behind the cash register, I see a slight smile tug at Nicole's lips, and I know she knows that my mom had to return the hat because she couldn't afford it. And I also know that Nicole kind of likes that.

I know my mom was a total jerk to her, and I know Nicole has to deal with horrible, demanding people all day, but still. It makes me hate her a little. Which then makes me hate myself a little because come on—who hates a salesperson? And then I start to feel bad that I feel bad for hating her, because shouldn't my loyalties always lie with my mom? Ahhh!

By the time we're finished eating dinner at the sushi place across the street (I barely have three pieces since I'm full from my burger and frozen yogurt) I'm exhausted from all the emotional upheavery, and so as soon as I get home, I decide to take a nap. I'm a big fan of naps, especially late-night ones. I don't think they really count as time spent sleeping because you always end up waking up and then staying up later than you would have if you hadn't napped.

So really it's more like displaced sleeping.

My dad's car wasn't in the driveway when we pulled in, which meant he was probably off at some job site or scoping out a property. The weird thing about my dad and his job is that even though it doesn't seem like he's making much money, he's never—at least as far as I know—considered looking for some other kind of work. He just keeps pumping money into the business, taking out different loans and mortgages, making it almost impossible to turn a profit unless he gets an immediate sale. It seems crazy if you ask me, but of course, no one ever does.

Once I'm in a tank top and leggings, I snuggle into bed with my phone next to me. I run my finger over the Internet icon, willing myself not to do it. But I already know I'm going to. I'm like a junkie.

I pull up Jace's Facebook page. I hardly ever go on here anymore. I did a lot in the beginning, when we first stopped talking. But I made a promise to myself that I would stop, that it was just too hard to see his pictures, to read his status updates, to know what was going on his life.

But it's like a drug, and today, I can't stop myself. I flick through his pictures. The ones I know almost by heart. Jace with his friend Evan at a Rays game. Jace with his dad on vacation at Daytona Beach. Jace with his basketball team after a game.

I stay on each picture for a few moments, running my eyes over his face, his clothes, his hands, looking for any new detail I can find. I hold my breath when I get to the last pictures, wondering if there's going to be any new photos, any new images that will give me details about what Jace has been up to.

But there aren't.

I put my phone down on the pillow and stare up at the ceiling, wondering what he's doing right now. Is he with another girl? Is he doing homework? Is he eating dinner, out with friends, getting ready to take a nap like me?

You could text him, I think. The thought sends a delicious, dangerous little shiver up my spine.

I tiptoe out of bed, feeling like a thief in the night, and open the top drawer of my desk. Inside, there's a scrap of paper with Jace's phone number scrawled on it. I wrote it down after I deleted his number from my phone, just in case I ever needed it again. The paper is folded into a tight square and wrapped with Scotch tape, and on the front, I wrote "DO NOT OPEN THIS UNDER PENALTY OF DEATH."

Which was a really stupid thing to write, since of course I wasn't going to *die* if I opened it. No one even knew it existed except for me. I run my finger over the words on the front. Part of one side of the Scotch tape is pulled up, from a near miss I had a month or so ago.

Of course, I think as I put the folded square back into my desk, the paper is pointless. I know Jace's number by heart.

I crawl back into bed and tap the number into my phone, staring at the numbers on the screen. Then I type Hey—am going to Courtney's dad's wedding, I hope that's okay.

No, sounds too lame, like I'm asking his permission. I erase it immediately, then try something else.

Hi—know we haven't talked in a while, but didn't want it to be awkward when we saw each other at the wedding so thought I would say hi ☺

Hmm. I read it over, then erase the smiley face. What I really need to do is call Brooklyn and ask her for advice. She comes up with the best texts and e-mails. It's like her hidden talent. But there's no way I can do that, because she would tell me not to text him at all. And now that I've made the decision to do it, there's no going back.

I delete the part about me saying hi. Because that sounds really fake and also like maybe I'm just looking for an excuse to talk to him. Which I am, but still. There's no way I want him to know that.

I decide I'm thinking about this way too much, and so before I can stop myself, I delete the whole last text and then quickly type something else.

I hit send before I can obsess about how it sounds, and then slide my phone under my pillow. I'm not going to check to see if he wrote back until I wake up.

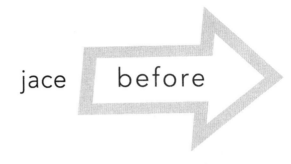

jace before

Saturday, May 22, 8:35 p.m.
Sarasota, Florida

"See?" Evan yells, standing up and pointing at the TV screen. "Do you see how amazing that was? How cool it looked when I jumped into the pool?"

We're at Whitney's house, and instead of watching a scary movie, we've somehow ended up watching the video of Evan jumping into his pool. He's already loaded it up onto YouTube, I guess this afternoon, despite his busy sweater-buying schedule.

And when he found out that Whitney had Apple TV, he insisted that we watch it. YouTube really shouldn't allow you to post videos so quickly, I think, watching as Evan beams at his own craziness.

"It looks cool, doesn't it, Jace?" he asks.

"It does." I'm not lying. It does look cool, if you can get over the craziness of it. When Evan jumps off the roof, he sort of scissors his legs in the air. I don't think he did it on purpose—I think he was just scared and a little panicked—but it still looks badass.

"I can't believe you did that," Whitney says, and shakes her head. "I mean, weren't you scared you were going to hit your head and die?"

"Courage," Evan says, and takes a bite of his pizza, "is doing things you don't want to do even when you're scared. Bravery isn't about not being scared; it's about facing your fear and doing it anyway."

I resist the urge to roll my eyes, then get up and head to the kitchen for another soda.

While I'm in there, my cell phone vibrates and I look down. A text. From someone who's not in my contacts. From an 860 area code. **Hey Jace, it's Peyton. Courtney told me you were coming to the wedding so I just wanted to reach out in case it was going to be awkward.**

I blink my eyes, not really sure I'm seeing what I'm seeing. *Peyton* is texting me? Peyton has the *nerve* to be texting me? Is she crazy? *Just wanted to reach out in case it was going to be awkward.* Ha! Of course things are going to be awkward.

Why is she going to the stupid wedding, anyway? She lives in Connecticut for God's sake. Only one of us should be allowed to go to the wedding, and it should be me because of geographic desirability. Who cares if she's family and I'm just the son of the couple's friends?

"Who texted you?" Evan asks, walking into the kitchen behind me.

"No one," I say, shoving my phone back in my pocket. I'm not replying to that. If Peyton thinks she can just text me out of nowhere, and pretend like everything's okay with us, then she has another thing coming.

Evan gives me a look.

"What?" I ask. I open the fridge and grab another soda. Although now that Peyton texted me, I feel like I want something harder. A beer, a shot, anything. I scan the shelves of the refrigerator, but there's nothing. Either Whitney's parents don't drink, or they know enough to keep their booze out of their teenage daughter's reach when they're not at home.

"Come on, Jace," Evan says. "Who texted you?"

I think about lying, but to do that would give Peyton more power. So I reach into the refrigerator and pull out a soda and uncap it. "Peyton."

"Peyton?" Evan exclaims. "What the fuck?"

I give him a dirty look.

"Screw her," he says.

I don't say anything.

"Right, Jace?" he asks, not sounding so sure.

"Right."

"Do you want to talk about it?"

"No."

"Okay." He hoists himself up onto the counter and looks at

me. "But maybe you will at some point, right? Maybe at some point you'll tell me what happened between you guys?"

"Probably not."

"How come?"

"Because nothing happened," I say, starting to get really annoyed. I start opening cabinets in Whitney's kitchen, looking for anything I can eat or drink to distract myself.

"Um, I don't think you should be doing that," Evan says. "It's not your house; you shouldn't just be going through the cabinets like that."

"Oh, now you're the morality police?" I say grumpily.

"You don't have to freak out, dude."

"Look, I'm sorry," I say. I close the cupboard and run my fingers through my hair. "I just didn't want to get that text, you know?" Why the fuck did she text me? I'd just stopped thinking about her, and now, in one day, I've had two reminders of her. First Courtney, and now Peyton herself.

Maybe I shouldn't go to the wedding. I'm obviously emotionally fragile.

"You sure you don't want to tell me what happened?" Evan asks. "It might help you to talk about it."

I sigh. Maybe I should tell him. It would be good to get it off my chest. "Well," I say. "We—"

"Hey!" Whitney says, appearing in the kitchen. "What are you guys doing in here? Because if you're looking for alcohol, I keep it in my room." She grins.

"We were just talking," Evan says. "If you could give us—"

"We were just finishing up," I say. "And I'd love a beer if you have one."

"Sounds good." She grins. "Let's go up to my room."

Thirty minutes later, we're in Whitney's room, and I have a good buzz going. There's a movie playing on the big flat-screen TV she has in here, but I'm not really watching it.

None of us are really watching it. We're just kind of hanging out and talking.

"Let's tell secrets," Kari says. She reaches over and grabs another drink off Whitney's nightstand. I had no idea she was such a lush. Not that I'm judging, but she's had two beers in half an hour and is now apparently going for a third. The weird thing is, it doesn't even seem to be affecting her. Maybe it's because she's from New York. In movies, kids in New York are always getting into bars without getting ID'd.

"No way," Whitney says. "I already know all your secrets." She's sitting in a beanbag chair in the corner of the room, and Evan has his head in her lap. A few minutes ago she started stroking his hair, which just kind of seemed wrong. Not that she's stroking his hair, but just that she's doing it in front of us. It's like . . . I don't know, weirdly intimate.

I pull my phone out of my pocket and read Peyton's text for the millionth time. Maybe I should text her back. Maybe I should tell her it won't be awkward, maybe I should tell her that I'm looking forward to seeing her, or at least ask her what she's been up to.

But then I think about what happened, and I get filled with anger. Forget it, I tell myself. And this time, I delete the text. As soon as it disappears from the screen, I'm filled with regret. I shouldn't have done that. Now how am I going to read it over and over?

God, I really shouldn't have started drinking. I don't drink all that often, and so when I do I start getting all emo and shit.

"I'll go first," Kari says. She grins. "When I was thirteen, I stole a lip gloss from Duane Reade, and I got caught and the police came."

Whitney rolls her eyes. "Lame."

"That is not lame!" Kari picks a pillow up off Whitney's bed and tosses it at her playfully.

"Yes, it is."

"Fine, then you tell one."

"I will," Whitney says. She clears her throat like she's getting ready to make some really big revelation. "You know how finals are coming up?"

We all nod. How could we forget? It's all anyone's talking about, even though they don't really matter. In fact, I could technically bomb all my finals and still be valedictorian. It's already been decided.

Whitney looks over at her desk, a mischievous smile playing on her lips. "Well, I have a copy of the math test in my top drawer."

"You do not," Kari says. She takes another pull of her beer.

"I do," Whitney nods. "Hannah Hewitt gave me a copy."

Evan sits up and looks at her seriously. "How much do you want for it?"

"No way." Whitney shakes her head, her short blond curls bobbing up and down. "I'm not selling it."

"Are you crazy?" Evan says. "You have to sell that shit. You'll get rich!" I can already see him working the math out in his head—how much they could charge for each copy of the test times how many people will actually buy it.

"I'm not going to sell it," Whitney says. "I don't want tons of people using it. I need it. I'm not doing so well in math."

Evan looks disappointed.

"But you can look at it if you want," she says. "It's in my top drawer."

"Can I make a copy of it?"

"No." She shakes her head. "You have to come over here if you want to use it." She licks her lips and smiles.

Kari and I look at each other, raising our eyebrows, and I can tell that we're both thinking the same thing. Whitney and Evan are going to hook up.

"Okay," Evan says agreeably. Then he gets up and goes over to her desk. "Where is it?" he asks.

"In the top drawer." She watches as he opens it and then starts rummaging around in there. "It's all folded up."

He pulls out a paper. "This is it?"

"Yup."

We all watch as he unfolds a picture of David Beckham, shirtless and in some kind of tighty-whitey looking underwear. Evan looks at it, shocked. Whitney collapses back on the beanbag chair in giggles.

Kari rolls her eyes. "That was so stupid," she says. "I knew you were lying the whole time."

"You did not!"

"I totally did," Kari says. "Your math average is an eighty-eight."

"So?" Whitney says. "You know I want an A."

Kari rolls her eyes again. "Ridiculous."

"Whatever, Kari," Whitney says, still giggling. "Why don't you tell a real secret then if you think fake secrets are so dumb?"

"I did." Kari props herself up on Whitney's bed. "I told you about the time I stole something from Duane Reade."

"That was lame."

This conversation is kind of lame, if you ask me. I'm in a bad mood about the whole Peyton thing, and the beer I drank is definitely not helping.

"It wasn't lame," Kari says. God. I hope these two aren't going to start fighting or anything. The last thing I need is girl drama. I can't stand girl drama. It's just so unnecessary. Which is why I'm not going to text Peyton back. She's obviously just trying to get drama going. Well! I am not going to be privy to that. I don't do drama. And if she thinks she's going to suck me, in, well, then she's got another thing coming.

"It *was* lame," Whitney says.

"At least it was true," Kari shoots back.

"So what? Stealing something when you were thirteen? Who cares?" She stares right at Kari, a smile playing on her lips. "Why don't you try telling us a real secret? One that actually means something?"

"I don't have any real secrets." But Kari's sitting up now, giving Whitney a death glare, which makes me think that she does have a real secret. A real secret that she doesn't want to tell.

"Why don't you tell Jace your secret?" Whitney giggles.

"Shut up, Whitney," Kari says.

"What secret?" Evan asks. "What, do you want to bang him or something?"

He laughs, but Kari flushes.

"Oh, shit," Whitney says. But you can tell she likes it.

"Whatever," Kari says. "So what? I had a crush on Jace for, like, a week when I first moved here. Big fucking deal." She looks at me. "I was over it in like, a day."

"How come you never said anything?" I ask, racking my brain for clues that she might have liked me. But I can't come up with any.

"I did," she says. "Remember? I sent you that—"

She cuts off as the sound of a door opening and closing

downstairs echoes through the house. "Whitney?" a man's voice calls.

"Shit!" Whitney says, her eyes widening and her skin turning pale. "It's my dad."

"I thought he wasn't going to be home until late!" Kari starts gathering up all the beer bottles and dumping them in the closet.

"He wasn't supposed to be," Whitney says.

"Is he going to flip out?" Evan asks. "Because if he calls my mom, I'm never going to be able to—"

"Yes, he's going to flip out!" Whitney says. "I'm not supposed to have people over, much less boys drinking in my room."

"Whitney?" her dad calls, the sound of his footsteps coming up the stairs. "Are you home?"

"Jesus," Evan whispers.

"Quick!" Whitney says. "Everyone hide."

Evan dashes under the bed, and Kari grabs my hand and pulls me into the closet. She shuts the door behind us just as Whitney's dad opens the door to Whitney's room.

"Ah," he says, "there are you are. I was calling your name."

The closet is kind of cramped, but I'm afraid to move because I don't want to make any noise. My parents probably wouldn't really care if they find out I was over here, but I don't want to get Evan in trouble if it can be avoided. The last time something even remotely like this happened, he got grounded for two months, and it was horrible. He got super depressed. He's like a puppy. He needs socialization.

"Sorry," Whitney says. "I must have fallen asleep."

"With the lights on?" her dad asks.

"Yeah, I just . . . I fell asleep studying for my math final."

Kari starts to laugh, and I put my finger to my lips, signaling her to be quiet. She buries her head against my shoulder to muffle her laughter, and before I know it, I'm also trying not to laugh.

We get ahold of ourselves a couple of seconds later, and when we do, she pulls away and looks at me.

And then, before I know what's happening, she kisses me.

the trip   peyton

Saturday, June 26, 12:34 p.m.
Bradenton, Florida

"So I'll be in charge of the GPS," I say, pulling it out of the box and plugging it into the cigarette lighter. I hope I can get a really good look at the map before Jace notices what I'm doing. Otherwise I have no idea how the hell I'm going to be able to get Jace to drop me off in North Carolina. North Carolina is a big state. I need to get dropped off in Raleigh, and if he drops me off in, like, Wilmington or something, that's not going to be good.

Actually, I don't even know if Wilmington is close to Raleigh. Not even a little bit. This is why I need to look at the map. Why didn't I try to figure these things out before I left? I should at least have a little working knowledge of geography if I'm planning on uprooting my life to a new state. I mean, that's so irresponsible.

"Okay," Jace says.

I tap through the GPS screen, accepting the agreement that basically says if we crash the car and die because we're looking at the GPS, then it's our own fault. Then it asks me the address of where we're going. What to do, what to do . . .

And then I have a brilliant idea.

"I think we should probably stay in North Carolina for the night," I say. "That will be a good place to stop, don't you think?"

"I guess." He shrugs.

"Good." I enter us to Main Street in Raleigh. Now we'll be in the middle of the town, and how hard can it really be to get from there to Creve Coeur? Even if I have to take a taxi, that won't be too bad. Things are looking up!

I slide the GPS into the holder and affix it to the windshield, then reach into the backseat and rummage around in my bag until I find my pink fleece blanket. I push my seat back and cuddle up under the blanket, getting ready to sleep. Hector assumes his normal position, with his head on the seat right next to mine. How cozy!

"What are you doing?" Jace asks.

"Having a nap."

"Having a *nap*? Nuh-uh, no way." He shakes his head.

"Why not?"

"Because we're supposed to be sharing the driving. I'm not just going to sit here and drive the whole time while you get a free ride."

I feel like telling him that there's no way this is a free

ride, that I am definitely paying for this ride, if not with money then with my pride. But I don't say that. Instead I just say, "Of course I'm going to share the driving with you. I'm not a freeloader."

"Good," he says.

"You do the first couple of hours, though. While I take a nap."

"Why do you need a nap?" he asks. "You just woke up not that long ago."

"It's noon."

"So?"

"So the brunch started at nine."

"*So?*"

"So! Some people wake up early before things like that. You know, to shower, get ready, that kind of thing?"

Jace is one of those lucky people who looks amazing even if he hasn't showered, shaved, whatever. I used to think it was so sexy—that he could just roll out of bed and still look perfect. But now I just find it annoying.

"Whatever." Jace shakes his head, and I lean back and close my eyes. He turns the radio on and starts flipping through the channels.

"Can you turn that down?" I ask.

"No." He shakes his head and stares straight out the front windshield. "Whoever's driving is in charge of the music."

"Fine," I grumble, deciding not to argue with him. I'll torture him with Taylor Swift later. Jace hates Taylor Swift, which makes no sense. How can you hate Taylor Swift? She's so innocent and cute. Not to mention talented. Everyone loves her. Look at the way America totally rallied around her that time Kanye West was mean to her. Jace thinks Taylor Swift is too modest, that it's all some big act. Like how every time she wins an award she acts all surprised.

"Welcome to the Dr. Laura show," comes through the speakers, and Jace goes, "Oh, perfect, I love this show!"

"Dr. Laura?" I moan. "Please, please do not make us listen to this."

"Why not? She gives good advice."

"Sure," I say, "if you believe all women should stay home with their children and that no one should have sex before marriage."

"I didn't say I agree with her on everything, but she does give good advice. She cuts through people's bullshit."

I snort.

"What was that for?"

"What was what for?"

"You snorted."

"No, I didn't."

"Yes, you did."

"Jace," I say, sighing. "I don't snort."

"Whatever."

"*Whatever*," I say. "Can we please just not talk? In a few minutes, I will be asleep, and then in a couple of hours, we can stop to go to the bathroom and then we'll change places. Okay?"

"Fine."

But I don't fall asleep. No matter what I try, I can't. I just lie there with my eyes closed, pretending to be asleep. And I hate to say it, but Jace is kind of right. Dr. Laura gives okay advice.

Like when she tells the woman whose daughter watched another girl getting bullied that her daughter was just as much to blame as the bullies.

And when she tells a man that he should stop supporting his deadbeat father who doesn't have a job and has been married four times.

Or when she tells a mother that it's okay to not let her son hang out with his cousin because the cousin is a terror and slammed the son into a bookshelf and made him start bleeding all over.

And then, right after she reads a commercial for some kind of at-home business that sounds like it's definitely a scam, she takes another call.

"Sarah, welcome to the program," Dr. Laura says.

"Hi, Dr. Laura, thanks for taking my call," Sarah says. She sounds nervous, like a lot of people do when they call Dr. Laura, probably because they know they're about to get yelled at. "My question is about my boyfriend. Um, he lives in Colorado, and I live in Washington. And I'm just wondering at what time does it become ridiculous for us to stay together?"

"How old are you and how old is he?" asks Dr. Laura.

"We're both in college. I'm a sophomore and he's a junior."

"Well," Dr. Laura says, "in my opinion, that is way too young to be in a serious relationship. But if you do make the choice to do so, you need to give yourself the chance to really get to know the person, and there's no way you can do that when he's hardly ever around."

"Okay," Sarah says. But she doesn't sound convinced. And then she does something that makes me groan. She says, "But we see each other at least once a month."

"Yes, but once a month does not allow you to really get to know a person," Dr. Laura says, firmer this time.

"But we talk on the phone every day, sometimes for hours."

I squirm in my seat, wanting to yell at the radio and tell Sarah to stop contradicting Dr. Laura. Dr. Laura doesn't like that, and now Sarah's really going to be in for it.

"Well, miss, if you want to spend your college days holed up in your dorm room with a cell phone talking to some guy you're most likely not going to end up with, then that's your business."

"But I haven't met any guys at college who are even close to being as good as Brant."

Jace guffaws. "Brant!" he says. "What a tool name. She should dump that loser."

"You would say that," I mumble, before I remember that I'm supposed to be asleep.

"What?" He glances at me.

"Nothing."

"No, what did you say?"

"Nothing," I say. "Just that you would think it was stupid to have a long-distance relationship. I mean, isn't that what you decided?"

I see his Adam's apple bob as he swallows. He shakes his head and frowns. "That's not what I said. I never wanted—"

"Stop," I say, realizing my mistake. I shouldn't have even brought this up. The last thing I want is to get into some big explanation of our relationship, where Jace tries to tell me why he ended things, and how it has nothing to do with me and blah blah blah. "I don't want to talk about it."

"Peyton—"

"I don't want to talk about it."

"Yeah," he says. "That figures."

"What does?"

"That you don't want to talk about it," he says. "You never want to talk about anything."

"Ha!" I push Hector gently back into the backseat, then reach down and pull the lever on my seat so that it shoots up. "What a crock! I'll talk about anything, anytime, anywhere."

"Oh yeah?" he challenges. "Then why are you running away?"

"That," I say, "is none of your business."

He nods in satisfaction. "That's what I thought."

I reach over and pull the lever on my seat again, sending it back down. "You know what?" I say. "Don't talk to me." Then I reach up and push the button on the radio, turning it off. "And I don't want to listen to this anymore. It's giving me a headache."

I lie back down, waiting for him to say my name, to tell me he's sorry, to try to talk to me again. But he doesn't say anything. He doesn't even turn the radio back on. He just keeps driving.

A couple of hours later, my bladder is dangerously close to overflowing, and so I'm the one who's forced to break the silence. I pretend that I'm just waking up, that I haven't been just lying there the whole time, trying to fall asleep. I made a big mistake when I turned the radio off because after that I had nothing to distract myself.

"Do you want to stop soon?" I ask, reaching up and stretching, as if I was sleeping and not just giving him the silent treatment.

"Fine," Jace says. "There's a Bojangles coming up in a few miles."

"Sounds good," I say nonchalantly, even though I'm about to explode.

Jace pulls off the highway at the next exit, and drives an agonizingly slow two miles to Bojangles. When he pulls into the parking lot, I rush out of the car and into the restaurant, hoping he can't tell it's because I really have to go to the bathroom, and instead thinks it's because I'm sick of him and can't wait to get out of his presence.

When I come out of the bathroom, Jace is standing in line, and I step in behind him, scanning the menu, looking for the cheapest items.

"Have you ever had Bojangles before?" he asks.

"No." I shake my head. "We don't have them in Connecticut."

He nods. "It's good. Like KFC, only better. But when we stop tonight in North Carolina we can go to the grocery store and stock up so that we don't have to keep eating fast food."

"Sounds good," I say, trying not to let him in on the fact that we're definitely not going to need much food tonight, since I'm going to be ditching him as soon as we get to North Carolina.

The line inches forward. "We'll have two number twos," Jace says. "Cheddar cheese on both, one with a Sprite, one with a Diet Coke." He turns to me. "That okay?"

I nod, then rummage in my bag for money. The food does sound good, and my heart does a little dance over the fact that he remembered I like Diet Coke, but I wish he'd picked something a little cheaper. I thought the South was supposed to be cheaper than the Northeast. Haven't they ever heard of the Dollar Menu? Disgusting, greasy, artery-clogging food for a buck?

But when the cashier adds everything up, Jace hands over his debit card without even asking me. "I got it," he says. "Don't worry about it, you can get me back later."

I think about protesting, but I'm afraid that if I do, he'll take me up on it. And I need to save my money. So instead I just say, "Thanks," and put my money back in my bag. Hopefully, whenever I get him back, it will be someplace a little cheaper.

We take the food over to a table in the corner and dig in.

"It's good, right?" Jace asks. He opens a little cup of ketchup, and sets it on the table between us so we can share.

"It is," I say, dipping a fry in the ketchup. He goes for it at the same time, and our hands brush against each other. "Sorry," I say, flustered. It's starting to feel a little hot in here.

"I knew you'd like it," he says.

"How?"

"Because everyone does."

"Oh." I keep eating, not sure what to say.

After a few minutes, he puts his sandwich down and regards me over the table. "So, seriously, are you going to tell me why you were running away?"

I sigh, "No. So stop asking me that. And I'm not running away anymore, so you can stop being so dramatic about it." I cross my fingers under the table, hoping he buys my lie.

"You're the one who was making it all dramatic back in your hotel room."

"Only so you would wipe the smarmy look off your face."

He opens his mouth, like he's going to protest the fact that he's smarmy, but then he changes his mind. "Fine," he says.

I take a bite of my chicken sandwich, although I'm suddenly not really that hungry anymore. I'm thinking about my mom. And about what happened. My eyes start to get all hot and prickly, and I blink hard. *I will not cry, I will not cry, I will not cry.*

"Sorry," Jace says. "I didn't mean to upset you."

I don't say anything.

He sighs. "Seriously, I'm really sorry, Peyton. I know you had your reasons, and it's not really any of my business. But if you ever want to talk about it, I'm here."

Somehow, the fact that he's suddenly being nice about it is making it even worse. And that he's not pushing me to talk about it is somehow making me *want* to talk about it. Because the thing is, no one knows the whole truth. Not Brooklyn. Not my dad. Not even my mom knows that I know. It's kind of too horrible to even say out loud.

"It's okay," I say. "You were just trying to be nice."

He nods, then takes another fry. "They have really good milkshakes here," he says, probably because he thinks I want to change the subject. "You can even get a chocolate peanut butter one."

Chocolate peanut butter is my favorite, and the fact that

he remembers this makes me lose it. I start to cry, right there at the table.

"Peyton," Jace says, his voice softening. "What's wrong?"

"Nothing," I say. "It's just . . . the reason I wanted to leave home, it's just . . . it's really horrible."

He doesn't say anything, and then after a second, he moves over to my side of the booth and wraps his arms around me. I melt into him, leaning my head against his shoulder. We stay like that for a few moments until I lean back, wiping my eyes.

"Peyton," he whispers into my ear, "I need you to know that I'm really sorry. About everything."

I don't know if he's talking about what happened with my parents, or what happened with me and him. He pushes my hair out of my face and he's looking right into my eyes and I really, really want him to kiss me.

But then a man walks down the aisle and sits down at the table next to us and starts slurping his soda noisily, and the moment is broken.

Jace pulls away and then, after a second, he moves over to the other side of the table. And I miss him. I don't want him to be back on his own side of the table. I want him over here, with me. Feeling that connection with him, for the first time in a long time, felt good, and I'm not ready to have it taken away.

Which is why I say, "Okay. I'll tell you why I was running away."

If he's surprised, he doesn't show it. He just nods, and I'm reminded of one of the reasons I liked him so much—he's completely nonjudgmental.

"Okay," he says, his eyes on mine. He leans back in the booth. "I'm listening."

And so I start to talk.

peyton   before ➤

"He's an asshole," Brooklyn declares. We're at the beach, lying on our towels and soaking up the sun. I kind of hate the beach, but Brooklyn loves it, so every once in a while, I do my duty as a best friend and go with her. I slather myself with sunscreen, get nervous that everyone's judging the way I look in my bathing suit, and try to avoid the water so that I don't get stung by a jellyfish or some equally disgusting sea creature.

"I know," I say, flipping through the new issue of *Cosmo*. All the articles are about how you can please your man in bed. Which obviously I won't be needing, so I don't know why I'm even reading this stupid magazine in the first place. "I just don't understand how I could have been so fooled by him."

"What do you mean?"

"I mean, he made me feel like he was such a nice guy, and then to not even respond to a text that I sent him? I mean, that's just common courtesy."

"Please tell me you're joking," Brooklyn says. She doesn't move from where she's lying on her lime-green towel, her face pointed up at the sun. "He completely blew you off after Christmas, are you forgetting that? How can you be surprised that he's not responding to your text?"

I decide to ignore this fact, and just keep on with the conversation we were just having. "Not to *mention* that he's going to be seeing me in a couple of weeks. Isn't he worried that I might go crazy on him or something? Like, what if I start to scream at him and make a big scene in front of all the guests? What if I scream, 'Jace Renault, you are a horrible womanizer, and I am here to say that in front of God and your family!'"

"Do you plan on doing that?" Brooklyn asks, her voice tinged with worry. She props herself up on one elbow and looks at me, her eyebrows raised over the huge black sunglasses she's wearing.

"Of course not," I say, even though the idea is kind of tempting.

"You know what you need," Brooklyn says, pulling her sunglasses off. Her eyes light up with excitement. "You need a new guy!"

"No." I shake my head. "Absolutely not. The last thing I need is a new guy. Guys are trouble. All they do is cause misery and heartbreak."

"Yeah, but think about all the fun you're missing out on," she says, grinning. "You could make a pact with yourself that you aren't going to get emotionally attached. You'd have a good time, and maybe you'd even get over Jace."

"You think?" I ask doubtfully. The thought of making out with some guy I'm not that into doesn't seem like the way to get over Jace. But maybe it would be. Don't they say that once you hook up with a guy, your hormones take over, making you emotionally attached to him? It's, like, the curse of being a woman.

"Oh, definitely," Brooklyn says, nodding. "It's hard to be upset about someone when you're making out with someone else. Now, who do you want to have a crush on? This is so fun!" She reaches into her bag and pulls out our yearbook.

"I don't know," I say. "Can't I just wait until I go away to college? Then I'll definitely be able to forget about him."

"That's a year away!" Brooklyn says. "Way too long. Plus it's not that fun."

"But it's summer," I point out. "How am I supposed to get a crush on someone now?" Having a crush on someone during the school year sounds a lot easier. That way you can lust after them in the halls. You know, from afar. I throw myself back onto my towel and close my eyes, watching the imprint of the sunlight flash and move on the backs of my eyelids.

"Good point," Brooklyn says, flipping through the pages of our yearbook. She pushes a strand of her blond hair behind her ear. "Maybe we should start going to more parties. Or maybe you should get a summer job at a place where lots of guys will be working. Like a sporting goods store."

"Oh, yeah, because that's not depressing or anything," I say. "Spending my summer dressed in some dorky polo shirt trying to sell people golf clubs."

"Think of all the flirting you could do! Actually, forget about the customers—think about the other employees! They'd all be guys." She bites her lip. "Maybe we should both get jobs there."

My phone starts ringing, and I know it's ridiculous and pathetic, but every time it rings, I think maybe it's going to be Jace. Which is so stupid. If he was going to respond to my text, he would have done it. I mean, it's been three weeks. I glance down at the caller ID, but the call is from a number I don't recognize. I pick it up.

"Hello?" There's a beat of silence on the other end of the line, and my heart slides up into my chest. Jace? "Hello?" I try again.

"Hello," a bright female voice chirps in my ear. "This is Maria Valerio from Visa, how are you today?"

"I'm fine," I say, my heart sinking. It's just a stupid telemarketer.

"Is this Peyton Miller?"

"Yes," I say. "But I'm not—" I start to tell her that I'm not interested, but before I can, she cuts me off.

"Good afternoon, Ms. Miller, I'm calling because your

account with us is currently thirty days past due, and we'd like to offer you a chance to rectify the situation before it gets put on your credit report."

"I'm sorry," I say as Brooklyn holds up our yearbook and points at a picture of Matt Swift. I shake my head. No way. Matt Swift is cute, but he's also really stupid. One time when I told him my grandparents lived on Cape Cod, he told me he always wanted to visit that state. "I'm not interested."

I'm talking to both Brooklyn and the lady on the phone. Brooklyn frowns and then goes back to looking.

But the lady on the phone says, "You're not interested in what, Ms. Miller? Paying your bills on time?"

"I'm sure I would be able to handle paying my bills on time," I say, rolling my eyes, not sure why I'm still on the phone. "But I don't want a credit card right now, thank you."

"Well, you should have thought about that before you opened an account with us," she says, getting all snotty.

"I didn't open an account with you," I say. I've been look- ing for someone to take all my Jace rage out on, since he's not calling me back and letting me yell right at him. Maybe this lady will fit the bill. I hate to get all angry at some ran- dom person, but honestly, she started with me first.

"Yes, you did," the woman says. "And your account is currently thirty days past due, almost sixty, which will affect your credit report when this information gets sent to the credit bureaus at the end of the month."

"What are you talking about?" I ask as Brooklyn holds up another picture. But I shake my head at her and then stand up and move away toward the snack bar so that I can hear the lady on the phone better.

"Your Capital One Visa," she says. "You have a current balance of ten thousand dollars, and with late fees and back payments, you owe us five hundred and twenty-eight dollars in order to get your account back up-to-date."

"But that's impossible," I say. "I don't have a Visa. That's what I've been trying to tell you."

All the picnic tables at the snack bar are taken, so I sit down on the curb of the sidewalk. The pavement warms my skin through the bottom of my bathing suit, and I slide my feet into the sand and wiggle my toes.

"We did receive one payment from you when you first opened the account," she says, totally ignoring the fact that I just told her I don't even have a stupid credit card. "But since then, there's been nothing, despite a bevy of letters and phone calls."

"But I haven't received any phone calls!" I say. "And how did you get this number, anyway?"

"This phone number was provided to us by DataTrax, a company that allows us to find phone numbers of people who have skipped out on their bills."

"But I haven't skipped out on my bill," I say. "That's what I've been trying to tell you."

"Are you saying that this account isn't yours?"

Is this woman for real? *"Yes."*

"So you didn't open it?" Her tone is skeptical, like she's used to people running up big bills and then trying to pretend they didn't do it.

"Yes!" I say. "I mean, no, I didn't open it!"

"Then who did, Ms. Miller?" she asks.

"I don't know!"

My heart is beating fast now. Because even as I'm saying it, there's a sinking feeling in my gut. A sinking feeling that maybe I do know who opened that account.

A person who likes to spend money.

A person who knows all my personal information.

A person who gets the mail every day and would be able to intercept any envelopes that were addressed to me.

A person who's my mom.

I tell Brooklyn that I don't feel good, that my stomach is bothering me, that I need to get home. She believes me, which makes me feel bad, but I can't tell her what's happening. I can't say the words out loud, can't say anything about it until I know for sure that it's true.

I don't remember much about the ride home, just that the whole time we're driving, rage was boiling up in my body, worse than anything I've ever felt toward Jace or anyone else. It bubbles and simmers the whole way, and by the time Brooklyn pulls into my driveway, my anger is so all encompassing that I feel like I'm going to explode.

"Mom!" I scream as I come barreling into the house. But there's no answer. "Dad!" I scream. Again, no answer. I stomp through the house, yelling their names as I go.

I peek back out the front window, realizing their cars aren't in the driveway, that they're not home. I don't know where they are or when they're coming back, but I don't care. I push my way into their room and pull open the drawer of my mom's nightstand so hard that it comes right off the track and lands on the floor with a thud.

My mom is horrible with organization, and so there's all kinds of stuff in the drawer. Old address books, old bills, lots of credit card offers, a bunch of flyers for gyms and stores and other things. My parents' room is very clean and neat, thanks to the cleaning service that comes twice a week. But if you look beneath the surface, it's actually a mess. Cleaning services can't help you when it comes to organizing. Especially if you don't want their help because you have something to hide.

I've become a banshee, tearing through every paper, my eyes not even really registering what I'm seeing. So I force myself to calm down a little bit and go through each piece slowly, opening anything that looks remotely like it could be from Visa.

But there's nothing.

I leave the mess on the floor, then fling open the closet and start pulling down the bins that line the top shelf. There are papers and things in here too, and I start methodically going through them. I don't care how long it takes—I'm going to find something. If there's nothing in here, I'll go to my dad's office. I doubt she'd leave anything in there, since it's my dad's work space, but if she's trying to hide something, who knows?

But it doesn't come to that.

I find what I'm looking for in one of the purple bins marked SHOES. There aren't any shoes in there, needless to say. And it's a really stupid thing to label a secret bin with, since my mom has a huge shoe rack and therefore wouldn't need to store her shoes on a shelf.

Instead, there are credit card statements. Dozens of them, all addressed to me. I start opening them one by one, my hands shaking the whole time, tears spilling down my cheeks, my heart pounding so hard in my chest I can't hear anything else.

I lay them all out, constructing the picture of what my mom's been doing.

Three credit cards.

Two Visas.

One MasterCard.

All in my name.

With a combined balance of around twenty thousand dollars.

the trip   jace

"Wow," I say, once Peyton's done talking. I stay quiet for a second, wanting to make sure I choose my words carefully. She's finally trusted me with something, and I don't want to give her any reason to regret that. At the same time, I think it's a little crazy that she's running away. "I can't even imagine what that must have felt like."

"It felt like a betrayal," she says simply. "Like the worst betrayal ever. Like my mom would rather have expensive shoes than a relationship with me."

"Yeah." I pick up my cup and take a sip of my soda, mulling over what she just said. "But you know it's not that simple, right? I mean, don't get me wrong, it was horrible what she did. But your mom has issues with money, obviously. It's not as simple as she likes her shoes more than she likes you."

It's the wrong thing to say. Peyton's eyes narrow, and for a second, I think she's really going to lay into me. But she just shakes her head and lets out a little laugh. "It figures that you'd take her side."

"I'm not taking her side," I say quickly. And I'm not. All I was doing was trying to point out that maybe her mom cares about her more than she thinks. "I was just trying to make you feel better."

"By telling me I'm overreacting?"

"I didn't say you were overacting! I was just saying that there might be a deeper explanation, that's all. You're not overreacting. I'd be freaking out if one of my parents did that to me."

"You still think I shouldn't be running away?" she challenges. I can tell what she wants me to say. She wants me to tell her that she *should* be running away, that she should be extremely pissed, that she should hurt her mom as much as her mom's hurt her, that I wouldn't blame her if she never went home again.

But honestly, I think the fact that she's running away is a little bit insane. I mean, when you think about it, it doesn't really make that much sense. What is running away going to accomplish? It doesn't help her to fix things with the credit card companies, it doesn't help her relationship with her mom, and it doesn't help her to feel like she's back in control. In fact, I can't think of one single good thing that it does.

But all I say is, "What does your dad think about it?"

"I didn't tell him."

"Why not?"

"Because it's . . . I don't . . ." She trails off, looking out the window, seemingly frustrated.

"Listen," I say gently. "I know it's a horrible situation. But did you ever think that maybe you should have stayed there for the summer, tried to work things out?"

She takes in a big breath, and when she talks again, her voice is shaky. "I don't want to deal with it," she says. "Why should I have to?"

"Because it's happening?"

"But it's not my fault."

"Peyton, a lot of things are going to happen to you that aren't your fault but still suck and have to be dealt with." Her eyes water, and I reach out and take her hand. "I mean, Peyton, this is serious. You might end up being responsible for this money."

"So you think running away is the easy way out?"

"I didn't say that."

"But do you?" She leans back in the booth and crosses her arms over her chest.

I take a bite of my sandwich in an effort to stall. I think about lying to her and just telling her what she wants to hear. But I don't want to do that. Finally I settle on, "I think that a normal reaction to what you're going through is to try to hurt your parents and to get as far away from everything as you possibly can. But I don't think that turning away from the problem is, in the long run, the best idea."

But she's not giving up. "Answer. The. Question."

I rub my eyes. "What was the question again?" It's a last-ditch effort to confuse her.

"Do you think running away is the easy way out?"

I sigh. "Honestly?"

"Yes, honestly!"

"Honestly I think it's always better to face things straight on and deal with them."

She shakes her head and then moves her straw up and down in her drink. It makes an angry squeaking noise as it slides through the plastic cover. "I should have known better than to talk to you about something like this." She cocks her head, and her eyes focus on the wall over my shoulder.

"Hey," I say, starting to get a little annoyed. "I've been nothing but nice to you. And if you didn't want my opinion, then you shouldn't have asked for it."

"Whatever." She picks up her sandwich again and starts to eat. And after a second, I do the same.

When we get out to the parking lot, Peyton holds her hand out to me.

"What?" I ask.

"The keys."

"Oh. Right." I pull them out of my pocket and hand them over, wondering if it's the right decision. It was one thing to tell her she was going to have to share the driving with me when I was tired and hungry; it's quite another once I'm recharged and she's mad at me. But still. I could use a nap. I know I gave Peyton a hard time about sleeping, but that brunch *was* a little early, especially since I was up so late last night.

We both climb into the car. Hector immediately starts nudging my hand, and I reach into the paper Bojangles bag and pull out the chicken sandwich I ordered him on the way out.

I feed him, and he slobbers all over my hands happily. "Hey, hey, chill," I say. But of course he doesn't listen. After about two seconds, the food is gone, and he licks my hands until he's sure there's nothing left. I pour some bottled water into my empty soda cup, and Hector laps it up, then flops back down in the backseat and sighs happily.

I wipe my hand off with a napkin, then put the napkin in the empty bag and drop the bag on the floor. I'll have to remember to throw it out the next time we stop.

"This feels weird," I say as Peyton slides the key into the ignition.

"What does?"

"Sitting in the passenger seat of my own car."

She doesn't say anything, just rolls her eyes and then starts the car. I know what she's thinking. That I'm complaining about being in the passenger seat of my car while she's dealing with her life falling apart. I decide I need to keep my mouth shut for a little while. Maybe she just needs some time to herself.

I lean back against her pillow and close my eyes. It feels nice and soft. I wonder how she gets it so soft. Mmm. It smells good, too. Girls are always keeping their stuff nice and soft and good-smelling. It smells like her, like vanilla and—

"Hey!" I scream as the pillow gets yanked out from under my head. "What are you doing?"

"Putting my pillow in the backseat," she says, and places it back there gently, like it's a child. Hector immediately claims it, laying his head down and giving another happy sigh.

"Putting your pillow in the backseat?" I repeat, shocked.

"Yes," she says. "It's my pillow. And that's where I want it right now."

"But I was lying on it!"

"But it's not yours." She shrugs, then reaches into her purse and pulls out a pack of gum, then pops a piece into her mouth. She looks down at the pack, considering, and then holds it out to me. "Gum?"

"No," I say. "I don't want any *gum*. I want you to let me use your pillow. I was really comfortable!"

"You can't use my pillow."

"Why not?"

"Because you have a dirty head."

This girl is unbelievable. "So you'd rather have Hector on

it?" I say. "He's a dog! And besides, my head is very clean."

She starts to giggle. "Oh, is it?" she asks. "Is your head very clean, Jace?"

"Real mature." I shake my head and then reach into the back and pick up her pillow. "I'm using it."

She pulls it from my hand. "You're not."

"I am."

"You're not."

It's in between us now, and we're yanking it back and forth, acting like children. But it's not really about the pillow. It's about the principle of the thing.

"Listen," I say, "you are riding in my car. So you have a choice. Either give me the pillow, or give me back my car, and I'll be happy to drive my ass back home. Where I won't need a pillow, because I will be curled up all warm and cozy in my bed."

Her eyes widen, like she's shocked that I would say such a thing. For a moment, I'm afraid she's going to tell me "Fine," and get out of my car and stomp away. I'd have to go after her, of course. I can't just leave her at some random Bojangles in the middle of . . . wherever it is we are.

"Fine," she says. "You can use the pillow." She looks at me out of the corner of her eye, shaking her head like she can't believe she's allowing such a thing. "I'll just have to wash the pillowcase before I use it again."

"Thank you," I say. "I appreciate it."

I place the pillow back under my head.

Peyton puts the car in reverse, takes her foot off the brake, and starts to back out of the parking spot. I close my eyes and settle in. I never realized the passenger side of my car was so comfortable. How nice. I wouldn't even mind if Hector wanted to cuddle a little.

And then there's a huge crashing sound as Peyton slams into the car behind us.

before jace

Thursday, June 24, 6:17 p.m.
Sarasota, Florida

"Did you even hear what I said?" Evan asks. "I said that we're going to have to up our marketing campaign!"

"Our what?" I repeat.

We're sitting outside of the Crazy Cow ice cream shop, eating hot fudge sundaes and killing time before we're supposed to meet Kari and Whitney to go bumper boating. Bumper boating is completely lame, and I'm in kind of a shitty mood, but whatever. Evan wanted to do it, and so did the girls, and I wasn't going to be the one to tell them it was stupid. I might be cranky, but I'm not a total asshole.

"What marketing campaign?" I lick up the last of my hot fudge sundae, then drop the container into the trash can next to our table.

"The marketing campaign for my pranks."

428

I resist the urge to put my head in my hands. "Why do you need a marketing campaign?"

Evan shoves his spoon into his sundae like a pitchfork and leaves it there. "Seriously, have you been listening to one thing I've been saying?" He leans back on the picnic table and looks at me, accusing.

"Of course I have," I lie.

"Then you would *know* that none of the good shows take unsolicited tapes. Apparently it's for legal reasons." He wrinkles up his forehead, like he can't even fathom the idea that a network might not want a bunch of kids sending them tapes in which they're risking their lives doing crazy, stupid things.

"Well, it makes sense," I say. "They don't want kids getting hurt because they think that they can get on TV."

"I guess," Evan says, frustrated. "But it doesn't help me any."

"I thought you were going to start posting your stuff on YouTube."

"I have posted some stuff on YouTube," Evan says, "but there's too much competition. We have to figure out a way to make it go viral. Which is why I need a marketing campaign."

"Viral," I repeat, distracted.

"Okay," Evan says, pulling his spoon out of his ice cream and waving it all around. Drops of liquid fly through the air and land on the picnic table. "What's going on with you? You've been all spacey ever since school ended. Are you getting nervous about graduation?"

"Why would I be worried about graduation?"

"Because it means that the real world is starting. No more messing around. We need to start getting serious about our future."

"You're going to start getting serious about your future?" I ask him skeptically.

"Eventually," he says. "I have hopes and dreams, too, you know."

"I know."

"So are you going to tell me what's been up?" All sound of joking is gone from his voice, and now he's just looking at me with concern.

"I don't know," I say, shaking my head. "It's this . . . it's this stupid Peyton thing. I thought I was over it, but lately I can't stop thinking about her."

"Oh, man," Evan says, letting out his breath in one big sigh. "I know what's going on here."

"What?"

"In fact, I was afraid this was going to happen."

"What?"

"Think about it, Jace. Think about it real hard."

I think about it real hard. *"What?"* I ask, trying not to lose my patience.

"Don't you think it's a little weird that just when you

start getting close to another girl, your obsession with Peyton kicks into high gear?"

"I don't have an obsession with Peyton," I say, even though it's a lie. "And I wouldn't say that Kari and I are getting close."

Ever since that night Kari and I kissed a few weeks ago, we've been kind of an item. After Whitney's dad almost caught us, the four of us all stayed quiet in her room until he left again, and then we snuck out the front door and went to see a movie.

While we were at the theater, Kari and I made out the whole time. It was nice, don't get me wrong. She's cute and I'm a guy—of course it was fun. And it was a nice distraction from Peyton. But when I got home, I wasn't thinking of Kari; I was thinking about Peyton and why she chose that night to text me and what it meant and what it was going to mean when I saw her at the wedding.

And then I started feeling guilty because Kari is really nice and fun and cute and it was a really shitty thing to do to hook up with her all night and then end up thinking about some other girl. And of course I didn't *set out* to hook up with Kari just to get over Peyton, and Kari was the one who kissed me first, but still. It made me feel like a shit. Obviously Kari likes me because (as Evan pointed out to me later) she pushed me into a closet and hid from Whitney's dad that night even though Kari was the only one who was actually allowed to be at Whitney's house.

"You guys have been hanging out for a few weeks," Evan says. "Doesn't that kind of constitute getting close?"

"I guess." Like I said, it's been nice. But not anything amazing. And the weird thing is, I kind of get the sense she feels that way too. That we enjoy each other's company, but that there's nothing deeper going on.

"So what's the problem, then?" Evan asks. "Forget about Peyton, man. Girls like that are bad news."

"Girls like what?"

"Girls who break your heart."

"Good point."

"And who live hundreds of miles away," Evan goes on. "If you ask me, you need to make this thing with Kari work. She's a great girl."

"Maybe you're right." Kari *is* a great girl. And she has one thing that Peyton doesn't have—Kari's never broken my heart.

"Of course I'm right." He finishes his sundae, then tips the plastic bowl up to his mouth and slurps down the rest of the melted ice cream. "See, the problem with you, Jace, is that you always want to make things more complicated than they are. You always want to analyze things and think about them. It's simple. One girl doesn't like you and makes you feel miserable; one girl does and makes you feel good. End of story."

I look at him in shock. "That actually might be the smartest thing you've ever said."

"Really?" He grins at me. "Thanks, man." He tosses his plastic bowl into the garbage. "Come on," he says. "It's time to meet the girls."

When we get to the bumper boat place, Kari and Whitney are already there, waiting. I give Kari a hug when I see her, determined to give this a real shot. Peyton Miller who?

"Evan," I say as I hand the cashier money for two admissions, one for me and one for Kari, "why is your camera in your back pocket?"

"It's not," he says.

"Yes, it is. I can see your pocket cam right in your back pocket."

The cashier gives me two paper bracelets, and I hand one to Kari.

"Thanks," she says and wraps it around her wrist.

Evan sighs. "Okay, fine," he says. "I was going to wait until we were actually on the boats to tell you this, but I was thinking that we could all do a flash mob."

Oh, dear God. I close my eyes and force myself to take a couple of deep, cleansing breaths.

"What's a flash mob?" Whitney asks, grinning. Apparently she likes the fact that Evan is completely crazy, which is good for Evan, but not so good for the sane people on this trip.

"It's when people all do a dance or something at the same time," Kari says. "Like out in public. And people look at them like they're crazy. Right?"

"Right." Evan nods.

"No." I shake my head. "I'm not doing a flash mob. No way."

The girl at the gate checks my bracelet and gives me a smile. "Hey," she says as I push through the turnstile. She's cute. Long blond hair. Nice smile.

"Hey," I say, grinning back. And then I instantly feel guilty. I'm here with Kari. Kari, who is perfectly nice and cute and fun. Kari, who I've been making out with for weeks. Kari, who is here with me, on this date, and probably doesn't appreciate the fact that I was just semi-flirting with the girl working the gate.

Although if Kari minds, she's definitely not showing it.

"I think a flash mob could be fun," she says. "But how can we really do it at a bumper boat place? And besides, aren't you supposed to plan those things out way in advance?"

We all file into the line that's forming in front of the entrance to the boats, waiting for the ride that's going on right now to be over. I take Kari's hand in mine, to make up for smiling at the girl working the gate. Kari seems a little surprised that I'm holding her hand. Probably because we haven't really done that much PDA.

And honestly, it's kind of awkward. We just kind of stand there, holding hands like kids or something. We're not relaxed, or loose, or romantic or anything. We're just gripping each other's fingers, like we're thirteen again or some shit. Very strange.

And then Peyton's face floods into my mind. Peyton. Who I'm going to be seeing tomorrow night at the wedding.

"Yes, technically you're supposed to plan things out in advance, but I didn't want to bring it up before because I knew Jace would flip out," Evan says. And then he starts going on and on about flash mobs.

I tune him out, trying to figure out why I'm so tense. Can it really be just because I'm going to see Peyton tomorrow? Or is it because of graduation on Sunday? *It's just a dumb speech*, I tell myself. *And she's just a dumb girl.* As soon as I think it, I instantly feel guilty. Yes, it is a dumb speech. But Peyton is not a dumb girl.

"Jace?" Evan's asking.

"What?" I ask, struggling to pay attention to what he's saying.

"Are you listening?" He's holding Whitney's hand as the line moves forward, but unlike me and Kari, they actually look like they want to be holding hands. Whitney's leaning into his chest, and he's rubbing his thumb against the outside of her hand. Who knew Evan could be so comfortable around girls?

Although I guess when you have a girl that you really like, who you can be yourself around, it's easy. Not that I can't be myself around Kari. I mean, why wouldn't I be able to? It's not like I'm hiding something from her. Well, besides the fact that I can't stop thinking about another girl. Another girl that I'm going to be seeing tomorrow.

"Of course I'm not listening," I say, shrugging and trying to make light of it. "You're talking about some kind of flash mob at a bumper boat place. Why would I want to listen to that?"

"Because you might get famous from it," Evan says. "I'll bet Peyton would be sure to notice *that*."

He realizes his mistake as soon as he says it.

"Who's Peyton?" Kari asks, frowning.

"No one," Evan says quickly.

Whitney's eyes narrow, and I can tell she's going to be grilling Evan about this later. Girls are always so protective of their friends. Guys would never do shit like that. Yeah, we look out for each other, but we also know when to stay out of each other's business. Damn. I'm going to kill Evan.

"Okay, fine," Evan says. "I'll tell you."

"Evan—" I start, but he cuts me off.

"It's Peyton Manning."

Kari laughs, but Whitney looks confused.

"He's a quarterback," Evan explains. "He keeps getting injured, and he's, like, kind of old, so . . ."

"Right," I say, surprised that Evan was able to come up with such a good lie so quickly. "I'm obsessed with him."

Evan nods sadly. "Poor little Jacey here keeps writing him letters and tweeting at him, but Peytie Pie just won't pay him any attention, will he, Jace?"

"Nope." I say, and shrug. "So anyway, about the flash—"

"Jace was even thinking about pretending to be a Make-A-Wish kid, weren't you, Jace?"

"No," I say through gritted teeth. "I wasn't."

"Yes, you were," Evan says. "It was right after that time you wanted me to film you with I LOVE PEYTON MANNING written across your chest while you ran up and down the hallways at school."

"You were going to do that?" Whitney asks, giggling.

"Of course not," I say. "It was just, um, a thought. I was joking."

"It seemed serious to me," Evan says, and shrugs.

Luckily, at that moment the line lurches forward and we all start to get herded into our boats. I slide onto the seat next to Kari. "You can drive," I tell her.

"Oh, no." She shakes her head. "I'm kind of horrible at it."

I shrug as she climbs over me and into the passenger seat.

"You're going down!" Evan screams from the boat next to us and honks his horn a bunch of times. A dad with two kids looks at us nervously, and I can tell he's thinking that he shouldn't have come to the bumper boats on a Thursday night, and that he can't believe how crazy teenagers are these days.

"Evan," I say, "relax. There are kids here."

"Sorry." He looks sheepish, and then he whispers, "You're going down."

"Sorry Evan's being crazy," I say to Kari.

She smiles. "I like it," she says. "At least he keeps things interesting."

She's right next to me, and even though the boat is really

small, there are still a couple of inches of space between our legs. She's sitting up ramrod straight, and I realize that I'm sitting up straight, too. Which isn't really how you should be sitting when you're on a date.

I shift my leg over a little so that it's touching hers, but now we're just sort of sitting there with our legs touching. After a few seconds, she shifts away.

The ride begins before I have a chance to think about what that even means, and we immediately start chasing Evan around the big pool of water. He's definitely acting crazy, driving the boat back and forth in looping circles, slamming into the wall and seemingly not caring if he and Whitney get completely soaked.

Whitney doesn't seem to think there's anything wrong with this, and in fact, she seems to actually like it. I wonder if maybe she's secretly as crazy as Evan.

"You're going down!" Evan yells again, and then slams into us. The other people in the bumper boats look at us kind of in disgust. But at least we're leaving them alone and just focusing on each other. That should count for some-thing, especially since not everyone does that. One time I saw this guy wearing a Budweiser tank top begin terror-izing the children on the boats, getting them all wet and laughing gleefully. He even made a girl cry.

"No, we're not!" Kari yells at them. "*You're* going down!"

"Oohh, this girl wants a fight!" Evan turns the boat around, driving the wrong way around the pool, and tries to smash into us head-on, which he knows is against the rules.

We're about to hit, but at the last moment, I yank the steering wheel hard to the left so that we miss them. Instead, we slam into the wall.

"Ha ha!" Evan yells from behind us, happy that he won his game of chicken. "Suckers!"

"Why'd you do that?" Kari asks me, sounding disappointed.

"I didn't want to crash into them that hard," I say. "We would have gotten all wet."

"It's bumper boats," she says. "That's kind of the point."

"Yeah, but you're not really supposed to be slamming into people like that."

"I guess."

There's an awkward silence, and I wonder why it was so important to her that we win the game of chicken. Then I wonder why I'm acting like kind of a dick about it. It's probably just my bad mood. I do that sometimes—get into a bad mood and then just not want to have any kind of fun.

But fuck that. I'm done letting myself get all worked up about Peyton. So I'm going to see Peyton. Big fucking deal. It's a stupid thing to be getting all weird about. Sunday is graduation, and then I'll have the whole summer in front of me before I'm off to college in the fall. And once I'm at Georgetown, I'm not going to be thinking about Peyton. She'll be just some girl that I knew in high school.

"It's okay," I say to Kari, shifting into reverse and backing our boat out from where it's wedged in the corner of the pool. "We'll get them now."

It's a sneak attack. We come up behind Evan and Whitney and slam right into them, shooting a spray of water over the back of their boat and soaking both of them instantly.

"Oh, that's it," Evan says, glaring at me as Whitney shrieks in glee. "Now it's on."

We spend the next hour riding the bumper boats over and over, and I do my best to get into it and to forget about Peyton. By the end of the night, it seems to be working.

Well. Almost.

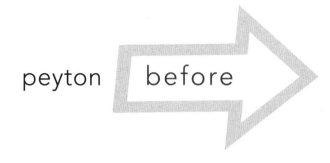

peyton | before

Thursday, June 24, 5:02 p.m.
Greenwich, Connecticut

"Did you bring a bathing suit?" my mom asks as I slide my suitcase down the hall toward the front door. It's the night before the wedding, and we're about to head to the airport for our flight to Florida. My dad was supposed to be in charge of bringing our bags out to the car, but he and my mom got into some huge fight a few minutes ago, and so now he's just sitting out in the car, pouting and waiting for us to load up our own stuff.

"Yes, I brought a bathing suit." I brought three bathing suits, actually. Because I'm going to be spending the summer in North Carolina, although my mom doesn't know that yet.

Brooklyn and I have spent the past two weeks crafting a plan. A plan to get away from Connecticut for the summer. A plan that will allow me to spend my summer away from my parents and their maybe-divorce, away from my mom and her lies, away from my obsessive Jace thoughts. (Not that I know for sure I won't be having obsessive Jace thoughts in North Carolina, but I figure it can't hurt.)

Here is our brilliant plan:

Stage One: I will go to the wedding and pretend nothing weird is going on. I will pose for pictures like a good girl and act like I'm having a great time. If Jace approaches me, I will smile and then act as if we are just acquaintances, and not like he is a boy who broke my heart. I will be like a Peyton made of stone, smiling and pretending everything is okay.

Stage Two: The morning after the wedding is over, Brooklyn will fly to Florida to meet me at the Sarasota Airport. We will then rent a car and drive to North Carolina, where we've rented an apartment for the summer. (Well— where Brooklyn's rented an apartment. She had to put it in her name, since she's eighteen, and I'm not. But I'm on the lease as a tenant.)

It's a surprisingly simple plan. And it was surprisingly easy to get Brooklyn on board with it. I just told her that I wanted to get away—that my parents had been fighting more, and I needed a break from being upset about Jace. North Carolina was even her idea—she knows a boy there, and I think she wanted an adventure.

Of course, we're going to have to find jobs when we get there, and figure out how to get around—we can't afford to keep the rental car for more than a few days.

But I can't think about any of that right now. I can't worry about the long term. Right now I just need to focus on the short term, on getting through this wedding and getting to North Carolina. I can worry about the rest of it later.

"Why do you have so much luggage?" my mom asks, staring at my bags. "You have more than I do." She says it slightly accusingly, like not having as much luggage as her daughter is going to make her seem like a loser or something. Which is completely ridiculous. Who cares who has more luggage?

"I just wanted to make sure I have enough for my college visits," I say. My parents think that after the wedding, Brooklyn and I are going to spend some time looking at colleges in Florida. They have no idea that I'm going to North Carolina and not coming back.

"I thought we went over what you're going to wear," my mom says, sighing. She and I spent almost two hours the other day going through a bunch of my clothes so that my mom could pick out what she thought I should wear when I make these imaginary college visits. It was a completely pointless exercise, but I pretended to go along with it, turning this way and that as she dressed me up in a bunch of business casual clothes as if I was her own personal Barbie doll.

The whole time I was resisting the urge to come out and yell at her about what she did. If I ever do confront her about it, I'm not sure what will happen. Maybe she'll deny it, maybe she'll beg my forgiveness, maybe she'll tell me I'm being silly, maybe she'll offer to pay it all back. But who really cares? The bottom line will still be the same. I need to get away from her.

"We did pick out what I was going to wear," I say, "but I packed a few other things, too. Casual stuff, in case me and Brooklyn end up hanging out with any of the students."

My mom nods, like this makes sense. "All right. Just make sure you don't drink." She shudders. "College kids these days are always getting drunk and making fools of themselves. And don't even get me started on college boys. They'll drop a roofie in your drink like it's nothing."

"Thanks for the moral lessons," I say sarcastically. It comes out sharper than I intended, and she looks up from tying her shoes. (Which, by the way, are these ridiculous Coach sneakers that cost two hundred dollars, and which she bought just for the plane. Who buys shoes just for a *plane ride*?)

"What's that supposed to mean?" she asks.

"Nothing." I shrug. Actually, come to think of it, I probably bought those plane shoes for her. Get it? Since she probably put them on her/my credit card? The thought sends me into hysterical giggles.

My mom frowns and then opens her mouth to say something, but before she can, the front door opens and my dad reaches in and picks up a bunch of our bags, then slams the door behind him as he heads back out to the car. Yikes. I guess he got sick of waiting.

"Thanks, Joe!" my mom calls after him sarcastically. She shakes her head. "Well, that was the last of them," she says. "So I guess we're all ready."

"Yup," I say. "I guess we're all ready."

I traipse out to the car, stick the earbuds of my iPod into my ears, and zone out until we get to the airport.

I've never been a fan of flying. Being stuck in the airplane, never knowing if it's going to hit turbulence, wondering what will happen if it crashes, not having any leg room, worrying that the person next to you is going to fall asleep and drool all over your shoulder . . . it's a whole big thing.

Unless you're flying first class, which my mom always wants to do, and which we *used* to do until the economy tanked and my dad got all concerned about money. Sure enough, my mom starts as soon as she gets on the plane.

"I really wish you would have let us fly first class, Joseph," she says. My dad hates being called Joseph. It's what my mom does when she's trying to shame and/or annoy him.

"Well," my dad says, giving her a tight smile, "if you'd like to earn the money to pay for the first-class tickets, I'd be more than happy to fly that way."

I tune them out, something I'm getting quite good at doing. I don't know why my dad even came on this trip— actually, that's a lie. I do know why my dad came on this trip. He came on this trip because my mom knew it would look weird to her family if he didn't come. People would ask questions.

Whatever. Not my problem anymore. *North Carolina, North Carolina, North Carolina,* I chant quietly to myself as I head toward my seat. It's a window seat that's, fortunately, a few rows up from my parents. I guess by the time they booked our flight, there weren't any seats left that were together. *Un*fortunately, my seat is next to two little girls, whose parents are sitting behind us. I guess they couldn't get their seats together either.

But the fact that they're letting two kids who appear to be no older than three or four sit together, while the two of *them* sit together, doesn't really make that much sense. Wouldn't it be a better idea to have one parent sit with each child?

"Sorry," their mom says from behind me, almost as if she's reading my mind. "They wanted to sit together."

"They're sisters," the dad explains. "Not twins, but Irish twins." He gives me a big grin and an expectant look, like he's waiting for some sort of reaction.

I look at him blankly.

"You know, Irish twins?" he asks. "They were born only eleven months apart."

I guess that's supposed to be some kind of joke about how Irish people are always having sex or something? So they're always having tons of kids are super close in age? I don't really get it, but whatever. It's actually kind of a prejudiced comment, when you think about it. Not to mention that this family definitely doesn't look Irish—they have dark hair and dark eyes and olive skin.

"I'm Sophia," one of the girls says.

"I'm Aleah," the other one says. They're wearing matching purple gingham sundresses, with purple shoes and purple bows in their hair.

"I'm Peyton." I stow my bag into the overhead compartment and then push past them toward my seat.

I flop down and turn my iPod back on, cranking up the volume and trying to calm myself down. It's not just the flying and the twins that are making me nervous. It's everything. This wedding. Jace. My plan to run away.

Why didn't I just get a Xanax or an Ativan the way normal people do when they're all tense and on the verge of a nervous breakdown? It would have been so much easier. But I have this weird aversion to any kind of pill that makes you feel like you're losing control. Although they say those pills don't actually make you feel like you're losing control; they just allow you to be calm, which obviously would be helpful right about now. Of course, I'd probably be freaking out about having some kind of weird reaction and/or allergy to the pill. Am I too anxious for anxiety pills? Hmmm. The thought is extremely alarming.

"Peyton?" One of the twins is tapping me on my shoulder. I quickly close my eyes and pretend to be sleeping. Tap, tap, tap. "PEYTON!" Then there's a poke. And then, to my complete shock and dismay, one of those twins pulls my ear-bud out of my ear. What the *hell*?

I turn and glare at her, but she's giving me the cutest smile ever. "Sowwy," she says. "But you couldn't hear me." Then she holds out her juice box. "Can you open this for me?" She wrinkles up her little nose. "The straw is stuck."

"Sure." I take the juice box and deal with the straw problem.

I replace my earbud, but five seconds later, it's yanked out again.

"Peyton?" the other twin says. "Can you help me? I lost my purple crayon. Purple is my favorite color. What's your favorite color, Peyton?"

I sigh. This is going to be a long flight.

When the plane touches down in Sarasota, I'm even more relieved than I usually am when a plane lands. I've had enough of playing babysitter. Which is what I've been doing this whole entire time. Tying shoelaces. Coloring pictures. Answering questions about flying and what the pilot does. (I didn't really know the answers, so I just kind of guessed. They're kids; they don't know the difference.)

"Well," I say as we're getting ready to debark, "it was nice meeting you, girls."

I give their parents a pointed look, hoping they'll at least thank me for taking care of their children while they read and relaxed. (I peeked over at them once, and the dad was reading *Marley and Me. Marley and Me!* It was so annoying for some reason. That book is, like, ten years old. He had to spend the time that *I* was taking care of his rug rats reading *Marley and Me?* Couldn't he have picked something a little more current?)

But the parents don't say anything. They don't even give me a smile. They're too busy pulling down their overhead luggage.

Ugh.

God, I'm in a bad mood.

"Can I meet you guys at the luggage carousel?" I ask my mom as soon as we're off the plane. She's wearing yoga pants and a pink Ralph Lauren short-sleeved polo shirt with huge Dolce and Gabbana sunglasses holding back her newly highlighted hair. She doesn't need sunglasses. It's nighttime. I've been resisting the urge to reach over and rip them off her head, maybe taking some strands of hair with them.

"Why?" my mom asks, shouldering her bag. "You have so much luggage. You should be there to pick it up."

"I *am* going to be there to pick it up," I grumble. "I just want to get a coffee first." Coffee always helps my mood.

"Sure, honey," my dad says, not because he's taking my side, but because he wants to piss my mom off. "We'll watch for your bags. You brought the Louis Vuitton luggage, right?"

"Yeah." I wonder if I can sell it to pay off my credit card debt.

I wait in line at Starbucks, ignoring the much shorter line at the Dunkin' Donuts, because I need something strong that's going to, hopefully, jolt me out of my bad mood.

The line inches slowly forward, and I tap my foot impatiently, then pull my phone out and text Brooklyn in an effort to distract myself.

We still on?

She texts back immediately: **Yes! Stop freaking out!!**

My biggest fear is that Brooklyn is going to back out of our plan. She's given no indication that she's going to, but that doesn't mean she won't. She could get strep throat. Or food poisoning. Or a broken ankle. People are always cancelling things. Especially me. I'm a huge canceller. I hope that isn't going to make it more likely that Brooklyn is going to cancel on me. Like cancel karma or something.

When I get to the front of the Starbucks line, I decide to switch it up and order an iced mocha. Skinny, because if I'm going to see Jace tomorrow, I don't want to be all bloated. Of course, all those hamburgers I've been eating for the past two weeks aren't going to help, but whatever.

I don't need to impress anyone. Once I'm in North Carolina, I'll meet a new boy. One who will bring me flowers all the time and take me out to fancy dinners and buy me tons of presents like jewelry and iPads and all sorts of stuff. And not in a skeezy way, either, the way guys do when they're feeling guilty or want to show off how much money they have.

Actually, no, forget that. I'm not going to get all caught

up in materialistic displays of affection. In fact, it's better for me to find a guy who doesn't have money. No way do I want to repeat my mom's mistakes. Plus I get the feeling that Jace and his family are kind of well-off. And I need the anti-Jace.

But anti-Jace can still bring me lots of presents. Flowers that he's grown himself. Little notes he's written on beautifully colored paper. Cookies he's baked, and books he's found in used bookstores that he wants me to read because they remind him of me.

Who needs Jace Renault? This is me, totally over him, la la la. This is him, disappearing from my mind.

"Skinny mocha latte," the barista calls out, and I pick up my drink, cheered by my new attitude and impending caffeine rush.

Brooklyn texts me again, and I check my phone.

Can't wait to c u! NC BAYBEE!

I smile and slip the phone back into my bag, then start to make my way through the crowd and over to the baggage carousel where my parents are waiting.

But a few seconds later, I stop short.

Because moving through the airport, coming from the other way, is Jace. He's wearing a cool-looking silver T-shirt, and his hair is pushed back from his face, and he's slouched over with his hands in his pockets and, oh, my God, he looks so hot and what am I going to do if he sees me?

I don't have time to run the other way. I don't have time

to do *anything*. My heart is beating fast and the room is spinning and my face is flushing and I don't—

Oh.

Wait.

That's not Jace. It's some guy with a lip piercing and spiky hair who actually looks nothing like him. Well. Okay. Good. False alarm. I mean, I didn't want to see him anyway.

I keep walking through the airport, my heart finally slowing to its normal rate. I guess that whole thing about Jace disappearing from my mind needs a little work. Sigh.

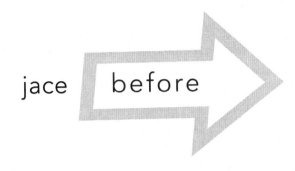

jace before

Friday, June 25, 10:07 a.m.
Sarasota, Florida

The night before the wedding, I can't sleep at all. I know it's ridiculous. I know it's lame. I know it's totally stupid. I know it's because of Peyton.

I toss and turn and toss and turn. Finally at around three in the morning, I give up. I play around on the Internet for a while, but the Internet is boring. I try to read a book, but I can't keep my mind on it. I try to work on my graduation speech, but I've already gone over the stupid thing so many times that if I work on it any more, I'm afraid it's going to end up being worse. Finally, I drift off to sleep at about five a.m. after watching a bunch of reruns of *The Office* on Netflix.

I'm woken up at ten the next morning by my mom knocking on my door.

"Jace?"

I roll over and blink at the clock, wondering what's going

on. My mom never wakes me up, because she thinks I'm the perfect son and therefore trusts me enough to set my own wake-up time. (Which is actually true. I am the perfect son. And I do know when to wake up. Never before eleven, har har har.)

"Yeah?" I call back.

"Someone's here to see you."

Peyton. It's the first name that pops into my mind. She has to be in Florida by now, right? The wedding's tonight at seven, so her flight probably got in last night. Maybe she came to my house to—

"It's Evan," my mom says. "He seems a little . . . worked up."

I sigh and swing my legs over the bed, then pull a sweatshirt on over my shorts and T-shirt. When I get to the door, Evan's standing on the porch, his hands in the pockets of his khakis, his feet shuffling back and forth. His eyes are darting all around, which makes me nervous. I have no idea what's going on with him, but I have enough to be dealing with. Graduation, a wedding, seeing Peyton . . .

"Hey," I say.

"Hello!" he says, immediately pasting a smile on his face. "There's my best friend in the world!"

Oh, Jesus Christ. "What have you done?" I ask immediately.

He looks wounded. "I can't believe you would ask me that."

"Really?" I cross my arms over my chest. "You really can't believe it?"

"No," he says, raising his chin in the air. "I can't. I've been nothing but nice to you, for my whole *life* even—"

"I didn't say you weren't," I interrupt him. "All I said was that it can't really be surprising to you that I would question what kind of scrape you've gotten yourself into that would necessitate you showing up on my doorstep at ten in the morning unannounced."

His look of outrage deepens. "I don't get myself into scrapes!"

"Really?" I ask. "What about the time you signed up to sell wrapping paper for the senior fund-raiser and then ended up spending the money yourself?"

"I needed that money—otherwise I wouldn't have been able to afford my prom ticket! And besides, I paid it back."

"What about the time you ended up involved in that vitamin pyramid scheme? The one where you almost got arrested for trying to sell diet pills to all the girls at school?"

"How was I supposed to know you had to be eighteen to take them?" he protests. "And besides, I got decked in the face because of that, remember?" He rubs his jaw, remembering.

"Yeah, because you can't just go around asking girls if they want to buy diet pills! Of course they're going to get pissed."

"That wasn't what—"

"Enough!" I hold my hand up. And then I start to feel bad. "Forget it. I shouldn't have brought all that stuff up."

Evan nods. "You shouldn't have," he agrees. "That stuff was in past, and I've really changed. Especially since I got together with Whitney."

I gape at him. "You guys have only been together for a few weeks."

"A few weeks is enough time. People can change like *that* if they're motivated." He snaps his fingers.

"I guess," I say doubtfully. "So then what are you doing here so—" I'm cut off by the sound of a yelp coming from the yard. I frown. "What the hell was that? If the neighbor's dog gets into my mom's flower beds again, she's going to flip."

I look around, but I don't see the dog anywhere.

"That's kind of what I'm here to talk to you about," Evan says, looking sheepish.

"My mom's flower beds?" I ask with a laugh.

He shakes his head, and then I get it.

"Oh no," I say. "Evan, please don't tell me you—"

"I got a dog." He steps to the side, so that I can see where his car's parked in the driveway. There's a dog in the backseat. When it sees us looking, it immediately starts whining and crying.

"Oh, Evan," I say, my stomach dropping. "You didn't."

"Why not?"

"You can't take care of a dog," I say. "You're too . . ." I'm about to say "irresponsible," but I'm pretty sure that would piss him off. ". . . impulsive."

"Thanks for the vote of confidence, Jace," he says, and

rolls his eyes like it's completely out of the realm of possibility that he would be considered impulsive. He puffs his chest out. "You'll be happy to know, then, that the dog's not for me. It's for Whitney."

"Okay." I peer at the dog gingerly. It definitely doesn't look like the type of dog you'd get someone as a present. Dogs that are presents should be clean and friendly looking, with their ears perked up and a big red bow around their necks. This dog looks . . . well, kind of scruffy. But whatever. If Evan's happy, I'm happy. "That's nice, Evan," I say. "I'm sure she's really going to like it."

"Well, that's the thing," he says. I close my eyes and wait for it. "She's allergic to dogs."

"Why in the world would you get her a dog if you knew she was allergic?"

"Well, *obviously* I didn't know she was allergic when I got her the dog." He shrugs. "But what's done is done."

"So take it back."

"I can't."

"Why not?"

"Because I got it from the shelter."

"And they won't take it back?" Not that I really blame them. If I'd gotten rid of a dog that looked like that, I wouldn't be excited to take it back either. I know that's a horrible thing to say. But it's true. Then I have a thought. "You didn't pay for that dog, did you?"

"Well, you have to give them an adoption fee, Jace,"

he says. "Shelters subsist on adoption fees and donations. Which reminds me, when was the last time you did any charity work?"

I look at him incredulously. "When's the last time *you* did any charity work?"

He nods. "Good point."

"Okay, so what are you going to do with him?" The dog is pawing at the inside of the window now, his front legs leaving muddy prints on the glass. "Is that how you tried to give him to Whitney?" I ask. "Because he's all dirty." She's probably not even allergic. She probably just didn't want a dirty dog.

"I never even got him to Whitney's," Evan says. He starts throwing his keys up in the air and then catching them. "I just told her I was coming over with a surprise, and she jokingly said 'I hope it's not a puppy, because I'm allergic.'"

"And what did you say?"

"I said, 'Of course it's not a puppy, I would never bring you an animal without asking your permission first.'"

"Okay," I say, "so then bring it back."

He sighs. "Jace," he says. "I just told you the problem with that."

"No, you didn't."

"The problem *is* they said all sales are final."

"All sales are final?" I shake my head. "That makes no sense. It's an animal shelter, not a Sears."

"Fine, they didn't say that." He stops throwing his keys up in the air and looks at me seriously. "But I can't take him back, Jace. No one wants him. And if no one wants him, they're going to put him to sleep. That's why I got him. He was on a list, you know, of dogs on their last chance." He lowers his voice at that last part, like he doesn't want the dog knowing about the last chance list.

"So then what are you going to do?" I ask.

"I'm going to find him a home."

"Good for you." I give Evan a good strong pat on the shoulder and then start backing into my house before he can try to involve me in whatever crazy scheme he's come up with to find a home for this dog. I can't help anyway—I don't know anyone who even wants a dog, much less a dog that looks like a big mess.

"But," he says, following me into the house, "I can't find him a home today."

"Why not?"

"Because it takes a long time for a dog to find a home! That's how he ended up at the shelter in the first place."

"Well, you should have thought of that before you got him. And anyway, why can't you keep him at your house?" I walk into the kitchen, then open the refrigerator and pull out the orange juice.

"Can I have some of that?" Evan asks, plopping himself down at the breakfast bar.

"That depends," I say. "How soon after you drink it are you going to leave?"

He gets a wounded look on his face, and I sigh. Just

because the dude was trying to do something nice for his girlfriend doesn't mean I have to be a dick. "I'm just kidding," I say, and pour him a big glass.

"Thanks." He drinks from it noisily. "I really am going to find that dog a home, Jace. I'm going to work very hard and find him a great home. I'll put up posters, I'll post ads on the Internet, I'll even take him door to door."

"Great."

"But I can't start on any of that right now."

"Why not?"

"Because I'm supposed to be going over to Whitney's with a present."

"Yeah, but you just said she's allergic to her present." I reach into the breadbox and pull out two slices of whole wheat, then pop them in the toaster.

Evan opens the pantry and pulls out a box of cereal, then begins fixing himself a bowl. "Yeah, but she doesn't know that. So now I have to bring her something else. And so I need someplace to leave the dog."

"Leave him at your house."

"Right," he says. "Like my parents are going to go for that. Anyway, I was thinking that maybe you could watch him." He settles back down at the breakfast bar and takes a big, slurpy bite of cereal.

"No." I shake my head. "My mom would never let me."

"Your mom would never let you what?" my mom asks, appearing in the kitchen.

"Let Jace have a dog," Evan says.

"Well, that's true," my mom says. "I love dogs but I don't know if it would be a good idea right now, since Jace is getting ready to go off to college."

"Oh, I wasn't talking about him keeping it," Evan says. "I was talking about him just watching one for me."

"Like dog-sitting?" my mom asks. She pulls down a bowl and starts making herself a bowl of cereal too. The same kind Evan has. I sigh.

"No," I say. "Not like dog-sitting. It's not even his dog."

My mom frowns. "Whose dog is it?"

"It doesn't have a home," Evan says sadly. His eyes are watering, which is a total fake. The dude never cries, especially not over a dog that he just met. "He was a shelter dog that they were about to put down."

My mom sets her spoon down and puts her hand over her heart. "That's terrible!"

"They weren't about to put it down," I say, slathering peanut butter on my toast.

"Yes, they were," Evan says. "They're one of those kill shelters, the kind that kill dogs if they don't get adopted."

"It's horrible the way people just discard dogs these days," my mom says, shaking her head. She sits down next to Evan with her bowl of cereal. "You really shouldn't get a dog unless you're equipped to take care of it."

"I know," Evan says, even though he just got a dog that he wasn't equipped to take care of.

"Anyway," I say, draining my juice. "Thanks for stopping by, Evan, and good luck with the dog. I need to go work on my speech for graduation on Sunday."

"I thought your speech was done," my mom says, a look of panic in her eyes. My mom's all worried that I'm going to get up there and blank out on my speech or something. It's, like, her big fear. Which is ridiculous, since all I have to do is read it.

"I just thought I'd put some finishing touches on it," I lie. "And practice reading it out loud."

"You don't want to sound too rehearsed," my mom says.

"She's right." Evan spoons up the rest of his cereal, then brings his bowl over to the sink. "If you sound too robotic, people are going to start tuning out. Of course, people will probably tune out anyway, but you can at least try to make it a little easier for them to listen."

"Thanks." I roll my eyes.

"So, look, can the dog stay with you or what?"

"No," I say at the same time my mom says, "Yes."

"What?" we both say, looking at each other.

"Why the hell would you want to let me have a dog?" I ask. "It's ridiculous. I begged and begged for a dog growing up, and you never let me have one."

"You weren't ready for the responsibility. And with your father and me working so many hours, it wouldn't have been fair."

"I'm not ready for the responsibility now, either," I try.

462

"I'm very irresponsible." I look at my empty glass of juice. "See how I just leave my dirty glasses around? I'm horrible with responsibility."

She waves me off. "Of course we'll take the dog in. How long?"

"Just a couple of days," Evan says. "Thanks, Mrs. Renault. I'm always telling Jace how lucky he is to have a mom as cool as you."

It's a lie. Well, half a lie. Sometimes he does say that, but it's only because his parents are so strict that anyone else's parents would seem cool by default.

"What about the wedding?" I say wildly in a last-ditch effort to derail this horrible plan. "Who's going to watch the dog while we're at the wedding?"

The wedding is at night, at this super-fancy resort, and so we're going to be spending the night there tonight. I guess they're having some big brunch tomorrow morning, and they gave my mom a major guilt trip when she tried to get out of it. Which means I have to go, too. Which means the night before my graduation is going to be a total waste.

"We can bring him with us," my mom says. "He can hang out in the hotel."

Great. A dog in my hotel room.

Just one more thing to worry about.

the trip peyton

When Jace's car smashes into whatever it is that's behind us, it takes me a second to realize what happened. It's like my brain can't comprehend or accept the fact that I hit something. I slam my foot down on the brake, which is pretty stupid, since we're already stopped.

From the backseat, Hector gives a little squeal.

I close my eyes. "What just happened?" I croak.

"What the hell do you think just happened?" Jace yells. "You hit someone."

"Are they . . . are they *dead*?" I whisper.

"No, they're not dead, you hit their car, not them." He's unbuckling his seat belt and stepping out of the car. There's man in a button-up shirt with a receding hairline standing behind us, his face so red and so mad that for a second I think he's going to explode into a fireball.

464

I put the car in park, then unbuckle my seat belt and take a deep breath. Hector is just sitting in the backseat, not making a sound. I check him over before I get out, to make sure he's okay. He looks fine, physically, which is good. But he's just sitting there quietly, which is kind of disturbing. I mean, usually he always wants to whine and wiggle around. The fact that he's being so silent means he knows something bad is going on.

"It's okay, boy," I whisper into his fur, wishing I could just stay in here with him. How could I have hit someone? I know the answer. The truth is, I was distracted. I was thinking about what Jace said in the restaurant, about how running away wasn't going to solve anything. Deep down, I know he's right. It's not going to help anything. It's not going to help me figure out how much of the credit card debt I'm going to be responsible for. It's not going to help me figure out how to confront my mom.

Does this mean I'm a coward? Does Jace think I'm a coward?

"I just need the summer," I whisper to Hector. "I just need the summer to not have to deal with it, and then I'll figure it all out, I promise."

Hector whines and turns his head, then puts his front legs on the back windshield and starts pawing at the glass.

I sigh. I know I should get out and see what's going on. I take another deep breath and then step out of the car.

"What the hell have you done to my *car*?" the man I hit is yelling.

Jace doesn't answer him, just peers down at the cars, looking at the damage. And there's kind of a lot. At least, it kind of looks like there is. The whole back bumper of Jace's car is hanging off. I immediately burst into tears. Something like that is expensive. Extremely expensive. You have to pay thousands and thousands of dollars for body-work. I know because one time my mom got into a fender bender and it cost like two thousand dollars in body-work and my dad was so pissed he threatened to take her Navigator away and make her buy something that had lower insurance premiums, like a Corolla.

"Why are you crying?" the man roars when he sees me standing there. "You're the one who hit me! I'm the one who should be crying!" He's waving his arms all around, his face flushed and sweaty. God, he's scary. I look at his car, but I can't see any damage.

"There's nothing wrong with your car," Jace says. He's been inspecting it while I've been crying. "So you can be on your way."

"I will not be on my way!" the man screeches. "We are calling the police."

"Knock it off," Jace says and rolls his eyes. "It's a stupid fender bender. I'll get you my insurance info." He turns and heads toward the car to get his insurance card.

"Were you driving the car, young lady?" the man demands.

I open my mouth to answer, then quickly shut it. He's probably going to try to nab me on some kind of insurance technicality or something. Like say that since I was driving, I have to pay everything out of pocket.

"Because if you were, you need some driving lessons. The first thing I always tell my daughter, the *first thing*, is that you need to check your rearview mirrors. Didn't you take driver's ed?"

I did take driver's ed, but it actually wasn't that helpful. It was four of us all in one car, and you spent most of the time just sitting there, waiting for your turn to drive. It was an hour-long class, so you only got, like, fifteen minutes of driving time once a week.

At the end of the six-week class, you got a percentage off your insurance. Which will come in handy now. Because my insurance will probably have to pay, won't it? Or will Jace's? God, I wonder if I should call my dad. He knows about stuff like this. Of course, I'll have to make something up, something about how I was driving with Brooklyn and crashed the rental car. He's not going to be happy, especially since—

"Here you go," Jace says, shoving a crinkled up piece of paper into the man's hands. "There's my insurance information."

Jace pulls out his cell phone out and snaps some pictures of both of the cars, and the man does the same.

Then the guy grumbles something about "crazy female

drivers," gets back in his car, and drives away. How rude. I mean, couldn't he at least have said something about crazy *teenage* drivers? Why does it have to be female drivers? I'm a very good driver. Well, usually. I mean, I'd never gotten into an accident before this.

When it's time to get back into Jace's car, I know enough to slide into the passenger seat. Hector does a little whine and then lies down in the backseat and stays quiet. Jace climbs into the car next to me, his face dark and stormy looking.

"I'm really sorry," I say. "I should have looked behind me."

He doesn't stay anything, just sits there, looking out the windshield, his hands gripping the wheel.

"I'll pay for it," I say.

He still doesn't respond.

"I'll make sure it all gets paid for, I promise."

He still doesn't say anything.

My eyes fill back up with tears, and after a second, Hector slides his paws onto the back of my seat and starts licking my face. I don't even care about all the disgusting dog germs that are getting all over me.

"You can drive me back to the hotel if you want," I say to Jace. "If you do, I'll understand. Or you can take me back to Courtney's, and she can help me get home."

I can tell he's really mad. After a second, he turns the key in the ignition, makes a big point of adjusting the rearview mirror and then pulls out of the parking lot.

When we get to the highway, I'm sure he's going to start

heading back to Siesta Key. But instead, he continues on our route, driving north toward the Carolinas.

Jace doesn't talk the whole rest of the way through Florida and into Georgia. It's actually pretty unnerving. I don't know what he's thinking. I don't know what he's planning. I'm half afraid that maybe he's so mad he's going to drop me off on the side of the road somewhere, leaving me to hitchhike the rest of the way to North Carolina.

When Hector starts whining in the backseat like he has to go to the bathroom, I'm relieved. I have to go to the bathroom, too, but I'm way too nervous to say anything.

Jace reaches over and pulls the GPS out from the little holder on the windshield, and starts punching something in, probably looking for a rest stop.

"I can do that," I offer, trying to sound equal parts apologetic, thankful, and helpful. "It's probably safer for me to use it. You know, since you're driving and all."

He snorts. Which makes sense. I mean, who am I to bring up safety? I'm the one who just got into an accident in a car that wasn't mine before I even started driving. He finds what he's looking for on the GPS, then slides it back into the holder.

Ten minutes later, he pulls into the rest stop, still not talking to me. He gets out of the car and starts walking Hector over on the grass. I'm not sure exactly what I'm supposed to do, so after I minute, I unbuckle my seat belt and head inside.

I use the restroom, then buy myself the cheapest food I can find—a snack-size bag of potato chips and a can of generic diet soda. Total cost = three dollars. At the last minute, I add a second bag of chips and a bottle of water for Jace. I figure doubling my budget is worth making the effort to keep him happy.

Well, maybe not *happy*, exactly. I mean, even I know that a snack isn't going to make up for the fact that I smashed his car. But maybe we can move past it. Maybe it will become one of those funny little road-trip stories we'll tell people later. Like party conversations, ha ha ha.

But when I get back to the car, Jace is standing behind it, scowling down at the bumper.

"I got you some snacks," I say.

He takes the water from me, pulls off the cap, and takes a long sip. Then he takes the chips.

"You're welcome," I say.

He still doesn't say anything, just keeps looking down at the bumper.

"Okkkkaayyy," I say. "So are you going to just ignore me the whole rest of the time?"

"I'm not ignoring you."

"You're not? Because it seems pretty much like you are."

"Why would you think that?"

"Because you haven't been talking to me for the past four hours!"

"You wrecked my car."

I roll my eyes. "I didn't *wreck* your car," I say. "It still runs, doesn't it?"

"I'm not sure," he says. He picks up the bumper and pushes it up against the frame of the car. When he holds it like that, it almost looks like you could just glue it back on. They probably have some kind of special glue you can buy at an auto parts store for like, ten dollars. That's what happened when Brooklyn got her brakes done. It was going to cost her four hundred dollars if she took it into a shop, but instead she got this kid in our class to do it for eighty dollars after she bought the parts at AutoZone.

"It might be something we can fix ourselves," I say, crouching down. I hold up one edge of the bumper, but when I do, the other side droops down and scrapes the paint. Oops.

"Don't touch it," Jace says, running his hands through his hair. "Jesus."

"Sorry." I feel my eyes start to fill with tears. I blink as fast as I can, not wanting him to know he's having this kind of effect on me.

He sighs. "No, I'm sorry," he says. "I'm being a douche. You didn't mean to crash my car."

"I *didn't* mean it," I say, shaking my head vehemently. "I swear. I should have been looking where I was going. But it was a total accident. And I really am going to pay for it, I promise. I'll send you however much it costs."

Of course, I have no idea how I'm going to get said money, but I'm so desperate for Jace to not to not be mad at me anymore that I'll pretty much promise anything. Besides, it's the right thing to do.

"The insurance will probably cover it," he says. He rolls his head around, stretching his neck. "Look, we should probably find a place to stay."

"A place to stay?" Hector is pawing at my legs, so I crouch down and rub his head until he starts to calm down a little.

"Yeah, a hotel. I'm exhausted, and there's no way I'm going to let you drive."

I nod. "That's fair." I take a deep breath. "Can we stay somewhere cheap?"

He nods. "Sure."

I want to ask him if he expects me to pay for his room, too, but I don't. If he says yes, I don't know what I'm going to do.

We all climb back into the car. Hector sits on my lap this time. He smells kind of gross, but I don't mind. It's comforting, having him close to me. Besides, he's just a dog. He has no idea that my life is a disaster, that I'm on a road trip with a guy I can't stand, or that my mom did something horrible to me. All Hector knows is that he's in this car, right now, driving, while I pet him.

And that's enough to make him happy.

I just wish it were enough for me.

Half an hour later, Jace pulls up in front of the Residence Inn in downtown Savannah. It's definitely not the cheapest hotel, but it's one of the only ones around that seemed like it was in a safe area, close to our route, and most importantly, took pets.

When we get inside, Jace walks right up to the front desk.

"We need, um, two rooms please, I guess," he says. He looks at me for confirmation. I nod. "And we have a dog."

"And which room would you like the dog to stay in?" the front desk clerk asks happily. Her nametag says MIA.

"Mine," Jace says. I'm about to protest, because it would be nice to have Hector curled up in bed with me, but then the front desk clerk says it costs an extra seventy-five dollars for the pet fee. Jace hands over his credit card and pays for the rooms, I guess expecting that I'll pay him back later.

"If you want to go out to eat, I recommend the Distillery," the clerk says. She swipes Jace's card and gives us a smile. "It's right around the corner and it's delicious."

"Thanks," I say.

Jace signs the receipt Mia gives him, then goes outside to park the car and bring Hector in. I wait in the lobby with our bags.

When he comes back, we walk through the bar area and down the hall toward our rooms in silence. Even Hector seems subdued, trotting along next to Jace compliantly, not even noticing the other hotel guests smiling at him and remarking to each other about how cute he is.

"Well," I say as I slide my key card into the door of my

room. It beeps and blinks with a little green light. "Um, I guess I'll see you in the morning? And I'll, uh, I'll pay you back for the room then."

"Yeah," he says, sliding his card into the keypad of the room across the hall. "I guess I'll see you in the morning."

He disappears through the door, and I stand there for a second, already missing him. Finally I shake my head to clear my thoughts, and then walk into my room.

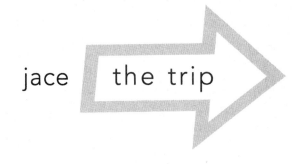

jace   the trip

Saturday June 26, 7:45 p.m.
Savannah, Georgia

I wasn't that mad at Peyton for crashing my car. I swear to God, I wasn't. Shit, it could just as easily have been me. I've been in a couple of fender benders since I got my license, and it's not like it's that big of a deal. I mean, what does it really matter? No one got hurt. And my insurance is going to cover the whole thing anyway, so it's not like it's going to be expensive.

So no, I wasn't mad at Peyton. I was mad at myself.

Because when she slammed into that car behind us, I realized something. *I didn't want to call off the trip.* She crashed my car, she'd been being kind of bratty to me, I was probably going to miss my stupid graduation because of her, and still *I didn't want to call off the trip.*

And when I thought about it, the only reason I could think of for how that could be was because I wanted to be with

Peyton. I wanted to stay with her. Peyton, who acts like she can't stand me, who acts like she doesn't want anything to do with me, who got into an accident with my car that is probably going to cause my insurance rates to go through the roof, and I wanted to stay with her. What the hell is wrong with me?

This is what's going through my head as I lie on my bed in the hotel room in Savannah. Finally, I can't take it anymore, and so I hook Hector's leash on and take him outside.

There's a field across the street from the hotel, and I walk Hector over and onto the grass. It must have been raining in Savannah earlier, because the grass is wet, and within a couple of minutes Hector's paws are a completely muddy mess.

I say a silent prayer of thanks that the hotel room I'm staying in has two beds. Maybe I can towel him off just enough so that he's not dripping, and then put him in the bed next to me. It's just dirt, right? It's not like it won't come off in the wash. Of course, the sheets are bright white, so . . .

My phone rings, and I sigh and reach into my pocket. It's definitely going to be my mom. Every time she's called, I've sent it right to voice mail, knowing that she's going to be bothering me about how I need to get home in time for graduation. I don't understand why stupid graduation means so much to her. Whether I'm there to give a big speech or not doesn't change the fact that I'm valedictorian.

But it's not my mom calling. It's a number I don't recognize.

"Hello?" I try to balance my phone against my shoulder as I grip Hector's leash with two hands. There's a leaf floating by, and apparently this is a big concern to him. So big that he feels the need to chase it, practically pulling my arm out of its socket in the process.

"Jace!" a girl's voice says. "Thank God! We thought you were dead!"

"Who thought I was dead?"

"I don't know," she says. There's a pause. "Actually, I guess only your mom thought that. I pretty much knew you weren't dead."

"Who is this?"

"It's Courtney!"

"Oh. Sorry. I didn't recognize the number."

"I'm calling from Jordan's phone." She lowers her voice. "Listen, I don't know where you are or what you're up to, but your mom's really worried. She says you have graduation tomorrow night, and she hasn't been able to get in touch with you. She's about thirty seconds away from calling the police."

"I know she hasn't been able to get in touch with me," I say. "I've been sending her calls to voice mail." I pause, waiting for Courtney to tell me that wasn't a very nice thing to do. But she doesn't. "And anyway, I told her I wasn't going to graduation. So I don't know why she's freaking out."

"Okay." Courtney's silent for a minute. I watch as Hector sniffs around, pawing things and eating grass. "So what do you want me to tell her if she calls?"

"She's *calling* you?"

"Well, yeah," she says. "She's worried about you, and she thought that maybe you'd come to hang out with me and my friends."

"Why would she think that?" I ask. "I told her I was—" I shake my head in frustration. "Actually, never mind. Just tell her that I'm safe, okay? And that I'll be home soon."

"Okay." There's a silence again. "Jace?" she asks finally.

"Yeah?"

"Are you with Peyton?"

I hesitate. I don't want to lie, but on the other hand, I don't want Courtney telling my mom any details, either. The less my mom knows, the better. Which is exactly why I'm not taking her calls. "Is this off the record?"

"Off the record?"

"Yeah, like are you going to tell my mom what I'm telling you?"

"No," she says. "I'll tell her you're safe and that you'll be home soon, but that's it."

"Then yes, I'm with Peyton."

"That's what I thought," she says. And I'm pretty sure I can hear a smile in her voice.

I walk Hector around for another half an hour or so, figuring it's probably a good idea to tire him out before I take him back to the room. I feel bad that he's been cooped up in the car all day. Not that he seems to be holding it against me. In fact, just the opposite. He seems totally happy, wagging his tail and trying to meet everybody that walks by.

We have to cross over the grass to get back to the hotel, and so by the time we get to the sidewalk in front of the building, his paws are leaving muddy prints all over the pavement. There's no way I'm going to be able to just towel him off. And if he jumps on the bed like this, it's going to be a mess.

It's wishful thinking to expect I can keep him on the floor. Last night at the hotel in Siesta Key he jumped right up on the bed as soon as the lights went out and then nosed his snout under my pillow. Don't ask me why he thought that would be a comfortable position, or why he turned over sometime in the night and slept on his back. Dogs are just weird.

"I really, really don't want to give you a bath," I say to Hector as I slide my key card into the gate that separates the hotel from the sidewalk. "But it looks like that's what's going to have to happen. Do you like the water, Hector?"

He wags his tail and looks at me happily, but I'll bet once he gets into the water, it's going to be a big debacle. Maybe I should just keep him dirty. At least I know what kind of dirt I'm dealing with. I'll just make sure to leave a big tip so that the housekeepers won't—

"Ahhh!" Peyton screams. She's on the other side of the gate, trying to pull it toward her at the same time I'm trying to pull it toward me.

"Oh," she says once she walks through and sees that it's me. "Hi."

"What are you doing?" I ask suspiciously.

She shrugs. "Just going for a walk. I was going to see if there was a gas station or something where I could grab something to eat."

"Why would you want to eat gas station food?" But as soon as the words are out of my mouth, I realize the reason. She's broke. Which explains why she bought those chips and waters at the rest stop, instead of going for something more substantial.

"What the hell happened to him?" she asks, looking down at Hector and ignoring my question about the gas station food. "He looks like a big muddy mess."

"Nothing happened to him," I say, suddenly defensive. I pull Hector's leash back a little bit, so that he's closer to me. "We were just going for a walk. Dogs get dirty on walks sometimes, Peyton." I roll my eyes like she doesn't know anything about dogs.

"Yeah, but he's reeeally dirty." She kneels down on the sidewalk, and Hector puts his front paws on her knees and licks her face. "What'd you do, let him walk through mud puddles?"

"No." Yes. "Anyway, I have to go give him a bath."

"A *bath*?"

"Yes, a bath. Dogs have baths, Peyton, when they're dirty."

She stands up and grins at me. "No, I know that. I'm just surprised, that's all."

"By what?"

"By the fact that you're going to give him a bath."

"Why?" I'm somehow insulted.

"I don't know." She shrugs. "It just doesn't seem like the kind of thing you would do."

"Well, I'm going to."

"Okay."

"Okay."

We stand there, looking at each other for a moment.

"Well," she says finally. "Um, let me know if you need any help."

"I won't."

"Well, if you do—"

"If I do, I'll let you know. But I'm pretty sure I won't."

"Okay. Well, see you tomorrow." She pushes past me through the gate, and even though I'm so annoyed at her, even though I can't stand the fact that she's acting like I'm so incompetent that I can't even give a dog a bath, I have to resist the urge to reach out and pull her toward me.

I shake my head and pull Hector through the gate and down the hall toward our room. This time, as we pass other hotel guests, they wrinkle up their noses and look at Hector like he's disgusting. Which I guess he kind of is, but really. You'd think people would be a little nicer.

He'll be fine after he has a bath. A bath that I can handle on my own, thank you very much. A bath that I definitely won't be needing Peyton's help with.

the trip peyton

Saturday, June 26, 8:17 p.m.
Savannah, Georgia

The gas station in Savannah is surprisingly well-stocked and surprisingly cheap. I don't know if it's Southern pricing or what, but I was able to get Oreos, a Diet Coke, two bags of chips, and some nacho cheese Combos for only six dollars. Six dollars! What a score.

It was so cheap that at first I thought maybe it was one of those things where the food is about to go bad, and so everything's marked down. But I checked the expiration dates, and they weren't even close. So yay for nonperishable Southern snacks!

I walk quickly back to the hotel, munching on a bag of chips as I go. It's a nice walk—it's still a little light out, and the Georgia air is warm and slightly humid against my skin. I decide to take the long way around the building, and go through the front lobby of the hotel instead of the side gate.

For the first time in a few days, I start to feel happy. *It's all going to work out,* I tell myself as I walk through the automatic doors. *It's going to be fine.*

The girl at the front desk, Mia, has her iPod on, and she's dancing to whatever song she's listening to as she enters something into the computer. She smiles and gives me a little wave.

"How's your room?" she asks.

"It's great!" I tell her. "Thanks."

She smiles, revealing the gap between her front teeth. "Let me know if you need anything else."

"I will."

Everyone here is so friendly and relaxed! There are people sitting at the bar as I pass by to my room, and they're laughing and joking around with each other. One of the women gives me a little wave as I go by, and I wave back. I guess this is what people mean when they talk about Southern hospitality. I wonder if this is how it's going to be in North Carolina, too.

I hope so. I could totally get used to it.

I push open the door to my room and dump my snacks on the bed. I decide to have a nice long hot shower, then watch *Jersey Shore* reruns or something equally mindless while I eat.

I grab a pair of fleece pants and a tank top out of my suitcase, bring them into the bathroom with me, undress, and then turn the shower on full blast. I push it as hot as I can stand it, letting the water wash the stress off me as the stream beads down over my body. I stay in there for a long time, and when I finally turn the water off, I feel relaxed and loose.

And honestly, when you really think about it, why shouldn't I be? I'm only one day away from being in North Carolina, only one day away from having my own apartment, only one day away from starting my new life. Who cares what other people are going to think or say? Who cares if I'm making a big mistake? People probably told Bill Gates he was making a big mistake when he dropped out of college. Same with Mark Zuckerberg. Of course, those guys were tech geniuses, and were actually working on something that they were going to bring to market. Or whatever you call it when you make a new product.

But maybe I could bring something to market. One time at the ninth-grade bake sale I made these amazing brownies because I messed up the recipe on the back of the chocolate chip bag. People were raving about them all day. I could open a brownie shop. And then expand into cookies and cakes. I've always wanted to learn how to make cookies and cakes in the shape of things, like on those shows where they build pastries up to look like people or cartoon characters. I could totally do that.

I'm so cheered by my new life as a retail and/or Internet entrepreneur, that I'm humming a little tune to myself as I get out of the shower and get dressed.

I'm just about to turn the TV on when there's a knock on my door. I ignore it, figuring it's probably housekeeping or maybe that nice girl from the front desk, coming to set a chocolate on my pillow or something. They probably do things like that in the South.

I rip open my bag of Combos, and pop one in my mouth.

The knock comes again. Geez. These Southern people might need to learn that being friendly is only friendly when the other person actually wants it.

"Peyton?"

Oh. It's Jace. Well, that explains it. He's definitely not going to be practicing Southern hospitality. He's lucky if he even practices Northern hospitality.

I creep to the door and peer out the peephole. He's standing there in a white T-shirt and a pair of dark green track pants. His hair is all messed up, and there's a big smear of dirt on the front of his shirt.

Hector is standing next to him, wagging his tail.

"PEYTON!" Jace says, and knocks again. "Are you in there?"

I sigh and unlock the door. "Of course I'm in here," I say. "Where else would I be?"

"I've been trying to call your room for the past forty-five minutes," he says. "Why didn't you answer?"

He peers past me into the room, all suspicious, like he half expects that I'm going to be throwing a party or entertaining a gentleman caller or something.

"I was at the gas station, remember?"

"For an hour?"

"No," I say, even though I was probably there for longer than I should have been, picking out my snacks. There were just so many to choose from. "Not for an hour. But then I was in the shower." I cross my arms over my chest, suddenly realizing that all I'm wearing is a thin tank top.

"Well, can you help me?" Jace asks.

"Jace," I say seriously. "I think you're beyond help." I think it's a pretty funny joke, honestly, but Jace doesn't seem to agree.

"Ha ha," he says, rolling his eyes. "But seriously, I need help with Hector. He won't listen."

"What else is new?" I look down at Hector and give him a fond smile, because honestly, how can I not love a creature that is giving Jace a hard time and not listening to him? And that's when I realize that Hector is now an even bigger mess than he was when I saw him outside after his walk.

Now not only is he covered in mud, but the mud seems to have been diluted by water and soap. It's dripping off his fur into dirty, gritty puddles that are collecting on the wood floor of the hallway.

"What happened to him?" I wrinkle my nose. "He's all soapy and dirty." I didn't even know you could be both soapy and dirty at the same time.

"I was giving him a bath," Jace says. "And he wouldn't

sit still. Every time I would try to rinse him off, he would jump out of the tub."

"He jumped out of the tub like *that*?"

"Yeah, and ran all around my room making it a disgusting mess."

I bite back a laugh.

"It's not funny!" Jace says.

"You're right," I say, nodding mock seriously. "It isn't."

Jace sighs. "Are you going to help me or not?"

"I thought you didn't need my help." I give him a challenging look.

He gives me one right back. "We all need a little help now and then, don't we Peyton?" I know he's talking about the fact that I needed him to drive me to North Carolina. Or, as far as he knows, Connecticut. I hate that he's bringing that up. But he does have a point.

"Whatever," I say, holding the door to my room open. "Come on in."

Okay, so giving Hector a bath with Jace was actually kind of fun. Once we let go of the idea that there was any chance that we, Hector, or the bathroom were going to stay clean, and just took it for what it was—a big, disgusting mess—it went a lot more smoothly.

"You hold him while I rinse him, okay?" I tell Jace.

"Okay," Jace says. Hector is in the tub, just standing there, looking at us like we're crazy. He doesn't seem to mind the water, but you never know when he's going to get excited and want to play or cause mischief.

Jace holds Hector gingerly around the stomach, and I pull down the shower sprayer to rinse Hector off. "It's okay, boy," I say. "It's just some nice warm water, it'll feel good."

Hector acts like he understands me, and raises his head up to the water. "Good boy," I tell him.

"You know he can't understand you, right?" Jace asks.

"Yes, he can," I say, even though I know it's not true. "He's a very smart dog."

Jace scoffs at me.

"He is!" I say. "And he doesn't like you saying that he's not smart, do you, boy?"

As if on cue, Hector works his way out from Jace's hands and puts his front paws up on the side of the tub.

"Hey, hey, hey," Jace says, lowering him back down into the water. "What are you doing?"

"I told you," I say. "He didn't like you saying that he doesn't understand English." And then I add, "And also you were hardly holding on to him. You don't have to be afraid of him, Jace, he wouldn't hurt a fly."

"I'm not afraid of him!"

"Then what's the big deal?"

"Nothing." He shrugs. "I just don't like him."

"Why not?"

"Because he's a pain in the ass."

"God, you are really mean, you know that?"

"I'm mean?" he says, and shakes his head. "Okay, fine, Peyton, you want to know why I'm being weird around Hector?" He takes a deep breath and then looks away from me and down at the bathroom floor.

"Yes!" I say. "I do want to know why you're so weird around Hector." I take the showerhead and point the stream of water down around Hector's back legs. He wags his tail, shooting little drops of warm water onto my arms.

"Fine," Jace says, "But don't say I didn't warn you." He takes another deep breath in and then closes his eyes for a second. "When I was seven I had a dog. He was a golden retriever named Mork. That was the year I was getting teased at school, and Mork, he . . . he was always near me. He was the only one didn't care about my speech impediment."

"You had a speech impediment?" I ask, frowning.

"Yeah," he says. "That's why I got teased."

I frown. "You don't have it anymore."

"I had to work with a speech therapist," he says. He sounds annoyed. "But anyway, back to Mork. He was my best friend." He gets a faraway look in his eyes, and I'm not sure, but I think he's even getting a little choked up. "At least, he *was* my best friend. Until that year's Christmas morning."

"What happened on Christmas morning?" I ask. My stomach is already clenching in dread, anticipating where this story might be going. I cannot deal with stories that have to do with animals dying.

But I can't just tell Jace to stop. Obviously this is something that has scarred him for life, something he feels like he needs to get out. And more importantly, he's decided to pick *me* to talk about it with. It makes me feel connected to him, and I can't help it, but I love that feeling.

"On Christmas morning, I came downstairs." He shakes his head, getting that same faraway look on his face. And I know it's not my imagination now—he really *does* have tears in his eyes. "And I immediately ran to look in my stocking. There it was, on the fireplace, with Mork's stocking right next to it." He swallows hard, and as if by instinct, I reach over and take his hand. If he's surprised that I did that, he doesn't show it. His fingers tighten around mine, and my breath catches in my chest. I don't know if it's because the moment is so emotional or because we're holding hands, but my body suddenly feels like it's on fire.

"And I immediately called for him. Mork! Mork! But he didn't come. I looked at my parents, you know, and asked them where he was. Usually he slept with me in my bed, but I'd been so excited about Christmas that when I woke up, I hadn't thought to look for him." He sniffs. "And then my parents told me he went to the farm. But he wasn't at the farm, Peyton. He . . . he *wasn't at the farm.*"

"Oh, my God," I say. A lump rises in my throat, making it hard to breathe. "That's horrible. What did he die from?"

"Cancer."

"Cancer?" I frown. "And you didn't notice he was sick?"

"No." Jace shakes his head. "I was only seven, after all." It's very brief, less than a second even, but I think I saw the sides of his mouth twitch. Almost into a smile. Which makes no sense. Why would Jace be smiling? Unless he's thinking about Mork and remembering him fondly. Or unless . . . I snatch my hand away from his.

"You're lying!"

"No, I'm not." He shakes his head sadly. "Poor little Mark."

"You said his name was Mork."

"That's what I said . . . poor little Mork." But I can still see the smile playing on his lips.

"You jerk!" I say. "I cannot believe you would make up a story about a dog with cancer!"

He laughs. "Oh, come on," he says. "It was funny. You should have seen the look on your face."

"Of course there was a look on my face," I say, throwing my hands up in the air, exasperated. "Anyone would have a look on their face when they heard about some poor kid losing their dog."

Hector whines.

"See?" I say. "You're upsetting him with all this talk of dog diseases. Have a heart."

"I have a heart!"

"No, you don't."

"Yes, I do," he says. "Look, I'll prove it to you." He

reaches into the tub and wraps his arms around Hector, suds and all. "Oooh," he says in a baby voice. "Ooooh, Hector, you're such a good boy, oooh, I love you, Hector."

Hector's tail immediately starts wagging, and he pushes his snout into Jace's face and starts licking it. "Oh, Hector, you're so sweet," Jace says. "You're just the best dog."

Hector moves and Jace's elbows slip, causing Jace's whole upper body to slide over the side and into the tub. For a second, everyone freezes. I'm afraid Jace is going to be mad, since now he's soaking wet, but instead he just says, "Oooh, Hector, that's okay," and then slides his whole body into the tub, clothes and all.

Hector gives a happy bark, glad to have a friend with him, and then plants his front paws on Jace's chest.

"Oh, my God," I say, laughing as water sloshes over the side and onto the bathroom floor. "You're soaked."

"Oh, you think that's funny?" Jace asks me playfully, and then before I know it, he's pulling me into the tub with them. But there's not really enough room for the three of us, and so Hector jumps out and then starts running back and forth in front of the tub, getting soap suds and water all over the bathroom.

I'm laughing hysterically now, my pajamas and tank top totally soaked.

When I catch my breath a few moments later, I realize that I'm lying on top of Jace. I can feel his chest underneath me, and the warmth of his breath on my cheek. Our legs are tangled together in the water, and my whole body flushes hot.

"Sorry," I say. I don't know why I'm saying it. He's the one who pulled me in here with him, not the other way around. But he pulled me into the tub as a joke, as a way to get back at me for laughing. He was just messing around, and the last thing I want is for him to think I planted my body on top of his on purpose.

"What are you sorry for?" Jace asks. His voice is deep and husky, and I pull my gaze toward his face. He's looking right into my eyes, and then he reaches up and slides a finger down the side of my face, over my cheek, and down over my collarbone. His touch is soft and sends shivers exploding through my body. My heart is beating so fast and my stomach is turning and I feel like I should say something—anything—but I can't.

Which turns out to be okay. The fact that I can't talk, I mean.

Because before I can say anything, Jace pulls my face toward his and kisses me.

before jace

Saturday, June 25, 6:58 p.m.
Siesta Key, Florida

I am going to be totally cool. I am going to be totally cool and totally in control of the situation. There is nothing to get all worked up about. It's just a stupid wedding. Yes, a stupid wedding that a girl I have a history with is going to be attending. But fuck that. My history with Peyton was a long time ago. Well. If you consider three months a long time ago. Which I do.

When the ceremony starts, I sit there with my parents, scanning the rows of people, trying to look for Peyton without being all obvious about it. I'm so distracted that I don't even hear the vows. Not that I really care. In my opinion, weddings are pretty much bullshit. I'm not saying that I don't believe in marriage—I just have a hard time understanding how you're supposed to be all happy and excited for the couple getting married when you're pretty sure their marriage is going to end up completely shattered.

Take Courtney's dad, for example. Here he is, getting married, taking vows, promising that he's going to love and cherish this woman forever. When really, he already promised to love and cherish Courtney's *mom* forever. Which he obviously didn't do. And now he's pledging his undying devotion to another woman? Why should I believe him this time?

But whatever. No one wants to hear that shit. They just want to be all weepy and blather on about how beautiful it all is.

After the ceremony, everyone files into the huge ballroom at the Siesta Key Yacht Club for the reception. Of course my parents are among the first people to get there. My mom has this obsessive need to be on time for everything.

"Did you make sure you fed Hector, Jace?" my mom asks as we walk in. "Because it's very important that we get him into a routine."

"Yes, Mom," I say, struggling to keep the annoyance out of my voice. "I fed Hector." It's true. I did feed him. Of course, I don't mention that I forgot to bring his dog food, so he had to make do with a McDonald's quarter pounder. He loved it. I never saw a dog eat something so fast. I guess they don't get much beef at the pound.

"Good," she says, not even suspecting that he wasn't

eating his special, wheat-free, sugar-free, organic-whatever dog food that she picked up for him. I don't know why she's so concerned about Hector and his routine. It's not like we're keeping him.

A waiter wearing one of those long-tailed tuxedos passes by with a tray of hors d'oeuvres, and I reach out and snag two of them. You always have to make sure to take double food at these kind of fancy-pants events, because if you don't, you end up hungry. You never know when the waiters are going to come by again, or when dinner is going to finally be served.

I start inching away from my parents little by little, heading toward the bar. The one good thing about weddings is that if there's open bar, no one's ever IDing. And I'm definitely going to need a cocktail to calm my nerves.

Finally, my parents run into some couple they know, and start chattering away. After an awkward introduction ("This is our son, Jace; he's graduating tomorrow, can you believe it, he's valedictorian!"), I excuse myself and start walking toward the bar.

But before I can get there, a voice calls my name. A female voice.

"Jace!"

My stomach flips.

I turn around.

But it's not Peyton.

It's Courtney.

"Courtney," I say as she runs up to me and gives me a hug. "You look great."

"Thanks." She's wearing a long red dress. I guess she decided to change out of her bridesmaid dress before coming to the reception. Which I think might have been a good choice. I don't know anything about fashion, but I'm assuming that huge bows and green fabric aren't exactly what a nineteen-year-old girl wants to be wearing.

"It's so nice to see you!" she says. "Have you met my boyfriend, Jordan?"

"Not officially. We never really got a chance to talk at the Christmas party." I hold my hand out to the guy standing behind her. "What's up, man?"

"Not much," he says. His eyes are darting around the room, and he seems distracted.

I wonder if this is really weird for him. He's Courtney's boyfriend and also the son of the bride. Yup, Courtney's dad married Jordan's mom. Courtney and Jordan were together before their parents were, but still. That's got to be so weird. Are the four of them all going to live together now or some shit? I want to ask, but honestly, it's really none of my business.

"Don't mind him," Courtney says. "He's just looking for his friend B.J."

"What the hell," Jordan says, his eyes settling on something over my shoulder. "I told that asshole not to wear white!"

I turn around to see a kid about our age walking through the door, wearing a tight white suit, a white tie, and a white fedora. He's even got on white shoes. When he sees Jordan, he tips his hat and gives him a big smile.

"Excuse me," Jordan says. "I have to go talk to him. But I'll see you guys later—you're sitting at our table, right, Jace?"

"He is," Courtney says. Jordan gives her a kiss on the cheek and then heads over to the kid in white, who's now doing the moonwalk on the dance floor, even though no one else is dancing and the music that's playing is definitely not moonwalk appropriate.

"Should we get a drink?" Courtney asks.

I nod, then take her arm and lead her through the crowd to the bar. She orders a Diet Coke, and after a second, I order a Sprite, mostly because I don't want to seem like the jerk who ordered alcohol at her dad's wedding when she was drinking soda.

"So are you excited about graduation tomorrow?" she asks. She takes a sip of her drink.

"Not really." I plop down onto a bar stool. "It seems kind of pointless."

"Graduating?"

"Not *graduating*, just the graduation ceremony itself. Most of those people I never want to see again in my life."

"But then isn't it a good thing?" she asks. "To celebrate moving on?"

"I guess." I shrug. "But it's like we're all supposed to be moving on to the real world, celebrating this big achievement together. I don't know, it all just seems melodramatic and over the top."

"Yeah." She looks down into her drink thoughtfully, swishing the little red cocktail straw around in the liquid. "Your mom said your speech is amazing."

"My mom told you that? Jesus." I take another sip of my Sprite, then signal the bartender. Fuck this soda shit. I need something stronger.

"Well, she told my dad," Courtney says, "who told me."

I cringe. "Sorry."

She shrugs. "It's okay."

Ever since Courtney started dating Jordan, her dad hasn't exactly been thrilled. I don't really know the particulars, but for some reason, he doesn't like Jordan. I don't know why. Courtney's always struck me as someone who has her head on straight when it comes to things like relationships, and I don't think she'd be with a bad guy.

Anyway, Courtney's dad doesn't like Jordan, and it seems like lately he's been doing this weird thing where he's always trying to talk up other guys to Courtney, namely me. As if she and I are going to end up together or something. Which is ridiculous. Courtney's a really pretty girl, but there's never been anything like that between us. Ever. She's like my sister.

"I just wish my dad would stop trying to get me

interested in other guys. He needs to realize that I love Jordan, and that we're going to be together whether he likes it or not."

"Why doesn't he like him?"

She sighs. "It's complicated." She bites her lip. "But the thing is, he can't make my decisions for me. Especially when it comes to relationships. Hell, *I* have a hard enough time controlling who I fall in love with."

"I hear ya," I say. I understand exactly what she means.

Right then more than ever.

Because at that moment, Peyton walks into the ballroom.

Her dark hair is pulled back on the top, the rest of it loose and flowing around her shoulders. She's wearing a blue-green dress that's tight and yet sophisticated at the same time.

Her body has always driven me crazy.

She looks even better than I remember.

My body feels numb and my mouth goes dry.

"Bartender," I call again, louder this time. "I need a drink."

peyton before

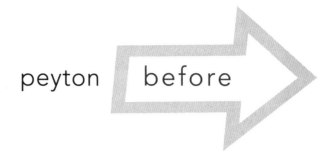

Friday, June 25, 8:10 p.m.
Siesta Key, Florida

I walk into the reception late, which is a bit of a tactical error on my part. Actually, a lot of a tactical error. I thought that if I got there early, if I got there *first*, I'd be forced to sit at some table with my parents, waiting and wondering when Jace was going to show up. Definitely not good for my mental state.

So I decided that arriving late, when I was pretty sure he'd already be there was a good strategy—that way I could just come in and find my seat and not have to worry about watching the door every five seconds, wondering when he was going to show up. Then, when I was finally ready, I'd very casually scan the room until my eyes landed on him, and then I'd just make sure to ignore him for the whole night.

Of course, this plan had not been decided on lightly. At

first I thought maybe I should be the bigger person, that I should go up to him and at least say hello. Brooklyn and I even spent a whole afternoon in my room coming up with opening lines. It was like a scene from a movie, where the heroine keeps practicing what she's going to say when she finally gets up the nerve to talk to the guy she likes. Of course, in those scenarios, it's usually a guy she's never talked to in her life, not a guy who she has a kind of history with and thought she was in love with. *Thought* being the operative word. As in, past tense.

After we came up with the perfect opening line ("Hi, Jace, it's nice to see you. You're looking very well," which would be followed by me pushing past him and going to talk to some imaginary person whom I just noticed was at the wedding), I realized that was a horrible plan. To be the better person, I mean. After all, he never replied to my text. And taking the high road is overrated anyway.

So I changed my plan to just ignoring him.

As you can see, I've spent way more time thinking about this than I should have.

Anyway, getting to the reception a little bit late meant my parents left their hotel room before I left mine. And so I had to walk into the reception alone, which was kind of intimidating, and a little bit humiliating. What if Jace saw me and thought my parents weren't even at the wedding and I'd come by myself just because I wanted to see him so badly? Like some kind of stalker or something?

I do my best to ignore the butterflies in my stomach, then walk with my shoulders back and my head held high right to table eight, which, according to my place card, is where I'm sitting.

There's no one at my table yet, which makes no sense since I got here late. Shouldn't people be seated? But it seems like everyone's at the bar, eating hors d'oeuvres and ordering drinks and having a grand old time. Damn. I should have come later. Or at least made sure someone was sitting at my table before I sat down.

God. What a disaster.

I sip water from my goblet, then grab an hors d'oeuvre from one of the tuxedoed waiters as he goes by. The thing I've learned about hors d'oeuvres is that you have to get them while you can—otherwise, you end up having to wait forever just to get some food.

I pop the pig in a blanket into my mouth, wondering why they'd have pigs in a blanket at such a high-level affair. Then I realize that if Jace lays his eyes on me now, he's going to see me sitting here all by myself, eating a hot dog. Which is *so* not the first impression I want to give him. I quickly swallow what's in my mouth and decide not to eat any more until other people sit down.

But now I don't know what to do with my hands.

I take another sip of my water.

"Our table's over here!" someone shouts. I look up to see a guy about my age dressed in a white suit and white shoes weaving his way through the crowd. He plops down into the seat next to me.

"Howdy!" he says. "Who are you? And are you here for the bride or the groom?" He sticks his hand out to me, almost knocking my water glass over in the process. I can't tell if he's drunk or just crazy.

"Um, I'm Peyton," I say, moving my glass to the other side of my plate and safely out of his reach. "And the groom is my uncle."

He nods. "I'm here with the bride." He pulls a sparkling white handkerchief out of his pocket, blows his nose, and then stuffs it back in his pocket. Ewww.

"I'm sorry," I say. "Are you Jocelyn?"

"Jocelyn?"

"Yes," I say. I point down at the card in front of him. "Because the place card says I'm supposed to be sitting next to someone named Jocelyn."

He peers down at it. "Oh, no, that's my girlfriend." He leans in toward me, like he's about to let me in on a secret. "Actually, she's my ex-girlfriend as of 12:17 a.m. last night. Or this morning, whatever." He reaches for his water glass, and downs the contents.

"I'm sorry," I say. "Um, that you guys broke up."

"Yeah, it was really horrible," he says. "I just . . . I don't understand what women want, you know? " He shakes his head sadly. "Do you?"

I'm about to say that of course I understand what women

want, that I *am* a woman, but then I realize that would be a lie. How can I know what women want when I hardly know what I want myself? "No." I sigh. "I don't think anyone knows what women want."

"That's what I've been trying to tell people," he says, gesturing around the wedding, as if maybe he's been going up to each and every guest, trying to convince them that no one knows what women want. He points a finger at me. "You're smart, I can tell."

"There you are!" Another guy comes up to our table, sounding a little frantic. "Jesus, B.J., can you stay in one place for one second?" This new guy sets a white ceramic cup full of coffee in front of B.J. "Here, drink that." He shakes his head, and I recognize him as Courtney's boyfriend, Jordan.

"Hi, I'm Jordan," he says, holding his hand out to me.

"I'm Peyton."

"Oh, right," he says, his face breaking into a smile. "Courtney's cousin. She talks about you all the time."

"She does? Good things, I hope."

"Always." He smiles again, and slides into the seat on the other side of B.J. And then, suddenly, Jordan's smile fades. "Ah, shit," he mutters.

I follow his gaze to where Courtney's crossing the room, walking toward us with another girl. They both look stunning—Courtney's in a floor-length red gown, and the girl she's with is wearing a tight baby-blue dress that hits just below her knees, her hair swept to one side.

"What?" I ask.

"That's Jocelyn," B.J. says morosely into his coffee. "That's my ex-girlfriend."

"Oh." I clear my throat. "Um, so you guys are both going to be at this table, then?"

"Yup," B.J. says. He leans in close to me. "Listen," he says, "I might flirt with you, you know, to make her jealous. I want her to know that I'm desirable and that other girls are interested in me." He inches his chair toward mine.

"Oh, I'm sure she already knows that," I say.

"No, she doesn't. So if I kiss you or something, just know that it's all part of the show."

Great.

"You're in my seat," Jocelyn says to B.J. when she gets to our table.

"I'm sorry," he says, looking around like he doesn't know where her voice is coming from. "I thought you weren't talking to me."

"I'm talking to you," she says. "I'm just not dating you. Now move."

"No." B.J. shakes his head. "I want to sit here." He scoots his chair even closer to mine and gives me a smile, like he wants to sit there so that he can be close to me.

"Who the hell are you?" Jocelyn asks. She puts her hand on her hip and glares down at me.

Lovely. Now I'm going to get my ass kicked by some girl

I don't know, over some guy who I don't know, and don't even *care* to know. "Um, I'm Peyton."

"Jocelyn," Courtney says, grabbing her arm, "come on, you can sit over here with me."

"I don't want to sit over there with you," Jocelyn says. "I want to sit there, in my seat."

"You heard Courtney," B.J. says, waving Jocelyn away like she's some kind of gnat. "You go sit over there. I'm going to sit with Peyton." He puts his hand on my arm and gives me another smile.

I smile back tentatively. I don't know what's worse— pretending to be going along with B.J.'s flirting and maybe getting into a fistfight with Jocelyn, or not going along with it and dealing with whatever craziness B.J. might come up with to punish me.

Joceyln's eyes widen when she sees B.J.'s hand on my arm, and for a moment, I'm pretty sure she's going to hit me. Or him. Or both of us. But at the last second she changes her mind, and her face breaks into a wide smile. But it's not the kind of smile you give when you're happy. It's the kind of smile you give when you're up to something bad.

Sure enough, a minute later, she's heading off to the dance floor, where she grabs some random guy and starts grinding on him. It's kind of a spectacle, actually, since no one's really even dancing yet. And Jocelyn's kind of rubbing all over the guy. And he's definitely older than her. Like, twenty-five at least.

Jordan looks at Courtney, but Courtney just shrugs. "We have to let them work it out," she says.

"We're not going to work it out!" B.J. declares. "You two need to stop babysitting us. We're breaking up." He motions for a waiter who's holding a tray of champagne flutes, grabs one, and downs it in about one second.

Great. Somehow I've ended up at the crazy table. Why is this stuff always happening to me? Why aren't I sitting with my parents, over in some corner somewhere, listening to adults talk about property taxes and kitchen renovations and school districts and all the other ridiculous things parents talk about?

Then again, this is a lot more interesting. At least I won't be bored. In fact, I realize I haven't thought about Jace in, like, ten minutes. That must be some kind of record or something. I guess being about to get your ass kicked will do that to you.

Courtney slides over to me and smiles. "I like your dress," she says.

"Thanks. I like yours, too."

"How's everything going?"

I paste a smile on my face. "It's going great."

"Really?" she says. "Because—"

"Excuse me," a voice on the other side of Courtney says, "but I think you're in my seat."

I look up. And there he is. Jace. The wind immediately gets knocked out of me, and red-hot lust shoots through my body. He looks amazing, even better than I remember. Tall. Dark hair. Blue eyes. He's wearing a white button-up shirt and gray pants, and his tie is loosened around his neck. His sleeves are rolled up a little bit, showing off his forearms, which are tanned and muscular.

"Oh." Courtney sounds surprised. She looks at me. "This is . . . I mean, this is *my* seat." She points to the place card. "And I was talking to Peyton."

"Yeah," Jace says. "But I want to sit there."

Courtney looks at me, her eyes asking me if it's okay. And what can I do? I can't say no. If I say no, Jace is going to realize that he's having an effect on me. And what is it that they always say? The opposite of love isn't hate, it's indifference?

Well. I will show Jace Renault that I am totally indifferent to him, thank you very much.

"It's fine," I say, and shrug.

And then, before I know what's happening, Courtney's getting up, and Jace is settling into the chair next to me. He reaches out and grabs my water glass, then takes a swig.

"That was my water," I say.

"Sorry." He holds it out to me. "You want it back?"

"Not *now*."

He shrugs and then takes another sip. "So how are you doing?"

He looks at me, and I look at him, and something about the way he's doing it, something about the way he's looking at me is sending shivers up my spine. He's looking at me the same way that I've been wanting to look at him. Like maybe he wants to take me into the coatroom and get me naked or something.

And that's when I know.

It is definitely not over between me and Jace Renault.

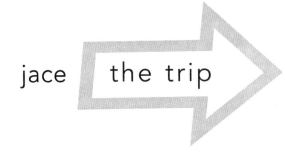

jace | the trip

I don't know how or why that happened. One minute I was telling that stupid story about my fake dog having cancer (which was pretty scummy, I'll admit), the next minute I was goofing off and splashing around in the bathtub with Hector, and then somehow, I was kissing Peyton.

I couldn't help myself. It was like I had to have her. Her body was pressed against mine, and I *needed* to kiss her. If I'm being totally honest, I've been wanting to kiss her all damn day. I'm actually surprised I lasted as long as I did.

And the kiss was good. Really, really, *really* good.

I pull her down closer to me, my hands on her face and in her hair. I want the kiss to go on forever. But after a little bit, she pulls back.

"Hi," I say, giving her a lazy smile.

"Hey," she says. She rests her head on my chest, and for some ridiculous reason, we just stay like that, me holding her in a bathtub while I stroke her hair.

Hector is gone—I don't really know where he is, but it definitely cannot be anywhere good. He's probably messing up the room. But I don't care. Right now all I care about is Peyton, about making this moment last forever. It sounds cheesy, but I don't give a fuck.

We stay like that for maybe twenty minutes or so, alternating between kissing and just lying there. Finally, she props her head up on her elbow. "We should get out of this tub," she says. "My clothes are soaking wet."

I grin. "Or you could just take them off."

"Funny." She pulls herself up and out of the tub, and after a second, I follow. She hands me a fluffy white towel off the rack in the bathroom, and I get to work drying off my hair.

"I need some dry clothes," I tell her. "I'll be right back."

I head back to my room and change into a clean T-shirt and a pair of track pants. When I get back to Peyton's room, she's sitting on the edge of the bed with Hector. She's changed into a soft pink T-shirt and a pair of black yoga pants, her hair hanging in curly tendrils down her back.

"Hi," she says.

"Hi." I sit down next to her. But suddenly, something feels . . . I don't know, *different*. Like the spell was broken or something. Now that we've kissed, I'm not sure what I'm supposed to do. Kiss her again? Turn on the television? Act like nothing happened?

"So," she says.

"So." I look at Hector. "You dried him off."

She nods.

"He looks clean."

"Yup." She nods again.

Wow. Talk about awkward. This is what I hate about things like this. It's like they can't ever just be normal. They always have to be some big deal. Like, we just kissed. So what? Let's kiss again, that's what I say.

"So, are you hungry?" I try. "Maybe we should order food or something."

"I got food from the gas station."

"Oh. Right. Well, what do you want to do?"

"I think . . ." She twists her hands in her lap nervously. "I think that maybe I should go to sleep."

I blink at her, unable to believe what I'm hearing. "You think that you should go to *sleep*?"

She nods.

"But it's not even ten o'clock!"

"We need to get on the road early tomorrow."

"Bullshit."

"What?" She looks at me, sounding shocked that I would say such a thing.

"I said bullshit," I say. "I just kissed you, and you're

freaked out by it, and so now you want to do what you always do. Just run away and pretend it didn't happen."

Her eyes widen, and flash with anger. "Are you kidding me?"

"No." I cross my arms over my chest. "I'm dead serious."

"You think I'm freaked out because you kissed me?"

"Yes."

"I'm not."

"You are!"

"I'm not!"

"Then why are you acting like it?"

She springs off the bed, like there's too much anger in her body to keep it still. "Okay, fine," she says. "I am freaked out, Jace. I'm freaked out because for some reason, I can't stop thinking about you. I can't stop thinking about how it feels to kiss you, about how happy I was when I thought we were going to be together, about how even though I feel like I should hate you, my heart knows that I don't."

"You don't have to be freaked out about that."

"Yes, I do," she says. "I do have to be freaked out about it!"

I stand up and go to put my arms around her, but she pushes me away. "No," she says. "Every time I let myself get close to you, I end up getting hurt."

"Every time?" I ask. I'm still standing close to her, and it's taking every ounce of my self-control not to reach out and kiss her again. "I don't think we've gotten close enough times for there to be an 'every time.'"

"Yes, we have!" she says.

"Name one time."

"Last night." She crosses her arms over her chest. "We . . . I mean, we . . . you know what happened between us last night, and then I found out that you lied to me."

"I didn't lie to you," I say.

"A lie by omission is still a lie," she counters.

"Oh, really?" I say. "Because if we're counting lies by omissions as lies, then I'm not the only one we should be talking about." It's kind of a horrible thing to say. It's not fair to her to bring up what I'm talking about.

"What are you talking about?" She frowns.

"Nothing," I say. "Just forget it." I shake my head and grab Hector's leash off the nightstand and clip it onto his collar. He's just sitting there on the bed, his head down, almost like he knows we're fighting. It actually makes me kind of sad. Just because me and Peyton are pissed at each other doesn't mean we should be scaring poor Hector.

"No," Peyton says. "I don't want to forget it." She stands in front of me, blocking my way to the door.

"Peyton," I say. "Stop. I don't want to talk about it. I'm going back to my room."

"Of course you are," she says, giving me a bitter laugh. "That's what you do, right, Jace? Everything's always some kind of big joke, you never want to talk about anything real, like why you kissed me last night, or why you lied to me, or why you just stopped talking to me after Christmas."

"You think that's what happened?" I say. "That I just stopped talking to you?"

"You didn't?" She crosses her arms over her chest, daring me to contradict her.

"No! I mean, I did, but it wasn't . . ." My thoughts are spinning around now, making my brain all confused and crazy. I take a deep breath. "It's not that simple. And besides, I told you I didn't want to talk about it."

"Of course." She steps out of the way, and I'm halfway to the door before she speaks again. "Don't worry about tomorrow, Jace," she says. "I can find my own way home."

Suddenly, I'm super pissed off. Like, *really* pissed off. I don't know why, since it's not like she said anything horrible, and let's face it—her giving me an out is going to make my life a whole lot easier. I might even be able to make graduation.

But it's just the way she says it—in this completely detached voice, like she's taken all her anger and hurt and folded it up into a little square and then deposited it into some box somewhere that's out of reach. It's the same shit she pulled with me over the spring, the same shit that caused her to be the only girl who's ever broken my heart.

"Oh, really?" I say. "You can find your own way home?"

She nods. "I wouldn't want you to have to express your feelings or anything. We all know what a horrible thing that would be."

"Right," I say. "And you know all about expressing your feelings, right, Peyton?"

"More than you."

"Really?" I counter. "Then why didn't you tell me your parents were getting divorced?"

Her face changes in an instant. Her eyes go wide and her skin goes pale and I want to take the words back, I would do *anything* to take the words back, but it's too late—they're hanging there, over us, their meaning permeating the room.

"Peyton—" I take a step toward her.

"No." She puts her hand up, stopping me, and the look in her eyes tells me she's serious. "How did you know about that?"

"Your uncle told me."

"My uncle told you? But that's—" She bites her lip, so hard that it starts to turn red. Her eyes narrow. "Just. Go."

"Peyton, let's—"

"I'm serious, Jace," she says. *"Go."*

"No." I shake my head. "I'm not leaving you. I'm not giving up on this again."

"Fine." She grabs her key card and her purse off the nightstand. "If you're not going to leave, then I will."

"Peyton." I try one more time, but it's useless.

She walks out, leaving me standing there, alone, in a hotel room that isn't even mine.

the trip peyton

Saturday, June 26, 9:47 p.m.
Savannah, Georgia

By the time I get outside the hotel, tears are streaming down my face. They're the worst kind of tears—the kind that are hot and angry and devastating, the kind that slide silently down your cheeks and leave salty tracks on your skin.

For the first time, I realize the drawback to the weather in the South—it's never cold enough that your tears will freeze on your face before they have a chance to fall down your cheeks. And so you can't deny that you're crying.

I don't know where I'm going or what I should do. I'm alone in downtown Savannah, and it's probably not a good idea for me to be wandering the streets alone at night. I have no phone, and I hardly have any money, either.

And then I remember the restaurant the front desk clerk recommended—the Distillery. She said it was within walking distance, and she made it seem like it was a popular place. I don't know what else to do, so I start walking toward downtown, and sure enough, a couple of blocks later, I see it.

There's a big neon sign outside, with umbrellaed tables set up on the sidewalk. The inside looks warm and welcoming, so I brush my tears away and walk into the restaurant.

"Welcome to the Distillery," the hostess says, picking up a menu and giving me a smile. "One tonight?"

Her voice has a gentle tone, and the fact that she says "one tonight" instead of "just one" makes me feel like I'm out enjoying some time to myself, and not like a big loser who has no one to go to a restaurant with.

"Yes," I say. "One tonight."

She shows me to a cute little table in the corner of the restaurant, and puts the menu down in front of me.

When the waitress, a gorgeous African American girl with short hair and a bright white smile, comes over, I order a Diet Coke and the Southern chicken tenders.

While I wait for my food, I think about Jace. I wonder what he's doing—if he's back at the hotel, if he stayed in my room, if he went back to his own, if he left. He said he wasn't going to, but come on. Why would he really stay?

I cannot believe he knew this whole time that my parents were getting a divorce. Does that mean Courtney knows, too? Does that mean it's really happening? I feel the tears starting up again and I swipe at them angrily with my napkin.

I am not going to start crying in here. I can't—someone

would definitely ask me what was wrong. The vibe in here is a cheerful one. Pretty much everyone is hanging out and talking, clinking their glasses together as they order more drinks and toast to whatever it is they're all so damn happy about.

When the waitress sets the chicken fingers down in front of me, at first I'm not that hungry. But I force myself to take a bite, and they're so good that by the time I'm on my third or fourth bite, I'm inhaling them.

And as I eat, I keep thinking about Jace.

I think about every single thing he's ever done to me. Every single time he let me down. And yes, when he said he hasn't let me down enough to make it an "every single time," he was right.

But when you're in love with someone—or at least, when you think you are—once is enough.

I met Jace over Christmas, which I think gave us kind of a weird start to begin with. Christmas is such a magical time. The lights, the sparkliness, the tinsel, the cold and snow outside mixed with the warmth inside.

Okay, that was cheesy, but it really is true. Who wouldn't want to fall in love around Christmastime? It was like the deck was stacked against me right from the beginning.

I'd just found out that my parents were getting divorced. At the beginning of December, they sat me down in the dining room over a dinner of roast chicken and potatoes (made by my mom—I should have known something was up when she offered to cook dinner) and told me.

Not like it was a shock. I mean, I live in the same house with them. I could hear their screaming fights and my dad had been sleeping in the guestroom for months. But it still hit me like a sucker punch in the stomach. Which is weird now that I think about it—that I had that reaction—because on some level, I didn't really believe them.

I remember calling my sister at college, and she seemed to agree with me. "They've been talking about divorce for years," she said. "I doubt it's really going to happen."

Of course, Kira was completely out of the loop—she'd been away at NYU for two years, and she'd spent the summer in Europe, backpacking around with her friends. On the rare occasions she did come home for a weekend, she'd end up spending most of the time out somewhere with her high school friends, or holed up in her old room, studying.

My parents would put on a great face—making sure not to fight when Kira was around, making sure we all ate dinner as a family on the nights she was home.

Looking back, I probably should have seen that as odd. Why would they need to put on some kind of show when their older daughter was in the house?

Anyway, there's no way Kira could have had any idea how bad things had gotten between my parents. She didn't know they were up late into the night, having screaming fights that would last forever. She didn't see me when I'd sneak out of bed and put on my iPod so I wouldn't have to hear the yelling. (Eventually, I started plugging my iPod into the outlet by my nightstand, putting my playlist of soothing pop songs on repeat, and falling asleep with it on, so I wouldn't have to hear my parents at all.)

But even though things were bad, I still didn't really believe they were going to divorce. They were always threatening each other with divorce. They'd yell at each other all the time about how they were going to leave each other.

True, they'd never actually sat me down and *said* they were getting divorced before this, but still. It somehow seemed more like another show they were putting on instead of a major marital decision. My mom even dabbed daintily at her eyes with a cloth napkin while they were telling me, and my dad reached over and gripped my hand like he was afraid I was going to start crying or something. The whole thing just seemed so staged and fake.

Anyway, after the big divorce reveal, my mom decided that she and I were going to Florida to spend Christmas with Courtney and her dad. I wasn't all that psyched to go—not that I cared that much about Christmas, but I wanted to spend the school vacation hanging out with Brooklyn. But my mom was insistent.

I felt bad and guilty about leaving my dad alone on Christmas, and so before we left, I pulled the box of Christmas decorations out of the attic, and dressed the mantel with our stockings. Then, right before my mom and I left for the airport, I stuffed my dad's stocking with the things I knew he would like—Lindt chocolates, butterscotch truffles, a new pair of socks, and a gift card to his favorite sports store. I signed everything as being from Santa.

The first day we were in Florida was, I think, the first time I realized the whole divorce thing might actually be real.

Courtney and I were sitting out by her pool, enjoying the fact that it was almost eighty degrees and sunny—in December!—when we heard the sound of my mom crying coming through the kitchen window.

"It's going to be fine," Courtney's dad soothed.

I'd never heard my mom cry like that before. It gave me a weird sort of twisting feeling in my stomach, and anxiety bloomed in my throat. Courtney turned the page of her magazine loudly, pretending she hadn't heard them, and after a moment, I did the same.

That night, she invited me to come to a Christmas party at her boyfriend Jordan's mom's (Jordan's mom was also Courtney's dad's new girlfriend. Awkward.) house.

"I don't think so," I said, shaking my head. "I think I'm just going to stay here."

"And do what?" she said. "Read? Watch TV?"

I didn't know that the big deal was—both of those seemed like wonderful options, especially since I was in the middle of watching the first season of *Downton Abbey* on

Netflix and it was really starting to get good. I loved all those English accents and regency clothes. Or frocks, as they called them.

"Yeah." I shrugged. "Or maybe wrap some presents." It was a lie. I'd wrapped all my presents back in Connecticut, and brought them to Florida like that.

"You're coming," Courtney said.

"I have nothing to wear."

"You can borrow something of mine."

I shook my head.

"Come on," she said. "You can't just stay inside all night, you're only here for a few days. Don't you want to take advantage of the weather?"

I didn't really see how standing around inside Jordan's mom's house was any different from sitting around in Courtney's dad's house, but whatever. I needed to snap out of my funk, and I knew she was right—staying home wasn't going to do it.

"Fine," I said, shooting one last longing look toward where my computer was sitting on the nightstand in the guestroom. "I'll go."

"Yay!" She grabbed my hand and pulled me into her room so we could find something for me to wear.

I figured there'd be no way I'd be able to fit into any of Courtney's clothes, but surprisingly, she had this really pretty red dress that was perfect. It had a slightly poofy bubble skirt and a fitted top that plunged down in the front and gave me just the right amount of cleavage. I looped a long silver jingle-bell necklace around my neck, slid my feet into a pair of Courtney's strappy silver sandals (they were only a little bit too small), and lined my eyes with a sparkly gold shadow. By the time we left, I was a feeling a little bit better and a lot more festive.

The party was in full swing when we pulled up. We walked right into the house and through the great room, through the sliding glass doors and to the back, where most people had spilled out onto the lanai and were standing around, mingling and drinking champagne.

I'll admit that I noticed him right away—he was sitting on an expensive-looking lounge chair, and the light from the pool was illuminating his face, and I thought he was cute. Okay, fine, I thought he was gorgeous. He took my breath away in a way that no guy had ever done before.

I couldn't take my eyes off him all night.

"That's Jace," Courtney said finally, when she caught me looking. "Do you want me to introduce you?"

I shook my head. One, I wasn't that bold. And two, guys who looked like that didn't usually go for girls who looked like me. It wasn't that I thought I was ugly—I knew I was cute, passably pretty. I didn't have guys falling all over me, and I wasn't going to win any beauty pageants, but still—I did okay. Jace, however, seemed like he was way out of my league.

But when Courtney went off with her boyfriend, Jordan,

leaving me to fend for myself, Jace decided to introduce himself.

I was over by the veggies and dip tray, working my way through a piece of celery, when he came over and picked up a plate.

"You're not double dipping, are you?" he asked, giving me a mock serious look.

I shook my head, not trusting myself to speak. First, I had a mouthful of vegetable, and second, he was even cuter up close than he was far away. My heart started pounding in my chest, my body flushed hot, and I had to take two big deep breaths to calm myself down.

When he was done loading his plate, he popped a tomato into his mouth and then reached out and tweaked my necklace. The jingle bell rang.

"Cute," he said. "I like jingle-bell necklaces."

"Oh," I said. "Me too." I realized how stupid it sounded, so I quickly added, "I borrowed it from my cousin." I licked my lips, which were suddenly completely dry. "Courtney's my cousin. I'm here visiting her from Connecticut."

"Cool," he said. He wiped his hand on a napkin and stuck it out for me to shake. "I'm Jace Renault. My mom's best friends with Courtney's mom. And my dad's best friends with Courtney's dad."

"Wow," I said, shaking my head. "That's gotta be awkward."

He nodded. "Super awkward." He leaned in and whispered in my ear, like we were sharing a secret. "Although if you ask me, I think it's pretty dicky for a dude to leave his family for another woman." His breath tickled at my skin, making every nerve in my body stand on high alert.

"Well," I said, "on the surface, yeah, it seems like an asshole move. But what if it's true love?"

"True love?" He was still standing close to me, although he'd moved back just a little bit, and now his eyes were on mine. "You really believe that?"

"In true love? Or that Courtney's dad found it with another woman?"

He cocked his head. "Both."

I bit my lip and thought about it. "No," I said. "I don't believe that it's true love. But I do believe in it. At least, I think I do."

"Why don't you think it's true love between them?" he asked. "Have you ever seen them together?"

I shake my head. "Just an instinct. Besides, haven't they only known each other for, like, less than a year?"

He nods. "So, you don't believe in love at first sight?"

I shook my head no. "But I do believe in lust at first sight." I was shocked that I had the nerve to say this, and my face felt warm.

"Really?" The sides of his mouth slid up into a grin. "Interesting."

My heart was racing now. While we'd been talking, we'd moved a few steps over to the side, and now we were a little bit removed from the party, almost like we were there together.

"So what's your name?" he asked.

"Peyton," I said.

He looked at me, seemingly taking it in, like my telling him my name was one of the most important things he'd ever heard. He nodded. "Peyton," he said, and I couldn't help but think that the way he said my name was super sexy. "That's a really nice name."

Yes, I thought as I took a sip of my ginger ale. I definitely believed in lust at first sight.

We ended up talking for the rest of the night—sitting in the corner, sharing one of the big chaise lounge chairs that dotted the lanai. He sat next to me so casually, just sort of leaned back next to me so that our legs were touching, like it was the most natural thing in the world for us to be sitting on the same chair.

He was wearing khaki pants and Nike sandals, which was so not appropriate for a party like this, but he somehow managed to pull it off.

Every time the bare skin of my ankle brushed against his, he set me on fire.

We didn't talk about anything important, really, that first night. Mostly just gossiped about the other people at the party. A couple of times I caught Courtney and her boyfriend, Jordan, over in the corner, glancing at us and whispering, and I knew what they were thinking: that something was going to happen between me and Jace.

I knew it wasn't true—like I said, guys like Jace never really gave me the time of day. He was probably just bored at a party where he hardly knew anyone, and had found someone his own age to pass the time with. That didn't stop me from getting a secret thrill out of the fact that Jordan and Courtney were talking about us.

But when we left that night, I thought that was it. I dodged Courtney's questions, rolling my eyes at her suggestions that Jace was flirting with me. She asked me if I thought he was cute, and I copped to it, because honestly, it wasn't really a matter of opinion. But that was it, I told her. I was never going to see him again.

I had a hard time falling asleep that night.

But by the next morning, I'd forced myself to forget about him.

Until Courtney and I were out shopping for bathing suits— so not my favorite activity, but she was determined that we were going to go to the beach. (Of course, I hadn't brought a bathing suit specifically because I wanted to avoid the beach, but Courtney was insistent.) She'd offered to let me borrow one of hers, but there was no way that I was going to set myself up for that kind of humiliation. A party dress was one thing, but a bathing suit was another story.

I was in the dressing room of this place at the mall called

Swimming with Sharks, trying on a particularly unflattering tankini—wearing a tankini in the first place is kind of like putting a big sign on yourself that says you don't feel comfortable in a bikini—when my cell phone rang, flashing a Florida area code and a number that I didn't recognize.

Figuring it could be my mom calling from my uncle's house or something, I picked it up.

"Hello?" I balanced my phone against my shoulder as I tried to slide the top of the tankini over my body. It wasn't working. My boobs were slipping out of the sides, and the front gave me that weird smooshed-boob thing that sometimes happens with sports bras.

"Peyton?" It was a male voice I didn't recognize.

"This is Peyton," I said, preparing myself for a telemarketer. I had put my number on that no-call list, but I heard it took a few weeks for it to kick in. I didn't even *have* the ability to switch my cable provider or anything like that, but did these telemarketers care? No. They kept calling and pushing, and of course I was way too nice to just hang up because I figured their job must really suck, sitting in a hot call center all day and probably earning about eight dollars an—

"Hey, it's Jace."

"Who?" I asked. Not because I didn't know who it was, but because I was sure I'd misheard. The bottom of the tankini fell to the floor, leaving me standing there in just my underwear and the top of the bathing suit.

"Jace Renault? We met last night at the party."

"Oh," I said. "Right." There was an awkward pause, and I tried to come up with something brilliant to say. I couldn't, so he forged on.

"I hope you don't mind that I called you—I called Courtney's house and your uncle gave me your cell number."

"No, I don't mind." Mind? Now that the shock had worn off, my heart was beating in my chest, and all I could think about was that Jace was on the phone. He called Courtney's dad to get my number! I sat down on the little bench in the dressing room, trying not to think about whatever kind of germs were lurking on there.

"So what's up?" he asked. "Are you busy?"

"Busy? No, I'm not busy." There was a pause. God, he must have thought I was some kind of idiot, incapable of making conversation. "Are you?"

"Am I busy?"

"No. Yes. I mean, what are you doing? What are you up to?" God, this was going from bad to worse.

"Not much," he said, and I heard what sounded like the squeak of springs, like maybe he was lying down on his bed or something. I tried not to think about his body, stretched out on his bed, his shirt slipping up just a little bit, showing his rock-hard stomach. I wasn't sure his stomach was rock hard, but I had an idea it would be. I blushed.

"So why are you calling?"

He laughed. "Getting right to the point, are you?"

"No, I just meant . . . I mean, if you went to the trouble

of getting my number from my uncle, you must be calling for a reason."

"I was wondering if maybe you wanted to grab lunch in a little while."

My heart caught in my chest. Before I could answer, there was a knock on the dressing room door. Courtney. "Hey," she said. "Are you in there? How does it look?"

"Is that Courtney?" Jace asked.

"Um, yeah." I was about to add that we were at the mall trying on bathing suits, but I was afraid if he knew I was out, he would take his invitation back. I knew that wanting to go to lunch with him so bad was pathetic. But what was even more pathetic was letting him think that I didn't have a life, so I said, "We're out shopping for bathing suits."

"Really?" he said, sounding interested. "That's kind of hot."

"We're not in the same dressing room," I said, rolling my eyes. Why did guys always get so turned on by the thought of two girls being naked together? Couldn't they be satisfied with just one?

"I wasn't thinking about Courtney."

"Oh." I was breathless. I couldn't help it. He had a hot voice.

"Peyton?" Another knock on the door. "Are you on the phone?"

"Yeah," I called. "Just a second."

"I should probably let you go," Jace said. "It seems like you're busy."

"Yeah," I said, holding my breath and hoping that he'd bring up having lunch again.

"So what time are you going to be done shopping? Do you want to meet for a late lunch or something? Like maybe around three?"

"That sounds great."

"Okay." I could hear him smiling through the phone, and that made me smile. "I'll pick you up at Courtney's?"

"Sounds good," I said, trying to act like it was no big deal, that I always got asked out by super-hot guys a day after meeting them.

We hung up, and I opened the door to the dressing room, forgetting that I was wearing only the top of a bathing suit and my underwear.

"Oh," Courtney said, frowning. "You're not dressed."

I grabbed her arm and pulled her into the dressing room. "Jace Renault just called me."

She smiled. "I knew it!"

"Shhh!" My grip on her arm tightened. "Do you swear you didn't tell him to?"

She shook her head. "I would never!"

I knew it was true. Courtney would never do something like that, ever.

"Okay." I bit my lip. "We're going to have a late lunch."

"Well," Courtney said, tossing my clothes at me. "That settles it. Forget bathing suits. We need to get you something for your date."

So we did. I bought a pair of skinny jeans and this shimmery off-the-shoulder top with a matching spaghetti-strap tank top that was sexy and casual and perfect.

I bought new lip gloss and a sparkly mascara and I spent two hours getting ready. And by the time Jace came to pick me up, I felt beautiful.

He took me to this really cool Hawaiian fusion restaurant, and I had fish tacos that were so good I could hardly stand it. When we were done eating, we walked around Siesta Key Village, poking into souvenir shops until we got bored, and then headed down toward the beach. We talked about everything and anything, and it was pretty much perfect.

As the sun went down, we sat on the beach, letting the warm water lap at our feet. Honestly, it was the most romantic thing that had ever happened to me.

As the sun dipped down, Jace turned toward me.

"Make a wish," he said.

"Why?"

"You always make a wish when the sun goes down," he said, inching toward me on the sand.

He smelled like the ocean, and when he pulled me close, electricity zinged through my body, setting my nerve endings on fire.

"Did you just make that up?" I asked.

"No." He shook his head. "It's, like, a thing."

"Okay." I shut my eyes tight as the sun disappeared,

looking like it was dipping right into the water. When I opened them, I turned and looked at him. His eyes were shut tight, his hair ruffling in the breeze. After a moment, he opened them.

"What did you wish for?" I asked.

"If I tell you, it won't come true." The sides of his mouth pulled up into a grin.

"I won't tell anyone."

He looked at me seriously, pretending like he was thinking about it. Then he shook his head. "Nope."

"Fine." I shrugged. "Then I'm not telling you mine."

"I don't want to know yours." His face was moving closer to mine, and now his lips were right there, teasing me.

"Yes, you do."

"How do you know?"

"Because it was a really good wish."

"Really?" He was even closer to me now, so close that I could feel the warmth of his skin against my cheek, the whisper of his breath against my forehead. He reached down and took my chin, tilted it up toward him gently.

"Yes," I said, almost unable to speak. "Really."

"So you're not going to tell me?"

"I'll tell you mine if you tell me yours."

He smiled. "Deal." And then, before I knew what was happening, his mouth was on mine. The kiss was delicious, soft and perfect and amazing, the kind of kiss you read about in books but don't think could ever happen to you, especially not from an amazingly hot guy you've only known for a day.

We kissed for what felt like forever, falling back onto the sand as the last slip of light dipped below the horizon.

When we finally stopped, my lips wanted his to come back, wanted to feel them forever. I know it sounds ridiculous, but it was true. He held my hand all the way back to the car.

I was going to be in Florida for the next few days, but he was leaving the next morning to spend Christmas skiing in Colorado with his family.

He told me he'd text me, but I didn't believe him.

But as I was climbing into bed that night, my phone was already ringing.

"Hello?" I said as I slid under the sheets in the spare bedroom of Courtney's house.

"It's me," he said, and I smiled.

We talked all night, until he had to get off the phone and head to the airport. When I got home to Connecticut, we picked up right where we left off. Talking all the time. E-mailing. Texting. We even talked about visiting each other over spring break.

I felt like maybe I was falling in love with him. Brooklyn thought I was crazy—she didn't understand how I could be so caught up in a guy I'd only spent a few hours with, a guy who was thousands of miles away, a guy who I had no idea when I would see again.

I understood her point, but I couldn't stop it. It was a force bigger than me. And whenever a voice in the back of my head would whisper that it wasn't real, I would ignore it. I wanted so badly to believe that it was.

In January, when my parents' fighting started getting worse, I'd bundle up in sweatpants and cozy socks, then take my cell out onto the deck and talk to Jace, the cold night air nipping at my lips.

We talked about everything. And yet, for some reason, I never told him that my parents were getting divorced. I don't know why. It wasn't that I thought he would judge me—we'd told each other plenty of personal things. Looking back now, I would have to say that it was because I was in some kind of denial. I didn't want to admit to *myself* that my parents were getting divorced, so why would I tell Jace that they were?

We went on like this for two months.

Until one day.

He just stopped.

Stopped returning my calls.

Stopped e-mailing me.

Stopped texting me.

It was like he just disappeared.

Finally, I broke down and told Courtney, asked her if she had any idea what might have happened. She called and asked him. It made me feel pathetic, but I didn't know what else to do. I was desperate.

All she could offer was that he said it was complicated, and that he wouldn't tell her any more than that.

So I did my best to forget him. And failed miserably.

The waitress brings the check over, snapping me out of my reverie.

"Here you go, hon," she says as she sets it down and picks up my empty plate. "Can I get you anything else tonight?"

"No." I shake my head. I'm not ready to go back to the hotel, but what choice do I really have? I can't just stay here all night drinking sodas. So I pay my bill and head out of the comfort of the cozy restaurant and back onto the street.

I'm sure it's just my mood, but the streets of Savannah somehow seem dark and dirty now, the people not as happy. The few that are out this late move past me, their hands in their pockets, not making eye contact. It's a little cooler now than it was before, and the wind kicks up a little, forcing me to keep my head down as I walk.

As I approach the hotel, I know I should go in the side entrance—the door that's the closest to my room, the door that will take me right back to where I need to go. It doesn't make sense to go around to the front—it's a longer walk.

But I want to see if Jace's car is still in the parking lot across the street—if he's still at the hotel or if he took off, leaving me here alone. Not that I would blame him.

But still. He said he wasn't going to.

And I can't help it. I want him to be here. I need to find out if he is.

So I circle back around to the front of the hotel, keeping my eyes down on the cobblestone pavement until the very last moment. And then, right when I'm almost at the door, I look up, over to the parking lot.

The lot is full, and I scan the cars for his. But it's not there. I know it, even though I keep looking. There's an empty spot—the same spot where he parked earlier. It's the only empty spot in the lot, which means that it must have just recently been vacated.

He left. Even though he said he wasn't going to, Jace left.

the trip   jace

Saturday, June 26, 10:27 p.m.
Savannah, Georgia

I left. Yup. I took Hector right back to my room, packed up the little stuff I had, headed out to my car, jumped in, and left. I didn't even care that I didn't check out. Let them charge me or whatever they fuck they want to do.

In fact, I hope they do charge me. I hope they give me some kind of bullshit no-checkout fee, or an expensive room-cleaning fee since I ended up leaving the room a big mess from Hector's bath. I don't care. I'll sue them. I'll get a lawyer and I'll sue them for whatever dumb charges they want to try to stick me with. There has to be some law against that, some kind of FCC regulations or some shit.

I reach over and turn the radio on angrily. I have no idea where I'm going. I just know that I have to get away from here, that I have to get away from Peyton.

Hector's sitting next to me on the front seat, looking at me quietly.

"What's wrong?" I ask him.

He whines a little and then inches over until his nose is on my lap. I swear this dog can sense people's emotions. It's crazy.

I reach down and give him a rub on his muzzle. "I'm sorry, boy," I say. "I shouldn't be taking my bad mood out on you. You didn't do anything."

In fact, when I think about it, Hector's the only one who's actually been supportive of me. He's just been happy to be by my side, not asking for anything except some attention and some food once in a while. He's very low maintenance, and he doesn't put any expectations on me. He doesn't keep secrets from me. He doesn't expect me to go to some stupid graduation and give some big speech. He doesn't expect me to just accept it when he doesn't tell me his parents are getting divorced. He just loves me no matter what. Even though I've been treating him like I don't care.

"I'm sorry, boy," I say again, and scratch his ears some more. He sighs in happiness, snuggles up closer to me, and then closes his eyes and immediately falls asleep. I shake my head, wishing my life were as easy as his.

I don't bother turning the GPS on. I just follow the signs and head south, figuring that at some point I'll end up back in Florida. I'm not in any rush to get back there, anyway.

My mom will be ripshit and I'll have to figure out what I'm going to do about graduation.

But I keep driving. Even though going home is going to suck, and even though I don't know exactly where I'm going, I need the miles to keep adding up, to keep putting distance between Peyton and me.

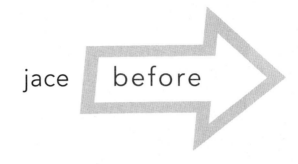

jace before

Friday, June 25, 8:18 p.m.
Siesta Key, Florida

I wanted to play it cool. I wanted to sit here at this stupid wedding reception, next to Peyton, and just pretend that she didn't mean anything to me.

But it's that fucking dress she's wearing. It's low-cut and tight and just . . . Jesus. Why would she wear a dress like that? Is she doing it just to torture me? I like the idea that maybe she had me in mind when she picked it out. Of course, she might be wearing it because she wants to get attention from other guys.

I look around the wedding suspiciously, trying to see if anyone is looking at her. I don't want to have to punch someone out, but I'll do it if I have to.

"So what's up?" I ask her. "How have you been?"

I see the indecision flick through her eyes—she's try-ing to decide whether or not to tell me to fuck off, to turn her back and keep talking to Jordan and Courtney. But instead, she just shrugs. "Fine. How have you been?"

"I'm good." I take another sip of her water, still wishing I had some kind of alcohol. I never did get a chance to get the bartender's attention.

"Getting ready for graduation?"

I nod. "Yup."

"That's nice." Her eyes slide past me, scanning the room, almost like she's looking for someone to get up and go talk to. I'm desperate to keep her near me, and so I say, "I'm giving a speech."

"You got valedictorian?"

I nod.

"That's amazing, Jace, congratulations." She smiles, and I can tell she's really happy for me. And even though I don't care about the stupid speech, even though I don't care about being valedictorian, I smile too.

Because the way she's looking at me makes me realize something—it is definitely not over between Peyton Miller and me.

Talking about my speech seems to somehow break the ice between us, and all through dinner, we're talking and laughing and kind of flirting.

I can't take my eyes off her. I think about why I stopped talking to her, about why I stopped replying to her e-mails and her texts. And suddenly, I'm so, so sorry. It's like my biggest regret in my whole entire life. I want to tell her that I'm sorry, I want to tell her that I didn't mean it, I want to tell her that I take it back, that we need to talk, that we need to be together, that now that she's here I never want her to leave me again. But I can't do that in front of all of these people.

Shit like that only happens in movies.

"Do you want to dance?" I ask Peyton as the plates get cleared.

"With you?" She looks at me skeptically.

"Yeah." I push my shoulders back in a false show of bravado. "I'm an excellent dancer."

"Oh, really?" She rolls her eyes, but she's smiling. "I wouldn't peg you for an excellent dancer."

I puff my lip out, pretending to be hurt. "Why not? You don't think I have moves like Jagger?"

"They weren't talking about Jagger's dance moves," she says, grinning.

I stand up and hold my hand out to her. "Come on," I say. "I'll show you."

She hesitates, and for a second I think she's going to say no. But then she takes my hand, and I pull her out onto the dance floor.

We dance for a long time, letting ourselves get caught up in the music. Most of the songs are fast, which is good. It keeps us from having that awkward moment where we have to decide if we're going to dance a slow dance, or if we're just going to go back to our seats.

But when the inevitable moment comes, and a slow song starts and the lights dim even more, it's not awkward. There's not even a hesitation on her part. She slips right into my arms, and it feels right. Perfect.

"Hi," I murmur into her hair, knowing it's a corny thing to say. But I can't help it. For some reason, whenever I'm around this girl, she turns me into some kind of lovesick fool.

"Hey," she says back. We dance the whole song, and when it's over, she pulls away from me slowly, almost like it's too much for her body to be away from mine. I know how she feels, because I feel the same way.

When another fast song starts, we decide to take a break and head back to the table.

I ignore the knowing looks that Courtney is giving me, and I ignore it when she leans over and whispers something to Jordan and he grins. They're probably making jokes about how Peyton and I are going to have sex or something tonight. I want that. Not to have sex with Peyton— although, actually, that's not really true, because of course I would love to have sex with Peyton—but to be like Jordan and Courtney. A couple who's giving each other knowing looks and sharing private jokes about other couples.

I know that at some point, Peyton and I are going to have to talk about what happened between us, about how

I stopped talking to her, about why she never told me her parents were getting divorced if we were supposedly so close. But I don't want to think about that right now. All I want to think about is how I'm never, ever going to let her go again.

When the waiters start to pour coffee, and everyone stands up so they can watch Courtney's dad and his new bride cut the cake, Peyton grabs my arm and pulls me toward the back of the room.

We stand there together, watching.

"If they smash it into each other's faces, it means they don't really love each other," Peyton reports.

"What?" I look at her, shocked.

"It's true." She shrugs. "Would you smash cake into the face of someone you really liked?"

I think about it. "No. Probably not."

We watch as the bride cuts the cake, and then the bride and groom each hold a piece, feeding each other daintily.

"Well," I say, "I guess they're really in love."

Peyton shakes her head. "Give it a minute."

So I do. And just when I think I'm in the clear, Jordan's mom takes her piece of cake and shoves it into Courtney's dad's face. Then he shoves his piece into hers. The crowd whoops and claps.

Peyton turns to me, grinning. "See?"

"So they don't really love each other."

"Nope." She shakes her head, and then the grin slips

from her face, and she's looking down at the ground. I wonder if she's thinking about what happened between us, and the fear that she might decide she wants to get away from me slides up my spine.

"Hey," I say, clearing my throat. I put my hand on her arm. "Do you want to go back to my room?" She looks at me in surprise, like she can't imagine I would suggest such a thing, and I put my hands up in surrender. "No, no," I say. "I just mean so that we can talk. About, um . . . you know, what happened."

She takes in a deep breath, and then she nods. "Okay," she says finally. "Let's go."

We slip quietly out the back of the ballroom, the crowd still hooting and hollering.

peyton before ➡

Friday, June 25, 9:45 p.m.
Siesta Key, Florida

This is so not a good idea.

Going back to Jace's room, I mean.

I know he's a jerk. I know he just stopped talking to me after making me feel like maybe he was falling in love with me, after making me feel like maybe all those e-mails and text messages and late-night phone calls and the way he kissed me on the beach at Christmas really meant something.

And after Jace stopped talking to me, I made a promise to myself that no matter how much I was hurting, no matter how much I cried, that I wouldn't ever let him suck me back in.

I broke that promise, obviously, when I texted him. And now I'm really breaking it, by dancing with him, by talking to him, by letting him take me back to his room.

But I can't stop myself—it's like a wave of emotion that's bigger than I am. It's wrong and perfect and delicious and warm and cold at the same time.

Is this what love feels like?

When we get back to his room, he unlocks the door and turns the light on.

The room's a mess. Not dirty or anything, just messy. His suitcase is open on the bed, and a bunch of clothes are strewn around the room, on the floor, on the bed, even on the chair that's sitting in the corner.

"Wow," I say. "Someone needs housekeeping. Why'd you throw your clothes all around the room?" I realize I don't really know Jace that well. Maybe he had some kind of anger-fueled fit or something. "Did you . . . did you have a fit?" I whisper.

"No," he says, rolling his eyes. "I didn't have a fit. I had a Hector."

"A what?"

The sound of jangling comes from the bathroom, and then the cutest dog I've ever seen comes running out, a red T-shirt in his mouth. His little tail is wagging, his ears are perked up, and when he sees me, he drops the shirt and rushes up to me like we're long-lost friends.

He jumps, putting his front paws on my super-expensive dress, but I don't even care.

"Hi, buddy," I say, falling to my knees on the floor. "Oh, you're so cute!"

"Yeah," Jace says, sitting down next to me and giving Hector a pat on his head. "If by cute you mean a total menace."

"Awww, how bad can he be?" I ask, burying my face in Hector's fur. "He's adorable!"

"Adorable can mean trouble," Jace reports.

I snort. "Don't I know it." I look up at him, hoping he can hear the accusing tone in my voice, hoping he knows that I'm talking about him.

"Peyton," he says quietly. And I can tell he knows exactly what I'm talking about, exactly what I mean when I said that if you're cute you can be trouble. "We need to talk."

I nod. Suddenly there's a twisting in my chest. I'm scared. Scared that whatever he says isn't going to be enough, that whatever explanation he gives isn't going to make up for the fact that he broke my heart, smashed it to pieces, and didn't even stick around to make sure I'd be able to be put back together.

He takes my hand and pulls me up onto the bed, and once we're sitting there, he doesn't let me go. Hector lies on the floor, chewing on one of Jace's socks.

Jace takes a deep breath. "I'm sorry I just stopped talking to you like that," he says. "It wasn't right."

I nod, waiting for the explanation. I'm looking down at the floor, but there's just silence. He doesn't say anything, and it's almost like maybe he's waiting for me to say something.

But I'm not going to. I'm not going to let him off the hook like that, I'm not just going to tell him that everything's okay because that would be a lie. Everything *isn't* okay—it's one thing to dance with him, to feel his arms around me, to go back to his room with him. But let's face it, this is just me losing my self-control for a little bit.

At some point, he's going to have to give me an explanation about what happened, about why he just disappeared, about why he just stopped responding to me. And it's going to have to be a good reason. Otherwise I'm going to have to walk out of this room, I'm going to have to leave him here, I'm going to have to move on with my life, even if it's hard.

I look up at him, praying he has some amazing explanation. Okay, fine, right now I would take any kind of explanation, anything that would allow me to understand why or how he could do something like that, why or how it was that I had him all wrong.

But instead of saying anything, he leans down and brushes his lips against mine. Sparks and warmth flood through my body.

"Peyton." He whispers my name, and his eyes are asking me if this is okay. And when I don't stop him, he kisses me again. This time the kiss is deeper, more delicious, more searching.

His tongue moves against mine, and his hands are on the back of my neck, his fingers sending shivers up my spine. I kiss him back, my mind a complete mess, my body on fire. I'm not thinking about anything but this kiss.

We stay like that for a while, just kissing, until finally, we fall back onto the bed. I'm breathless, my thoughts spinning and turning and jumbling, taken over by the feelings that are rushing through me. The moment swallows me whole, and it's only me and Jace, here, on the bed, together. It's endless and perfect and beautiful and I never want it to end.

"Wait," Jace says. He sits up and shakes his head.

"What?" I ask, trying to catch my breath.

"We should . . . I mean . . ." He runs his fingers through his hair, brushing it back from his face. I love the fact that I have this effect on him, that I might be driving him as crazy as he's driving me. "We should talk first."

"Okay." I sit up and lean back against the heavy cherry headboard of the bed, trying to hide my disappointment. All I want to do is keep kissing him. But I know he's right—it's better if we talk first, if we get to the bottom of things. And the fact that he's the one that's bringing it up just makes me want him more. It's like a double-edged sword.

From his spot on the floor, Hector begins to whine.

"So," Jace says, taking a deep breath and standing up. "I'm going to take Hector out, and then you and I can talk."

I nod. "Sounds good."

He cocks his head. "Are you hungry?"

"Hungry? We just ate at the wedding."

"Yeah, but that food doesn't count." He wrinkles his nose. "Too fancy. You want to order pizza?"

I didn't think I was that hungry, but now that he's said it, pizza sounds amazing. "That sounds really good," I admit.

"Okay." He nods. "Walk first, then I'll come back and order us some food. And then we'll talk."

"Perfect."

He walks out the door and I let out a happy sigh, running my hands up and down over the sheets. As I do, my hand accidentally brushes something off the bed and onto the floor. At first I think it's the TV remote, and I reach down to pick it up. But it's not. It's Jace's cell phone. It must have fallen out of his pocket.

I go to set it on the nightstand next to me, but when I do, my eyes fall onto a text message on the screen.

From someone named Kari. **Miss you**, it says.

Miss you.

Miss. You.

The two words reverberate through my head, through the room, getting bigger, taking over everything.

Miss you miss you miss you miss you ruining everything miss you.

Before I can even think about what I'm doing and whether or not it's right, I open the text history between the two of them.

Kari: **Hey cutie, when will you be back?**

Jace: **Tomorrow morning.**

554

Kari: Am I still going to graduation with you and your family?

Jace: Yup. Can't wait!

Kari: Miss you.

My heart squeezes, and I set the phone down on the bed and then sit there for a long moment, staring at it.

Maybe it's a relative, I tell myself. *A cousin, or an older aunt or something. Miss you could mean miss you and your family and cutie could be like if you were talking to a kid or something.*

My fingers are on autopilot, and they scroll through Jace's phone until they land on the name.

Kari.

I hit call.

It only rings once before she picks up.

"Hey, sexy," a voice says.

A girl's voice.

A girl who's my age.

I hang up the phone.

Tears prick at my eyes, but I blink fast, and then, just like that, the sadness is gone. I shut it off, the way I've shut off all kinds of things these past few months—my parents getting divorced, my mom using my credit card, everything.

And then I walk out the door of Jace's room, and force myself not to look back.

before jace

Friday, June 25, 10:29 p.m.
Siesta Key, Florida

I walk Hector down behind the restaurant of the yacht club, hoping that he doesn't poop on the grass. I have a bag, but the last thing I really want to be doing is picking up dog poop. And this is definitely the kind of place where if you don't, someone will notice and say something, like, "Hey, shitbag, clean up after your dog."

I let Hector sniff around for a while until finally he lifts his leg and pees.

"Come on, boy," I say, running him back up the hill to my room. I want to get back to Peyton. I want to kiss her more, and I want to talk to her about why she didn't tell me her parents were getting divorced, about how much that hurt me, about how even if she *did* hurt me that not talking to her was a stupid thing to do, about how much I regret letting my idiotic pride get in the way.

But when I get back to my room, she's not there.

"Peyton?" I call out. But there's no answer. I knock on the door to the bathroom, but she's not in there either. "Where is she, boy?" I ask Hector, before realizing that's a really stupid thing to do, since (a) Hector wasn't here when she left and (b) he's a dog, and therefore can't talk.

My phone's sitting on the nightstand, and I pick it up so that I can call her. Maybe she had to go tell her parents she was leaving the wedding, or maybe she decided to order the pizza and go pick it up herself.

When I pick up the phone, though, I see there's a new text from Kari.

Miss you.

My heart jumps into my throat. But there's no way Peyton could have seen it. She wouldn't have looked in my phone. She wouldn't have done something like that.

But then where is she?

I try calling her, but she doesn't answer. In fact, it goes right to voice mail. I don't know what room she's in, so I call the front desk.

"Hi," I say. "I'd like Peyton Miller's room, please."

The operator connects me, and I listen as the phone rings on the other end, over and over and over, until finally a recording picks up and says that the person I'm trying to reach isn't there.

Okay, so she's not in her room. Which is actually a good thing. She must have gone and picked up the pizza.

I look at my phone, thinking about Kari. Shit. I'm going to have to break up with her. And I should probably do it before Peyton comes back. I'm going to have to tell Peyton about it, too, which is going to suck.

I shake my head. Whatever. Peyton and I will make it through this. Yes, it's going to be messy and mixed-up and we're going to have a lot of talking to do, but I don't care. If we're ever going to work out, we're going to have to start being honest with each other.

I sigh and then pick up the phone and call Kari.

"Hey," she says when she answers. "Why are you pranking me?"

"What are you talking about?" I ask.

"You just called me a few minutes ago, and then you hung up."

"No, I didn't."

"Yes, you did."

"No, I didn't."

"Jace!" She laughs. "You did."

"My phone must have called you by accident," I say.

"I don't think so," she says. "It rang, and I picked up the phone and said 'Hey, sexy' and then you hung up on me. It wasn't very nice."

Bile rises up in my throat. I pull the phone away from my ear and scroll through the call log. And there it is. An outgoing call to Kari, made ten minutes ago. An outgoing call that must have been made by Peyton. Shit, shit, shit.

"Hello?" Kari's saying. "Jace, are you there?"

"Yeah," I say. "I'm here." I'm already on my way out the door, grabbing my keys and shutting the door behind me, shrugging on a sweater and walking down by the fountain and the garden path, scanning the area for Peyton.

"Is everything okay?" she asks. "You don't sound like yourself."

I take a deep breath. "No," I say. "Everything's not okay."

before | peyton

When I leave Jace's hotel room, I don't really know what to do, so I go to my parents' room (my mom gave me a key just in case I needed it), and grab the keys to the rental car that got us here from the airport.

I slide my phone into my purse, shutting it off just in case she decides to call and yell at me for taking the car. Although even if she does, who cares? I mean, what's she going to do? Call the police? Big deal, I'll call the police on her for stealing my identity. I get behind the wheel of the car and drive. I don't really know where I'm going, just that I need to get away from Jace, need something to keep my mind occupied until tomorrow, until Brooklyn comes, until I can escape to North Carolina and forget about Jace Renault for good.

jace | before

Saturday, June 26, 10:41 p.m.
Siesta Key, Florida

She took it well. Kari, I mean. Of course, she didn't understand what the hell I was talking about at first, mostly because I was babbling, but also because I ran into Courtney's grandma while I was walking, and she stopped me and wanted to have this big discussion about iPads.

Seriously. I'm enmeshed in the biggest emotional drama of my life, and the lady started asking me about *iPads* and if I thought she should get one. Like I'm fucking Steve Jobs or something. I was perfectly polite to her, but she seemed a little miffed that I couldn't give her more info on the specs. I really don't understand why old people always think everyone from the younger generation is some kind of tech genius.

Anyway, Kari couldn't understand why I hadn't mentioned Peyton before, and at first I'm pretty sure she thought I was making the whole thing up just to have a reason to break up with her. But by the end, it seemed like she believed me, and she was cool about it. "Jace," she said. "I hope we can still be friends. Because honestly, we were better that way." On some level, she definitely must have felt the weirdness between us too.

So now I'm roaming around the grounds of the yacht club looking for Peyton, not really sure where the hell I should go or where she might be. I finally end up ducking into the main building, not because I think Peyton is going to be there, but because I spot Courtney's grandma lurking around outside, and I really don't want to have another run in with her.

I look around the lobby, but obviously Peyton's not there. Why would she be hanging out in the lobby of the hotel?

And then, suddenly, I have a brilliant idea. An idea so obvious that it's actually not even that brilliant. I'll just find out what room Peyton's in, and then go and find her! Even if she's not at her room right now, she's going to have to come back to it sometime, right?

I make my way over to the front desk clerk, a twenty-something guy wearing a nametag that says WADE. It would be much better if Wade were a woman. Women I can sweet talk—you give them a sob story, a little smile, compliment them on their looks, and you can usually get what you want. (Not that I usually manipulate women like that, of course. That's way too douchey. But desperate times call for desperate measures.)

"Hello, sir!" Wade says as I approach. Okay. So Wade is perky. Hopefully, he's perkily going to do what I ask him.

"Hey," I say. I shake my head and try to look sheepish. "I forgot my room number."

"No problem, sir!" he chirps. Seriously, he chirps. I've never really heard a guy chirp before, but whatever. To each his own. He puts his fingers over the keyboard of the computer that's in front of him. "Can I have your name, please?"

"Well, see, that's the problem," I say. "The room isn't in my name."

"No problem, sir," he says. Only this time he doesn't sound so sure. I take this as a very bad sign. "Just tell me the name of the person under whom your room is booked."

I rack my brain, trying to remember Peyton's mom's first name.

"Michelle," I say. "Michelle Miller."

Wade clacks across the keys. "Hmm," he says. "Are you Peyton?"

"Am I . . . ?" For a second, I'm confused, but then I get it. The room is in Peyton's mom's name, and Peyton must be listed on the account as the only other person who's allowed to have access to it. And since Peyton can be a boy's name too, I guess Wade here just assumes that I'm Peyton.

"Why, yes," I say, puffing out my chest. "Yes, I am Peyton. Peyton Miller, yup, that's me."

"Okay, Mr. Miller," Wade says, "I'm just going to need to see your ID."

Fuck.

"Um, my ID's in the room." I hold my hands out and shrug, like, *Oh, well, what can you do?*

"Oh no!" Wade puts on a really upset face, like he can't take the fact that now he's going to have to tell me some bad news. "That's really too bad, Mr. Miller, because unfortunately we are not allowed to give out room information or replace keys unless we have identification." He pushes the desk phone toward me. "Is there anyone you can call who can come down here and help? The person who booked the room, perhaps?"

"No." I shake my head sadly. "The person who booked the room is . . . unavailable."

I stare at Wade, waiting for him to do something.

But he doesn't.

He just folds his hands in front of him and stares at me.

"So, what am I supposed to do?" I persist. "I need to get in my room. My dog, Hector, is in there, and he probably really needs to go out."

I figure I can get him with the dog story for sure— after all, I seem to be the only person on the face of the planet who doesn't fall to pieces when Hector gets brought into it—but instead, Wade gets a shocked look on his face.

"Sir," he says, and then takes in a deep breath, like there's a situation that now has to be dealt with. "Dogs are not allowed at this hotel!"

Shit. "Oh," I say. "Well, um . . ." I rack my brain desperately for something that can save the situation. But I can't think of anything. And now Peyton and her mom are probably going to get some sort of bullshit pet charge on their bill or something.

I wonder if I can offer Wade some money to just forget about this whole thing. He doesn't seem like the type to take a bribe, but you can never really tell now, can you?

And then my eyes land on his bracelet. It's one of those plastic bands that come in all different kinds of bright colors—his is yellow—and on it are the words I'M A BELIEBER.

I've been on Facebook and Twitter enough to know that this means the dude likes Justin Bieber. So I quickly turn on the charm.

"Oh, my God!" I say, pointing at his bracelet. "You like Justin, too?"

He looks at me, then puffs his chest out. "Justin who?"

"Is there more than one?" I scoff.

His mouth drops. "You? *You're* a belieber?"

"Um, yeah," I say, "for years." I'm not sure if Justin has even been around that long, but whatever. "I love his music, and honestly, I don't understand why more guys don't like him."

"That's what I always say!" He looks around then motions me forward, like he wants to let me in on a secret. I step closer to the desk, and he lifts up the cuff of his sleeve and shows me a tattoo. It says JB in curly script.

"So cool!" I gush, when in actuality, all I want to do is lunge across this dude's desk and grab his keyboard so that I can find out what room Peyton is in. "Anyway, aren't beliebers supposed to look out for each other?"

He hesitates.

"Come on!" I say. "You know Justin would want it."

He sighs, then looks around to make sure we're alone. "Fine," he whispers. "I'll tell you the room number and I'll even forget about the dog. But I'm not doing this for you, I'm doing it for Justin!"

I'm so thankful that I almost reach across the counter and hug him. "Thank you, thank you, thank you," I say. "Dude, you have no idea how much I appreciate it."

He gets to typing, but then, like some kind of nightmare, all of a sudden from behind me comes the sound of someone screaming my name.

"Jace! Hey, Jace!"

I don't turn around, willing whoever it is to just go away.

"JACE!" The person is really screaming now.

I just keep grinning at Wade.

"I think that guy is looking for you," Wade says, looking at something over my shoulder. He wrinkles his nose in disgust.

"Oh, no," I say. "He must think I'm someone else."

"JACE RENAULT, IT'S ME B.J. FROM THE WEDDING!!"

The voice is getting louder, and I lean in toward Wade, trying to get a peek at the computer screen. "Did you find the room number yet?" I'm about to start sweating.

Wade goes to open his mouth, but before he can say anything, I feel a pair of arms wrap around my shoulders from behind and grab me tight. What the *hell*? I struggle to get out of the embrace.

"Jace!" B.J. says, and grins. "You're here!"

I shake my head, trying to communicate to him with my eyes that I'm in the middle of a scheme, and that he should just go away.

But of course he doesn't get it.

"Jace! It's me, B.J.! From the wedding?" He frowns. "Are you okay? You don't look so good."

"Excuse me," Wade says from behind the computer. His eyes, which had brightened up a little when we were bonding over being (albeit fake) beliebers, are now dark and stormy. "I'm going to have to ask you to leave this desk, otherwise I'm going to have to call security."

I think about protesting, about trying to convince him that I really am Peyton Miller, but I'm smart enough to know when I'm licked.

I sigh and move away from the desk as Wade starts mumbling something about how I'm not really a belieber, how a real belieber would never be so deceptive. Shows what he knows. One time I was at a Barnes & Noble when a new Justin Bieber book came out and I got run over by two eleven-year-old girls who were so excited to buy it that they lost all sense of real decorum.

"What's up, my man?" B.J. says, and claps me on the back like we're old friends. "Why did that guy want to call security on you? Did you try to sneak alcohol into your room?" He nods sympathetically, like he's been there, done that. Which is not that hard to believe.

"No, I didn't try to sneak alcohol into my room," I say. I resist the urge to start screaming at him, and then maybe throttle him around the throat for good measure.

"Then what is it?" He lowers his voice. "Drugs? Because that's not cool, dude. Crack is whack!"

I shake my head, my anger starting to dissipate. How can I be mad at someone who's so obviously clueless? "No, it's not drugs," I say. "It's a girl."

"Pffft!" he says, shaking his head. "Chicks! They're crazy, aren't they?"

"Not this one," I say. "I'm the crazy one. The crazy one who fucked everything all up."

"Man, that sucks," B.J. says. He crosses his arms over his chest. "So what are you going to do?"

"I don't know," I say. "I have no fucking clue."

He looks thoughtful for a moment, his lips sliding over to the side, pursed in concentration. Then his eyes light up. "I know!" he says. He reaches into his pocket and pulls out his phone. "I'll call Jordan!"

"Jordan?"

"Yeah, you know, Courtney's boyfriend? He's the best when it comes to figuring out chicks."

"Um, no, that's okay," I say. The last thing I need is people who are pretty much strangers trying to help me with my emotional problems. I mean, talk about humiliating.

But B.J. doesn't seem to want to listen, and ten minutes later, Jordan's walking into the lobby. Wade is still giving us death looks, so I herd everyone over to the lounge on the other side of the room.

"Oh, sweet," B.J. says, his eyes lighting up. "They have a pool table."

He picks up a pool cue and starts swinging it around like a samurai sword. "So what's up?" Jordan asks, reaching out and taking the pool cue out of B.J.'s hands. "Why did you guys ask me to come down here?"

"Jace needs women advice," B.J. reports. He starts racking up the balls.

"No, I don't," I say.

Jordan nods. "Peyton, huh?"

I nod sheepishly. "Yeah. Courtney told you?"

"Yeah. So what's the deal?"

"Yeah, what's the deal?" B.J asks, then leans over the pool table and breaks the balls. One goes flying over the side of the table and onto the floor. "Oops," he says. It rolls across the marble floor until it hits the side of a man's foot. "Sorry," B.J. says.

The man gives him a dirty look, but B.J. isn't fazed.

He just puts the ball back on the table. "Do over," he says. "Okay, guys?"

"Fine with me," I say.

"Whatever." Jordan says. He grabs a pool cue and I do the same. "So what's going on?"

"Well," I say, really thinking about it. "We met at Christmas, and then I broke up with her."

B.J's mouth drops open. "You *broke up* with her? Dude, are you crazy? Peyton's hot."

"There's more to relationships than hotness, B.J." Jordan says. He leans over and shoots the orange solid into the side pocket effortlessly.

"Don't I know it," B.J. says. He shakes his head. "Jocelyn's hot, and that's not even close to being enough." He looks at me like he's letting me in on a secret. "With girls, you have to worry about their emotions."

"So why'd you dump her?" Jordan asks me.

"Because I found out she'd been keeping a secret from me." Jordan and B.J. exchange a glance.

"Been there," Jordan says.

"Courtney kept a secret from you?"

"No, *he* kept one from *her*," B.J. reports. He bends over the pool table to take his shot, but the ball only goes about two inches before rolling to a stop on the felt.

"So what happened?" I ask.

"I broke up with her," Jordan says. "Because I was a pussy."

"Yeah," I say. "Been there, dude." It's my turn, so I lean over the table and concentrate on the shot. I put all my energy into sinking the yellow ball, and it works. It goes right into the pocket. "So what happened?"

"I made myself miserable because I couldn't tell her how I felt," Jordan says, shrugging. "And finally, she found out the secret on her own."

"She found out on her own?"

"Yup. And she was totally pissed."

"So what did you do?"

"I had to make it up to her," he says. "And she didn't want to forgive me, so I had to work at it." He shakes his head. "If there's one thing I've realized, it's that you have to be honest. Even if you're scared, even if you're worried that you're going to get your heart stomped on, even if you think that the truth is going to ruin everything, you have to put it out there. Because otherwise, you're fucked." He leans over and sinks the solid blue ball into the middle pocket. He says this whole thing completely matter-of-factly, and the thing is, I believe him. I believe he knows what he's talking about.

I've seen him and Courtney together. I've seen the way they look at each other like they're the only people in the room. They seem connected. I want that with Peyton. And I know Jordan's right—in order to have that kind of relationship, you have to put it all out there, you have to be willing to let yourself be vulnerable.

Otherwise, there's no way you're going to be able to have anything real.

"Now," Jordan says, "the only question is, is she worth it?"

"She's worth it," I say. God, is she worth it.

"Then you have to go find her."

And again, I know that he's right.

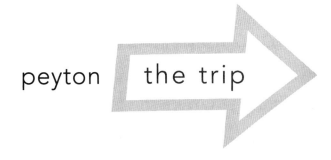

peyton | the trip

Saturday, June 26, 10:53 p.m.
Savannah, Georgia

When I get back to my hotel room in Savannah, I'm starting to consider maybe having a mini meltdown. I mean, I have no clue what I'm going to do. I don't know how the hell I'm going to get to North Carolina. I don't have a car. I hardly have any money. I don't even have a *phone*.

I plop down on the bed, wondering if maybe I should just call my mom and have her come get me. Or maybe my dad. I could tell him about why I wanted to run away, about what my mom did to me.

But doing that would mean I would have to speak the words out loud, and I really don't know if I'm ready for that. Besides, I don't *want* to go home. I want to go to North Carolina. I want to get my apartment in Creve Coeur. I want to stay there for the summer until I can figure out what the hell I'm going to do.

I stare up at the ceiling. Maybe all I need is a good night's sleep. Maybe tomorrow morning I'll be able to come up with a plan. I mean, there has to be a way. People are always finding ways to do things with little to no resources. It's, like, the basis of civilization. Maybe I can take a bus, or maybe I can find one of those cash-advance places that are super shady and charge you, like, triple the money when you go to pay it back.

I turn on a rerun of one of the Real Housewives shows, and then slide under the covers, determined to just fall asleep. But it's not working. I can't stop thinking about him. About Jace. About how he knew my parents were getting divorced, about how that was the reason he stopped talking to me.

I'd spent so much time obsessing about what went wrong, and the possibility that maybe he'd somehow found out about my parents had never crossed my mind.

Of course, the absolute worst part about it is that I'm the one who did this. I'm the one who pushed him away. I'm the one who didn't tell him something important that was going on in my life. All that time we spent on the phone—all that time I spent getting to know him, making plans, getting close, and I didn't tell him. I should have told him.

Even so, I can't put all of the blame on myself. He's the one who just blew me off like it was nothing. He didn't even bother to ask me about it.

And what about the fact that he was kissing me last

night, while the whole time he had a girlfriend? A girlfriend who was texting him all "I miss you" and blah blah blah. And yeah, I was kissing him in the bathtub tonight even after knowing that. But you can't really blame me. I mean, it was a physical reaction that couldn't be controlled.

Anyway, that's two strikes against Jace. Two strikes and you're out. I mean, when you think about it, that's how it should be. Who wants to stick around for a third strike? Anyone can have one slip up, but after the second, it's probably not an accident.

My thoughts swirl around my head, keeping me awake and driving me crazy, until finally, at around three in the morning, I fall into a fitful sleep.

I'm woken up by a knock on the door. It's so loud and violent that at first, I think it must be coming from the TV. But when I blink my eyes open, the clock on the nightstand says 10:07 a.m., and the TV is off. I must have turned it off at some point during the night.

I sit up in bed. Shit, shit, shit. This is not how my morning was supposed to go. I was supposed to be awake by six or seven, showered and clean, my stomach full of free continental breakfast. I was supposed to be bright-eyed and bushy-tailed, ready to come up with a brilliant plan for my future. But instead, I'm still in bed, being assaulted by aggressive knocking on the door. Probably housekeeping. Don't they know that checkout isn't until noon?

I throw my legs over the bed and pad to the door, yanking

down the right leg of my pajama pants, which has slid up to my knee.

"I'm still in here," I call. "I'll be out at noon, you know, when it's time for *checkout*."

"Oh, no, you won't!" a voice says. "You will open up this door right now, young lady."

My heart pounds in fear. Whoever that is sounds like they mean business. Real business. The only other times I've heard a tone like that is when I'm watching reruns of police shows, and there's some wanted man in a house somewhere who won't come out. But I'm not a criminal. And I don't have a warrant. Unless . . . we never called the police after we got into that accident earlier. Maybe they traced the car or something back to me, and now I'm going to get in trouble for leaving the scene of a crime!

I tiptoe to the door and peer through the peephole, expecting to see a policewoman or two, uniformed and holding handcuffs, ready to take me to jail. Then I would definitely have to call my parents. No way do I have enough money to bail myself out of jail.

But there's no police officer on the other side of the door. There's just a tall woman, with perfectly highlighted light brown hair that's pulled back into a low bun. She's wearing a cream-colored T-shirt, dark jeans, a sheer black cardigan, and gold ballet flats. Maybe she's undercover? She doesn't look like the type of person who would be sent out to pick up criminals.

"Can I help you, ma'am?" I ask politely. Something shady is definitely going on here, and if she doesn't identify herself, well, then, I'll just call 911 and the real police department can get to the bottom of this.

"Yes," she says. "I think you can help me. I'm looking for Jace Renault."

"Oh." I think about it, not sure I want to admit that I know Jace, that he was just here with me last night. What if he's in some kind of trouble? Of course, he left me, so if law enforcement is looking for him, it would serve him right if I turned him in. But if it *is* about the car, then there's a good chance I could get in trouble, too. "Who am I speaking with, please?" I ask.

I watch through the peephole as the woman in the hall-way takes a step back, like she can't believe I've asked such a question. "Who am *I* speaking to?" she asks, moving back toward the door and pounding on it again with her fist. Yikes. We've got a live one here.

"I asked you first," I counter, not wanting her to know that I'm secretly terrified.

"My name is Piper Renault," she says. "I'm Jace's mother."

Oh. Well. I guess that explains it.

Mrs. Renault isn't at all like what I imagined. I know it's stereotyping, but I thought she'd be this really stuffy, sort of boring, plain-looking woman. She's a professor of women's studies, so I'd just assumed—I mean, aren't all those women's lib people always kind of crunchy-looking? I thought they didn't like it when women wore makeup or bras or anything that put their sexuality on display.

But Mrs. Renault is really pretty. She's wearing this amazing shade of lipstick, and I kind of even want to ask her what it's called, but she's definitely not in a mood to talk makeup.

When I unlocked the door and let her in, the first thing she did was start barging around my room like she owned the place. "Jace!" she called, opening the bathroom door roughly and peeking in. "Come out! The jig is up!"

Yikes. The jig is up, even. She opened the closet next, but of course Jace wasn't in there.

"He's not here," I say. "Um, he left." I wish I had some more information to give her because she seems like maybe she's about to start really tearing this place up, and I don't want to be the one to get in trouble for it.

"Ha!" she says. She gets down on her hands and knees and looks under the bed.

"I swear," I say. "Mrs. Renault, Jace isn't here."

"Then where is he?" She taps her foot against the floor impatiently, waiting for me to tell her where her son is.

"I don't know," I say. "I don't . . . I mean, I think he's probably on his way home."

"On his way home! I truly doubt that." She looks around the room one more time, and then her gaze settles on me. "So what is this? You two decided to run away together or what? You want to get married or something?"

"Married?" I'm shocked she would even think that. "God, no. We weren't running away to get married."

"Then what? Tell me why Jace would skip out on his graduation to be with you!"

"Jace . . . what? He skipped out on his graduation?" I frown. That makes no sense. "Why would he do that?"

"I don't know!" She throws her hands up in exasperation. "But it's tonight. Tonight at seven o'clock. Which means that if he's not on his way home right now, he's going to miss it!" She looks at the clock and then crosses her arms over her chest.

I take a deep breath. "Mrs. Renault, I'm sorry about Jace and his graduation. And I swear, if I knew where he was, I would tell you. But I don't. He left here last night, late. He, um . . . we . . . we got into a fight."

She looks at me and opens her mouth like maybe she's going to yell at me again, or tell me that she doesn't believe me, or demand that I tell her everything I know. But at the last moment, her face crumples. She sits down next to me on the bed, just looking down at the floor. After a moment, she wordlessly reaches over and grabs the bag of Combos that's sitting on my nightstand. She slides her hand into the bag, pulls out a few, and pops them into her mouth.

There's an awkward silence as she just sits there and eats, and I just sit there being nervous. She holds the bag out to me, and I don't really want any, but I feel like it would be rude not to take some, and so I eat a couple.

"I was probably too hard on him," she says. "I pushed him, I know that I did."

"No," I say, shaking my head. "I'm sure you were fine."

"No, I wasn't. He doesn't care about school. Yes, he's smart, and that's great, but he's not into all the accolades, all the trappings and things that go along with it. He doesn't need to impress people." She dips her hand back into the bag. "Unlike his mother."

I want to tell her it's okay, but I don't. Because honestly, it's kind of not. I mean, look at my mom—she's so concerned with putting on a good face, with making people think that she has all kinds of money, and for what? It definitely put a huge burden on her relationship with my dad, and it's basically ruined our relationship, even though she might not know it yet.

Jace's family actually has money, so it's funny how his mom just picked something else to focus on—she wanted everyone to know that Jace was super smart, to parade him. around like he was some kind of golden child or something.

"I'm sure you did the best you could," I say, figuring I need to give her a break. At least she's here, and at least she's admitting what she's done.

Jace's mom blows out a big breath and then hands me back the empty bag of Combos. "Sorry I ate all your Combos," she says. "I'll buy you a new bag."

"That's okay," I say. "I was done with them anyway." I set the empty bag back on the nightstand. "So you drove all night to get to Jace?"

"No." She shakes her head. "I took a flight first thing this morning. As soon as the credit card showed the charge at this hotel, I headed for the airport. I was going to drag him back on a flight this afternoon, then get him home and ready for graduation tonight."

"How did you know what rooms we were in?"

"I told the woman at the front desk that Jace was using my credit card and that it was technically a stolen charge that could be disputed and cancelled unless she told me."

I nod. "You're a good mom."

She sighs. "It doesn't feel like it." She reaches into her bag and pulls out her cell phone. "He won't answer my calls."

"Well, I'd call him for you, but he probably won't answer my calls, either."

"Because you guys had a fight?" she asks.

"Yes."

She nods, thinking about it. "So if you're not running away to get married, then what are you doing?"

"Didn't he tell you?" I ask. "I didn't have a ride home from the wedding. My ride got—" I grope around for a word. Delayed? Cancelled? "My ride kind of ditched me. And so Jace said that he would drive me home."

She frowns. "That's what he told me," she says. "But don't you live in Connecticut?"

581

"Yeah," I say. "How'd you know that?"

She waves her hand like it should be obvious. "Of course I know where you live, Peyton. Over the winter you were all Jace could talk about. Peyton this and Peyton that." She looks at me out of the corner of her eye. "What happened between you guys, anyway?"

I swallow, not sure how much I want to reveal to her. She is Jace's mom after all, and pretty much a total stranger. But then I think, whatever, screw it. Keeping things from people hasn't gotten me all that far—I'm stranded in a Savannah hotel room with no money, after all—so maybe it's time to turn over a new leaf.

"I kept something from him," I say. "Something pretty big. And when he found out, he got mad and just stopped talking to me."

She nods. "That sounds like Jace. Unfortunately, he's a product of his parents. Stubborn like me. Shuts down and avoids conflict like my husband when he really cares about someone." She gives me a thin smile. "Do you really think he's on his way home?"

"I really do."

"Not because he's excited about graduation, though."

"No," I say. "Not because he's excited about graduation."

"Ah, well." She stands up and shoulders her purse, then turns around and looks at me. "Do you . . . I mean, are you okay here? Do you need a ride somewhere?"

I think about asking her to take me to the airport, but

then what would I do once I was there? I have no money for a flight, and as soon as that became obvious, she'd most definitely call my parents. Same if I asked for a ride to the bus station. She'd start asking me all those annoying questions adults love to ask, like where I'm going and who's going to meet me and blah blah blah.

"No," I say. "My friend's coming to pick me up."

"You sure?" She's standing up now.

"I'm sure."

"Okay." She sighs, then turns around and heads to the door. "Thanks, Peyton," she says. And then she's gone.

I look at the clock next to my bed. Ten thirty. Only an hour and a half until I need to be out of here. Ninety minutes to come up with some kind of plan. I can do it.

But first, I reach over and pick up the phone. I hesitate for a second, then dial the number that no matter how many times I deleted from my cell, I could never delete from my heart.

It rings, and I hold my breath, hoping against hope that he'll pick up. But he doesn't. It goes right to voice mail.

"Jace," I say. "Hey, it's Peyton. I wanted to let you know that your mom was just here. She, um, wanted to make sure you were still going to graduation, but she . . . she seemed like maybe by the end of it she wasn't mad at you. She was just happy that you were okay. At least, I kind of led her to believe you were okay, even though I'm not really sure if you are. Are you okay? I hope so. You should . . . I mean, maybe you should call your mom."

I hang up the phone.

And then, after a moment, I take a deep breath and head for the shower.

jace | the trip

I haven't left Savannah. Well, that's not exactly true. I've left Savannah, but I haven't gone that far. I drove around for a while last night, going in circles, not knowing exactly what the hell to do. Go back and get Peyton? Say fuck it and go back home? Finally, I ended up at some diner about twenty miles away, where I've been sitting for most of the night.

Every five seconds, I change my mind. Go back and get Peyton. Go home and go to graduation. Fuck everything and just sit here for the whole day, then deal with everything later. Why the hell am I suddenly so indecisive? Usually I know exactly what I want and how to go after it.

My phone has been blowing up with phone calls from my mom all night and all morning. So when I'm ordering what seems like my fifteenth cup of coffee, and my phone buzzes with a voice mail, I don't really give it much thought. Until I look down and see that it's from a Savannah area code.

Peyton. Maybe she wants me to come back and get her, maybe she's going to tell me she's sorry she ever lied to me, that she needs me, that she can't believe what a horrible thing she did.

I pick up the phone and play the message.

"Jace," she says. "Hey, it's Peyton. I wanted to let you know your mom was just here . . ."

What the *fuck*? My *mom* was just there? The thought of Peyton and my mom hanging out makes me want to break out in hives. Also, why did my mom drive all the way to Savannah to find me?

I knew I shouldn't have used my credit card to pay for the room! She probably tracked it and found out what hotel we were at. I can only imagine how pissed off she must be.

Although from what Peyton said, it seems like maybe my mom isn't all that mad about graduation—that she's actually just worried about me. I sigh, feeling like an asshole. I should have at least texted my mom to let her know I was okay.

I pick up my phone and tap out a quick text. **Mom, I'm okay. Not going to make graduation, obviously. But I'll be home soon, and we'll talk then.**

The reply comes almost immediately. **Thanks for letting me know, Jace. I love you and I'm so glad you're okay.**

I hold my phone in my hand, wondering if I should call

Peyton. She did call me, after all. And even though she didn't *specifically* ask me to call her back, it would be rude not to. Wouldn't it?

Before I can talk myself out of it, I call the hotel and ask for her room. But when they connect me, it just rings and rings. The thought of her leaving makes my throat hurt. I don't want her wandering around Savannah by herself, with no money and no idea where she's going. I should never have left her.

I look down to where Hector's sitting at my feet. He was in the car for the first couple of hours I was here, but when the waitress peered through the window and saw him, she told me I could bring him in as long as none of the customers complained. He's been chill, Hector—just lying still, his head on his paws. The waitress brought him a plate of sausage biscuits and gravy, which he wolfed down in about two minutes. I think he's in a food coma.

I don't know what to do. Go back? Don't go back?

What I need is some advice. But who can I call? I dial Evan, but he doesn't answer.

I scroll through my phone until I find Courtney's number, and before I can think about whether or not it's a good idea, I push call.

"Hello?" she answers, her voice sleepy. "Jace? Are you okay?"

"Yeah, I'm okay," I say.

"Jesus!" she says. "Do you know your mom's been going

587

crazy? She found out you're in Georgia, and she's on her way there. I tried to call you, but you weren't picking up."

"Yeah, I know. Listen, are you with Jordan?"

"Yeah, he's right here next to me," she says. "Why?"

"Can I talk to him?"

"Oh, no," she says, sounding wary. "Why? Are you involved with drugs or something?"

"No." I shake my head. "Just . . . can I talk to him?"

"Sure." I hear the sound of her waking Jordan, the blankets rustling, and then his voice comes over the phone.

"Yo," he says.

"Hey," I say. "Remember how you told me about how I had to be honest with Peyton, no matter what?"

"Yeah." There's another rustling sound, like maybe he's sitting up in bed or something. He sighs. "You didn't do it, did you?"

"How'd you know?"

"I could just tell. You weren't ready."

"Well, I think I'm ready now."

"How do you know?"

"Because I can't stop thinking about her."

"Not enough."

"I would do anything for her."

"Anything?"

"Yes."

"Even put yourself out there, giving her the opportunity to tell you to fuck off and stomp all over your heart?"

"Yes."

"Okay," he says simply. "Then you need to go get her."

"But what if—"

"What if nothing," he says, cutting me off. "If you love her, if you really mean it, then there's nothing else to talk about."

"There isn't?"

"No," he says, sounding exasperated, like maybe I still don't get it. "You have to just go get her. Enough talking. It's time for action."

I swallow. Just go get her. I know he's right. So instead of even saying goodbye, I hang up the phone and throw some dollar bills onto the table. Then I grab Hector's leash and slip out the door.

No more talking. It's time to go get Peyton.

the trip peyton

Sunday, June 27, 11:07 a.m.
Savannah, Georgia

I thought I heard the phone ringing while I was in the shower, which made my heart jump and leap, thinking that maybe it was Jace calling me back. I'll admit that part of the reason I left him that message was because I wanted him to call me back.

I wanted him to call me and be all—"Hey, Peyton, thanks for telling me about my mom, what exactly did she say?" And then I would be all, "She was really worried about you, Jace, but I told her not to be, and then I calmed her down, and by the end, it seemed like maybe she'd even grown as a person." And then he'd be all, "Oh, my God, Peyton, you're amazing and way better than my stupid girl-friend Kari, will you marry me?"

I mean, it's not like I did anything amazing when his mom showed up here, but still. If I'd wanted to, I could have gotten her all riled up and told her Jace and I were getting married because I was pregnant with his love child.

Which actually would have been pretty funny. If she'd been in a different frame of mind, I'll bet she might have even thought it was a funny joke.

I towel-dry my hair and then dress in a pair of jeans and a red tank top, pulling my still-a-little-damp hair up and twisting it into a loose ponytail. Then I head down to the lobby to grab one of those carts so that I can load all my luggage up onto it.

I have to be out of my room at noon, but no one ever said anything about being out of the *hotel*, now, did they? My plan is to sit in the lobby with my computer, Googling and researching until I figure out some kind of plan.

If worse comes to worst, I might have to call Courtney or Brooklyn and ask them to wire me some money. Although I probably won't have to do that until I get to North Carolina. I mean, I should have enough for a bus ticket, at least. On the East Coast, you can get a bus ticket from New York to Boston for, like, nineteen dollars. Nineteen dollars! And it seems like prices are definitely a lot lower in the South.

When I get back to my room with the cart, I load it up and then slide it out into the hall. Jace might have been right when he called me high maintenance. Why the hell am I bringing all this stuff to North Carolina? Did I really think I was going to wear all of it? Not to mention that all these bags make it super inconvenient to travel.

Of course, I couldn't have foreseen the way things turned out—I thought I was going to be driving in a car with Brooklyn, not having to carry all this stuff onto a bus.

But still. I really did not need all this junk, I think, as I make my way to the lobby, carefully pushing the cart in front of me. I didn't need the matching shoes and earrings for each outfit, I didn't need all those different colors of nail polish and all those different summer dresses. I could have packed a bunch of shorts and tank tops, which would have fit nicely into one bag. Where the hell did I think I was going for the summer anyway, the Riviera?

The thought is actually kind of disturbing—that I might be the type of girl who has to bring all her stupid, overpriced designer clothes with her everywhere she goes. I don't even like half of these clothes, and only wear them because it's what my mom wants me to wear. And I'm not actually even sure if *she* likes them, or if she just thinks she *should* like them because they're expensive.

I push the cart angrily into the lobby as fast as I can, hating the idea that I might be like my mom in any way.

"Whoa," Mia, the girl from the front desk, says when she sees me coming. "Do you need any help with that?" She doesn't wait for my answer, just comes over and starts helping me steer the cart into the lounge.

"Thanks," I say.

"Are you checking out?" she asks. "Because if you are, you can take the cart outside, you know."

"I am checking out," I say, pushing a strand of hair out of my face. "But I thought maybe I'd hang out in the lounge here for a little bit, just do some work on my computer before I get on the road." Hopefully, she can't tell that I'm going to be spending that time figuring out exactly *how* I'm going to be getting on the road.

"That's cool," she says, shrugging. "Stay as long as you want." She hesitates a second, then leans in close to me. "Did, uh, everything work out? With that woman?"

"That woman?"

"Yeah, your friend's mom? She seemed a little worked up. I'm sorry I gave out your room numbers like that, but she said she was going to call the police."

I smile. "No, it's fine. You did the right thing."

She smiles. "Good. Do you want any breakfast? It's free."

"Sure," I say nonchalantly.

She waves at the buffet—it's small, just some bagels, coffee, and cereal, but still. It's food. And it's free.

"I'll check you out, and just let me know if you need any help with your bags." She grins again. "We can get one of the guys to do it for you next time."

She starts walking back toward the front desk, then stops and turns around. "Is your friend checking out too?"

"My friend?"

"Yeah, the guy you were with. The hot one."

"Oh," I say. "Yeah, he's checking out, too."

I almost say he checked out last night, but then I catch myself. Probably doesn't give the best impression if I checked in with a guy, and then he left in the middle of the night. I mean, talk about sketchy. She'll probably think I'm some kind of prostitute or something. I'm not even sure they have those in the South. Isn't it all religious and conservative down here?

She disappears back behind the front desk, and I sit down and open my laptop.

After about twenty minutes, I'm starting to feel a little bit defeated. Yes, there are some cheap bus tickets, but the next two buses aren't leaving the station until three o'clock. Which means I'll have to find something to do here for the next four hours.

And then I'll have to figure out a way to lug my bags all the way to the bus station. Either that or spend money on a cab.

And *then*, when I get to the bus station in North Carolina, I'll still be thirty minutes away from my apartment in Creve Coeur. Which means another taxi. Not to mention that the bus doesn't get to North Carolina until nine o'clock tonight, and I can only pick up the keys to my apartment at the rental office between eight and eight. Which means I'm going to have to find a place to stay in North Carolina for the night. Which means I might have to sleep in the bus station.

I take a deep breath in, then search some different bus lines, but it's all the same story. Okay, I think. I can sleep in the bus station. It's not *that* horrible, when you really think about it. People do it all the time. And who says I actually have to sleep? I could just stay up all night, read a book or something. Not that I have a book. Why didn't I bring a book? And of course I don't have a phone, so if there were some kind of emergency, I'd be in trouble.

But I'm sure they have pay phones there. Maybe I could call Brooklyn or something, and get her to call me right back. Then we could stay up all night talking. I should probably call Brooklyn anyway. She's got to be worried about me. She's probably tried calling me like three million times by now.

Okay. I can do this. It's really just about changing your mind set, about not looking at the negative side of things. When you think about it, is a day or so of travel challenges really going to make me scrap my whole plan? I've come so far already. I just need to figure out the safest way to do things without spending a lot of money.

Just take it a step at a time, I tell myself.

Okay.

Step One.

Get from here to the bus station.

I could take a cab, but that definitely wouldn't save money.

And then I have a brilliant idea. Why not take a *bus*

to the bus station? There has to be a city bus that goes there, right?

I Google the Savannah city bus schedule, my fingers flying over the keys. The nearest bus stop is about half a mile away. And the next bus to the Greyhound station comes in twenty-five minutes. Not bad. So I can walk the half mile to the bus stop, take the bus to the bus station, then hang out there until it's time to go to North Carolina. Of course, I have all my bags. And it's like, almost ninety degrees out.

But whatever. How bad can it really be? A little exercise will invigorate me!

Cheered by my new plan, I grab a bagel from the restaurant, and slather it with peanut butter. While I'm eating it, I take two cartons of orange juice and put them in my purse. I'm going to need the hydration.

"Bye!" Mia says as I wheel my stuff through the lobby. She's smiling, but her face turns doubtful as she looks at the big pile of suitcases I have. "You need some help?"

"No thanks!" I say brightly, and continue wheeling. I don't want her to ask any questions. The last thing I need is for her to figure out that I'm going to be wheeling my bags half a mile in this heat. She'd probably think I'm crazy.

"Okay," she says. "Well, thanks for staying with us! Good luck on the rest of your trip!"

"Thanks," I say, wondering if she'd still be wishing me

luck if she knew I was going to be stealing this luggage cart so that I can wheel my stuff to the bus stop.

Probably not, but I decide to pretend she still would. If there's one thing I'm going to need, it's luck.

the trip jace

Sunday, June 27, 11:37 a.m.
Savannah, Georgia

I'm trying my best not to speed. I really am. The last thing I want is to get a speeding ticket or get into an accident. But I'm so anxious to get back to Peyton that I can't help it. I keep the car at five miles over the speed limit, reminding myself that speeding isn't going to get me there that much faster, and that if I get pulled over, it's going to take even longer to get back to Savannah.

By the time I pull into the parking lot of the Residence Inn, it's all I can do to keep from jumping out of my skin. Checkout isn't until noon. So I'm betting she's still here. Where else would she be? She *has to* still be here.

The thought that I'm going to miss her sends me into a panic, and I run from the parking lot and across the street to the hotel, jumping up onto the curb, rushing through the automatic doors and down the hall to Peyton's room. But when I get there, the door is open, and two women in maid uniforms are stripping the bed.

"Can I help you?" one of them asks, turning around and looking at me.

"Um, no," I say. I head back down the hallway and into the lobby, looking around. *Think*, I tell myself. Where would she have gone? To the airport? The bus station?

"Hey!" the girl at the front desk says. Mia, I think her name is. "You're back!"

"Yes," I say. "I'm back. I'm, um, I'm looking for my friend."

"The girl you were with?" she says. "She left about half an hour ago."

"She left?" My heart sinks. "She didn't . . . I mean, did she tell you where she was going?"

Mia shakes her head. "No. But she stole one of our luggage carts. I don't care or anything, I mean, I'm sure she had her reasons. But just to let you know if she doesn't return it, they're going to charge your credit card three hundred dollars."

"Thanks," I say, my mind racing.

If Peyton took one of the luggage carts, it means that she's probably walking somewhere. But where would she go?

"How far away is the bus station?" I ask Mia.

"Five miles, maybe?" she says. I guess Peyton could have tried to walk five miles, if she was desperate. "But there's a bus stop about half a mile from here."

"Can you tell me how to get there?"

She pulls a piece of paper out from behind the desk and draws me a little map, giving me directions to both the bus stop and the bus station itself.

"Thanks," I say. "I owe you one."

"No problem," she says. "Good luck."

I'm going to need it.

I'm back to my car in a flash. Hector's sitting in the front seat now, his ears perked up like he knows something's going on.

"We're going to find her, boy," I say as I put on my seat belt. "Don't worry."

I pull out onto the street and head for the bus stop. It's relatively easy to find, although a lot of the way is uphill. I can't imagine how hard it would be to push a whole cartful of suitcases in this heat.

I see the bus stop sign at the end of the street.

But when I get there, there's no sign of Peyton.

I park the car and get out, looking up and down the street, searching for any sign of her. But there's nothing. I walk into the two cafes that are on that road, scanning the tables for Peyton. But she's not there.

I get back in the car and lean my head against the seat.

Hector does a little whine next to me, and I reach over and scratch his ears. "What do you think?" I ask him. "Where's Peyton?"

He wags his tail at the mention of her name.

I sigh.

I don't know what else to do. Maybe I should call Courtney. Or Peyton's parents. Maybe I should drive to the airport. Or the bus station.

I put my car into drive and start to head toward the bus station. But I don't have far to go.

Because a few blocks over, I find Peyton.

She's sitting on the curb, crying.

the trip | peyton

Sunday, June 27, 11:49 a.m.
Savannah, Georgia

I missed the bus. I walked all the way here, pushing that stupid cart that I stole, and when I turned the corner, I saw the bus pulling away from the station.

I was so far down the street that I couldn't even run after it. It was kicking up dust, groaning on its wheels and emitting exhaust into the June heat. I stopped pushing. I leaned my head against the cool metal of the luggage cart.

Then I pushed it to the side of the street, walked into the café that was on the road, and bought a bottled water. I wanted to sit inside for a little while, because I was hot from the walk, and the air conditioning felt nice. But I was afraid someone was going to steal the stuff on my luggage cart. I'd already seen a few people pass by on the street, and look it up and down, like maybe they were thinking of waltzing off with it. And the stupid thing was too big to bring in with me.

So I headed back outside to guard my stuff. No one seemed to know when the next bus was coming, but they did tell me where the bus station was.

So I decided to walk.

I got about three blocks before I realized it was time to sit down and have a good cry.

And so now here I am. Sitting here. Having a good cry. I told myself it was only going to be for a few minutes, but I think I've definitely been here for at least ten or so.

There's the sound of a car pulling up to the curb, and I look up, half expecting to see a cop or a meter maid or someone standing there, telling me to get the hell off the street.

But it's not a cop.

And it's not a meter maid.

It's Jace.

He's stepping out of his car and walking toward me. His hair is all rumpled and he's wearing the same T-shirt and track pants he had on last night and there's a little bit of stubble darkening his cheeks. He looks, as always, amazing.

"What are you—" I start.

"Stop," he says, and shakes his head. "Don't talk." He sits down on the curb next to me.

"Don't talk?" I repeat dumbly, even though he just told me not to.

"No. I mean, yeah, you can talk, but—" He shakes his head again like he's trying to clear his thoughts, and then he stares down at the pavement. He's so close that our knees are touching. "I need to say some things," he says, moving his eyes up so that he's looking right at me. "And I don't want you to say anything until I'm done."

My pulse starts to quicken. "Right," I say. "Now you want to talk and I'm just supposed to—"

"Peyton," he says, putting a finger on my lips. "Please." His eyes are on mine, and he's looking at me so longingly, like he really needs to say what he came here to say. So after a second, even though I'm mad, I nod.

"I should have never stopped talking to you the way I did," he says. "It was stupid. *I* was stupid. I found out that you hadn't told me about your parents, and I freaked out." He sighs. "It was my stupid pride. I let it get in the way, and I've been paying for it ever since."

"Why?" I ask.

"Why what?"

"Why did you freak out?"

He hesitates for a second, and I hold my breath, praying he's going to say what I want him to say. "Because I was falling in love with you."

Electricity zings through me, and my heart leaps. "If you were falling in love with me, then why did you stop talking to me?"

"I told you. It was my stupid pride. I . . . I was afraid." His eyes are still on mine, and whatever's passing between us is so intense I'm having a hard time looking at him. "I was afraid that maybe it was real. And I was looking for any excuse for it not to be. And so as soon as I found an out, I just took it."

"Why, though?" I ask. "Why didn't you just ask me about it?"

"Why didn't you just tell me?"

I think about it. Really think about it. "Because saying it out loud would have made it true," I say. "And then I'd have to think about all kinds of other fucked up stuff, like my mom's issues with money and how my parents were still both living in the same house, not even thinking about how that might affect me."

He nods, then finally pulls his gaze from mine. He looks down at the ground. Tears fill my eyes, remembering the betrayal, remembering how much I did—*do*—love him. I want him to tell me we can forget it, that we can move on, that we can just be together. But I know it's not that easy.

"We can't do that to each other," he says finally. "We can't go around keeping secrets like that."

"I know," I say. "I think . . . I mean, I've always known that. I think that's maybe why I told you about my mom and the whole credit card thing."

He nods, then kicks at some gravel on the road with his shoe. "So now what?"

"I don't know." I shake my head. "It's too . . . it just seems like every time we're together, everything gets so complicated."

He takes a deep breath. "So the question is, can you deal with complicated?"

"We live so far away," I say. I feel the familiar twinge of hope stirring in my chest, and my first instinct is to squash it, to tell him that there's no way we can work out, that we don't make sense, that we've screwed everything up way too much to ever go back.

I look away, squinting in the sun. I take a deep breath in. And then I remember something. Something I haven't told Jace. "I wasn't really going home," I say. "I was going to trick you into taking me to North Carolina."

His eyes widen in shock, and then he nods. "It's that bad at home, huh?"

I nod.

"So maybe . . . maybe you can stay in Florida for the summer," he says.

"Right," I say. "Like my parents are going to go for that."

"How can they really stop you?" he asks.

"Where would I stay? I have no money, no job . . ."

"Well, you could maybe stay with me," he says slowly. "Or Courtney. You know her dad is going away for the whole summer on his honeymoon." He gets a thoughtful look on his face as he reaches into his pocket and pulls out his phone.

"Who are you calling?" I ask.

"My mom."

"Your *mom*?" I ask. "But she's—"

He holds a finger to his lips, motioning for me to be quiet. "Mom," he says. "It's me." I hear her start to yell at him on the other line, and then she must catch herself, because she lowers her voice. "Yeah, I know," Jace says. "We can talk about it when I get home. But Mom, can Peyton come to graduation with me? And if we get home in time, can she stay with us for a few days?" He rolls his eyes. "Of course separate rooms, Mom, geez."

A second later, he's off the phone. "It's all set," he says. "We'll fly back to Florida tonight, and worry about my car later. You can go to graduation with me."

I shake my head. "I want to," I say. "I do. But . . ."

"But what?"

"But what about all the stuff you said, about me running away from things?"

He tilts his head, thinking about it. "When we get to Florida," he says, "we'll call your dad. We'll tell him everything that happened, and we'll come up with a plan."

The thought twists my stomach into a ball of anxiety. But Jace reaches out and squeezes my hand, and I immediately feel better. I nod slowly. "What about Kari?"

He shakes his head. "Kari and I broke up."

I narrow my eyes at him. "When?"

"Last night. When you took off, I called her and ended it." He shrugs. "It's always been you, Peyton. Always."

I feel my eyes fill with tears, and I look down at the ground. We just sit like that for a few moments, in the middle of the Savannah summer, him holding my hand, me thinking about what all of this means.

"So I go to Florida with you now," I say slowly, "and stay for a few days. And then what?"

"And then we'll figure it out," he says. "You can talk to Courtney, talk to your parents." He squeezes my hand. "It'll all work out."

I'm not sure if he's talking about me and him, or about the whole situation. I raise my eyes to his, and he reaches out and wipes away the tear that's sliding down my cheek.

"Peyton," he says. "It's going to be okay. I'm going to take care of it, okay? And I'm never going to let you go again."

And for the first time in a really long time, I believe it.

All of it.

That everything's going to be okay.

That he's going to take care of me.

That we're going to be together.

And then he kisses me.

And it just might be the best feeling ever.

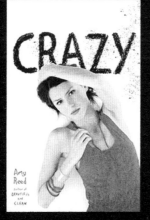

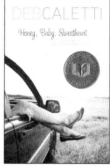

Love. Heartbreak.
Friendship. Trust.

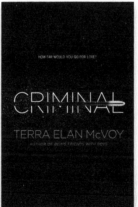

Fall head over heels for
Terra Elan McVoy.